THE SLEEP
THAT RESCUES

C.J. HENDERSON

FIRST EDITION
10 9 8 7 6 5 4 3 2 1
Published in September 2009
ISBN: 1-934501-15-8
Printed in the U.S.A.

Published by Elder Signs Press
P.O. Box 389
Lake Orion, MI 48361-0389
www.eldersignspress.com

THE SLEEP
THAT RESCUES
C.J. HENDERSON

2009

Over the years, I have gotten to work with all sorts of people. Some of them have been quite easy to work with . . .

Some . . . have not.

And some have proven to be simply a delight.

Of them all, however, one comes to mind above the rest. Competent, jovial, insightful, generous—all good words to describe them. So are talented, gracious, subversive and magnanimous.

There are some people in this world who simply possess all the right attibutes for working with others. Some have to put forth a great deal of effort to make this appear easy. For others, it just looks natural.

Of all of those with whom it has been a pleasure to work, however, one has stood head and shoulders above the rest.

Thus, this book is dedicated to:

William Shatner

A gentleman and a scholar of brobdingnagian proportions, and someone whose innumeral kindnesses I can never repay.

"In bed my real love has always been the sleep that rescues me by allowing me to dream."

—Luigi Pirandello

"How many of our daydreams would darken into nightmares were there any danger of their becoming true."

—Jean Cocteau

"The more a man dreams, the less he believes."

—H.L. Mencken

PROLOGUE

IN-FUCKING-CREDIBLE.

Johnny sighed, his tired muscles tingling as the beautiful Kara folded warmly against him. Finally. His heart skipped repeatedly, missing multiple beats in an explosion of overwhelming happiness his conscious mind could not—had no desire to—keep in check. He could feel the power of the thumping muscle throbbing, racing within his chest, beating wildly—expanding at the very touch of her.

Her–

Man, thought Johnny, his mind reeling from all he had been through, this is unbelievable.

Suddenly—all of it—all the hundreds of endless battles, the bloody killing, the continual, mindless, hideous slaughter—the on-and-on of it all—the desperate fights and comical brawls, the monumental swordplay and the multiple variety of traps he had avoided, the bizarre puzzles he had unraveled and the seemingly supremely formidable enemies he had conquered—all of it finally felt satisfying.

Real shame.

It was worth it, he thought, his breath coming in ragged, billowing sighs. Looking down at the dazzling beauty pressing herself hard against him, his mind's defenses softened, his weariness evaporating as the energizing phrase whispered once more in his mind–

Oh yeah, it was most definitely worth it.

"My Johnny," the near-fainting woman sighed. "My wonderful Johnny . . .,"

The youth felt his whole body begin to tingle—to tremble in a manner he could only imagine was ecstasy. He could not begin to actually describe the feeling. There was nothing in his past experience to compare it with—amusement park thrill rides, his small, experimental experiences with alcohol and drugs, first fumbling attempts at sex—nothing. There was nothing in his short life to compare with what he was feeling at that moment.

"Has any woman," Kara murmured, her voice fading into his chest, "ever had such a hero?"

The words were electricity to him. The lad tried again to find something in all his days to hold against the sensations coursing through his mind, but he could not. What held him then was something totally new, a sensation completely beyond the pale of anything he had ever felt before—beyond, he knew, what *anyone* had ever felt since the beginning of time.

It was more than just some simple rush or thrill; what he was feeling, he was certain, had to be something the universe had fashioned uniquely just for him—a complete and overwhelming aliveness no one had ever previously known. It pumped through his veins, jolting his brain with a fiery vitality that shamed his wildest dreams.

Man, what a blast this was, he thought. What an adventure, what a god-damned life. I mean, really—is there anyone in the entire universe who's luckier than me?

His mind was still staggered. Since first he had set foot in El Dorado, his old senses had come alive, been transformed, been so, so alert, so magnified, so warily active—everything had been so unbelievable. So totally, completely, galactically unbelievable. The endless fighting and killing and drinking and whoring, the sheer unrestrained wildness of it all. His mind had never been more clear, more focused. His life had never before had such purpose. Such meaning.

"Tell me you'll stay this time," the panting redhead moaned. There was shame in her velvet voice, self-knowledge that she was being brazen, perhaps even unforgivably so. It did not matter to the young woman, however. She did not—could not—care. Gathering all her strength, she drew her lips close to her hero's ear and whispered the words he had been waiting to hear.

"Tell me you'll be mine—mine forever."

I mean, it's a real shame, ain't it?

The young man's wild heart raced even faster. Wiping away the dripping sweat on his brow, he laughed at the impossibility of it all—and the foolish-ness of her question.

Would I mind staying this time, he asked himself jokingly within his mind. He knew exactly how quickly he would do so—and how impossible such a thing actually was.

Would if I could, babe. Would if I could.

Still, even as his pragmatic side joked, the parts of his mind which had come alive so recently, that had battled for so long, against the most impossible odds, waiting for the moment he was experiencing then—when Kara would finally be his—they were practically frozen by indecision. They had worked at obtaining the impossible goal for so long that having finally obtained it, they could scarcely imagine what to do next.

"Kara," Johnny whispered, crushing his long-sought prize to his chest, unable to say anything in response other than the name he had practically worshipped for so long. Closing his eyes, he smelled her hair once more, felt her soft frame molding to his own, ran his hands over the silk-covered curves his fingers had ached to touch since his first sight of her.

"Kara."

He whispered her name once more in a soft, fragile voice, a tone he had found little use for over the numbing months of the rescue campaign. He said the perfect word differently than ever before, however. This time, he uttered it with a new syllable, coating it with a lacquer of hope—a boldness he had not dared previously.

The word for how long he had adored his Kara—yes, *his* Kara, not Princess of the Eternal Lands, not Goddess Priestess of Hypelsina, but *his Kara*—was "endlessly." Since he had arrived in her land, time had possessed no meaning—not for John der Lance, J the Conqueror, Johnny—not for any of the men he had been, the times they had lived, or any of the places they had trod—not since any of them had first seen their dear Kara, learned of her, discovered her plight, vowed to save her.

Time had held no meaning for him, not since then, and not now, either. Not now that he was finally next to her—his queen, his woman—the unobtainable suddenly in his hands. At last he was with her. Breathing her scent, tasting her, holding her, crushing his lips against hers. At last.

Finally.

"My Lord," the girl said with satisfaction as her mouth came away from Johnny's. Smiling, she hugged him tighter as she added, "I still can not believe that our ordeal is finally over."

Over, thought the young man. It's all over.

So, we got another one, huh?

What was that?

Johnny's head whipped around. Kara seemed not to have heard the faraway voice, but he had. Disembodied though it was, still it came to him clear as the waters of Mondropoor's diamond lakes. It was a dull, cynical tone—the voice of . . .

Of what, young Jonathan?

Johnny paused. He had not heard the Oracle's voice since the elder's second death.

Old man, are you really back? he thought, broadcasting the joyous desire as strongly as he could. Hoping against all hope that the wily shaman could have somehow cheated the black robe once again, he thought, Can you help me?

Help you—again? How can I help you again? Now? Now, when it is over.

The question did not have the sneering tone the Oracle so often employed. Indeed, it seemed . . . how could Johnny describe it? Puzzled, perhaps. Confused.

Confused, wondered Johnny with a growing sense of dread. The Oracle . . . confused?

The idea was ridiculous to him. Ludicrous. Tossing the notion aside, laughing at it, the newly crowned boy king aimed his thoughts at the Oracle once more.

Old friend, he asked, his spirits rising ever higher at the arrival of his mentor during his moment of triumph, *can you not tell me what to do next?*

It is over.

The Oracle's words rang grimly in Johnny's head. He should know what the old man meant, he knew he should know. But, though he had always been able to decipher the sour elder's meanings in the past, somehow he could not grasp exactly what he was being told this time. As he continued to puzzle over their meaning, however, the Oracle's words came to him once more.

It is over.

What do you mean, responded Johnny. *Yeah, I'd say it better be over. I did it all. I beat the Vandelesh, drove out the Clan of Kerzil. I recovered the Silver Cup, divided the Yarl, killed Trobor and rescued Kara. I lead my knights and conquered all of the vast plains of Dy'gra.*

How do they get this way?

Johnny's emotions boiled. He had won through. The battle was his. The princess was his. But . . . something was wrong. These voices in his head, out of nowhere, saying words that had no meaning. And the Oracle on top of that. Not telling him anything, simply repeating the same words again and again . . .

It is over.

"Stop saying that!"

Kara looked up, her mostly blank eyes filling with a semblance of confusion.

"My Lord," she said with surprise, pulling herself a small space away from her savior. Half-aware, half-frightened, she asked, "why do you rage so? What is the matter?"

"It's . . ." Johnny stopped, confused. Trembling. How to explain? What could he say to make his goddess love understand when even he did not?

It is over.

No one's sure. We got no threads yet, really.

Johnny slammed his hand against his head. Letting go of his love, he staggered several paces from her, hitting himself again—then again. He could not think—could not concentrate—not against the confounding chatter of all the voices overlapping within his mind. For so long his purpose had been simply, perfectly clear—find his mentor, learn the ways of magic and the sword, reach the kingdom, defeat the baron in battle so he could prove his worth, take up the quest, gather his band, turn back the hordes, overthrow the ruler of the savage lands, save the princess once she was kidnapped, and then, and . . . then . . .

It is over.

Oh, my God.

The words etched with needle cruelty across Johnny's heart, ice crystals bonding with glass, screeching in his ears.

Yeah, just somethin' new the chump generation has found to goof themselves up with.

And then he remembered—not all of him—not all of it. Just a part. A tiny part lodged off toward the back of his brain. Suddenly, thought, memories returned. He could see once more the needle from the corner of his eye, could remember the offer. He felt the laughing joy anew, the thrill of not being able to turn it down, not thinking for a moment he had any reason to do so.

It is over.

J the Conqueror continued to hold Kara, great tears breaking free from his closing eyes. His cheeks went wet, his body heaving as he cried for joy. He had finally triumphed. Victory was his. At long last, it was over. He had conquered all. He had won every prize. It was over. He was, undeniably, the greatest in all the land. There was nothing more to prove. The princess was his. The kingdom was his. There were no more battles to fight. No more tests. Nothing lay in his path any longer.

It was over.

But, as he tried to arrange it all in his mind, his hands trembled, sending shivers through his beloved. Sensing his distress, Kara held him all the closer, shutting her eyes as she asked;

"What is it, my Lord? Tell me."

Johnny smiled. Unable to hear the back of his mind, unwilling to shatter the image which far too much of his brain had accepted as truth, John War-ren Marshall—not John der Lance, not J the Conqueror, not even Johnny, hero of the plains, simple John, son of Robert and Grace Marshall—stopped struggling . . .

And in that moment, he heard a new voice. Not one from the back of his mind, not his mentor, not the faraway pair he could not see, it was not any voice he had ever heard before. Indeed, it was composed of qualities unlike any he had ever heard in all his life. Not human, not electronic, not from a cartoon.

"Johnny," it beckoned, a flat, hissing whisper that sounded of dream and reward, "Listen to me, Johnny . . . bit by bit . . . follow the gold."

You see his eyes—just there—that. Did you see that?

"The city of gold . . . bit by bit . . . you can find it, Johnny. Only you can find it."

That was it—I've seen this. That was it.

And, in a flashing instant, Johnny fell into the beckoning oblivion.

We just lost him.

Knew it, answered the other voice. Told ya . . .

And this time, Johnny accepted his fate–

I seen this before . . .

And the darkness that had waited so patiently finally fell across him as the two dispassionate ambulance workers pulled the sheet over his face and began making out their report . . .

I seen this before . . .

Even as young John Warren Marshall began his greatest quest, searching the final unknown beyond for a city of gold he could see ever so clearly through his blood encrusted, long-closed eyes and the cotton sheet covering them.

CHAPTER ONE

"**M**R. MORCEY, LOOK OUT!" cried the older man. "There's another one."

Paul Morcey did not waste time looking about, quickly ducking instead as a screeching bundle of wings and fangs and leathery fibers violently slashed the space over his head. Claws raked the air wildly, grasping at the balding man, trying to at least snag his foot length pony-tail as he dove for the floor.

"Guooooffff!" Air rushed out of the ex-maintenance man as he slammed against the marble walkway. His move had been neither well-planned nor well-executed, but it saved him from the terror's razored attack.

"Leave these nasty t'ings to me boys, now," shouted a large black man over the increasing din. "Dis be our job."

Stepping forth into the open, a compact automatic weapon in each hand, the towering figure made a rolling motion with his shoulders. Instantly, well-trained men appeared in response to the silent signal—behind him and at each side.

"Ah, me brothers," he said in a thick accent that spoke of exotic islands and the reality of pain, "let's kill us some bad t'ings—*now!*"

Gunfire rocked the museum halls in response to the command. Shotgun blasts tore through creature flesh, splattering fluids, pulping narrow eyes and conical ears, shredding wings and leathered bones—and more. Two of the things went down in immediate response to the opening fusillade, shrieking a foul, terrible noise that almost sounded like language. Instantly, three more of the gruesome shapes appeared out of the shadows, each of the new trio markedly faster than the first.

"Second team, news flash," the balding man shouted into his headset, desperate to be heard over the reverberating din of the gunfire. Pointing at the new arrivals, he bellowed, "we got company!"

The shooters turned, one too slowly. Fangs clamped on the man's neck just above his protective vest, tearing into his flesh. Bone snapped. Leather lips smiled. Blood pulsed in a wild arc, showering across the polished stone flooring as well as those standing nearest the victim. As multiple weapons swung toward the thing's direction, it let go its now-dead prey and beat its massive wings furiously, trying to gain height even as its fellows dove toward the marksmen. Gunpowdered thunder shattered the night once more, missing their mark by inches, tearing gouging holes in the marble wall beyond.

"Damnit, Pa'sha!"

The bellow swelled from a tall, thin man with intense, blazing blue eyes. Small boned, but square-shouldered, he pointed around wildly at the priceless paintings all about the invasion force with one hand, tugging at his tie with the other, as he screamed into his throat mike over the gunfire.

"Remember where you are!"

"Goward man, right," snapped one of the gunman, a wiry deep-black Jamaican. Nodding, he added, yelling to the others, "De teacher speak most cool—wrong bang bang and kiss goodbye the gentle mystery of dey Mona Lisa's smile."

"Also most terrible law suits and other annoying t'ings, my brothers, don't you know?" answered their boss. "Okay, me Murder Dogs," he shouted to his men. "Show de man we know our business."

"Yes, daddy man!"

Pa'sha's forces returned to their defensive crouches. They moved forward slowly, their guns frozen in their grasps, their eyes scanning the walls and ceilings carefully. The men watched the areas ahead of themselves, as well as behind, their minds constantly repeating the warning that the things they were waiting for could come from any direction. Ignoring the mounting tension as well as the beads of sweat gathering across their brows, the force continued sweeping forward, weapons ready, waiting for their targets, following the lights—eyes searching–

"Left—up—the Warhol section!"

Those designated as part of A-Sweep followed the line of direction, their weapons ready. As the lighting man marked the designated coordinates with his hot flash, the B and C men fired without question at the first thing that moved into sight. Black it was, large and powerful with wings spreading some eight feet across. It was a screeching fast flier that slashed at the lights hitting it, somehow spilling a warm foul line of darkness into the beam from some beyond realm.

"Avoid!"

The men's eyes widened, several of them freezing in place. Pa'sha roared into his mike.

"Damnit, all—move it now! Get out o'de way!"

The mercenaries scattered, backing rapidly away from the fetid, light-absorbing pus as their first projectiles struck their targets. The shotgun man's blast sent a shatter of pellets through the thing's shoulder at the wing, turning the meat and sinew of the joint into a splintered ruin. The rifleman's first bullet tore a chunk from out its neck. His second sliced a flapping ear neatly off the leathery head. Both men silently cursed their missed shots. Despite being hit cleanly, the thing continued to fly for a moment, then wobbled off course and shattered its skull against the marble wall. Bone and stone both cracked loudly. The vaporous ooze vanished in an acrid flash as the broken thing slid down the wall.

"Good shooting," called out their boss. "Dese t'ings be devil fast—lucky we are to hit them at all. B Team, you're up. C, prepare."

"T'anks, Pa'sha daddy."

The big man smiled. Watching carefully for any other beasts that might appear, he flipped his throat mike upward and began making a report of the recent action. Readjusting his night vision goggles at the same time, he listened to a response coming from someone not within the same chamber. From the look on his face, it was clearly evident the big man was not happy with what he was hearing. Across the room, the woman watching from the corner stayed glued against the wall.

Who in hell *are* these people, she wondered. Her eyes wide—round, unblinking. Back slick with sweat, she stared mutely as another round of gunfire tore two more of the impossible creatures apart. Her gloved fingers tapped unconsciously against the marble slab chilling her spine.

And, while we're busy speculating, a nervous voice from the back of her mind asked, could you explain just what in Hell it is they're blasting to bits?

The woman was not part of the team shooting up the museum. She was not even armed. She had no idea who the men before her were, why they were there, or what the creatures were they were slaughtering with such precise determination. She did know a few things, however. For starters, she could see that the men were dangerous, and good at their work.

Unlike her, they did not stare open-mouthed at the flying, vicious horrors whistling through the hallways. They were not frightened of the claws or fangs, or the fact that the things they faced could tear apart the fabric of space to open inter-dimensional rifts. Unlike the woman, they seemed, if not complacent about it all, at least somehow used to the idea of creatures of which no one else had ever heard. Indeed, so unflapped by the beasts were they that they were coldly, coolly and quite rapidly disposing of the things one after another as if they were nothing more than bats or over-sized moths.

In fact, the woman suddenly realized they were making short work of anything moving that was not a part of their team. Realizing what that calculating efficiency would almost certainly soon mean to her personally, the woman told herself;

So, there's your question, little girl. Do you stay where you are and eventually get yourself discovered, or do you move and get yourself shot?

"Dearon," Pa'sha bellowed into his throat mike, "what's holding up de lights? Why we still walking around in monster-protecting darkness?"

"I found the problem, daddy-man," came his answer, broadcast to the assault leader through his headset. "Someone cut the main feed wires. Dey also jam the security back-up."

The man in the basement cursed under his breath as he worked feverishly to untangle the mess before him which had once been the museum's central electrical main.

"Can you at least get de back-up lights running again?" asked Pa'sha with frustration.

Well, the woman told herself after hearing the big man's request, that should answer your question.

Deciding that risking death was better than risking discovery the woman carefully felt for the doorknob she knew was somewhere behind her. Normally the doors to the security hallways would not open for anyone without the proper codes to use at the punch pad. But, with the power throughout the museum neutralized, minor problems such as that had been eliminated. The woman moved slowly, quietly, working with precise care in her attempt to avoid being detected by the heavily armed force.

The hundred questions she had already asked herself buzzed through her head again, some of them for the fiftieth time—who *are* these people, what are they doing here, what were those things they were fighting, and why here? Why now? What the goddamned Hell is going on around here, how long has it been going on, why hasn't anyone ever heard anything about these kinds of things before, how can this be happening–

There was more, but she silenced all the trembling voices within her mind with ruthless efficiency.

It doesn't matter, she told them, harshly shouting down their protests. Who needs to know? Who cares? What does it matter if they're filming a movie, it's the end of the world—what the hell difference does it make?!

It certainly won't make much difference if they catch you, another voice within her head whispered. Or *kill* you.

The woman nodded. She did not believe the assault team knew anything about her. They were not worried about her. Indeed, it was painfully obvious to the woman that catching her had nothing whatsoever to do with why they were there. But, getting in their way seemed more than possible.

Move your behind, she told herself. We're not bleeding for this job.

As the woman inched the door open she did not bother worrying about the noise it might make. There were too many shouts and gun shots for anyone to hear a set of squeaking hinges. She still moved slowly, however. The men tearing up the museum were equipped with night vision equipment and were checking every corner with a thoroughness she found both impressive and frightening. Her only chance lay in the fact that the things they were fighting, or hunting, or whatever they were doing, were airborne and fast-moving.

No one's looking for slow little us down here on the boring old floor, she told herself calmly. And that's the way it's going to stay. All we have to do is keep our cool and we'll be out of here in no time.

Once the door was open some nine inches she stopped its forward motion and began instead to slide herself along the wall toward the opening. Her back moved along the cold marble, her black leather outfit gliding noiselessly across the stone. She inched through the near-foot wide opening she had created, only her breasts and the barest edge of her skull mask grazing the door's brass edge. Once on the other side she closed it again, somewhat faster than she had opened it. Then, safely in a less violent darkness, she finally let go her self-control and quietly indulged her violently pulsing nerves.

"Jesus," she breathed, half-gasping, half-crying—her voice angry, but still a whisper. "Jesus H. Christ, what in all the hills of Rome *were* those things? What in six goddamned Hells *were* they? I mean, I . . . that's nothing you find in the encyclopedia. There haven't been any Discovery Channel specials about 'the flying goddamned lizard monsters of Manhattan's museums.' So, what, what . . . what in all the damn . . ."

The woman felt a tear forming in the corner of her left eye. Surprised, embarrassed, angry, she forced herself to take a deep breath, then another, then another.

I will not cry—nothing can make me cry.

Although her resolve was fearsome, the woman could not completely control the panic flooding her. Now that she had removed herself from the immediate danger beyond the door, her nerves were rebelling. The deep breaths could not help her. Sliding down the wall, she hit the floor hard as tears began to roll down out of the corners of her eyes, soaking her mask.

"Damnit," she cursed, a fist striking the floor, "Damn, damn, damnit all, damn."

You're getting hysterical, the voice from the back of her mind whispered in caution.

"Of course I'm getting hysterical," she snapped to the air, louder than she should have. "Who wouldn't get hysterical after what I just saw?"

Reaching up, the woman pulled off her mask. Three feet of wet, dark red hair tumbled out from beneath the black wool, sticking to her neck, ears, forehead.

That's enough, she told herself. Control yourself.

Repeating the words of her long-dead mentor snapped her back to her usually controlled mindset. The still rational part of her brain kept talking.

Whatever those things were, they weren't ghosts or demons, they were just creatures of some sort—flesh and blood. If those men doing all the shooting didn't have any reason to cry over them, neither do you.

The woman's tears stopped abruptly. She clamped her teeth together, forcing her chin to stop quivering. Then, pushing herself up off the floor, she gave herself a reminder.

Remember yourself. You're Joan de Molina, the woman they call the Pirate Queen. You're stronger than this. You're the best thief in all the world.

"Really," she questioned herself quietly, desperately working to regain her composure while she muttered under her breath, "Some thief. You break in, disable the security and lights, and for all the time you've had free access to this entire place, you've got precious little to show for it."

Well, the night's not over, the back of her mind answered. A smile crossing the redhead's lips, she pushed herself down the hallway. Picking up speed as she reassembled her usual attitude, she quickly mapped out her exit strategy.

There's still time to make tonight work, she schemed. Whatever is missing, the bangbang boys will take the fall for it. No one's going to identify that kind of destruction as my handiwork. After all, blowing the hell out of places isn't my M.O. All I have to do is make a quick grab and get the hell outside.

Scanning the doorways as she moved, Joan quickly retrieved her sense of direction. She had come at the request of a collector, an exceedingly rich individual who thought little for the boundaries by which most were expected to live. He had hired her to make off with a particular painting he wished to add to his private collection. That piece, however, if indeed it still was in one piece, was back in the gallery with the gunmen. Obtaining that at the moment was out of the question.

However, she thought craftily, the Antiquities Section is just around the corner ahead. Gold with inlaid jewels, thousands of years old, priceless beyond measure—even if there's no buyer, just the insurance return will cover a year's expenses.

Seeing the right door ahead of her, Joan de Molina, the beauty widely regarded as the greatest professional thief in all the world smiled softly. She would grab an armload of trinkets and hit the sidewalk before any more time was wasted. It was not the score she had intended to make, but it would do. Her hand touching the doorknob, she thought to herself;

Funny, that almost looks like light coming from under the door.

Then, she pushed her way into the Hall of Antiquities, and stared into the face of Hell.

CHAPTER
TWO

"**OH, CHRIST!**"

Joan could not—refused to—believe her eyes. What? *What?*

As the security door swung open before her she saw that the main chamber of the Antiquities Hall was filled with a blazing light, but not one created by any man-made source. What she saw, no—actually she more *felt* the illumination than saw it—was a dull, bubbling shimmer, a pale green dashed through with flashes of putrid orange and purple. The light did not shine outward from its source, but rather it somehow *throbbed* forth, oozing forward a space, only to then retreat backward and then ooze forward once more, over and over in dull repetition.

Oh, God, she thought, her mind stiffening, terror itching its way into every part of her once more. Oh, my dear God . . .

The light moved nosily. Somehow, the grotesque shimmer sent a muffled echo bouncing off the stone walls as it pulsated wetly within the room. The sound it made was heavy, thick, squealing—like the slap of a damp rug against a chamber filled with half-empty balloons.

God, oh God, ohmyGod, *ohmyGod*–

The woman's mind raced, her nerves screaming again as panic flooded through her, chewed at her logic. What now, she wondered—amazed, frightened. What in *Hell* have I stumbled into now?

Shutting her eyes, hating the tears that had begun again, she whispered weakly as her legs began to shake;

"What now?"

Nothing took note of her words. The light demanded all attention. It pulsated outward in sickly vibrations from the left-hand side of the room. More specifically, it flowed back and forth from the inside of a golden cup. The vessel was an oversized thing, one made more rightly for the hand of a small giant. Covered with intricate carvings of grossly exaggerated figures, inlaid with rows of rubies and vertical lines of what appeared to be platinum, it was a repellant goblet despite its obvious value. Vague loops of a pallid yellow mixed with a thin, watery brown began spiralling through the crawling shafts of light, making the effect harder to follow by the moment. Odd as all of this was, however, neither the light nor its cup were what had captured the Pirate Queen's attention.

Holding the cup was a nearly naked man, or more correctly, a nearly naked humanoid some seven feet tall. An ordinary man the figure might have once been, but somehow it had been changed, transmuted—corrupted. The thing still stood on two legs, but its appendages seemed to no longer respond to a central sense of gravity. Not bending in any recognizably human pattern, they instead moved more like the limbs of a child's rag toy, or the tentacles of a sea creature.

"Tsk, tsk, tsk," the man/thing made the noise by moving its sloppy tongue over the roof of its mouth. The simple sound became a sinister note in its elongated maw, directed at another figure there in the room. Staring at the man barring its path, it articulated words with a struggle, annoucing;

"Not much surprise, you showing up here."

"Don't make me hurt you, Laub."

"Tsk, tsk, tsk," the man/thing slurred the simple sound once more. The noise of it froze Joan's blood, but not enough to make her do anything foolish. So far neither of the others in the room had taken any notice of her. The Pirate Queen remained stock still, barely breathing, determined to keep the situation that way. Beyond, the creature spoke once more.

"But at least, finally, we two shall make an end to our little contest—yes?"

Wobbly things the one-time man's pale legs were, barely able to support their master's weight. Above them, a corpulent waist hung down sloppily on both sides as well as in the front and even the back, the effect resembling melting ice cream, drooling over the edges of its cone. The hairless torso above the midsection, however, was a reedy thing, narrowing upward into a shoulderless junction where the figure's arms seemed to emanate almost directly from its neck. Long and gangly they were, ending in hands with rubbery, queerly slick fingers. The shaved head that crowned the form was an odd, lumpened object, looking mainly like a sack filled with congealed mush. Bluish veins pulsed in odd rhythms across the top of it, bulging to what seemed to be the bursting point. If the thing had ears, or any features that might constitute a face, they were hidden from Joan's view.

"Now," drool spilled over Laub's impressive maw. "Won't that be pleasant?"

The wrinkled skin of the figure appeared to be a foul shade of olive, but Joan could not be certain of even that small fact since the colors emanating from the cup transformed the look of everything within the room. From the ceiling to the floor, all the objects touched by the putrid light pulsating within the chamber were made to appear alien in some fashion or the other. Even the man confronting the thing with the cup in its grasp did not seem completely normal.

"This is your last chance, Laub," the man standing in the creature's way answered calmly—evenly. With a confidence Joan could not fathom, the all too average looking individual snapped an order to the monster mere yards away from him.

"Put the cup down," he told the heaving thing, "and we'll try to get you fixed up."

"Fix me? Fix me *up?* Tsk, tsk, tsk . . ."

The thing raised its eyes upward in mock confusion, then sent its empty hand to scratch at its hairless brow. "Tell me, detective, what is there to fix about *me?* Now, now that I am a being transformed unto perfection."

Joan watched the man with more than casual interest. There was something about him that tore at her insides, compelled her, made a long-unused part of her ache. Yes, like the others she had just run from, he was cool and collected in the face of horror, but there was something more. Something that stirred the Pirate Queen. There was a power to him that riveted her, that tore her breath away, something special, something–

Fool, the back of her mind hissed at her. Idiot, what are you playing at? Get *out* of here.

Good idea, she admitted, wondering what had taken her so long to come up with the idea in the first place.

Thinking herself on the edge of breaking down, Joan pushed herself back against the door, her hand again searching behind her for the knob. Whether she was close to finding it she could not tell. For some reason she could not tear her eyes from the events unfolding before her.

Focus, her mind snapped at her, but she could not. The confrontation being acted out before her had stolen her attention completely. Although in far more control than most people would have been in the same situation, still she was paralyzed—helpless to do anything but watch, her mind desperately attempting to fathom what was going on throughout the museum.

"Really, detective," said the misshapen thing identified as Laub, its words sinister, almost reptilian in their texture. "I believe you're the one who needs fixing. You're the one who needs some work done."

"Damnit, Laub—give it up," snapped the man, his hand inching toward the inside of his jacket. "Don't make me do something I don't want to do."

"Ah, me oh my, poor little london thing," answered someone—no, something else—some thing which now spoke through Laub, "you really are a simple creature, aren't you?"

The detective—as he had been called—stopped moving for a second, obviously stunned by his adversary's words. His clear eyes went wide—unblinking. Joan studied what she could see of his face. She could tell that something the awful creature with the cup had said had prompted a memory within the man, something he either did not wish to face, or perhaps something he could not believe he had to face once more.

"Well," he managed after too-long a pause, "I guess that seals that. You're not actually Laub anymore, are you?"

"Ah, london thing, so certain you were that you were blessed—made superior—ready to challenge gods. Observing you is always so amusing, like watching a dog that has discovered a back door into a garbage dump and thinks itself anointed, rather than simply just another eater of trash."

London's hand pulled a shining, black .38 revolver out from under his arm, a highly polished weapon he had named Betty years ago for reasons he could no longer remember. He leveled the revolver at Laub, giving the pulsing monstrosity a final chance to obey his instructions. Cocking the .38, aiming carefully, the detective spoke evenly, trying to reach any vestige of the one-time human being that might still remain within the thing before him.

"Laub, if you're still in there, forget this, all of it. It's over. You've been tricked. You've got to fight this thing or you're done for!"

"Fight *me?* You give this sad waste too much credit."

The words curled harshly from Laub's amused lips. The sound of them was grating and bitter, certain syllables beginning to jumble, straining Laub's throat, fading beyond human ability to perceive them. "None can fight *me— why, you of all people should know that.*"

"Yeah," asked London, pointing his weapon directly between Laub's eyes. "That so? Seems to me last time around I made a mess of your plans."

Laub shifted from foot to foot.

"Isn't that right . . . Q'talu?"

ahhhhhhhhhhhhh, it's so good to be remembered

The words sounded in the detective's head alone. As London realized that the takeover of the would-be sorcerer before him had become complete, he tightened his trigger finger sending a bullet flying directly for the bridge of Laub's nose. Despite its great speed, the projectile did not manage to reach its target. The sound of it disappeared before it could reach anyone's ears, swallowed somehow—dissipated. The bullet traveled with something close to its natural speed for half the distance across the room, then it slowed and simply stopped, hanging suspended in the ever-changing light.

poor, foolish little london thing, you are powerless to stop me this time

"What makes you so sure?" asked the detective.

The woman against the door watched the scene before her, half-fascinated, half-terrified. Sweat pooled in her hair once more, dripping around her neck, down her back, under her tunic. Her legs felt weak, her head swimming. Suddenly only able to hear London's half of the conversation, the tableau before her took on an even more unreal quality. She could sense that the detective was still in communication with the thing holding the cup, even if somehow she was no longer privy to both sides of their exchange.

We've got to get out of here, the part of her brain trained toward survival warned her. Go. Turn the knob. You got in, now get out. Now—*do it.*

The fingers of her hand moved across the door once more, slowly, inching, feeling for the knob, but only absently. Even as they continued to search, she told herself;

Not yet. I have to know what's going on. What is all this? And who is this, this London person?

She stared at the detective, wondering, finding herself fascinated beyond all reason. As the panicked voices in her head urged her again to flee, she cut them off, unable to tear her eyes away from the man before her.

Who are you, mister London, to make me feel this way?

Joan's thoughts were cut off as the detective's weapon fired again and then again. Both bullets were stopped in the same manner as his first shot. This time, however, the thing with the cup struck back. The lips of it mumbled an unintelligible sentence and suddenly a raging billow of solid crimson light flew from the vessel's bowl, splattering against London. He screamed in response. The sound was wild and primal, as if the pain he felt were enough to reach not just his own nerves and heart, but deep into the recesses of his mind as well, affecting not just him but all the howling, primitive ancestors locked away within his brain. The thing he had called Laub chuckled softly, then unleashed a second torrent of scarlet devastation.

Again the detective spasmed. He had already dropped his weapon, his fingers clenching and unclenching uncontrollably. This time he fell to his knees, slamming the floor harshly, reflections of his pain bleeding out of him.

Can you resist me again? How many times, I wonder . . . for how long can we make this dance last?

The thing that was now Laub moved its lower limbs in an obscene manner, twisting and spinning as it chuckled over the wounded body before it.

I would be most grateful to your slight flesh if it could keep itself together for a while longer . . . that I might enjoy this moment which I have waited for . . . for so very long

London did not answer, at least not directly. He lay on the floor, still howling, tears leaking from his burning eyes. Even his screams were lost, the sound of them trapped in his throat, his mouth opened wide and round, but remaining soundless. The Laub-creature chuckled again.

now, little london thing . . . now you will come to join me . . . first you, then the lisa, she that should have been mine so long ago, then all your world . . . your universe . . . consumed . . . finished . . . and those billions of lives all around you . . . any beyond . . . just the beginning

The detective clawed at the marble flooring. His fingers bent against the stone, nails breaking. Struggling, unable to get his muscles back under his own control, he worked frantically, awkwardly, desperate to find his way back to his feet. He knew he could not make it in time. His struggles were pointless, but they amused his enemy to no end.

finished, you are . . .

The thing turned its hand, aiming the cup at London once more, but this time in a different manner. The lips of Laub mumbled for a last time, calling up a more deadly spell. The cup in its hand glowed a fierce black.

this is your end

London made it to one knee, just in time to watch Laub's body crumple and fall to the floor. As the detective blinked, he realized there was someone behind the sorcerer—a woman. She had something in her hands, a ritual club, taken from the same display case Laub had broken open just before he had arrived.

Who? He wondered. Why?

Panting, his arms weak and burning, his spine unresponding, he struggled to stand erect, tried to speak, almost falling back to the floor for his efforts. Then, even as the Pirate Queen darted across the room to catch him, the screech of police sirens filled the air.

CHAPTER
THREE

"JOAN," A LONG-UNHEARD VOICE asked. "Joan, didn't I ask you to set the table?"

What? Where am I?

Joan de Molina looked about her. Where was she? She recognized something about the look of the plain room; some vague thing about it that caused some long unused portion of her brain to recall various details of it—verifying that she had been there before. Oddly, despite its extreme ordinariness, the feel of the place held something disturbingly awkward about it.

What's bothering you, she asked herself. Think—look around, observe.

Joan fought the urge to give into her panic, shoved aside all of the bizarre, unbelievable things she had seen in the last handful of minutes. Steeling herself, she shut her mind to everything else and concentrated on only what was happening to her at that moment. As she looked about, the woman could plainly see she was no longer in the museum. Somehow she had been transported away from the combatants in a fraction of a second to what appeared to be an average living room in all respects, but one where the ceiling was unusually high.

No, that was not all that struck her. The couches, the television, coffee table, arm chair, everything in the room seemed normal in its design, but like the ceiling, abnormally high—tall. Large. Somehow, Joan was certain she knew the place. But from where? And when . . .

And how? How did I get here? What happened to the museum, that thing—London?

The thought of the man who had collapsed into her arms a split-second earlier made her eyes dart to her hands. He was gone. As were her gloves. Indeed, her entire work suit seemed to have vanished. And as for her hands–

My hands, her mind flashed, what's happened to them?

"Joan," came the thick, female voice again—shriller, its edge harsh and nasty—growing more recognizable. "Are you going to answer me?"

They're so small. So tiny—what in the . . .

"Joan?!"

Joan de Molina looked around the room once more. She fought the growing panic stabbing at her, needling her to surrender herself unto it. As she did, bits of her confidence slipping aside, she finally recognized the room she was in. At last, she knew where she was, *when* she was–

Oh God, oh no—

"Joan, you little bitch!"

Mrs. Perryman came into the room, staggering—as usual—her puffy, redden face exploding through Joan's memory.

Oh God, my hands aren't small, they're a child's hands—I'm a child, again. The furniture isn't big—I'm small. I'm a child. I'm, I . . . how? *How?!*

"You can't do a single thing you're asked, can you?"

Not here, not, not again, her mind pleaded with dread. It can't be—it's not . . . it's not *fair!*

Joan looked up into Perryman's bloated oval face. How could she have forgotten that voice? That tormenting, horrid voice? Could it have been that long?

"Maybe you're just one of those who likes the belt," the woman asked, reeling as she spoke. "Is that it?"

Joan stood still, not moving, not speaking.

The fingers of the horribly tall woman before her started to fumble near her waist, struggling to undo the belt holding her pants closed. She was wide enough all around to not need the services for which it was designed. She wore belts only to satisfy her sense of fashion, and to keep them close at hand.

Joan's mind flashed with frightened memory, her normal courage deserting her. What could have happened, she wondered. How? How had she returned, back to the horrible foster home that the state had picked for her, back to the screaming, the abuse, the beatings, the meals denied, the lies—

Oh, she never does her work, never does what we say. I don't think she's stupid, just lazy, and always stealing, why, it breaks our hearts, but we have to beat her, we just *have* to—she's impossible. You don't understand, she presents herself to others so well, but she's a monster, just—

"A monster," Perryman's slurring voice sneered as it had so many times in the past. The horrible, terrible past Joan had thought long gone—buried.

Forgotten.

"Just a monster."

The hand went up in what seemed slow motion, the leather length snapping sharply in the air. Down it came, Joan frozen by the scene, not understanding what had happened to her, watching the belt buckle descending toward her face. The flashing metal square turned over and over as it fell, the belt's descent clearly discernable.

Run!

Joan should have been able to easily avoid the approaching blow, but she could not move. She agonized as she remembered how she had wanted to do so so many times back then. But then, she had wanted to do so many things, had wanted to strike back, wanted to cry, to dodge, to run, to scream—

—*flash*—

The blow never landed. At the moment she should have felt the buckle rake across her forehead as it did years earlier, Joan suddenly transformed once more. Younger she became, dressed in black, standing at her parent's grave sites. Two young people who had married against their parents' wishes—mother beautiful and clever, Asian and poor, father English, descended from long-faded nobility, pockets full of gold but his heart empty until he had found his love.

"Mommy," Joan managed to croak, looking down into the deep, rectangular holes before her.

Two wonderful years they had enjoyed with each other before her birth. Poor in those days, cut off from their families, abandoned, shunned, cast out, they were still fabulously happy with their lives for they had each other. Then, they had their Joan. And their lives found a center.

"Daddy . . ."

The beautiful baby girl whom, once she arrived, they could not live without. For seven years she compensated for all they had given up to be with each other—and more. Smart and artistic, her talents seemed limitless, her smile as wide as the ocean, her grace and beauty enormous, plentiful—timeless.

Not again, the back of her brain screamed, paralyzing itself with fear, her mind's voice racked with tears. Don't make me live it again.

—flash—

Whatever was controlling her did not listen to her request. Shifting time again, it whisked her to the moment she knew was coming, four days before her eighth birthday. On the way home from the store with presents and party fixings and minds filled with bold plans for the future, a driver, more concerned with the cell phone conversation he was having with his friend, more interested in the chances of some sports team to make the playoffs than he was with watching the road, stole the lives of the parents of the perfect girl waiting at home.

Joan remembered hearing the door, wondering why her father would knock. "Silly daddy," she called. Had he forgotten his keys, did he have his hands full—what game was he playing now, she had asked herself.

Oh, daddy . . .

Joan remembered how she had giggled, opening the door, waiting to see what her father was doing now to make her laugh. She felt again the horrid flood of confusion and fear as she had seen the policeman on the other side of the door.

"Are you Joan," he had asked. She remembered his eyes, unblinking, determined. "Joan de Molina?"

She had nodded. He had spoken again. He had not told her of bloody, twisted metal, of her mother's neck snapped clean by the government's mandated, insisted-upon, demanded under penalty of fine and/or imprisonment airbag. He did not say anything of her father, crushed by the other driver's car, his once handsome face torn to shreds by stabbing glass and ruptured steel. There was no need. His eyes told her everything. Hers filled with tears, her throat with screams.

—flash—

Again the scene changed. This time Joan noticed a shard of light and then suddenly, everything mutated, including herself. She found herself older now, in her third foster home. The place where they allowed her to have pets. The place where her older "brother" delighted in maiming the animals she tried to shelter. She felt the fur in her bed again, the wet fur . . .

—flash—

Forward again to the Brenton home. The place where the wife constantly sniped at her husband and her own child and Joan to stand up straight.

"Walk right," she would fume. "Stand up straight. You look like a pack of freaks."

She watched the husband, the son, struggling to comply, to understand, to endure.

"Are you hunchbacks? Stand up straight. Stand straight. Stop bending over backward. Sit right."

Her eyes began to fill with tears as the voice keened on and on.

"What's wrong with the bunch of you?"

—flash—

Older then—seventeen. Ferris. Ferris Miller. She remembered his face, his touch. His words, always sweet. She thought she was in love. Maybe she was. Maybe he was, too. She recalled him too fondly still to think otherwise.

He had treated her with respect, spoken to her of gentle futures, showed her kindness she had forgotten existed in the world—in other people. He had told her of his dreams, of foreign lands he wanted to visit, of the doctor's degree he wanted to earn, the people he wanted to help.

Oh, Ferris, oh my poor, dear Ferris . . .

Tears broke free from Joan's eyes as she remembered the night they had gone to the concert. The stadium was in the wrong part of town. They had, of course, known better, but she had wanted to go and he could not deny her. They were, after all, seventeen, they were immortal—everything was sure to be all right for such a perfect pair as they. As the scene recreated itself around her, Joan touched Ferris' arm once more.

"Run, darling," she screamed. Somehow hoping to change history, to save the dead hero she adored by turning him into a coward she would hate, "Run—get out of here."

Ferris smiled, not understanding. How could he? What was there to run from? His face stared at her, his mouth forming a question. His smile—so beautiful. Joan's throat caught, her heart skipping a beat, wishing the moment could be frozen in time forever, that she could stare into her darling Ferris' eyes for all time. But, it could not.

In an instant, at the appointed time she saw the thugs approaching again, their leering faces, grasping hands. Again their laughter made her stomach churn. Again their knives flashed. Again she and Ferris turned over their valuables, but it was not enough. Not content with their money, her single piece of valueless jewelry, the drunken trio turned to abusing her. When Ferris tried to defend her their faces lit up. It was, of course, just the party game for which they had been waiting.

"No, Ferris, no," she pleaded with her love, then with his attackers. "Leave him alone!"

Of course, as they had a lifetime ago, the quartet did no such thing. Again they screamed with glee as they viciously stomped on her beloved Ferris, kicked him, crushed his heart and kidneys, his face and spine. Fourteen days he would live on—blind in one eye, mostly unconscious. Fourteen days of a wheezing, pitiful Hell for the girl who soon after would learn never again to trust or hope or dream.

Or cry.

—flash—

Joan watched the doctor approach down the white and blue-tiled corridor once more, heard again his telling her the end had finally come. She felt herself standing numbly as she had that night, walking out of the hospital, seventeen and alone, leaving everything she knew behind.

No more tears, she had promised herself. No more screams. No more suffering. None. No more.

Never again.

Armed with a righteous and burning anger, a pure but unfocused hate aimed at everything around her, the wounded girl had walked until she could no longer move and then she had sunk to the ground and slept. Under a tree, she remembered, in someone's yard. Alone—forever.

The time flashes came more quickly thereafter. Memories flooded over her, briefer bits of the past flinging themselves at her, swirls of different existences overlapping, searing bits of memory burning the woman's mind as they forced themselves on her once more—many for the first time in years.

She saw again her evenings as a call girl—laughing, cooing, giving her marks the useless things they thought they wanted, waiting for them to sleep or use the bathroom, waiting for any three minute moment in which she could rifle their wallets. Social Security and credit card numbers, driver's license serial codes, it took so little for her to be able to empty their bank accounts, destroy their credit, transfer their stock holdings, to ruthlessly steal their lives as others had stolen hers.

—flash—

She saw various officers of the law again, policemen and judges and lawyers, people she learned to use to her long-lasting advantage by allowing them to use her for a moment. Her body began to tremble with rage. Crimson hatred, long-locked away, began to bellow fiercely, to beat against the restraints behind which she had hidden it so many years in the past.

—flash—

And then, when she thought the madness which had somehow enveloped her would break her completely, suddenly the pain disappeared. As the moment changed once more, she recognized where she was immediately, and a smile broke through her pain, calming her racing heart.

"Dancer . . ."

It was that same hole-in-the-wall cafe in Manchester, long since torn down, and she lived again through her first meeting with the Dancer. He was the most legendary of the world's great con artists. He was also the man who took Joan under his wing and taught her all he knew of the many and varied ways people could be convinced to hand over all their belongings to a trusting smile. Their laughter had been cruel, but she had at least learned to make the noise once more.

"Oh, my God," she said, still not understanding what was happening to her, now not caring, grateful for the chance to once more hold the dear old man's hand. "Dancer . . ."

After their three years together, bilking the rich and stupid of the world, her mentor realized that he had shown her all he had to offer. Knowing she needed something more, the venerable Dancer had taken Joan to Austria, to Herr Rabe. Under his tutelage, her skills as a thief had been honed.

—flash—

"Quite a life you've had."

Joan blinked. Gone in a last explosion of light were all the memories—all the forgotten bits she had ignored for so long. Gasping for breath, the woman found herself once more in the Antiquities Room of the museum. She was on her knees. The detective London was still there, next to her, holding her hand. Laub was still there with them as well.

"What the hell just happened here?" Joan gasped for a moment. Then, she sucked down a deep breath, exhaled, and snapped her next words off in anger. "Who are you? And all those shoot 'em up specialists out in the gallery?"

"Can I thank you for your help, first?"

"No. You can . . ." Stopping in mid-sentence, the woman pulled away from London, rubbing her arms furiously as she demanded, "That, that thing," her hand pointed to the still twitching remains of Laub. "What the Hell was that all about? And that damned cup, and, and . . ."

Catching hold of herself, Joan rose to her feet. Her eyes scanned the timepiece on her wrist—only seconds had passed. Amazed but accepting, she checked her possessions quickly, making certain she still had everything with which she had entered the building. Satisfied she was leaving nothing behind, her hands brushed her ears. Smiling, she said;

"On second thought, who cares? We've got to get out of here."

"No time for that," answered London. "The police will be here any moment."

"So—they don't have to find us here when they finally lumber in." Grabbing the detective's arm, she urged, "come on. We can get out of here before they arrive."

"No," London answered calmly. "I need to explain what happened here to them, make them understand it enough so they have the good sense to keep it quiet." Pushing himself up from the floor with Joan's help, the detective looked about for his .38.

"Besides," he said, "Paul and the others, those 'shoot 'em up specialists' as you called them, need time to escape. I'm sending out vibrations that will lead the police to us first."

"You what?"

Joan stared at London with disbelief. She was not about to doubt his words—not after what she had already seen. But, what was wrong with him, she wondered. How could he invite such trouble? How could she look into his eyes and see what she saw? No man had the right to affect her so.

Footsteps sounded in the hall, rough and loud, moving rapidly. Turning to the woman, the detective offered, "A woman with your talents, you can make it out of here in plenty of time, you know. Even woozy I can still handle a few cops on my own."

London smiled warmly as he slid his weapon back into its holster. "Besides, I owe you one. Get going," and then he added, unconsciously, "if you want."

Joan de Molina looked into the detective's face once more. She knew no man could be trusted. She knew there was no percentage in sticking her neck out for anyone—certainly not in getting mixed up with the police. Then, she felt London's warmth coming through the air once more—the vibrations of which he had spoken—and something long frozen within her snapped, brittle pieces of old chains falling away into nothingness.

"I'll stay. After all, like you said . . ." Joan stepped close to London as she spoke, then impulsively put her hand behind his neck and pulled his face to hers. Kissing his lips, she purred, "you owe me one."

And then the door was flung open, and a half-dozen weapons were aimed at the pair.

CHAPTER FOUR

SMOKE SWIRLED IN THE air between the man and the woman. Joan de Molina looked around herself at the close, gray metal walls as they continued to vibrate. Taking another deep drag of the cigarette she had waited too, too long to have, her attention focused for a moment on the wrist of her free hand then flashed back to London.

"You know," she said, holding out her unshackled wrists for the detective to inspect, "this is not the way these people usually do things."

"I know," answered London, a thin bit of a smile curling one side of his mouth. The two sat in the back of a moving police van, unescorted and unrestrained. The woman was referring not only to the lack of anyone travelling there in the rear of the vehicle with them as an escort or the apparently forgotten, but absolutely, under-all-circumstances, required handcuffs, but also to the fact that the two of them had been permitted to travel together.

"It's true," the detective agreed, "normally, standard operating procedure would've been for them to have kept us separated to keep us from talking to each other."

"Can't get our stories straight between us that way," added Joan.

"You're right," agreed London. "But I thought it might be a good idea to put a little stop to all that."

Joan merely raised one eyebrow at London's comment. It was a half-flirtatious, half-"explain yourself" gesture. The detective obligingly continued.

"When one of them moved in to cuff us, I waited for a moment of contact—where I could actually touch him, his bare flesh, I mean—then, I planted a suggestion in his mind to put us both together, leave us alone and, of course, drop the usual bracelets."

"You did all that, did you?" The woman lowered her eyes to flirtatious slits. "Why? Do you chafe easily?"

"Not really," answered the detective. Glancing at the Pirate Queen's ear rings, he added, "but, you know, handcuffs, that steel/silver look. Gold seems to be your color."

Joan looked at London with only a touch of skepticism. She nodded with appreciation at his words, but her mind still reeled from all they had been through. After everything she had seen earlier in the museum she was not about to dismiss anything the detective had to say simply because it went against something she used to believe. For Joan de Molina, twenty minutes in the past the world had ceased following the rules she had learned throughout her life up until that point.

Still, she was curious. More than curious—intrigued. Aroused. Grateful for her cigarette, both in its role as comforter and as prop, she continued, feigning more confusion than she actually felt, admitting to more than she ever would have even half an hour earlier.

"I understand what you're saying, I do . . . but, ah, I still don't . . ."

"What you need," interrupted London, "are some explanations. First off, let me apologize to what happened to you in the museum. The flashbacks of your life."

The police van came to a sudden, too-fast stop, one which slid the detective and Joan along the metal bench welded into its wall. The two slammed against one another, then against the wall separating them from the driver. In no hurry to move away, Joan feigned helplessness and nuzzled her head against London's chest coyly, pulling herself erect once more by using his shoulders for leverage. London, of course, was not fooled by her act. But then, he was not meant to be fooled. Joan brought her head to eye level and stared at the detective, fixing him with a pouting look. What she saw in his eyes told her he probably had not minded the contact very much.

"So," she purred, her tone one of wounded dignity, "you caused all of that, did you?"

London nodded, his eyes almost sheepish. Joan dug one of her fingers playfully into his chest and asked;

"All right, then . . . two questions—why and how?"

"I'm sorry, but I had to know who I was dealing with. Even though, thank you very much, by the way, you'd just saved my life and, through extension, the entire world, ah . . ."

London actually colored—a slight involuntary shade change, barely noticeable—but the Pirate Queen's heart skipped nonetheless. He rolled his eyes slightly as he continued;

"I'll explain that later . . . but anyway, I still needed to know who—and what—you were. What I mean is, you weren't supposed to be there in the museum any more than any of we were, so I needed to know . . . why were you there? What were you up to, what'd you want, where'd you come from? I had to know everything and I had to know it quickly."

Joan nodded—accepting, fascinated.

"The invasion I made of your mind," London continued, well aware of the woman's feelings toward him, "was pretty much the same thing I did to the cop who put us in here. Of course, I didn't have to learn anything about him—just plant a few orders."

"And . . . you do things like this often?" she asked the detective, her voice half-awed, half-admiring—wondering if he knew what she was beginning to realize—smoke curling from her still smiling lips.

"Actually, I've never tried anything like this before," he answered honestly, his New York accent fading slightly as his Southern roots warmed his voice. "And really, I do apologize, Ms. de Molina . . ."

"Oh, my," interrupted the woman, her tone sounding almost wounded, "after what we've been through, sharing minds and all, I don't think you need to be so formal. Call me Joan."

London dipped his head in a shallow nod. Giving the woman a bit of a smile in return, he continued.

"As I was saying, I apologize, Joan," the woman smiled back, nodding in approval. "aka, the Pirate Queen, but I've never entered someone's mind like that before. I wasn't even certain I could do it. But, with all that was going on, I had to know that you weren't one of Laub's people, or some other part of Q'talu's plan—not that you'd know who-slash-what that is."

"Q'talu," replied Joan matter-of-factly. Crushing out her cigarette on the wall of the police van, black embers crumbled as she added, "an interdimensional god of some sort that was responsible for the destruction of Elizabeth, New Jersey, and most of lower Manhattan back a few months ago. Right, Mr. Theodore London, aka, the Destroyer?"

The detective nodded dumbly, his eyes going wide, mouth drying. Joan continued.

"Every twenty-five hundred years, give or take an hour," she told him, her voice purring, her eyes amused, "Fate picks a person to place in the way of those things that would destroy us. This time around, it was your turn. You were just a normal man up until that moment, now you're the closest thing this world has to an actual superhero—yes?"

London was shocked. Nothing he had read in the woman's mind had indicated she had any prior knowledge of him and his activities—nor that she had any particular psychic or extraordinary abilities. As best he knew, no one outside of his circle of investigators knew anything of what they had done. He had gone to great lengths to make certain of that. Turning his head at an angle, he probed the inside of his mouth with his tongue as he looked Joan over carefully. Finally, he asked;

"I'll bite. How do you know anything about me?"

"Same way you know about me, Houdini," the woman answered. "When you made me live my life over, you were in contact with me, sucking up the information you wanted. I can believe you've never tried to pull that little trick before, elsewise you would know that while you were getting all your questions answered about me, I was learning all I wanted about you."

London stared dumbly. Joan laughed. Holding up her hand once more, she touched the detective's chin softly with a single finger. Then, turning it gently, she dug the tip of it softly into the cleft in his chin.

"Oh, poor man, hims not used to having women play his game without a handicap." Gently flicking the bottom of his nose with her finger, Joan pulled her hand back.

"Yes," she said," you're the man Destiny moved out as a roadblock to stall off things like this Q'talu. Thanks to you, he, it, whatever you want to call the great slimy beast, has been barred entry to our dimension. But," she continued, her voice growing more serious, "it can still reach over and cause havoc through useful idiots like your friend Laub. As time goes on you think . . . no, I'd guess it's more like hope, isn't it, you *hope* this creature's reach will grow strained and scenes like this incident with Laub won't happen any more."

London regained control of his facial features, blanking over the surprise Joan's knowledge had forced him to show. Pursing his lips, he had to strain to maintain his composure as she went on with her playful lecture, letting him know how much information he had carelessly let slip through his fingers.

"Still, despite all the monster hunting, you're an interesting man, all in all," Joan purred. "Six foot one, two hundred and ten pounds, owner of your own business, partnered with an ex-janitor and saddled with a weepy chestnut curled dim-bulb you can't figure out how to ditch."

"Excuse me," said London, his attitude frosting over suddenly, "that wouldn't exactly be my description of Lisa."

"Oh, wouldn't it," asked the woman. Turning her body, half to face the detective directly, half to allow herself to stretch out before his eyes, she told him, "don't be too sure. Remember, I've had the full tour inside that locked-down dome of yours. Because of the way you sprang things on me, I didn't realize what was happening at first, but now, well, let's just say that maybe I know some things you don't."

When London only answered her with an uncomfortable silence, she nodded sympathetically.

"I understand. Believe me I do. But facts are facts, and out of a misguided sense of loyalty, you feel you have to keep up the pretense of a relationship with your former client."

"I think . . ."

"No, Teddy, you're not thinking. You're letting your feelings blind you to the truth. The menace you wanted to protect her from is gone. Locked away. Finished. But, you're thinking that if it ever gets out it's going to come after her again."

The detective sat on the metal bench, his mouth open the slightest crack. No words came out, however, for he simply did not know how to respond.

"A man in love would have done something about it by now. But you, you've spent most of the time since you met poor little Lisa Hutchinson keeping her at a long arm's length. You're a proper couple, to say the least. The fact you haven't slept together would be telling, but why go there—you two've barely kissed."

Joan let a small laugh escape her lips. She used the inward rush of air which followed it to subtly move her body in an attractive fashion. As the detective sat silently, she dropped her voice an octave as she speculated;

"Hummmm, she is such a child. Maybe it's the age difference that's holding you back—you and her more than ten years apart . . . not like us . . ."

London pursed his lips uncomfortably, defenseless in the face of the facts the woman had pulled from his head due to his carelessness. As he cleared his throat nervously, she almost laughed once more, but spared him the embarrassment.

"Whatever it is," she continued, "there's no ring on little Lisa's finger, and no thoughts in all your wide male skull about putting one there, either. You're a bachelor, Teddy London, have been ever since your Jenny died . . ."

A hiss of motion blurred the small space within the back of the van. Without seeing what happened, Joan found herself moved back several feet from London. Or, more precisely, where London had been. As the woman turned, she found the detective suddenly sitting behind her. His eyes had narrowed to slits. His smile was gone, replaced by a thin harsh line.

"Hit a nerve, did I?"

The detective did not answer.

"Well, touché, mister," she spat, her tone growling, not backing down. "Now maybe you know how it feels to have all the worst parts of your life pulled up and flung in your face, all your deepest secrets pawed over by some stranger."

As London softened slightly, the Pirate Queen lowered her tone, reaching into the back of her mind for tricks she had not needed in nearly a decade.

"You apologized to me, so I'll do the same. That was mean of me. You were only doing what you had to when you . . . I can't believe I'm actually saying this . . . when you *read my mind*. So, let's just say we're even now." Then Joan extended her hand toward the detective.

"Friends?"

London looked at the hand before him, delicate despite the heavy black glove. The woman was a thief—without morals or scruples. But, he reminded himself, she had also saved his life. Indeed, the woman had been the one to stop Laub, or more importantly, to stop Q'talu, where he could not. That she had had luck and surprise on her side did not matter, he forced himself to admit. She could just have easily slid back into the hall and disappeared. But, instead she had acted decisively when most people would have been gibbering in fear, screaming in terror or heaving up the contents of their stomachs. After that, she had stayed by his side and risked the police to be with him. Although he had no intention of being disloyal to Lisa, still he felt more than slightly responsible for Joan's current situation.

You told her she could run, the back of his mind snapped. She chose to stay. Let her take her chances.

With what she knows, another voice within his brain offered, a deep tone, one of his more ancient ancestors, would that actually be wise?

I think we're stuck with her.

Yeah, came yet another of the detective's ancestors, and she knows it.

Women. You can't trust 'em. This is going to be nothing but trouble. She's . . .

Pretty interesting. Good looking. And like she said, ain't no one got a ring on their finger with our name on it.

Other voices began to stir, all throwing in their opinion. Ever since his first contact with the supernatural, London had been privileged to be in a form of mental contact with the stored memories of all his ancestors. At many times he found their combined knowledge, spanning the millennia as it did, could offer useful, often wise, council. There were other times, however, when he was simply on his own. Knowing he had reached one of those moments, the detective cut off their flow of comments, then took the Pirate Queen's hand and shook it warmly.

"Friends," he agreed. "At the least—friends."

"So," said Joan, feeling herself at ease in the company of a man in a way she had not allowed herself to feel in years, "what next?"

"Next," said London, "we've got to explain everything that happened in the museum to the cops and get ourselves out of their grasp."

As the van began to slow, Joan asked why, as long as he was giving the police mental orders, London could not have simply told them to allow the two of them to leave.

"That would've only been a temporary solution," he explained. "There was Laub's body to deal with, the cup to be gotten out of the reach of the general public. If this story fell into the media's grasp as a mystery—who shot up the museum, what was the creature discovered there . . ."

"Creatures," Joan corrected him, remembering the things Pa'sha and the others had gunned down.

"Well, there you go," agreed London, his eyes twinkling at her quickness. "The police have to be convinced to cover this all up from the beginning. I've got to have a chance to talk to whoever can do that by laying out all our cards on the table and hoping for the best."

Joan considered the detective for a second. From their shared moment when he had inadvertently allowed her access to his memory pool, she knew he was telling the truth. He had allowed his friends to escape detection, drawing the police's collective attention down on himself so that he would be the only one to deal with them.

And why, she thought, why so he can make certain the great unwashed masses aren't upset with tales of bogeymen. My, my, my sweet Mr. Teddy London, aren't you the interesting one?

At that moment the van came to a sudden, jerking halt. It had stopped previously more than once, but this time both the detective and the Pirate Queen could tell it had finally reached its destination. Before another word could be said by either of them, the van's engine went silent. Seconds later the sound of keys were heard in the door lock. The two moved apart unconsciously, their eyes turning toward the rear of the van.

While London straightened his jacket, Joan's hands busied themselves with her hair, shoving it this way and that, pulling it forward over her shoulders and ears. Then, as the pair watched, the two doors at the back were opened and a quartet of policemen stood waiting, the closest to the door motioning to them both to exit the vehicle.

"I think I'll let you do the talking," whispered Joan. She smiled at him again, brushing the back of his neck with the fingers of one hand as they moved to leave.

London nodded slightly in response. The formerly bickering voices within his head gave him a single message, all of them gravely letting him know he was moving into deep trouble. He did not need any of them to confirm that they were not talking about the police.

INTERLUDE

D AVID HARDY LOOKED AROUND himself. He had just returned to his home after another long day. Of course, for Hardy, arriving home in the middle of the night was nothing unusual, had not been for years. His work demanded his presence in the lab for hours on end sometimes— often. Actually, recently those times had increased to where "some times" had become "all the time." But, for now, anyway, he was home, peacefully sitting in his dining room, hands palm down on the table—alone in the dark.

Quiet, he thought. I love when it's quiet.

He let his gaze wander across the walnut breakfront standing against the wall in front of him, taking in the various prizes his wife had discovered in curio shops and street stalls and even a few moldering barns across the face of Europe—the Richard Redgrave christening cup that had thrilled her so dearly, the candlesticks she found in Venice, and her vases–

"What were they," Hardy mused, trying to remember what was special about the two small-mouthed pieces of pottery. Somehow out of the swirl of antique terminology his wife continually tried to teach him, which he always seemed to forget instantly, he somehow remembered the phrase, "Royal Lancastrian ware."

That was it. He did not know which Lancaster the vases were from, or what made them royal, he just remembered the vast sum they had cost him. In fact, every place his eyes wandered within the large room, an object could be seen, the price of which instantly reminded him as to exactly why it was he needed to pound away in his lab, constantly swimming forward, struggling to keep himself ahead of the always nearing crest. Working, endlessly working, all so he could support a family it seemed he never saw anymore. All so he could feel fortunate just to sit in the dark in his own home in the small hours of the morning.

Alone.

"Alone," he said the word aloud, but quietly, thinking, yeah—that's me, all right.

Of course, at such a late hour, no one else in his home was awake. His wife, his children, all of them would be asleep for at least another few hours. Hardy sighed at the thought. He had his house—the downstairs, anyway—all to himself. Peace and quiet. No one to disturb him. The same way he found himself almost every time he came home, anymore.

Staring out the sculptured bay window overlooking the main yard, Hardy forced his vision through the darkness, straining to make out various details on his grounds. He loved his garden so, the opportunity it occasionally still afforded him to cut himself off from the world, to do something slow and honest and natural. When he and his wife had first purchased their estate, they had hired a service to take care of everything outside the house, the planting, weeding, trimming, et cetera. But Hardy had found the final effect the gardeners created a bit too manicured, too perfect. He wanted it to look somehow different, rougher—more random, more realistic, more honest. Eventually he had cut their services back to mowing the lawns, pulling the weeds and pruning the trees, leaving them the "grunt" work while he took over the creative challenges.

Aided by the reflected light of a brightly clear, full moon, his eyes came to rest on the crescent-shaped patch of gladiolus he had installed the year before. The favorable winter had been kind to all the yards in the neighborhood, but he felt as if his had been especially blessed. Through the spring, while the snow was still on the ground, first the various strains of crocus had broke forth, soon followed by the tulips and daffodils which had bloomed in multi-colored abundance.

At least I know how to do something right, he thought, his gaze captured by the moonlit yard beyond the window.

He took in the sight of his delicate stand of Lily of the Valley, the violets, bleeding hearts—all the others. All of them had rushed to meet the new rain, filling every corner of his two acres with their delicate beauty. His four stands of rose bushes had offered enormous yields as well. And the irises—both the small, regular-sized ones and the towering, three foot tall, bearded variety— his wife had filled vase after vase and still there had been plenty of color left outside to please the eye in every direction.

"You're looking fine," he told the remaining gladiolus. "I hope you're all happy this morning."

Hardy felt silly speaking to his flowers, especially when he was still inside. He was glad no one was about to hear him for, sitting in the dining room, he could not even claim to be talking to his blossoms for their health, following the assurances of those progressives who believed it beneficial for plant life if their owners chattered to them.

Wake up, moron, the back of his mind whispered to him. They can't hear you.

"I know, I know," he answered aloud, although quietly, "it's just that they're easier to talk to than anyone else around here these days."

Regrettably, David Hardy was a man who had lost sight of his life some time back. He had not only just recently begun to realize the fact, but also the enormity of it. His children, both of them from a previous marriage, though still young had grown distant toward him. Cold, really. Part of it was their new life style, the extravagant extra frills that had come from the rush of money his work had brought. Part of it was resentment toward their father at the way he had abandoned their mother.

True, she had been ill, and life had been hard for her, raising the pair practically alone with their father always in the lab. And he had always been in the lab, it seemed. Always late, always staying later—working endless hours and never bringing home enough money. For years it had been that way, always having to make due with less and less. She had never been a robust sort, and so her breakdown had come as only a mild surprise to those who knew the family. But Hardy's reaction to her infirmity had surprised everyone—even himself.

At the same time his wife had needed to be hospitalized, David Hardy had finally made the breakthrough he had always sworn he was on the verge of making. It had been one of those amazing accidents, a series of events never to be duplicated which gave him the answer for which he had been looking. The timing of it, sadly, had been one of those cruel twists of fate, one to which even he felt he could have responded to in a better fashion. Sadly, however, he had not.

Come on, now, don't get into that again. Really, what else was I supposed to do?

David Hardy had asked himself that question many times before that morning. Every time his answer had been the same—silence, and a sad lowering of his eyes. Guilt over his actions had sniffed at his heels since the first trip to the doctor's office. He had loved his first wife—he had. He knew he had. But somehow, of all the possible voices in his head to listen to, he had chosen the worst one to give his attention.

Due to his breakthrough, bonus money had begun to pour in by the truckload—riches were suddenly his beyond anything he had ever thought possible. In a matter of weeks his wife found herself in a rest home, shunted there perhaps for life—her years of constant devotion conveniently forgotten.

A shallow man, really, that was what he had to consider himself. He had always thought he loved his wife, but he found with the arrival of his new station in life, he was suddenly completely incapable of the type of loyalty she had shown him. His new wealth obscenely inflating his self-importance, Hardy quickly divorced his helpless wife to take up with his assistant. Soon, Ms. Della Gorstein, blonde and sensual, fifteen years his junior, easily young enough to be his daughter, not nearly old enough to be the mother of his children, was his wife.

David Hardy was a well-envied man. He had shed himself of his "baggage companion" and managed to not lose his new-found fortune or his children while doing so. After years of blind toil, struggling to bring a vision to reality, he had a mansion, riches and a beautiful companion to share them. He had those members of his family around him which he wanted nearby, and had been able to dispose of the one of whom he was bored. To all intents and purposes, David Hardy's life had reached perfection.

Hardy stared out the window a moment longer. He smiled at his beautiful gladiolus, only days away from opening in the wonderfully temperate June weather New York had been blessed with that year. Then, as he had taken to doing whenever he had the chance, in those rare moments whenever he found himself safely alone, the man with the perfect life put his face in his hands and began to weep.

He would not stop until the rapidly approaching sunrise mocked him with the advent of another glorious day.

CHAPTER FIVE

"SO, MR. LONDON, I'M told you wanted the opportunity to say a few words?"

Police detective William Krandell was a large man—Caucasian, clean shaven, approaching middle age, but hiding it well. His shoulders were broad, his features blunt, his head bald. Even when smiling, his mind relaxed, the officer was a fearsome figure. Whenever he put on his standard interrogation face, however, his intimidation factor went up greatly.

"I'm told there was some bit of a story you wanted to share with us?"

A usually pleasant man, one actually thought of as quite the joker by his family and friends, he showed no trace of his lighter side at that moment. No, for interrogations the lieutenant always brought up the side of his personality that knew no humor. Doing so was a tactic he found most useful, the wearing of his extra personality, "Mr. Sinister," as his captain had nicknamed the persona he used for criminal interviews. The police detective was expecting no trouble from the pair before him. They might take a little extra time, he admitted, but a challenge was always welcome to a man like Krandell, one who too quickly had grown too good at what he did.

"Yes, I do," answered the detective in a matter-of-fact tone his interrogator found a touch flippant. "And, I'm hoping that your captain, or someone equally high-up, is on the other side of the two-way as well," he added, indicating the wall-length slab of glass behind them reflecting their images.

"It'll save us all a lot of time."

Krandell frowned internally. Second to second, the two suspects were proving to be something other than what he had anticipated. True, a state licensed detective with a small, but clean, one might as well say exemplary, record, and a known museum raider and antiquities thief were both types he expected to be at least somewhat cool under pressure, but there was something wrong here—something more.

He was used to being handed the toughest interrogations. That was to be expected. And yes, there was nothing inflated in his expectation that people brought in for him to fix under his personal microscope would display some sense of urgency. But, not the type of urgency like he was reading from the two before him. They were concerned—but not for themselves. Indeed, as far as their personal futures were concerned, the pair seemed cool; too cool—smug, even. In fact, the attitude they projected was one of authority, as if they were the ones in charge.

What the shit is goin' on this time, he wondered, not able to gauge the situation with his normal ease. Studying the couple sitting on the other side of the table, he thought, maybe there's something stewing around here I'm not keen to yet. I mean, what's the deal with these two? Why all the special treatment? Why'm I seeing the two of them together? Why aren't these two in separate rooms? Whose screw up is this?

Aloud, however, Krandell revealed nothing of his frustration or anxiety, expertly holding his cards close to his vest. It might take him a bit longer, he allowed, but he would crack his prisoners if it took all night.

"So, you want to save time, you say," asked the officer, fishing, looking for something to explain the odd ticks he was getting from the man and woman before him. "Now, why would that be, eh? Got somewhere important to go?

"Some pressing date—you and the Pirate Queen here?" When his identification of Joan's alias failed to elicit a response from either her or London, the lieutenant continued to prod, looking for the crack in their armor he knew he would inevitably find sooner or later.

"What's the matter, Red? Didn't think we'd identify you so quickly, did you?"

"Please, I think you're the police," Joan answered in a voice that promised trouble. The woman caused Krandell to turn for some reason he could not explain, undercutting his powers of anticipation. Point one to them, he thought. "That makes you predictable and pedantic, sometimes amusing, usually boring, but I've never thought of you as completely incapable. Not even here in provincial little America.

"Then again, considering our present host," Joan smiled, lighting a cigarette, "I suppose I should admit that I am well known for my generosity."

"I'm not," grunted the detective harshly. "Put out that cigarette."

"Arrest me," sniped the woman.

The Pirate Queen arched her body and threw the force of the motion at Krandell with the snap of her exhale. Her nose wrinkled with condescension, a minute thing, but enough of an insult to the officer to snap his concentration once again. He stared at Joan and thought for a moment—too many emotions slamming one against another for him to act.

"Detective Krandell," interrupted London, forcing the man's eyes to shift again—point two, "let's get down to business, shall we? What are we charged with—breaking and entering? Perhaps, but you won't be able to make it stick."

What the hell is up with this guy? Where's he going with this? Krandell could sense that none of the usual lies were about to follow. This one's got a new angle. Okay, pitch to me, asshole. I love a good game as much as the next guy.

"Theft?" continued London. "Nothing's missing, so that won't stick, either. I hear there are bullet holes in the walls, but as you know, Joan wasn't armed, and you'll find none of the slugs your people are going to recover are from my .38, so you're at a loss there, too. You can get us for trespass, obviously, but you've got bigger problems on your hands."

"Like what?"

"Excuse me? Are you telling me you don't know, Krandell?" London stared unblinking, his eyes boring into the officer's, his look finely calculated to transmit actual surprise. "How 'in the dark' are they keeping you?"

"I'm not the . . . you . . ." Lieutenant William Krandell found himself sputtering, caught himself before London could pull him in any further.

Okay, he told himself, calm down—do it! You been coasting on your rep. Now, a hard nut comes along and suddenly you're acting the rookie. Tough it up, dickweed.

"Ohhh, you feeling better now, officer," asked Joan with a trace of a sneer. Holding back the urge to laugh, she taunted Krandell, saying, "You poor lamb. Try taking deep breaths, one-two, one-two, you'll be all right."

"Shut up, bitch," snarled the officer. His fist slamming against the table, he shouted, "who the goddamned hell do you two think you are? I'm in charge here."

"Yeah, right," answered London, his tone halfway between bored and urgent. "Look, Krandell, for your own good, I think you'd better drop the badass approach and start thinking about working with us. Trust me, the time you and this city have is definitely running out."

"Tick tock, tick tock," added Joan through a sarcastic smile. She beamed it at the officer, wagging her index finger back and forth as she spoke.

Point three, he growled to himself, knowing that the redhead was well aware of just how completely she was getting to him.

"You people think you're some kind of comedians," snarled Krandell. The interrogator regretted his words, but had no others to give. He knew he was making a mess of things. His usual competence was evaporating, rushing away from him. He felt like the worst kind of rookie, but he could see no reason for any of it. Whatever it was that was rattling him about the pair across the table from him, he could not peg it. Regretting his words even as he heard them, he finished his sentence, saying, "You think that this is all some big joke."

"Drop it, officer," snapped London. Krandell's head snapped back as if he had been struck. Leaning forward across the interrogation table, the detective added, "we do not have the time to waste."

"You god'suckin' punk," Krandell felt his face going red, felt his internal pressure rising. He knew he was stumbling, but he could not contain his rage, "I'll cut you off at the knees. I'll bury your ass so deep in shit you'll have to take the elevator to find bottom!"

"No," whispered London in a tight voice, his words firing in a straight drill line into Krandell's brain. "You won't. You can't afford the luxury of the typical brute stupidity that normally motivates your kind. This is all too big for you. Now, you listen to me, you stumbling ape, you'd better get someone in here who knows the score and you'd better do it fast, or this city is going to come apart at the seams."

Krandell stared at the detective intently. He opened his mouth to speak, closed it, then opened it once more. Even after the long pause, still the policeman had found no words he wanted to say—that he even *could* say. His will seemed as if it was being sapped away—stolen from him second by second. There was simply something about the man across the table from the officer that was compelling him to obey.

The big detective tried to defiantly stand his ground, however, his hands clenching the edge of the table. Two beads of sweat broke out on his forehead, one remaining stationary, the other trickling down into his left eye. Blinking, Krandell began to shake, part of him urging obedience to London's dictates, another raging violently against the idea.

"Tick tock, tick tock," said Joan mockingly, her finger once more wagging in Krandell's face.

Red-faced and angry, the police detective released his grip on the edge of the interrogation room table. His arms coming up furiously, he started to move around the barrier, his intent obviously focused on the Pirate Queen. His speed was a surprising blur for such a big man.

London's was faster.

"Now, now . . ."

The detective was standing. Somehow he had made it out of his seat and around Joan's to cut off Krandell's approach. The Pirate Queen watched the scene calmly, a contented wreath of smoke pluming in triumph around her.

"Don't do it," London warned calmly.

As the officer lunged, the detective side-stepped, bringing his arm up to neck level, clotheslining Krandell as he tried to get hold of Joan. The larger man hit hard—throat against bone—instantly collapsing in a gagging fit.

Awww, damnit! thought London. That's just going to make things harder.

He had not wanted a physical confrontation with the lieutenant. He knew the man was unarmed—standard operating procedure for an interrogator—but he also knew there were at least three observers on the other side of the two-way glass who were armed. Working against the clock, London caught the sputtering Krandell. Then, holding the man upright, keeping him from hitting his head, the detective whispered in his ear.

"Don't you get it yet? Have you ever lost it like this? Is this normal for you? No. There's something more at work here. And if you and the rest of the trained gorillas around here don't catch on fast, we're *all* going to be in the soup."

Krandell waved his arms, gasping for breath. Before he could say anything, however, the single door to the room opened.

"Detective Krandell," a harsh voice snapped. "Perhaps you'd like to get a breath of air?"

It was not a request.

All right, thought London. Now things should get interesting.

CHAPTER SIX

THE STILL-CHOKING OFFICER TURNED to see his captain standing in the doorway.

"S-Sir," he stammered. "I . . ."

Krandell coughed, gagging on the sloshing egg of phlegm lodged sideways in his throat. He swallowed hard, pushing himself off the cement floor, clearing his throat with difficulty. The police detective looked sheepish, confused—how, he wondered, his brain almost paralyzed, could he have lost his temper, so quickly, to a pair like that, like *that?*

"Yes . . ., ah, air. Maybe I should . . . ah, yes, sir."

Krandell backed away from London, mumbling something else to his superior as he made his way out of the room, head hung low, eyes glazed. The captain nodded curtly, but with sympathy, then allowed the larger man a moment to clear the doorway. After that he closed the door softly so as not to embarrass his detective further. Then the officer turned sharply to face London and the Pirate Queen.

"So," he said, his eyes locking on London's eyes, "let's start this over. My name is Cantalupo. Michael Cantalupo. I don't usually have to interfere with one of my officers in something as routine as an opening interrogation. You want to tell me what's so different this time?"

"Be happy to," answered the detective. "Are you a man who can handle what I have to tell you, or are you going to crumple up on me like your boy Krandell?"

"You'll have to try me," answered Cantalupo. The captain, a balding, cold-eyed man with a wiry black beard and a nose that had known more than one violent encounter, sat down in the chair opposite London's. Turning to Joan, he threw his eyes at her cigarette in a gesture the woman recognized as a universal plea for a smoke. She slid her pack as well as her lighter across to him, nodding her generosity. He threw her a head movement she knew meant she had a small sliver of his undying gratitude.

"I like him," she said, beaming at the captain, just the right amount of imp in her manner to assure that everything was fine and that everyone was the best of friends again. Cantalupo lit up, grateful his inhale helped hide the smile he almost let slip. He made a mental note to be careful around the woman as he returned her cigarettes and her lighter. Then, welcome smoke pouring out of his body, he returned most of his gaze to London.

"Okay, we're all mellow campers filled with love for each other. Start talking."

"You've got a problem. More than one actually. And you're not sure what to do about any of them. First off, you've got a body you can't explain. And, my guess is that in the museum hallway where you found extensive damage from machine gun and shotgun fire you found several more, even less-human bodies that you're finding even harder to explain."

"So far so good," said the captain evenly, giving nothing extra away with either his tone or his expression. "Now tell me what it's all about."

"I will," answered London. Indicating the glass partition behind him with his thumb, he said, "but first, you've got to do something for me. You've got to shut down the recorders on the other side of that window and get the observers out of there. You want to hear what I have to say—fine. I'll talk. But to you, and only to you."

Cantalupo thought quietly for a moment. He knew what kind of a panic the city would have on its hands if he were to let be known even what little he already knew of what had transpired so far that night. If the press were to get pictures of the bodies he had seen the questions would be unending. So would be the complaints from city hall, and from higher above where the real power resided. A smaller man might have looked on the situation as a way to fame and recognition. Cantalupo saw only continuous, unanswerable questions and a nightmare of endless conflict.

Of course, the people have a right to know, he told himself. This would be like covering up the landing of a UFO, or the discovery of werewolves in Central Park.

Yeah, that's true, another voice in the captain's mind mused, but being the one to let the news out without approval from above isn't a very smart idea, either, and you know it. So, ask yourself this, Mikey, is this the kind of thing you want to end your career over?

Situations like the one confronting Cantalupo were not unknown in Manhattan. The island had a long history of disturbing occurrences, just as the police department had a long history of hiding the details. Finally, deciding he wanted—needed—to hear what London had to say, the captain gave the people on the other side of the glass barrier a hand signal to shut down operations. A light came on from behind the mirror which suddenly rendered it a simple two-way piece of glass. Over a speaker, one of the officers on the other side asked;

"You sure about this, captain?"

"Mr. London and his companion don't look as if they have anything dangerous in mind. Are you planning on doing me any harm, Mr. London—Ms. de Molina?"

"I might offer you another cigarette," Joan answered coyly.

When she said nothing more, and London continued to answer only with a look, Cantalupo simply raised an eyebrow. The gesture was understood and his people dispersed. After that, the captain settled back in his chair, indicating that he had done his part and was now waiting for the detective or the Pirate Queen to start talking. London obliged.

"Several months ago, captain, I stumbled into . . . what can I call it . . . another realm of reality, for lack of any better description, that has . . ."

The detective's words trailed off. He could feel the concerns of the man sitting across from him, could tell the officer was already confused enough—anxious enough. Cutting what he had prepared to say sharply, he adjusted, saying;

"Look, I'll be square with you—I don't know how to describe the things I've seen—that I've done. Do you believe in vampires, captain? People who can just lay their hands on your flesh and drain your life away? I didn't. Not up until a few weeks ago. I do now. I didn't believe in other dimensions, or flying lizardmen, either, but I do now. And, if you want to check your records, you'll find there are more than a few officers downtown who believe in flying lizardmen—as well as a few more of them who can't be here to testify one way or the other for having met some."

Cantalupo's fingers curled into fists in his lap. His fingernails dug into his palms. The public had never been told about the reports several months back of the restaurant that had been torn apart by what people claimed were flying creatures—giant bats, or dinosaurs, or something. Not by the authorities. When the police had been asked to comment on the stories that had spread across the city, they had officially laughed off the wild, tabloidesque stories.

Officially.

"Go on, Mr. London."

"Tonight a low-grade boob who thought he was the great-grandson of Merlin broke into the museum where your people found Joan and myself. His name was David Laub. He'd made a pact with a thing from another dimension. He would use a sacred relic from the museum to bring the thing into our world and it would reward him with treasures and power beyond measure."

London paused for a breath. The captain looked dazed. Blinking hard to drive away his fatigue, the detective started again, saying;

"Yeah, I know—it's a story you've seen in any number of bad horror films. But, you've got to trust me on this, that doesn't stop what I'm saying from being real. The thing mutated Laub's body from beyond, giving him the power to utilize the relic's magic. It also created the other things you found in the museum to be his helpers."

Cantalupo ground his teeth together. He could tell London was speaking from the heart. Of course, the captain reasoned, so do all sorts of crazies who came to the station house to confess to being alien warlords, and serial killers, who brought themselves to his domain to unburden their unstable minds of all manner of unbelievable nonsense, staring at him sincerely with forlorn eyes shaded by tin foil hats. But, London was not one of those. The captain knew it. There was simply something about the detective that forced Cantalupo to take him seriously—as much as he might not want to do so.

It's his eyes, the captain thought. Staring at London's face, the officer shuddered as he flinched from looking any deeper, repeating to himself, *his eyes.*

"So, what do you think we should do?"

"Honestly," answered the detective, "I'd destroy the cup. Tell the museum it was stolen. Do humanity a favor and have it melted down into slag, encase the slag in concrete and then throw the whole bloody mess off a bridge. Don't get any bright ideas about cashing in the gold or jewels and putting the proceeds in the widows and orphans fund. The metal, the gems, all of it's tainted. Just get rid of it, and have the people that do it wear gloves. As for the bodies—burn them. Bag them and send them to the nearest incinerator and be done with them."

"And the damage?"

"Blame it on extremists," answered Joan. Leaning back in her chair slightly, she exhaled another deep lungful of gray as she suggested, "You'll find that the cup was a Middle Eastern relic. Say that the weapons' fire strike marks throughout the place were the result of a heroic battle between the police and terrorists—they wanted their holy objects returned and didn't care how they did so. Actually, they were going to blow up the museum after they took back the artifacts of their culture, but luckily superior police work put you all on the scene on time to keep them from doing anything more than stealing the cup."

When London looked at the woman, one eyebrow raised, she smiled, reminding him, "Goward told you about the cup . . . and remember, what you know, I know."

Cantalupo stared at the pair across the table from him, wondering exactly what was going on between the two of them. Silently, he pulled his lips together into a straight line, pressing his tongue against the back of his tightly clenched teeth. Suddenly he knew exactly how Krandell had felt. He did not like the feeling. Not in the least.

Who is this guy?

It was eerie after all his years to feel so completely as if he were not in charge anymore. And yet, he had somehow known this would happen from the first moment he saw the two brought in—together, uncuffed. Indeed, he had sent Krandell into the interrogation chamber almost certain that the officer would fail in his attempt to get anything out of London and his companion.

"Captain," ventured the detective, "there's something you're not telling us, isn't there?"

"You're a clever man, Mr. London," answered Cantalupo, his voice taut, tinged with menace. "I'm going to tell you something you might not believe at first. And that is that I'm going to follow your recommendations."

London eyed the officer with slight suspicion.

"All of them."

The detective did not speak. He was being told what he wanted to hear, but he was positive he did not yet know the reason why. Cantalupo was convinced London was correct, of that the detective was certain. But, he was equally certain the policeman had not been convinced solely by what he had just heard. No, Cantalupo was agreeing with him too quickly. Too easily.

"Now," answered the captain, "you might think someone hearing what you have to say would need more convincing, but for reasons of my own, I don't. I believe you."

Joan and the detective looked at each other once more in silence. Both of them realized there was an overwhelming feeling of too-good-to-be-true in the air. As they waited, the captain continued. "You don't have to take my word on it, though. I have proof. You'll give me a moment, won't you?"

Without waiting for a reply, Cantalupo rose and went to the door. Opening it, he stuck his head into the hall and asked for an officer Fergeson to be brought to the interrogation room. While they waited, the captain explained.

"I believe you had dealings with officer Fergeson earlier this evening, Mr. London. He was in charge of the museum scene. If I'm right, I think you'll be able to explain what's . . . but then, why spoil the surprise?"

London felt a sinking pressure in his chest. As the wave of emotion overwhelmed the detective, Joan felt her own chest tighten. She looked over at London, her hand reaching for his, her fingers closing over it, consoling, pleading. Before either of them could say anything, however, the door opened once more.

Oh, no, thought London, his throat going dry, his pulse quickening. Oh, Christ . . .

Into the room came the officer with whom the detective had made contact at the museum, the one he had touched and cavalierly given instructions to place Joan and him in the same vehicle, with no handcuffs, alone. The man whose mind he had entered and played in as if he were rearranging a sock drawer.

I did to him what I did to Joan, he realized in an instant. I only wanted to . . .

Wanted to what? another part of his mind hissed. Take a shortcut, make things easy? Cheat?

"You!" Sergeant Carl Fergeson stood semi-erect, holding onto the officer that had been helping him move over the last hour. "It was you!"

London could see it in the man's eyes. All the horrors that the detective had known over the past few months, the countless rivers of blood he had spilled defending humanity, the terrible things he had seen and those equally terrible things he had been forced to do, the monsters he had faced and the monster he had at times become, all of it had flashed into the man's brain in their moment of contact.

"You, you . . . what *are* you? What did you do to me? What did you god-damn *do to me?*"

There were bandages on the man's hands, scratches on his face. The swelling around his redden, swollen eyes was severe. London shuddered as he realized the officer must have tried to scratch out his own eyes in an attempt to stop the barrage of visions.

"So, Mr. London," Cantalupo asked with a detached coldness, "you think you might want to tell me what you did to this man? And, maybe even *why* you did it?"

Before anyone else could say anything, Fergeson broke away from the officer holding him erect. Stumbling forward madly, tears streaming down his cheeks, he slammed awkwardly into London. Pawing at the detective, he blubbered madly.

"How? How could you, how can you live—knowing what you've done? Or . . . *is* it me? Is it *me?* Are these my memories? Did I do these things?"

The man's hands slapped against London's chest, fresh blood beginning to seep forth from underneath his bandages.

"Did *I?*"

What the hell did this guy do to himself, wondered the detective guiltily.

"*Did I?*"

As the officer who had been helping Fergeson pulled him gently away from the detective, everyone else in the room remained silent, hushed by the terrible howls of the crying policeman. Finally, London spoke.

"This, this," the detective aimed his hand at Fergeson, his gesture one of sorrow, "was an accident. I . . . I don't know what to say, but I do think I know someone who, ah . . . might be able to do something about it."

"I'm glad to hear that," answered Cantalupo with strained sincerity. Quickly giving the officer assisting Fergeson several instructions, the captain turned his attention back to London as the others left the room. "I think whoever they are you should get them here right away."

As London nodded quietly, hating himself for using his new-found abilities so recklessly, so foolishly, he looked over at Joan and suddenly realized that she was an even bigger complication than everything else that had happened that night put together.

Oh yeah, he thought, you're one smooth operator all right. Just a regular Obi-Wan Kanobi.

"And, Mr. London," Cantalupo's words took on an edge the detective could not immediately identify. "After this 'someone' of yours does what they can for Officer Fergeson, then . . ." the captain stalled for a moment, swallowed, then finally continued by saying, "then we'll get down to what I really want from you."

Oh great, thought the detective, this night just gets better and better.

INTERLUDE

IT WAS LATER THAT same morning, mere hours after dawn. Far too early, thought David Hardy, for people to be at work.

"God help me," he groaned through a drawn-out stretch and yawn. "It's positively way too damned early for me to be back here, anyway. That's for sure."

Having nothing for them to do, Hardy let his arms fall back uselessly to his sides. The outer lab beyond his office was still dark, its computers all on minimum attention, the testing stations cold and unmanned. None of his subordinates would be in for at least another two hours.

No need for them to come in, he thought. They don't have over-mortgaged mansions to pay for.

The scientist stared dully at the top sheet of the stack of printouts piled on the desk in front of him. The endless rows of figures continued to baffle the scientist as they had for the past several months. It was not through incompetence that their meaning still hovered beyond his grasp. He had worked at them as hard as any man could, had tackled the problem of unrestricted growth as it related to fragmentation from every angle, tried fourteen dozen different solutions in the last two weeks alone and nothing. No matter what he tried or in which sequence, it seemed, he was getting absolutely nowhere.

"If we restructure the base molecules," he muttered, his hand absently reaching for his already cold coffee, "then I leave the test subject open to repeat downward spiralling. If we don't restructure, though, then there's nothing to restrict the growth pattern . . ."

His eyes too busy to help, Hardy's fingers wandered about the desktop, searching absently for his coffee, touch working valiantly to replace his other senses. As the hunt proceeded, he wondered just how many times he could say the same words without making himself insane. How many different ways could he utter the same infuriating, progress-halting words without simply throwing back his head and screaming?

Hell, I'm there already.

And then, for a long moment, Hardy thought seriously about screaming—about actually throwing back his head and doing exactly what he had been thinking of doing. He imagined the joyous release that might be found in simply cutting loose and howling at the top of his voice, spitting forth the churning frustration that vexed him constantly.

Indeed, just the idea alone soothed him somewhat.

Ohhhhh, he thought, teasing himself with lies of contemplating such freedom, maybe I should.

Hardy's face broke into a smile, despite the fact he knew he was lying to himself. He did not care. He could feel his neck relaxing, the painfully knotted muscles loosening some.

Funny how lies keep getting you what you want.

Hardy ignored the whisper from the back of his mind. Snapping his conscience shut, he disregarded its admonitions once more with practiced ease. His body craved the release the self-deception caused and he went with the feeling, allowed himself to imagine shutting his eyes, arching his neck, and then letting loose with great screeching gusts of hot bellow until his teeth were shaking and his throat was raw. The pain of his short daydream sent more wattage to the welcome smile softening his tired lips.

"Now," said an unexpected, but cheerful voice from the doorway, "what is it that could possibly make our ever-so-valuable Dr. Hardy so happy this early in the morning?"

Hardy's distracted imaginings crashed and disappeared, folding themselves away into the locked box in the back of his brain at the sound of CEO Harlan Mortonson's voice. The doctor had been completely taken by surprise by the older man's entry into the complex. He had neither heard the outer door to the lab area as it was unlocked, nor noticed as the chief executive officer had crossed the room and opened his door.

Sloppy, he told himself. Stupid. He could have been standing there for . . . for, who knows *how* long? Stupid. Clumsy. Goddamnit, did I say anything . . . did . . .

Hardy growled at his panic, coldly shaming it into silence, accepting that if he had muttered anything the CEO should not have heard it was too late to do much about it. As he cursed himself mentally for his inattention, aloud he said simply, "Oh, Mr. Mortonson—good morning. What brings you down here to the dungeons so early?"

The CEO pulled a nearby stool toward him. The plush office stool moved quietly on its hard plastic wheels. The seat was comfortable, but Spartan, an ugly but functional thing which somehow seemed unfitting for a man of Mortonson's importance. Positioning himself upon the stool, however, the CEO seemed unaware of his perch's utilitarian aspects as he answered Hardy's question.

"My good doctor," he said with practiced smile in place, "since I'm not certain whether your time or mine is more valuable to this company, I won't risk a profit drop by wasting too much of either. That means, however, I'll have to skip all the usual pleasantries and get right to the point."

"Shoot, sir."

"Dave," the older man pulled himself closer to the table, leaning in as near to the doctor as he could, "I'm worried about you."

"Sir, we'll beat this problem. I've just got to put in more time. But don't you worry . . ."

"You're missing the point, son," interrupted Mortonson. The older man caught the opening notes of rising panic in the doctor's voice. Not understanding the reaction, hoping to dispel it, he continued in a calm but concerned tone, saying, "You're a valuable member of this team, and that, as I hope you understand, is the grossest of understatements. Let me be blunt—Future Images, Inc. would still be a risky tech stock, if it even still existed, without you.

"Now, now," the chief executive officer added softly as he winked at the doctor, telling him in a conspiratory tone, "of course, I know I'm supposed to act as if every good thing that happens around here happens because of my genius and hard work and all that silly putty, but since I was the genius that brought you on board, I feel safe enough there to let it slip—just this once, mind you—that we can't run this place without you. You know that, don't you, David?"

The older man smiled, not expecting an answer, plowing his course along the path he had picked when he first started talking. "You know that it was your foresight, your designs, your imagination that built this place. You don't actually need *me* to tell you that, do you?"

Hardy nodded absently. As he tried to pull the terror from his eyes, worked at calming his heart rate, relief flooded him as he realized Mortonson was just there to give him some kind of asinine pep talk. At the same time, however, the back of his brain continued to chatter at him angrily, his constant companions fear and anger screaming in his ears.

How long is he going to ramble? He runs the goddamned place, for Christ's sake, how can he be wasting his time down here? Why doesn't he just shut up?

Hardy struggled to keep the features of his face neutral even as his anger churned within him.

I'm moved, all right? Your stupid concern is touching me greatly. Now shut up and get out of here. Stop wasting my time before I don't have any more of it to waste, you sucking relic! *Leave me alone!*

The CEO continued to try and do what he could to relieve the tension that was plainly visible in the eyes of his most valuable employee. David Hardy's work would catapult the company to greatness; it would revolutionize their business, and a hundred others. The patents that came out of his eventual success would be worth billions—and that, everyone in the boardroom knew, was a conservative estimate. His voice at its silkiest, Mortonson worked hard at putting Hardy at ease, though he was still not able to get a handle on what could be upsetting the doctor so.

"I mean, from what I gather, the process is a success—only a lab success at this time, but still, a complete and unqualified success—correct?"

Yes, sir," Hardy admitted, his pained eyes staring into Mortonson's. "But that doesn't mean much in dollars and cents yet. Anything, really. I mean, yes, everything we've been working for works—but only in here. Yes, we can tell the world the process works, but we've got roughly some fifteen million dollars worth of equipment on hand backing up each test, with seven different specialists backing up the automatic systems. We're nowhere near a street-ready product."

Hardy broke off eye contact, afraid he might say too much if he continued to look directly at the older man. His gaze drifting toward his notes, he muttered;

"Nowhere. No where."

"You say that as if that were a bad thing." Mortonson shook his head, clearly saddened at the younger man's reaction. "David, yes, it would be nice if we were ready to launch. Clearly we'd put Hollywood, television and everything else out there all the way down to Slinkies and the good old ball and jacks out of business—which from the viewpoint of our stockholders would be, what was that Devo phrase, 'a monumental good thing'—but I don't think anyone expects that at this point. And if they do, then they deserve a good kick in the ass."

The CEO stood, his hands becoming animated, "My God, David, the latest tests show we're clearly ten years ahead of schedule on this product. A decade. The company had millions more budgeted to get us to this point."

"But, sir, home units are still . . . I don't know, I can't even guess how many years away that . . ."

"David," the CEO's voice dropped an octave, growing sterner, the older man's concern showing clearly. "Who cares? Everyone—*every one*—is as pleased as they can be with your progress. No one expected this project to be anywhere near the stage it's at now. Home units?"

Mortonson said the words with exasperated surprise, repeating them as if he could not believe they were having the conversation. "Home units? David, you're going to put yourself into an early grave if you don't stop working so hard."

Early grave? The back of Hardy's mind snickered at the macabre humor to be found in the phrase. Shoving the idea aside, the scientist thought, How? How do I tell him? How can I tell *anyone* the stupid mess I've made of things?

"I . . . I guess," offered Hardy weakly, "I just don't want to let you down, sir."

Mortonson shook his head. He knew that there was something troubling his top scientist, something far beyond what the man was admitting. And, how to discover what it might be was not the hard part. Deciding whether or not he should risk probing the situation any further was the big decision.

On the one hand the CEO certainly did not want to rock such an incredibly hard working and profitable boat. On the other hand, if the boat were to run itself onto the rocks, well, he had little use for that, either.

Sighing, the older man thought, feeling his ulcer churning despite the warm milk bath he had just given it an hour earlier, this is why CEOs get those great, big salaries the public think we don't earn.

Feeling it was still too early to pry further, he accepted the answer he knew was offered as a sop and nothing more and backed off a step. Standing, taking a short step away from his stool to indicate he would be heading back for the hallway, after only a few more words, he said;

"You're no good to anyone if you have a stroke. We don't want you burned out at forty, so I'll just say it once more. I'm concerned for your well-being, David. Are you certain everything is all right with you?"

"Yes, sir," Hardy answered, too quickly, lamely adding, "everything's fine."

"Really, son? *Really?*"

"Yes, sir, honestly," the younger man lied. "Thank you for coming down. I, I appreciate it."

"Well, all right," Mortonson nodded, then gave the doctor a smile. Stepping back to the outer lab, he forced a chuckle, pointing at Hardy as he added, "remember, I don't want you putting yourself into an early grave. I still need you around here to keep making me look good."

"Okay, sir," answered Hardy. With a near superhuman effort, he managed to create his own smile as he added, "yes, sir."

As the doctor watched the CEO finally leave, however, his mind flashed on the repeated black comedy, whispering to him, yeah, maybe you don't want us putting ourselves in an early grave, but if we don't, we know someone else who will.

A part of Hardy snarled, rebelled at the fact that he might not be in control, cursed him for myriad decisions he had made, tried to tell him that everything would be just fine—the scientist laughed sadly and dismissed all the notions. The feeling that he was in control, that he did not have anything to worry about had come to him often recently, but he knew it was nothing but ego trying to compensate for his failures to date. It was nice to think, even briefly, that everything was going to turn out just fine, but he knew better than that.

Sadly, he knew far better.

And with that Dr. David Hardy, his coffee finally in hand, returned to the problem that had been plaguing his team for months. The problem which he knew could be solved in time—if only he had some. The problem that, if he did not find its solution, would soon be, oh so literally, the death of him.

CHAPTER
SEVEN

L ONDON STARED AT THE prone body of John Warren Marshall as it lie motionless in its hospital bed. The boy appeared as close to death as one could be and still somehow offer the hope that his eyes might yet open, his lips move, a smile returned to them once more as if the last few days had all been some sort of mistake, a medical miscalculation and nothing more.

Christ, boy, wondered the detective, just what the hell happened to you?

Multiple catheters and I.V.s flowed from and to the teenager's body. London stared closely, noting that John's breathing was whisper shallow, his eyes closed. Careful scrutiny revealed that there was little to no rapid movement to be detected beneath the tight shut lids. And, as for the feeble breaths moving in and out of his lungs, it seemed quite apparent that those were being aided, if not completely accomplished, by one of the many machines surrounding the frail-looking teenager.

London stared at John's struggling body past the point where he had accessed the boy's tenuous situation. He continued to take in the view, not because he thought he might discern some new factor he had missed so far, but because he wondered why the police were seeking his council in the matter. The detective urged all his various ancestors to peek out through his eyes along with him, hoping someone might have a notion as to why Cantalupo might have asked him to observe the teenager. None of them, including London, had any worthwhile guesses.

All right, thought the detective, allowing himself an internal sigh, time for the direct approach.

"So," London asked finally, his curiosity more than a little aroused, "what's the story?"

"Young Mr. Marshall here was found in an alley in mid-town about four days ago." Cantalupo stared directly at the detective and his companion, his eyes never so much as glancing at John. Whether the officer wanted to keep the pair under strict observation, or he simply could not bring himself to look at the motionless youth any more, neither of them could say.

"His condition," the policeman continued, "has worsened steadily since his arrival. He has never regained consciousness, not for an instant, and yet the doctors have assured myself and his family that his brain activity is normal."

London and Joan exchanged glances, an action the detective immediately regretted. On the one hand, London wished the woman would simply go away. He disliked the disturbingly in-sync aspect of their relationship immensely. Part of him found it too much of a reminder of the mistake he had made with officer Fergeson. Part of him disliked being disloyal to Lisa.

Tell me, son, how exactly are you doing that?

The question, and several more like it, floated in the back of the detective's mind, mutterings of the ancestral voices he had learned to hear. It irritated him that an overwhelming majority of them were firmly against his way of seeing the situation.

She's awful cute.

Her eyes, boy, look in them. She's got the blazes for you, you know.

And you're not married, you know that, too. Don't you?

They were right, of course. He and Lisa were not engaged. They had nothing like even an "understanding," as the old phrase would put it. Indeed, the two had not yet even been on so much as an official date. He had, since first he had realized what his life had become, done his best to disentangle himself from her for her own safety.

If that's what you really want, one of his female ancestors confided, there's no better way to gain some of that distance than to take up with another woman.

He saw the sense in the statement. The situation was actually perfect for what he kept telling himself he wanted. He was practically blameless for Joan having come into their lives—his life. It was an accident. He was simply stuck with her now. Certainly Lisa would be able to see that.

And yet, the truth be told, the detective chilled at the thought of having such a perfect device for removing Lisa from his life. As much as he tried to ignore it, he knew he felt something deep and abiding for her—more than he could admit.

And why is that?

London could not answer his question. Indeed, he asked himself, why did he keep Lisa at arm's length? She was beautiful, and he was certain he loved her. And yet, he constantly worried about her presence, about growing closer to her, about everything that existed between himself and the woman for whom he had saved the world.

Saved the world for her, one ancestor voice broke in, you did more than that. You learned to step through time and space. You broke all the rules of God over how you felt for her.

Yeah, and now, he growled inside his head, I have this mess as a big thank you.

A mess created from the facts that Joan de Molina was also beautiful, and that he now also loved her. He had reached into her mind to find out who she was at the exact moment she had been aching with desire for him. He flooded his way into her consciousness at the singular instant that she was wishing to know everything about him. Now, their minds were imprinted on each others—their desires intertwined like an endless strand of spaghetti eternally looped over and over on itself. With every passing minute, his desire for her grew stronger, and he had only himself and his reckless use of his abilities to blame.

To be certain, London had tried to put distance between himself and the Pirate Queen as quickly as possible. In his attempt to dislodge her as rapidly and painlessly as he could, the detective had cleared her name with the police. Cantalupo, eager to begin working on both covering up the museum mess and to get London to their present location, had agreed there was no reason to hold her. Not only was the detective the only one of them he actually wanted for his own still-secret reasons, but there was also the fact that the captain did not really believe Joan was a part of London's organization, and thus not someone he was certain he could trust.

He had cleared her of all charges, left her free to go when jailing her could have been quite a feather in his cap, because he sensed that having her out of the picture would have made London as comfortable as it would himself. And, once he had done so she had insisted on coming to see young Mr. Marshall.

"After all," she had laughed, wrapping her arm around the detective's, "I'm an essential part of the London Agency, a valued team player, practically indispensable—that's my alibi, anyway, captain, and I'm sticking to it."

She might have found the whole thing amusing, but London did not. After everything that had happened to him since first he had become the Destroyer, he had been working hard to get his world back in order. Suddenly having a second woman in his life was not something he thought of as in any way uncomplicating things.

On the other hand, though, the detective also had found himself growing increasingly uncomfortable at the thought of her leaving. There was something about the so called Pirate Queen, the look of her, the feel of her skin, the depth to the scarlet of her hair, some maddening combination of factors that had begun an itch in London's mind which he could not shake. Even as he stared at the body on the pallet before him, tried to stare, forced his head to remain motionless, still he found his eyes wandering, straining off to the side trying to catch a glimpse of Joan. He felt like a high school student, gawking at a cheerleader in class, hoping the teacher would not catch him ignoring his studies.

Lord, what have I done to myself, he wondered. Instantly, a voice from the back of his mind whispered;

What have you done to us? Probably the same thing you did to ol' officer Fergeson.

The detective nodded grimly, refocusing his attention on what Cantalupo was telling them.

"Of course he was checked for signs of abuse—alcohol, the standard battery of drug tests—but he came up clean. No needle marks, not on his arms, between his toes or fingers, none of the usual injection sites. Nothing in his nostrils or his blood stream, either—nothing under his fingernails. No works found on him or near him."

The officer stopped for a moment, drawing a breath in through his nose. He used the action to pull himself to his full height, moving his head and shoulders as he sucked down the air. He closed his eyes for a split-second as well, cutting himself off from all the world except its atmosphere. It was only a moment, but it was one he needed.

The case John Warren Marshall was a part of had baffled him from the beginning. It was crazy. Impossible. And the more of his resources he poured into it, the worse it had become. Now, London had come into his life and he had two such cases on his plate. It simply was not fair, he decided. A just God would not give a man such a burden unless the one was the means to solve the other. Believing more strongly than ever that London was going to lead him out of the darkness surrounding the body before them both, he allowed the split-second of need to pass, opened his eyes once more, and resumed offering details.

"Not that we looked at destructive behavior all that closely. This was not the kind of boy who fit any such pattern. Marshall had no kind of a previous record—nothing. And his school lists him as a well above average student, advance placement, college prep courses, lots of extracurricular activities, hell, he was being courted by everyone from Harvard to the Air Force Academy. SAT scores less than fifty points off from perfect. Not the kind of loser who throws his life away on drugs."

Cantalupo sighed. Then he explained the frustrated noise.

"His parents, as you would expect, are shocked and confused. I know that parents often miss the most obvious warning signs, but it seems this time they didn't miss anything. As best we can tell, our boy Johnny here was as clean-livin' a lad as they come these days."

"Then what's happened to him?" asked Joan.

"That's what I want you to discover for me," answered the captain with a tired honesty. "I want to know what the hell happened to this apparently straight and narrow kid . . . and to all his friends."

When London and Joan simply stared, Cantalupo indicated the other beds around the room.

"This is a private ward. The only patients that have been in this room for the past two months have all shared this same, common affliction. What it is, nobody knows." The captain went quiet for a moment, then added, "But we know what it does."

Again London and Joan simply stood silently, waiting for Cantalupo to finish his explanation. After a second, the captain pursed his lips, moving his moustache back and forth several times. Taking a pair of deep breaths, he shut his eyes for a long moment, squeezing the fatigue out of them, and then he began again.

"For some two months we've been finding bodies, mostly males, some females, all races, all creeds, strewn throughout various parts of the city. There's been some variations, of course, but it's mostly been the same thing over and over. Young person, exceptional in school, often artistic, never in trouble. Oh, perhaps something minor, but never nothing really major. No, basically all of them were as upstanding and clean-cut as our Johnny here."

The officer turned, his hand pointing to the still slightly living body, his eyes finally taking in the sight once more. The withering shell made Cantalupo feel helpless, something the captain did not like in the least.

"All of them were found in the exact same condition," he continued, returning to ignoring John Marshall, "unconscious, near death, the reasons unknown. A few were found to have been drug users, casual usage, marijuana, I think one tested positive for a little coke, a couple had some slight traces of alcohol in their systems—content level never indicated nothing much stronger than beer—but that was it."

"You said you found them throughout the city," said London. "How about outside the city? Upstate? Jersey? Has there been anything about cases like this reported anywhere else?"

"Not that we know of," answered Cantalupo. "Of course, we've been keeping a tight lid on this to try and avoid a panic. If they're piling up bodies over in Newark, though, they're being awfully quiet about it. And believe me, we have our ways of asking each other questions about things like this. We've asked. This is a New York City problem."

London nodded, thoughtful, wondering. As his mind turned the fact over, Joan looked for another.

"You implied that there's been a steady stream of these cases, captain," she said. "Where are the rest of them?"

"In the morgue."

London's head snapped up, his eyes wide. Cantalupo's answer had not been what he had expected. His eyes blinked, darted to the captain, then returned to staring at Johnny as he asked;

"What did they die of?"

"We don't know," answered Cantalupo. "After nine, ten days they just sort of fade away. If it wasn't for the machines, they wouldn't last that long."

"How many so far?"

"Twenty-seven, Ms. de Molina. Why, does it make a difference?"

"I can think of some fifty-four people to whom it might make some difference," she answered, her voice going cold. She wondered at how correct she might be. Did John Warren Marshall have two parents in his life? Two people waiting at home who cared about him? Who were praying for him? Did they have any idea how this could have happened? Did anyone?

"So you have people in comas," asked London. "What does this have to do with me? And, please, captain, try to understand, I'm not trying to be belligerent here. I just want to know what it is you're looking for from me."

Cantalupo glanced around him, wanting to make certain that none of the hospital staff were close enough to overhear what he had to say before he answered. Satisfied that no one else was in the ICU with them, still the captain lowered his voice to just above a whisper.

"You want me to believe in all sorts of crazy shit—that the explanation for those bodies in the museum is that they were possessed by some demon thing from beyond, okay—fine. They were crazy-lookin' shit, and you've shown me more crazy shit, and the commissioner's office, off the damn record, it seems, is willing to confirm even more crazy shit. Okay—swell, great, wonderful. It's crazy shit day."

Cantalupo caught his voice growing louder, deeper—strained. Stopping himself with a slight jerk of his head, he forced himself back to a calmer place, then tilted his head at an angle as he said, "this is just some more crazy shit that's been dropped in my lap—do you understand? Twenty-seven dead kids, and more slippin' fast. All the same—no over-doses, no medical history to indicate such a thing was likely, nothing the doctors can do for any of them except plug them into their fancy hardware so they can lay around and beep at us all night."

The captain turned away from London and Joan, staring at the far wall as he continued.

"They operated on the first half dozen. They spread their ribs and they went in and poked around, checking their hearts and who knows what else. They took out their organs, one at a time, tossing them in pans, all lined up neatly. Sawed off the tops of their heads and pulled out their brains and . . ."

Cantalupo bit his lower lip. A tiny noise escaped his mouth, a gurgle of spit being forced through tightly clenched teeth. Then suddenly he went calm and continued.

"They, they didn't find anything. After six they gave up. 'Until we know more, further exploratory surgery seems rather useless,' the head doc told me. 'Seems rather useless' he says. Okay—fine, London—the doctors are rather goddamned useless here. We have their word on it. I'm here to give you the police's opinion. It's confirmed; we're as fucking useless as they are. So, voodoo man, how about you?

"Are you fucking useless, too?"

For a moment, London considered touching Marshall, trying to probe his supposedly still functioning brain for an answer. He rejected the idea with a shudder as soon as it passed through his mind, however. He was still reeling from his earlier, botched attempts to control such an ability. His arrogance in using it so cavalierly came from having seen such tactics manipulated in the past with a level of ease that made it all look so easy. Now, he had a policeman on the verge of going mad with which he had to contend.

"How about it, Teddy," asked Joan, her voice a velvet touch in his ears, her fingers brushing his neck playfully, "tell me we aren't *fucking* useless. I'd hate for us to be that kind of useless."

Yeah, he thought, his breath cutting off short. His face close to flushing as his attention turned to the desirable redhead, his body aching for her, he reminded himself, and you've got this little problem, too. Good going, smart guy. Can't wait to see your encore.

"Let's just wait for my other associate," answered London, hoping that the call he had placed from the precinct house would be answered soon. "After tonight, I'd trust her judgment over mine."

Yeah, spat a voice from the back of the detective's head, ain't that the truth?

Cantalupo nodded. Joan stroked London's arm. No one else had anything further to say. And, on the bed before him, John Marshall continued his laborious breathing, one mechanical bellowsful at a time.

CHAPTER EIGHT

"SO YOU'RE THE PERSON that's going to help officer Fergeson," asked Captain Cantalupo of the Asian woman standing before him. "And how exactly are you going to do that?"

"I am a psychometrist," answered the woman in a quiet but firm voice. "I am sensitive to time—to those things which have been already moved beyond our reach, as well as to that which is yet coming toward us." The woman swept back the edge of her lace veil, moving it from in front of her eyes. She had no need to extend her peripheral vision, of course. The motion was made to allow her to focus her eyes on Cantalupo, to fix him with their dark pits, to render him more compliant.

"The past is set in stone, easy to read. It should not be too difficult for me to find the portion of your officer's mind that is troubled and soothe it."

"And you are going to do this with a laying on of hands, are you?"

The woman, dressed in a black wrap which covered her from head to toe, stared at the captain for a moment, gauging his attitude. Absently adjusting her shawl once more, she said, "Yes, actually. Contact is not required, much as you could fire your gun off in a pitch black room and still hit a target. However, as light would most likely help your aim, so will even the slightest touch aid mine."

Cantalupo stared at the woman for a long moment. In the time it had taken for London, De Molina and himself to reach the hospital where he was hoping to secure more than one miracle, he had begun to develop some small doubts over the detective's ability to aid him. After all, everything he had seen, had been told, it was all so fantastic.

So London knew about the police files on the monster sightings that had come just before the Conflagration. So he was right about a few other classified matters, too, wondered the captain. So what?

These kinds of things can be faked. I mean, the things this guy expects me to believe. And now, this scary hoodoo chick . . . this is like some damn Bela Lugosi flick.

"Bela Lugosi, captain," asked the woman. "Aren't you dating yourself a bit?"

"I'm not that old," Cantalupo answered. Then, suddenly, the captain's eyes blinked. His brain screamed at him, reminding him that he had not spoken.

Did I, he wondered, his hidden panic edging itself into his conscious mind.

Speak out loud? Even a whisper? Did I maybe move my lips unconsciously? *Did I?*

As he sputtered, desperate to find a question that would allow him to remain in charge of the situation, the woman cut him off, speaking in a low, cold voice.

"Do not presume to consider me some sort of charlatan, captain. This close to you, the fact that we are standing on the same floor is contact enough for me to invade any part of your life I wish." As his eyes narrowed in sanity-rescuing doubt, her voice grew cold as she told him;

"You have eight keys on the ring in your right pocket. Fourteen dollars in your wallet. You have two credit cards—VISA and Discover—your wife insists you use the Discover card whenever you can because of their discount, or lower rate. You are actually not certain why she insists on this, but she does and you do as you are asked." The woman's smile was a thin and bitter thing. "It makes life easier."

Cantalupo stared, his mouth open more than half an inch, though he was not aware of his gaping lips or unblinking eyes. Probing into his mind a further touch, a minuscule fraction deeper, the woman added;

"Speaking of your wife, she is shorter than you, blonde—not natural. She does not particularly enjoy high heels, but she wears them because she knows you like them. Her name is Cynthia—Cindy to her friends, in private you call her 'Sinful.' You chuckle when you do so. She blushes. It reddens her entire face, runs down her neck, paling to pink just between her breasts. There is–"

"Stop it!" Cantalupo gasped for a breath, his hand brushing at the front of his forehead, searching for hair that had not been there for over a decade. Catching himself, the captain lowered his voice, adding, "Just stop it."

The woman nodded, satisfied.

"My name is Lai Wan," she said. "I apologize for going where I was not invited, but you must understand, I rarely go out in public. Being amongst people is not . . . comfortable for me. When their attention is focused on me, the discomfort grows. When they cast doubt in my direction it can become most painful. I have found returning the pain is usually the only way to end it."

"I, I'm sorry," answered Cantalupo, honestly. Shamefully.

"Do not feel sorrow," answered Lai Wan. "How could you know? Up until I received this curse, I would have felt as you. Done as you, shaken my head sadly at the freak."

"Then," asked the captain, struggling to understand, "you weren't born this wa—with this . . . ah, ability?"

"No," she answered. "Some ten years ago I was what you might call 'a normal woman.' I was about to be married. My life was ordered. I considered myself happy."

The woman closed her eyes absently, not noticing the sudden darkness as she continued.

"Then, fate sent a bus to change all this. The bus ran into a car. Another car, trying to avoid those two, lost control and jumped the sidewalk, pinning me to a building. The bus followed. I was not expected to live. And, indeed, I did not. I died on the operating table."

Cantalupo stared once more. Not wishing to discomfort the man any further, Lai Wan finished her story quickly.

"I am certain you have heard the same tale told before, of those who have found themselves floating above the operating theater looking down at their own bodies. I watched the doctors work, watched them give up on me. I cannot say if they brought me back, if I chose to return, or if some other force beyond either of us pushed me back--I have never been able to resolve this question--but from the time I opened my eyes in my hospital bed, the abilities I now use began to manifest themselves."

"Why don't you just use them now," interrupted London, The detective looked worn and tense. "Let's get this show on the road, all right?"

"That is why I am here," answered the soft-spoken woman in black with only a touch of sarcasm. "What shall we try?"

"I think we should start with Officer Fergeson."

Cantalupo nodded in agreement, indicating with a gesture which bed held the tormented policeman. The psychometrist needed no such directions; the pain emanating from the man cried at her, pierced the air—begged her for help. Lai Wan moved quietly, seemingly gliding across the floor to Fergeson's bedside. Once there, she stared intently at the officer, speaking to London over her shoulder. She gauged her volume so only he could hear her.

"You have been trying to do as I, knowing the pain it has caused me? You think now that you can simply snap your fingers and make anything happen you can imagine? Are you thinking yourself a *god* now, Mr. London?"

Though the woman's tone was low, her words rang with fierce reproach. The detective answered her quietly.

"After everything else we've seen, been through, I, I guess I just thought it would be easy."

"Starting something is always easy, Mr. London," agreed Lai Wan as she struggled to maintain her composure, her voice a dagger of sneers. Taking the seat next to the suffering policeman's bed, she added, "Like rolling a boulder off the side of a cliff. It is the controlling of what you have started that can be, oh, how would a person of your talents describe it? Tricky?"

The psychometrist made to continue, then noted once more the suffering man beneath her. Controlling her anger, she turned away from London, murmuring;

"I almost wish that I could leave this man to suffer, knowing it would gnaw at you. You need to be leashed in, before you cause real harm." Then, Fergeson suddenly spasmed, squirming beneath his blanket. Pity flooding her mood, the woman whispered;

"But then, to do so, that also would be 'playing God,' would it not?"

The woman placed her hand lightly on Fergeson's forehead. The officer had been restrained, not only strapped to his bed but gagged as well. It had been the only way the hospital's staff could find to keep him not just quiet and from further injuring himself, but from disrupting the entire ward, if not most of the hospital. At the first touch of Lai Wan's fingers, however, the policeman relaxed noticeably. While London, Joan and Cantalupo watched, the psychometrist stayed bent over her charge, her eyes closed, his rapid breathing suddenly shallow. Finally, however, she rose from her chair, returning to the waiting trio.

"He should be fine now," she answered simply. "You might call for someone to release his restraints. Especially the gag."

"What?" Cantalupo's surprise was mirrored by London's and Joan's. "That's all? That's it?"

"Yes," answered Lai Wan simply. Understanding the captain's need for words, she continued. "Mr. London allowed some of his memories to bleed into officer Fergeson's consciousness. I went to the part of his brain where those memories were and blocked them. I assured him that they were not his memories, that he had not seen the things he was remembering, had not participated in the horrible events he felt he had engineered. Like all memories, they could not be removed, but they could be recessed, turned away from—for the most part, forgotten."

"He won't remember anything?"

"I understand your concern for your man," answered Lai Wan, sincerely addressing the hope in the captain's voice. "But, I am sorry to say I can not be more specific. Such things vary from person to person. However, it is true that he does not want to remember any of the things he has accidentally seen. Thus, it is doubtful he would ever consciously remember them, or if he did, that they would bother him to any real degree."

"And what do we tell his family?" growled Cantalupo, suddenly rankled by the attitude of those there with him. "He has people out in the waiting room demanding an explanation."

"Why not just report that he took a blow to the head during the museum scuffle with the terrorists," asked Joan. "He suffered for his badge—make him a hero and let it go at that."

"You're just full of glib answers," snapped the Captain harshly, "aren't you?"

"Just trying to help the boss here," answered the Pirate Queen with a smile, running her hand along London's arm as she did so. "After all, we here at the London Agency are a well-oiled team."

Shaking her hand away, the detective snapped;

"That's enough."

"All right," answered the redhead, amused at his reaction, "so we'll skip the oil. Easier clean-up anyway."

Lai Wan eyed the detective coldly. Her gaze moved from London to Joan, then back to the detective. She did not know what had happened that night, who the redhead was, or why the newcomer would feel she could act in such a familiar manner. The psychometrist also did not care. As long as the stranger did not complicate matters, it was not her concern.

To Lai Wan, the only thing that really mattered was finishing with her current chore—removing herself from the hospital and all its grasping, painful surroundings—the thousands of aches and miseries bleeding into the floor and walls, begging her attention. As the decades of agony stored in every surface around her leached at her defenses, the psychometrist steeled her will against the waves of overwhelming pain, then spoke abruptly.

"So, that done, what else is there to keep me here?"

London indicated John Marshall's body.

"More of your handiwork?"

The detective shook his head, lowering it slightly, but it had been unnecessary. The psychometrist was only indulging herself in a bit of cruelty. Even from a distance, Lai Wan could sense that whatever was wrong with the boy on the far bed, it was a problem extremely different from Fergeson's. She had also instantly been able to sense that whatever the teenager's problem, the detective had not been the cause of it.

Crossing the room, the psychometrist stopped at the foot of Marshall's bed, staring at the varied assortment of tubes and monitor cables running away from his body. After a moment, she sat down in the standard chair next to the bed and reached out, prepared to find her way into the boy's mind, to search for what had happened to him and his fellows. It was nothing that worried her. The procedure was one she had performed hundreds of times. As with officer Fergeson, it was a simple thing, barely worth a moment's concern.

Clearing her mind, Lai Wan shut her eyes, slowed her breath once more, and then placed her hand lightly on John Warren Marshall's forehead. And, at that moment, she fell into utter darkness, completely lost in a void darker than chaos and blacker than night.

CHAPTER
NINE

*D*O NOT PANIC
    Slowed breathing, slabs of darkness, life-closing emptiness, soul disintegrating–

Do not panic

Despair melding with confusion, rolling waves of it sluiced through the silent corridors all about her, dripped from the ceiling, soaking everything in mounting, blurred discomfort. As the mournfully empty gray walls of sadness sliced toward her, a well-trained voice in the back of Lai Wan's head repeated the keying phrase again.

Do not panic

The familiar imperative—one of many she had spent so long to train herself to use automatically—finally caught her stunned attention, focused it, alerting all her protective systems automatically. Calming her, forcing her to observe rather than simply react, it adjusted her senses, working to suppress fear, to gently tap adrenaline as needed without awaking its production mate, terror.

Do not . . .

It was a simple, somewhat routine procedure for the psychometrist. It was not one she needed often—she was too skilled, too practiced at what she did. But, it was one that had served her well during the occasional—what could she call them—bursts of surprise.

panic

Those, of course, were the nightmares when the familiar had somehow been shattered and she had been called upon to use her abilities instantly—blindly; those frightening moments when her few years beyond her momentary experience with the grave were simply not enough to tell her what to expect next from a hostile universe. Especially those moments which had come her way over the last few months. Or, more specifically, those times when her life had crossed that of Theodore London. Those moments when she met creatures who could suck away her life with a touch, when she faced gods—*gods.*

Do not panic

They had all been horrid times—meeting such things, experiencing their vast and timeless indifference to humanity, touched the utter and complete knowledge that to them she was less than the dust which caressed atoms, a milliseconded mote of flesh that would last even less time than she mattered, which was no time at all.

Do not . . .

Those supremely unpleasant moments, like the numbing cold—what was that phrase she used for them—bursts of surprise—yes, they were exactly like that—like the numbing cold burst of surprise she was experiencing right at that moment.

All right then, so what exactly do we have here?

panic . . .

"Can you sense me?" she thought aloud, questioning the soul around her. "Can you feel me moving around? Let me tell you that I am not an enemy. What is happening here is that I have come to find out what has happened to you. You are still alive . . . are you not . . . John Warren Marshall?"

Lai Wan's mental essence floated in what should have been flourishing, active memory chambers of John Marshall's brain. The policeman had said the doctors' machines had listed the teenager as having full brain activity.

Once again, she thought, so much for the medical sciences.

Still, she had traveled within the minds of coma victims before. Their thoughts, perhaps surprisingly, like those of a conscious person, were always where they were supposed to be. All there, all in place, just merely silent, ghost-like, similar to catalogues lined on a shelf, waiting for someone to pull one down and flip through it. But that was not the case within the brain whose mind Lai Wan now shared.

Where are you, John Marshall?

The psychometrist stared about into the cloying darkness, swatting at the gathering clumps of it, wondering at what could have possibly happened to the teenager. He was a high school junior, an honor student—he had lived life for over a decade and a half, had packed away acres of book knowledge. His brain should have been filled with the electricity of youthful exploration. It should have been exploding with trillions of elaborate, cross-referenced memories, all nattering away at each other. His brain should have been a din.

Where *is* everything?

But it was not. Silence stretched away in all directions from Lai Wan's presence. There were no memories of any kind to be found within the confines of the boy's gray and quiet brain; there were no facts on file, no joys stored or surprises recorded, no secrets tucked in any of the corners; indeed, there seemed to be no thoughts left within him at all. Life without thought, without more than the slightest trace of soul. More than surprise was leaving the psychometrist cold at that point.

"John Warren Marshall," she whispered, voice tense—chilled. "Can you tell me where you are? Do you know where you are? Can you hear me?"

No answers were forthcoming. Used to even the dullest human brain being uncomfortably alive with blinding layers of chatter, Lai Wan suddenly wondered if London's blunders with the policeman and the de Molina woman had somehow interfered with her own abilities.

What have you gotten me into now, London—what kind of games do you think you can play, detective?

Lai Wan caught the bolting wisp of anger, quickly extinguishing the fear which had ignited it. Such a thought was not worthy of her. Steeling her resolve, she returned to her task, feeling gingerly at the atmosphere around her. Pressing forward gently, the woman interwove her astral self more tightly within the fabric of her surroundings, searching for any interference that would make a wonderful excuse to exit.

Nothing, she realized. Nothing at all. There were no anomalies, her senses were fine. Her astral form was traveling comfortably. John Marshall—technically alive, was simply, for lack of a better word, empty. The shrouds of spiritless twilight were draining away his soul, gathering it like unraveled thread. The thought of such a thing made the woman shake—tremble. She was gliding through what, until that moment, she had firmly believed to be an impossibility. The sudden, horrible reality of it was beginning to frighten her.

"John Warren Marshall," she whispered once more. "Where are you?"

Bracing herself against what she might discover next, Lai Wan banished further speculation as an option and began looking for actual answers. She wandered the barren landscape of Marshall's mind, moving from chamber to chamber with all her senses thrown fully open, trying to uncover the reason why his brain was so dissimilar from any she had previously entered.

A normal, simple answer, she thought, that is all I want. Something which does not involve . . .

The sentence froze in her head, her vocabulary missing the words she needed to complete her thought. Before she had met Theodore London she had used her abilities in a rational, scientific manner.

What, she asked herself. What do I even call these . . . things that follow the detective everywhere, that lurk around each corner of his life?

The psychometrist shuddered on all levels. Every time that Theodore London crossed her path, he brought with him nothing but danger and evil. Not evil men, not evil empires—no, nothing that simple. No, London brought with him pure and simple evil. The essence of evil—distilled. Refined. It seemed to wait for him everywhere. It challenged him, came snapping at his heels every time he went out of doors. And he felt no compunction whatsoever against bringing it to others.

To *her.*

Oh yes, she remembered, the disorienting pain of their first meeting flashing through her mind. She had felt it, been touched by it—it, them, they, whatever—the sharp and hungry voices from some other realm, land, dimension, continuum—she did not know what to call it; where it was—names, locations, such simple, restrictive niceties did not matter. All that mattered was what the voice she had heard that first time had promised.

Oblivion

The thought had terrified her when first it had been offered.

Other people get to die when they are crushed by a bus; why does this burden fall to me?

The voice had enticed her—wooed her—tempted her in a way nothing had before. The joy of it, she dreamed, no more thoughts invading hers, no more unfamiliar shocks—brush a wisp from a pillow, a tiny, unthinking gesture, and end rewarded with the chance to relive the blind agony of an animal as its feathers are ripped from its body and limbs—no more . . .

Dead, she hoped for an instant, finally . . .

Oblivion

Yesssssssssssssss

And then, London had slammed into her, brutally tearing her paralyzed fingertips from the contact point, ripping the alien intrusion from her mind and the flesh from her hands. She had talked within her head with a thing so large and ancient, so utterly devoid of any emotions save lust and greed and anger, that the moment had left her weeping inside over the fact that day after day she continued to remain alive.

Never again, she swore to herself, the horror of her surroundings beginning to unnerve her. *I mean it, this time. I will never work with this man again.*

At that point Lai Wan shoved all her thoughts on London from her head as she attempted to concentrate, struggling to find an answer for the puzzle of John Marshall—one that had more to do with science than "the powers of darkness."

All right then, she asked herself. *If you are in such a rush to leave this place, tell me why? What is wrong here? What is so different here?*

Stepping away from her emotions, thinking technically, the first thing the intruder had noted was how different the terrain of Marshall's brain was from those previous she had traveled. The memories and thoughts of others had always appeared as liquid to the psychometrist. A highly active mind, that of an imaginative person, would be filled with raging torrents of thought. The fact that Marshall remained in a coma should not have mattered. Memory was merely stored electromagnetic data. It did not disperse until death. And John Marshall was not dead yet.

"Are you," Lai Wan whispered. "Are you dead, John, and refusing to share the secret?"

The woman had laid hands on corpses, searching for the images her powers could uncover even in the departed. So far such had never been a problem for her. Mere death was no barrier to her talents. Indeed, she could read the past of inanimate objects if she so desired. But the woman was finding nothing within the boy with whom she had joined. Less personality than a piece of ice, less soul than a fragment of rock. Nothing but dry and dusty accesses. Ghostly, unlit, unused.

Silent.

No, she thought, not silent.

Curiously, there sounded a dull noise from somewhere in the background, a kind of distant background hum, far away, small, rhythmic. The psychometrist wondered at the distant beat, straining to remember any past time when she had experienced such a thing. Then suddenly, her attention was distracted from the tiny noise as she spotted *it*.

"Interesting."

Away on the hollow dark floor of Marshall's mind, Lai Wan caught sight of a puddle. One last moist spot of . . . what? Memory? Instinct? Active thought?

"We shall know soon enough."

Crossing to the pancake-sized circle of moisture, gliding effortlessly, the woman settled near the liquid stain and, stretching out her hand, sent her fingers into it.

"*Help me!*"

The words screamed at her so desperately that the psychometrist could not help reacting in panic. Instinctively she jerked her hand free, a precious few droplets of soul scattered by the violence of her motion. Immediately catching hold of her surprise, though, the woman forced her hand back down.

"John," she shouted desperately, "come back—talk to me!"

Her arm disappeared to the elbow, her sleeve drenched in thought, soaked with terrified emotion. Reaching down deeper, she grabbed for any link she could find to the dying boy. And then, from out of nowhere a netting of searing agony slashed across her flesh, making her cry out both in shock and pain. Although she did not break her physical, body-to-body contact with Marshall, her astral hand snaked back out of the puddle with such speed Lai Wan lost control of her spiritual form and fell to her knees. She tried to prop herself up with her hands, but the one was too damaged by the sudden contact. She collapsed in agony, falling on her side to relieve the clawing, frightful pain. Staring at her fingers, the psychometrist saw they had been burned.

What in heaven?

The woman stared at the puddle, walls shattering over her confusion. There was no steam, nothing to indicate heat. And even if there had been, nothing could affect her astral form. It defied all science. It was impossible.

It seems, she thought, staring at the flickers of thin smoke still wisping away from her swollen, throbbing fingers, that there are always new limits being imposed on what is and is not impossible.

Nothing even remotely like this had ever happened to the psychometrist before. Not in all her years. Not to any others with whom she had ever talked. Once again, without warning, her powers had taken her to a new and dangerous land.

"No," she said, finding her anger once more. "It is not my abilities that have brought me here. It is Theodore London."

The woman shut her eyes, ground her teeth, thinking on how every call from the detective had put her in worse danger, had caused her more pain. Standing, then floating once more, she thought indignantly;

What have you done to me now, London?

"He's lead you to my gold."

Lai Wan froze, suddenly desperately afraid. Where the voice was coming from, she did not know. It was not Marshall's, that she could tell instantly. A flat, hissing thing, it was composed of qualities unlike any she had ever heard before.

"Bit by bit," the horrid noise echoed, "he has lead you . . . to my gold."

At least, unlike any she had ever heard from the throats of human beings.

"Will you," it asked. "Will you follow the gold?"

Not again, she thought with dread—her essence brimming with knot-tying fright. Not this—

"Will you follow it . . . follow it bit by bit," the hissing whisper asked once more. "Will you follow the gold?"

Lai Wan cried out, gasped, then turned to leave the way she came.

"Who are you," the voice demanded, its words slippery with the curiosity of avarice. "What brings you to here? How came you to here?"

The psychometrist stumbled, then caught herself, floating in the darkness.

You can not fall, she reminded herself. There is no reality here save that which you impose. You are in charge.

Are you certain?

This is not a good time to be questioning ourselves.

Lai Wan trembled, bleeding tears of panic as she braced against the oncoming force. It was not a voice she had felt before, but it reeked of seniority and dismissal in a way that was gaggingly familiar. Burrowing their way into Marshall's mind through the vanishing puddle across the way, fingers of energy dragged themselves across the emptiness, straining to reach the woman in black.

"Will you come," the hiss continued. "Will you follow the gold?"

With a powerful flourish, the psychometrist threw her shawl up over her shoulders, shielding her body with its length. As she did, tendrils of energy jolted—splashing outward from the puddle. As they snaked toward her she slapped them away with the hand she had hidden beneath her shawl. A sinister laughter flooded the chambers of Marshall's mind, filling Lai Wan with loathing.

And fear.

There was pain in the brief contact, long and drawn across time, a pain far more intense than the burning she had experienced earlier. This was severe and cutting, like a migraine that could leave one's brain and crawl throughout their flesh. Instantly it shattered the locks bolting the entrance to her mind, breaking down her defenses one after another. Casually. With a brutal indifference she could scarcely comprehend.

Accept what you know, her defenses whispered. Believe, and act upon belief.

The stench of overwhelming power crawling toward the delicious smell of her, Lai Wan made to gather her composure. Wildly, she grabbed for it, forced it's return, tore after it as she felt the horrible length gathering itself, preparing to come at her once more. Then, finally recomposed enough to accept the inevitable, she vanished.

$$\blacklozenge \quad \blacklozenge \quad \blacklozenge$$

"What?" London spoke with surprise. In real time the woman before him had closed her eyes and then reopened them in a matter of seconds. "You're back already?"

"Yes," Lai Wan answered simply.

"Well," asked Cantalupo.

"Well, what, officer?"

"Look, lady," responded the captain. "I don't have this hoodoo stuff down yet, okay? Forgive me for just being some idiot normal type who doesn't have an autographed picture of Dracula on his nightstand. Did anything happen? Did you get anything? Learn anything—what?"

"Yes, Captain," answered the psychometrist. Holding up her hand, she amazed the assembly as they stared at the burn marks running from her wrist to her fingertips, some of them still sizzling. "I learned that working with the London Agency is never a simple proposition."

London snapped into action, immediately getting a nurse to treat Lai Wan's injury. As an orderly worked a cream into the blood-filled blisters, the detective placed his hand on Marshall's body where the psychometrist's had been, feeling for heat. The skin was cool, clammy to the touch.

"Laying on of hands again," snipped Lai Wan. "Haven't you caused enough trouble that way in the last few hours?"

London did not answer, his eyebrows folding, eyes turning to slits. Cantalupo stood numbly by, not knowing what to do next—as did the Pirate Queen. After the psychometrist's hand had been bandaged and she had been given something for her pain, she told the others everything that had happened within Marshall's mind. The police captain asked questions from every angle he could think of, but the answers all lead back to the scant little the psychometrist had been able to learn.

London merely listened, taking it all in, trying to perhaps find answers in the scores of questions her story posed. He stared into her facts desperately, looking for some kind of lead, the slightest of jumping off points. Nothing came to either him or any of the ancestral voices with whom he communicated.

Lai Wan noticed this.

"Nothing to ask, Mr. London?" The woman in black's tone was a challenge.

"I know what you want me to ask," responded the detective, weary of the way the world was turning that night. "But I know the answers. Yes, the same bloody, beyond-the-universe kind of crap is reaching for us again. Us, the big 'us,' the all six and a half billion of us. Yes. They're back."

"Or maybe they are simply still here," snapped Lai Wan. "Perhaps they never go away. Perhaps they are always on the other side of the wall, digging, probing, trying to eke their way through to us . . ."

London said nothing, not certain why the psychometrist was so upset. His head snapped slightly as she continued.

"Or perhaps it was your arrival that interests them all so. Maybe their boredom vanishes whenever you arrive, all filled with bluster and swagger, dragging us all headlong into danger, into death, all a . . ."

And then, the woman in black shuddered and went silent, folding inward on herself. Her veil covering her face, shawl hiding her body, she withdrew from the conversation, frustrated by her inability to do anything for the slowly dying boy on the bed, ashamed of her outburst, frightened of what she knew was coming back into all their lives.

"Anyway, Teddy," asked Joan, tired of waiting, uncomfortable in the silence. "What next?"

Cantalupo looked to the detective as well. Staring around the room at the other beds with their well-monitored, dying teenagers, back at Marshall, at Lai Wan's hand, and finally once more at the Pirate Queen, he thought of asking Lai Wan to try and read the others. Reminding himself of what the psychometrist had just told them, knowing that he knew those answers already, he responded to Joan in a voice that almost sounded relieved.

"Captain," London snapped suddenly, shaking himself into activity, "keep Marshall on life support. All the kids you've still got breathing, keep them that way. Whatever this goddamned thing is, we're not losing another life to it."

"And what do we do," asked the Pirate Queen, her eyes alive with interest. His own eyes heavy-lidded and dark, London snarled;

"What do we do now? Well, now I guess, we go back to doing things like detectives."

INTERLUDE

NERVOUS FINGERS DRUMMED AWKWARDLY, fumbling, following no recognizable pattern as they scattered themselves across the shining table top beneath.

Where are they, where are they; miserablegoddamnedbastards—where in God's name are they?

Dr. Hardy tried not to look around the lounge. However, sitting alone in the over-sized booth was making him anxious. His nerves tore at him, ridiculed him, terrified him—irritated him with whispers that sounded suspiciously like *I told you so.*

They're doing this to me on purpose. They *always* do this to me. And I always let them . . .

Of course you let them, a voice from the back of his mind gave him with a matter-of-fact tone. What choice do you have?

Sweat beaded across his hair line. A clamminess smeared itself in between his fingers, making him rub at them repeatedly. When it did not go away, he rubbed all the harder, not realizing what he was doing. Not caring.

Why do I even bother to show up when they tell me to, he wondered once more, pondering the notion seriously, when they never, never, never, never, nevernevernever get here at the time they say they will.

They never say they're going to be here, he reminded himself, answering his question with cynical precision. They just give me an order, "be at this place at this time." The "we'll get there when we feel like it" part is simply understood.

No, he heard another part of his mind laughing, not when they feel like it, when they know we've squirmed enough. When they know we're as stinking scared as we can get.

The fingers of Hardy's left hand closed around the stem of his drink while those to his right continued to unconsciously drum away. He toyed with the notion of downing the still cold martini, then thought better of the idea.

That's when they show up, when I'm ten seconds from pissing in my pants because I'm so goddamned scared.

You have nothing to be frightened over. You are in control of everything.

Hardy laughed. The part of his brain that kept assuring him that everything would be fine had reached the point where the scientist was beginning to think of it as high comedy. It was such a stolid, assured voice he was willing to believe it was being beamed into his skull—that no part of him could possibly feel that confident about the future.

Still, he thought, the laughter felt good—honest. Cleansing. The scientist toyed with the idea once more of just throwing caution down the stairs and saying the hell with everything and downing the drink, as an act of defiance if nothing else.

"Why not?" he mumbled. "Why the hell not?"

Because, he told himself, you need a clear head to deal with Gallbendo and his thugs, remember?

After another second, however, the notion that he could in any way, shape or form deal with Mr. Albert Gallbendo, or either of his usual shadows, became so ludicrous he tossed back the drink in his hand and signaled the bartender for another.

Well then, if that's the case, it that's all they're waiting for, the smug part of his mind asked him innocently, the part of him that had warned him against bringing those for whom he waited into his life, why aren't they here?

A tear formed in Hardy's eye. It did not roll down his cheek, it clung, welling, sucking at the moisture of him, desperate to escape a host it despised. Hefting his newly arrived drink greedily, the fifth he had ordered, Hardy drained it as quickly as the last one, dry gin dripping down over his chin. As his hand fell away from his face, the glass hit the table top roughly, attracting stares. Hardy sighed, then closed his eyes, knocking free the struggling tear.

"Hey look, boss—he's leakin."

Hardy shuddered involuntarily. His bladder contracted, flattened, desperately trying to expel its load. The scientist fought to contain it, desperate to not fall down past any further levels of humiliation in the eyes of the trio finally approaching the booth.

"David," came the familiar, hateful voice. "What's the matter? You not feeling well?"

Concern, thought Hardy, the contempt he felt for the men drawing closer almost sufficient to burn through his mounting fear, how appropriate.

Albert Gallbendo and the two of his thugs the scientist was most used to seeing slid into view. Hardy had no proof the two men with Gallbendo could be accurately described as his "thugs," of course. But the circumstantial evidence he had compiled in the matter lead him to believe that if he were to displease their boss in any way, that he would receive all the proof he could possibly need.

"No, no," Hardy lied badly, "I'm fine."

"Hear that, boss," said one of the pair who might just be thugs, a smiling man with a hard, broad chest, scarred hands and a twice-broken nose, "he's fine."

His companion, also large and scarred, also battered, but not smiling, felt the need to comment as well.

"If this is fine, I'd hate to see him when he was upset."

Hardy noticed something he had not before. The two gorillas never spoke to him. They, and the few others he had seen, only spoke to Gallbendo about him. Deep down, his fear understood why this was so. It was easily understood. They were extensions of Gallbendo, his powerful arms, his avenging fists. They were the voices inside their boss's head—the Gallbendo Greek chorus. When they finally spoke to him directly, he thought soberly, when he finally did become the focus of their attention, he would die. At the least, he would find himself in a terrible amount of pain.

"No, David," said Gallbendo with amazingly realistic sympathy, "are you sure? You have anything to eat?"

Hardy shook his head no, muttering a feeble joke "about drinking his dinner." Gallbendo would not hear of it. With a snap of his fingers a waitress was at their side, scribbling furiously. Hardy studied the man across the table from him. He was an awkward, humorous looking man—curly hair cut crew style, wiry but graying, overly large nose, crooked mouth, massive, well-sculpted arms built large by intense labor, shirt sleeves covering the tattoos Hardy knew were there, cheap things—loud and gaudy with no real artistry and, of course, the dead, baby-doll eyes.

"There," said the crooked mouth, "we'll have something out here in no time. Plenty of their best for everyone." Gallbendo turned his attention to his men.

"What are you two, statues? Sit down, already."

Of course, his attention had never really left Hardy. The dead, baby-doll eyes had stayed locked on the cowering scientist, examining him closely, as usual. They rolled over him greasily, stripping him of clothing, skin and organs, dissecting him down to his soul, looking to see what was there, what might have changed. Gallbendo was not probing for weaknesses. Of that Hardy was certain. The man with the large arms had catalogued all of David Hardy's various weaknesses long ago.

"So, Davey, tell me, what's new in the science game?"

"Not much, I'm afraid."

"And what does that mean?" Gallbendo said the words in a friendly manner. Reaching for a breadstick, grabbing one from the basket in the approaching waitress's hand, he broke it in two as he pretended to be deciding if he wanted to butter it or not. "Could you give us a few details, maybe?"

"I'm sorry," he answered. "There aren't any. Not anything new. Not anything you haven't heard before."

Hardy was a study in abject apology. He knew it was the worst approach possible. He knew there was no sympathy for a cringing coward anywhere within Gallbendo's heart. Standing up to the man might get him a beating, but it would also get him the respect he so desperately needed in dealing with the uncaring mass which had effectively become his owner.

"I, I don't know what else to say . . . we're years, *years* ahead of where we should be. We're sitting on a technology that will be worth billions, maybe trillions . . . the uses it will have are staggering, but it's, we . . . I mean . . ."

"David," Gallbendo interrupted, hand outstretched, a solitary finger held up to indicate silence, "you're working yourself up into an emotional state here. I'm not sure it's healthy for you. Com'on now, you've got to relax."

Hardy lowered his eyes, lowered his head, then shut his eyes, gritting his teeth in helpless frustration. Did he have any time left with these people? Was this the night they were simply going to get rid of him? Or would they hurt him that night, just enough to convince him that they meant business?

Hardy laughed a short, frightened note. The concept that he might not yet grasp the fact that Mr. Albert Gallbendo meant business struck his perverse side as a wildly funny idea. Excusing himself, begging forgiveness for the sick chuckle he pretended was a hiccup, Hardy said;

"I'm sorry, sir, sorry . . . it's just, I, I'm not sleeping much. Working, staying late, trying to get the last . . . if we could just restructure the base molecules, but somehow keep the user from falling into the damn repeat down spiralling . . . you see, it's the damn growth pattern . . ."

Hardy looked up, suddenly embarrassed. The glaze hardening in the eyes of the thugs seemed as impenetrable as the skin of a bowling ball.

"Well, there you go, Mr. Gallbendo," cracked one of the thugs, the one Hardy liked the least. "You see, it's the damn growth pattern . . ."

The second thug snickered. Gallbendo remained impassive.

What was he doing, Hardy asked himself, talking integral detailing to these monkeys? Did he want them to think he was making fun of them? Was he starting to think he should just get them to kill him and get it over with?

Maybe

The single word frightened David Hardy more than Gallbendo. The notion of giving up and just letting the trio there with him kill him entered his mind so easily, sounding so soothing, that he found himself frozen, unable to speak. Then, a curious note sounded in his head, and for an all-too-brief moment the scientist considered that them killing him was not the only way that particular equation could work.

"Was we supposed to understand any of that, boss?"

Gallbendo gave his man a frustrated sideways glance. The thug stuck the roll in his hand into his mouth, pushing it in with his thumb so it might block any other words he might foolish let escape. Then the man David Hardy feared so greatly turned to the scientist and made more soothing noises. He understood the pressures of Hardy's position. Trying to take care of a young wife, maintain a beautiful home, work a stressful job, it was all very trying. Yes, he understood completely.

After a few moments, Hardy actually did begin to calm down. Gallbendo's words, his voice, it was somehow soothing to him—as always. He knew, of course, that nothing had changed. When he had wanted to keep the good times going, when he had already gone through the fortune his initial discoveries had earned him to keep his new wife happy, he had taken far too much money from Gallbendo's outstretched hand, had promised far too much in return, and had quite foolishly promised it far too early.

And if that wasn't bad enough, a part of him whispered, there's all the other "help" they've extended. Then again, moving bodies around is more their line of work.

Inside, the scientist shuddered. A sudden clairty outlined his future for him. Eventually, he would succeed at work or he would continue to fail. Success would mean turning his work over to Gallbendo, something he would never be able to do without being found out. Success would ruin him.

And, if he continued to fail, if he never produced any work finished enough to turn over to Gallbendo, then his time would run out. And failure would kill him. Possibly him and his entire family. Sooner or later, himself, and possibly everyone to whom he was close—snap—gone in an instant.

But, his mind dancing at the knowledge, the fact that Gallbendo was bothering to create the charade of caring meant he would not be hurt that night.

Not yet, he thought, his heart skipping several beats. They're not going to hurt me tonight.

At that moment the food arrived. Multiple platters of fried calamari and glass bowls of salad, sides of Cajun-spiced French fries and bow tie carbanaro were set wherever there was room. Pitchers of beer and wine were squeezed in, and Albert Gallbendo made a huge show of making a toast and encouraging everyone to enjoy themselves.

Hardy shoveled a score of still-sizzling calamari pieces onto his plate, crushing the juice from a fat lemon slice over them, coating their hot fried batter with a snow storm of salt. Then, he attacked them with a frenzied hunger, a grateful voice echoing over and over in his head, just loud enough to be heard over his ravenous greed–

Not yet, it whispered repeatedly, not yet, not yet . . .

And Hardy devoured in joy, well aware that he had only been granted a reprieve, not a pardon.

CHAPTER
TEN

"ALL RIGHT," SAID CANTALUPO. "This is everything we've turned up so far. Where do you want to start?"

London and Joan sat in an interrogation room with the captain and a much changed Lieutenant Krandell. The man had put aside his former bluster, partly out of respect for that aspect of London which he did not yet understand, partly because Cantalupo had ordered him to do so. On the table between them were three hefty boxes of reports, two of them full to spilling-over.

"Cliché, I know," answered London, "but how about we start at whatever you consider to be the beginning?"

Krandell looked to his captain; Joan waited in smirking silence. Cantalupo made no reply, instead reaching into the box to his left and pulling out a handful of folders. Thumbing through them, he found the first of the cases, the one unrelated to anything at the time it was discovered simply because it had been the first.

"Name: Ben Felden, age: seventeen, high school student, top of his class at Brooklyn Technical . . ."

The late Benjamin Felden became something of a template for the fifty plus case files the captain would review with London and the others. Before they had begun, the detective had put a call through to one of his partners, Paul Morcey. The balding man had arrived at the station by the time they were going over the fifth case file. Before they had finished reviewing the ninth one, most of the major patterns the police had noted were already becoming apparent to both Morcey and London. By the time all the material gathered by New York's finest had been gone over, the following facts were obvious to everyone in the room.

All of the victims to date had been young. Most seventeen or under. The oldest had been twenty-two. There had been two nineteen year olds, one twenty-year old.

"Whatever's going on," said Krandell, "I think it's safe to say someone likes 'em young."

"Not necessarily," countered Joan. "Maybe only the young are attracted to whatever this thing uses for bait."

No one argued with her. It was a good point. It was also agreed upon that whatever the bait might be, it was something that appealed to the male of the species far more than it did the female. Close to ninety percent of the victims discovered up to that point had been male. Whereas sex seemed to matter, however, little else did. The victims were not predominately of any one race or any one religion.

"My notes seem to indicate a somewhat elevated IQ level," offered London. "Tally with your findings?"

"Yes," agreed Cantalupo. "All these kids were still in school, or they were graduates. Not all geniuses, but certainly on the high end of the learning curve." The captain grew quiet, wondering where the detective was going with his line of thought. Hoping for a trail he could follow, he asked;

"Think that's something important—something in particular?"

"Who knows?" answered London honestly. Sensing Cantalupo's disappointment, as well as growing antagonism from Krandell, feeling the intensifying waves emanating from the two men, the detective offered;

"I mean, I'm sure it means *something*, but who knows at this stage what that something is? You have to remember, captain, yes, I have a lot more experience with these bump-in-the-night kinds of things than you guys, but I'm still just a human being. I've got to puzzle this stuff out the same way you do." As Krandell gazed on sourly, London added;

"That's the way the universe works. When people hurry—any of us—they make mistakes. Ask your officer Fergeson if he thinks I'm infallible."

Silence filled the room, the raw edgy kind of quiet that gnawed at people. Before it could go on, Morcey tried to swing them all back in the right direction.

"If what we need to do is to identify this thing's brand of bait," started the balding man, "Then how about common interests? I gotta admit I didn't notice any real strong patterns myself, but . . . school clubs, or types of movies, I don't know . . . did anything else in their private lives outside of good report cards come up at a higher rate than just coincidence?"

"I did a lot of the home visits," responded Krandell. His tone indicated he had stored his hostility away—at least for the moment. As the others focused on him, he continued. "Saw about half their rooms. And yeah, there was a lot of similarity, but then, we're talkin' high school kids. They're always all into the same things."

"How long ago did you go to high school," asked Morcey. "These kids today, they ain't like we were. They got ten thousand different interests, and they got the Internet to feed 'em all the crap they want about whatever little bit of nonsense they figure is the greatest thing in the world."

"Good point," mused Cantalupo.

"I agree," added London. Then, turning back to Krandell, he asked, "Can you remember any actual, specific things from their rooms, like not if they all had posters, but what kind of posters they had? Or what kind of music, what kind of toys? Anything that popped up a lot?"

As Krandell started to think, Cantalupo began passing piles of folders out to everyone. Not all the files had photographs, of course. The first few deaths, before anyone suspected that the deaths were related, or that there might be some sort of connection beyond the accidental, had not been considered suspicious. At first, only the discovery sites had been gone over by forensics, not the victims' homes.

That had come later.

And a grand mistake that was, thought Cantalupo, rationing out the files. Another nice snafu, complete with more bodies we can notch up for the collection thanks to the incompetence of New York's Finest.

The captain blinked hard for a moment, chasing the bitter thought to the back of his mind. The rational part of his brain chastised him for deepening his already morbid depression, for assuming fault he could not possibly deserve. London sensed the darkness swirling about the man, understanding all too well the tendency to shoulder more responsibility for problems than one should. Quietly the detective reined in his senses, leaving the captain to his grief, not needing any more guilt on his conscience at the moment.

Going through the photographs taken for the individual files, the team began to find more similarities. There had been a strong interest amongst the dead in Japanese animation. Anime posters, toys and music CDs were spotted in a large percentage of the rooms of the deceased. Such items also reflected a high interest in action movies, comic books, science fiction and horror. Still, Krandell was not convinced.

"Ain't all kids into this shit these days?"

"Some of it," admitted London. "But where are the sports fans? Last time I looked, kids still seemed to like stuff like basketball and football. Anybody see a hint of sports anywhere?"

"And what about exercise?" asked Morcey. "Anybody see any weights, or running shoes? Any kind of exercise equipment, a jump rope, fitness magazine—anything?"

"And how about pictures of real women," asked Joan. "Batgirl and video game thieves with breasts the size of their heads are all well and good for little boys, I suppose, but did anyone notice any posters of actual women, any nudie magazines, or whatever they call such things these days?"

"I believe the word you're searchin' for is 'porn,'" offered Krandell.

"Thank you, Dr. Dictionary," the captain interjected dryly, stopping his man and the Pirate Queen before they could get into yet another row. "Now try answering the important part of her question."

The five thought for a moment; each rifled through a few of their folders, looking for anything they might have missed. No one found anything new.

"So, okay, this tells us something—right?"

Cantalupo asked the question with an air of hopeful expectation, as if this revelation should have given London some sort of neat, precise answer that would explain everything for them. The detective narrowed his eyes, answering the captain as best he could.

"It tells us our victims all appear to have been geeks. Geeks with similar interests, but it's all still pretty vague. We spotted a few of the same toys and things, but nothing that's going to lead us anywhere—not yet, anyway."

"You're wrong," Cantalupo rebuked the detective. "It gives us a hell of a strong profile. What I want to know is, what could really lead us somewhere, is it a profile of the kind of person for which something likes to put out bait, or is it a profile of the kind of person that goes for the kind of bait our something has to offer?"

It was a sharp deduction, and a major fork in the road of their investigation. Lai Wan's experience had definitely let them know they were not dealing with some sort of weird disease, that there was indeed some sort of hunter on the prowl. Still, if the group could determine the answer to the captain's question, they would be able to narrow the scope of their investigation significantly. His eyes open wide, unblinking, London shrugged slightly and admitted he had no concrete ideas yet to send them in either direction.

Silence curled its way through the room, infecting one person after another with its poison. Walls of it began to slide into place, one after another, cutting London and the others off from one another, the weight of it drying the atmosphere, making it cramped—stifling.

Despite the air conditioning, a sweaty clamminess began to manifest itself, straining the general mood. Having sat through hundreds of such sessions during his career, Cantalupo knew when an investigation was beginning to go nowhere. Also noting how long they had all gone without sleep at that point he suggested everyone grab fifteen minutes to take care of whatever business they might wish to attend to. Krandell headed for the men's room. Morcey followed him. Cantalupo headed for his office without specifying any goal or reason.

Noting the time, knowing Lisa would be at the office wondering where both he and Morcey were, worried about how their operation from the night before had turned out, London pulled out his cell phone. He had turned it off when they had first entered the museum for obvious reasons, but then never turned it on again.

You're just full of swift moves today, he thought as he punched in the speed dial number to her direct line. Lisa picked up during the first ring, grateful for the sound of the detective's voice.

"Teddy," she cried. "Where are you? What happened? There's news about the museum all over the television and radio. No one seems to have a clue what really went on, though. The authorities are withholding all information. There's nothing on the services about our kind of operation, though—the strongest rumor anyone seems to have is that it was a terrorist attack. Is everything okay? Is it over?"

"We took care of Laub," answered London cautiously. Lisa had not known the detective long, but she had known him long enough to recognize his style of skirting an issue. Not confronting him, but still fishing, she asked;

"Good. Then when will you be in?"

"I, I'm not sure. Something . . . new . . . has come up. I've been with the police since the museum . . ." London heard a sharp intake of breath over the phone. He reassured her hurriedly.

"I'm fine, I'm fine. Honest. Paul's here with me. We've, well, we've sort of been pulled in on a case the police are having a tough time with."

"Would that be one of . . . *our* kind of cases?" The nervous pause and rattled edge in Lisa's voice shook the detective. Lisa was frightened about something, of that the detective was certain. When he made a small, surprised noise, he did nothing to calm her fears.

"Teddy, what is it; what happened?"

London glared at Joan, who merely smiled, retracting her shoeless foot from the part of his anatomy she had teasingly brushed. Lighting a cigarette breezily, as if she had done nothing at all, she stared at him innocently then pouted a cloud of smoke at him as she mimicked;

"Teddy, what is it; what happened?"

And London froze. Hearing the smirking redhead speak the same words Lisa had spoken, the words he had heard through his cell phone, words no one else could hear . . .

Unless they were in my mind

And the Pirate Queen's smirk expanded into full-blown laughter, for London finally understood the depths of his carelessness, and for her, the look on his face was too priceless for words.

CHAPTER ELEVEN

L ONDON STARED AT JOAN for a long moment. As the others in their little group stayed on the same level of time as most of the rest of the universe, the detective unconsciously accelerated to a plane of existence that moved at an incredibly faster rate. There was nothing noticeable about his action. No science fiction movie effects accompanied his efforts. He simply wanted an extra moment to study the woman across the table from himself without making anyone else aware of what he was doing.

As he continued to stare, however, he was startled to see that the Pirate Queen was actually staring back at him—that she had moved herself to the same plane as easily as he had.

"How?" he asked, his voice heard by only her. "How can you be here with me? I'm not even sure how I managed it."

"Teddy, you really don't understand yet, do you?"

The woman spoke with a teasing smile warming her voice. She was enjoying herself, luxuriating in her small moment of triumph. Around them, the other officers Cantalupo had brought in to go over the files, all moved in millimetered motions, slower than snails, bunches of minutes passing between each beat of their hearts. Snarling, London forced his way back to the real time of the universe, grabbing Joan's wrist as he did so.

"Let's take the air."

Standing abruptly, the detective made a quick and curt "goodbye" to Lisa, then slid his phone back into his pocket while announcing that he needed to talk to his "valuable, practically indispensable team member" in private. Before any of the others could comment, London had jerked the Pirate Queen to her feet as well, and had moved them both halfway to the door. Several of the officers noted the rapid jumps in space made by the pair—all made awkward, uncomfortable efforts to show they had not noticed anything.

In the hall, the detective glanced about sufficiently to make certain the two of them had an adequate amount of privacy. Satisfied, he turned and moved forward, the intensity of his mood shoving Joan back against the wall.

"Look," he snarled, half-angry, half-desperate, "I know you know what the dreamplane is, because you know everything I know. Fine—you 'know' about it. But all you have is what they used to call 'book learning.' You understand it intellectually, but you haven't experienced it. You don't know what kind of fire you're playing with."

"And you do, I suppose," she responded. "That's why Officer Fergeson is the head of your fan club. And why you and I have become such good friends."

"No," London answered. "I *don't* know what it's all about. That's the point. Every time I think I do, something like Fergeson, or you, comes along to remind me how little I do know. But all that proves is that if I don't know much, you don't know *anything.*"

"It's nothing to get upset about, lover," answered the redhead calmly. Taking another drag on her cigarette, she told him, "normal people slide into it every day. Don't they?"

As she exhaled, the detective nodded.

"Sure," he agreed. "Day dreamers, people you look at and say, 'hey, you were in another world;' half the time they were. Consciously dreaming about making something happen seems to be the first step toward getting there. It's the same for technological advances. All through history, you've got four or five people all making the same leap forward at the same time. No phones or radios or anything like that to transmit ideas, and yet people in countries that don't even know each other exist stumble across the same answers at the same time."

London gulped, part of him not even wanting to discuss the dimension where wishes became reality. What was it, he wondered. Heaven? Hell? Some soulless patch of energy that merely generated concepts such as Heaven and Hell? The detective sincerely did not want to know.

"There's an ether that surrounds the world, that surrounds all of us. It's the reason two guys on opposite sides of the world can get the same idea at the same time, and the reason I could do what I did to Fergeson, and with you. This ether coats us all, keeps us all interconnected. It's where we get the ability to 'feel' someone watching us; it explains 'love at first sight;' it . . ."

The detective, ready to continue rattling off examples, cut himself off in mid-sentence, then jumped forward after a pause and finished, telling the woman, "Basically, if you truly believe you can do something, you can use the ether to do it. Period. You just have to believe."

The pirate queen enjoyed the last lungsful of gray relief her shrinking cigarette had to offer, then crushed it out on the wall behind her as she answered London honestly.

"Obviously I believe you. I've seen too much proof. But tell me, what keeps the world from filling over with little gods all trying to rule our sorry pathetic planet with whatever super powers they dream up for themselves?"

"I've talked this out with a professor I know," said London, to which Joan replied;

"Professor Goward . . . I know him, too. Remember?"

"As best we can tell," the detective continued, ignoring the Pirate Queen's barb, "the dreamplane only responds to thinking individuals. Babies are pure want, but they can't manipulate its forces. Only adults can do that, but most can't, because they believe they can't."

Now Joan stared at London, her eyes narrowing, drawing into slits as she waited for him to explain. His own eyes still, unblinking, he told her;

"It's doubt. We all learn it early on. And, once you have the slightest bit of it within you, once you learn to doubt your abilities, whether it's humility, or just an intellectual safety, once you wonder 'can I actually do that,' you've cut yourself off from the dreamplane. Doubt keeps people from being one hundred percent focused on something."

"That explains a lot."

London wondered what the woman meant. Staring into his eyes, Joan knew the detective could not follow her statement. That was to be expected, however, since she meant to confuse him. On the one hand, it was a standard trick, pretending to understand more than one does. In this case, though, the Pirate Queen was not trying to fool anyone. She understood London perfectly.

Since the death of Ferris Miller, Joan de Molina had been a completely focused individual. From that day on, she had pulled back into herself, learning her limits, pushing them, expanding them, shoving herself forward into anything that pleased her. Up until that moment, it seemed to the Pirate Queen that everything around her conspired to break her will. But, nothing ever did. She had stood against the tide and had simply forced things to move in her direction since that terrible, cleansing night.

"Don't fret, lover," she said in a small, knowing voice, her eyes filled with the same desire for London they had held when first she had watched him facing down Laub in the museum. "It all makes sense."

"To you, maybe," London answered. "But not me. And I don't think you understand as much as you think you do."

"What's to understand?" The Pirate Queen's words frosted slightly, her automatic defenses triggering. "I've spent my entire life being backed into corners that I've had to fight my way out of. Every single time I've come out the better—smarter, tougher—improved. This is no different."

"There are a few differences," countered London.

"None I can see," she whispered. Her hands sliding up the front of the detective's chest, she moved her fingers under the lapels of his jacket, then pulled him forward slightly as she added, "Not from where I stand. I took another risk, and from it I got exactly the reward I desired."

Joan was pleased to note that as she released her hold on London that this time he did not back away. Her eyes still locked on his, though the two of them were still standing in the hallway of police headquarters, she pulled him closer once more, rising to meet his descending face until their eyes were but a few inches apart.

"You really have no idea what you're dealing with here," asked London. "Do you?"

"No," she agreed, her voice all warmth and invitation, "I have a very strong feeling I don't. That's why I've got myself such a good teacher to guide me through."

Various precinct personnel had passed by them at this point. Plainclothesmen and uniformed officers stared at the couple, wondering who they could be, what they could be up to. Their minds wandered as they watched the two, their imaginations peppering the ether with the smell of sexual tension. Individual swirls of congratulations, envy, lust and approval poured over the two as they merged into each other's space.

"You might be willing to admit that you're out of your depth here, but I don't think you really have any understanding whatsoever as to just how bottomless this end of the pool actually is," said London. The disapproval in his voice was strong, but it was tempered with desire, and the sound of it made the redhead feel weak; intoxicated. "Once you make contact with the dreamplane anything is possible . . ."

"Anything?" Joan repeated the word with a sense of wonder, her breath catching in her throat.

"Yes," answered London, trying to be stern, hoping to wedge himself out of his current situation. "Anything. But there's always a price."

"There's always a price for everything, Teddy," agreed the Pirate Queen. Shifting her head on her long neck, Joan brushed the detective's lips with hers, sending frosted fire through his veins. "That's the way the world works, silly boy."

"This price is higher than you might think."

London gulped down a breath, forcing it into his lungs. Blinking, fighting the near-overwhelming urges burning their way through his mind, he told the woman whose arms encircled him, "Everything we do on the dreamplane is paid for on this side. Whatever energy it takes to fulfill some urge, it's simply sucked up from here—usually at random. Whatever force it takes, it's all billed to this world. Do you understand?"

Joan nodded, her eyes open, bright, sparking. Her body tight—hoping. Without a word, she moved forward and upward, this time planting her mouth firmly over the detective's. She kissed him long and hard, needing him, wanting everything he was in every way it could be had. And, driven by their unique connection, unable to resist the tides of emotion battering at him, London kissed her back—just as long.

Just as hard.

Somewhere in the middle of the embrace, both closed their eyes, falling totally into each other's existence. Then, they opened their eyes at the same time, seeing the unspoiled face of their partner. London simply stared, his mind calm for an instant. He had been fighting the moment for too long. Now that he had succumbed to it, he needed a space to sort things out.

For the Pirate Queen, on the other hand, the moment had been the triumph for which she had been waiting. She had seen London in the museum and had wanted him, unconsciously hungered for him—had known instantly that this was the first man she had discovered since . . . since she had given up looking, that could balance her scale, who could be what she needed. Who already was everything she needed. Staring at him, smiling, she heard his words of warning in her head once more.

"Once you make contact with the dreamplane anything is possible . . . anything. But there's a price."

There's always a price, Teddy, she had told him, acknowledging that she knew the way the world works. But he had continued, his voice practically breathless as he insisted;

"This price is higher than you might think."

I don't care–

"Everything we do on the dreamplane is paid for on this side."

I don't care–

"Whatever energy it takes to fulfill some urge, whatever force it takes, it's all billed to this world."

I don't care–

"Do you understand?"

Their eyes still locked Joan nodded slightly, then whispered;

"I understand."

As London reacted to her words, the Pirate Queen reached into her soul, throwing open its doors for the first time since the night she turned her back on everyone and everything in existence. The light she revealed blinded him for the moment, the force of its release staggering the redhead for an instant, as well. Her eyes focused intently on the detective's, she told him;

"The energy we use on the dreamplane, you said it's all billed to this world—right?"

London nodded, his face stern. Smiling, ignoring the warning feelings washing off the detective, Joan filled her throat with a laugh and then aimed her lips for London's once more as she said;

"Good. Let's run up a tab."

CHAPTER
TWELVE

JOAN DE MOLINA TUGGED on London, pulling him toward her, throwing herself backward through the wall. The detective tumbled after her, their bodies becoming insubstantial, their atoms sliding apart—then mingling. Around the pair the police station disappeared, the world racing away along with it, everything familiar to either of them simply vanishing, replaced by a vast and unimaginable landscape.

Red dust blasted in whirling cyclones across a flat and frozen plane of violet, crimson crystals scratching their way across the polished, purple surface beneath. In the distance, greenish-gray bolts of lightning splattered themselves against the mountain range that ran across the horizon, shattering great stands of rock, sending their ruin down to rumble across the gouged and gleaming plane below.

"Teddy," the Pirate Queen murmured, "oh, Teddy . . ."

Her hands tore at his jacket, ripping it from his body in long, straggling sections. Instinctively understanding how the dreamplane worked, she laughed as she simply puckered her lips and blew against the detective's chest, the rest of his clothes splashing away from his body, falling apart at their atomic level in response to the commanding pressure.

"Joan," snapped London, his face flashing from stern to worry, "stop it."

"Afraid to play," questioned the woman, her tone teasing. "This doesn't look good to you?"

With a shrug of her shoulders, the Pirate Queen shed her ordinary world clothing, replacing it with robes of gleaming silver. A mixture of silken threads and spider-spun precious metals, the cloth hugged her like wet paint. Floating several inches off the ground, Joan smiled, her arms open and inviting, her red hair brilliant, sparkled with gem dust, dancing in the air behind her.

"Don't you want just a taste?"

The question melted through London like sound waves repeatedly rippling the calm surface of a long lost mountain lake. The woman had not thrown mere words at the detective, but bubbles of emotion which burst against him, twining his hair, slipping across his exposed skin, dissolving beneath its surface.

"Joan, don't do this."

London resisted the temptation floating before him, fought against the heaving layers of desire burning within his mind and beyond. His entire body was filled with a crackling hunger, with a need so all-consuming he could barely concentrate.

"You don't know what you're doing."

"Oh, but I do, lover," she whispered. Drifting in the air just above him, arms outstretched, the Pirate Queen beckoned to London, drawing him to her.

"I wanted you the first minute I saw you. Your little mind meld trick only made me want you all the more. We're perfect for each other—two of a kind . . ."

Joan stretched her arms further, welcoming the slowly approaching London. The detective resisted her pull, not just because of Lisa, but because he knew their struggle would be affecting the outside world. How, to what extent, he had no idea, but he knew the longer he allowed them to play with the force of the dreamplane, the more likely it was the effects would not be to his liking.

And yet, as he stared at the woman before him, she opened to him the memories she held of the countless men who had desired her. A tumbling flood of naked emotion flashed around him, ten hundreds of thousands of male voices all whispering their hungering, crushing desire to possess the prize he would disdain. London gulped, his eyes riveted to the woman known the world over as the Pirate Queen. His unblinking eyes captured her dazzling radiance, the unbelievable, shimmering cosmic beauty of her, and suddenly it seemed he found his will evaporating, the need welling within him simply too hard to ignore.

"Teddy," she called, her voice softer than clouds, more delicious than happiness, "take what is yours."

His fingers cramped from the aching want of her. The detective reached for the floating woman, his body racked by a grasping hunger invading every muscle and fiber of him, a washing ravenousness which poured around and over and through him, a flood that swept both flesh and mind along in its path. Though a small part of his consciousness still screamed caution, warning against abandon, far too many of the voices within his head had been seduced by the sight of Joan since the beginning—the delicate feel of her in the air, the sound of her radiating flesh, the pulse of it wrapping all of them with an itching avarice they simply could not ignore.

Take what is yours, she had said, and London reached to do so, for in truth, everything about her was his, as everything about him was hers. They shared one mind now, two lives intertwined into one memory—a maze he had entered in the museum without realizing it. Though he struggled against accepting it, the fact was clear that in many ways the two had lead the same life. Both had lost their parents early on, had their first true loves torn away from them, lost the simple path most people are bound to by dull fate. Both had fought back against destinies they did not desire for themselves.

"I want you," London's voice growled, the noise of it thrilling the woman. "I've always wanted you."

Her eyes open wide, Joan de Molina stared down at the approaching London. His eyes traveled the length of her, starting at her toes and working their way over the length of her magnificent body. In truth, she had not had to change or sculpt herself to any great degree. Unconsciously she had used the power of the dreamplane to heighten the sheen of her skin, the depth of the color of her eyes, but they were small things—minor. Insignificant. More would have been an insult. Less would not have been noticed.

London knew who she was in every aspect. Since their melding in the museum, he knew her as he knew himself—in some ways better. He understood on the most intimate level everything about her—where her birthmark was, what made her ticklish, what made her despair, the depth of her navel, the sound she heard within her head when she drew a sharp breath, what it felt like when she cracked her neck by touching her ear to her shoulder—everything physical, and more.

"Then catch me."

Impishly, the Pirate Queen floated higher, drifting away from London's grasp. Inflamed, abandoning all pretense of even trying to halt his all-consuming desires, the detective flexed his knees slightly and then threw himself upward after the woman. Smiling, the redhead increased her speed, moving away from London. Smiling equally, he doubled his own speed, shrinking the distance between them rapidly.

Laughing in a clean and wild way, in much the manner of schoolchildren at play, their voices echoed off to the ever-crumbling, ever-renewing mountains in the distance and back again. Churning the air dramatically, their speed increasing with every second, they burned the atmosphere of the dreamplane, scorching it both with their rapid movements and with the heat of their mutual desire. In but a handful of moments their flaming bodies became fiery blurs, mere outlines barely discernable against the deep orchid of the sky.

And then, London's fingers caught hold of Joan's ankle. Drawing her legs upward toward her body, the Pirate Queen was not trying to break the detective's grasp—she merely desired to pull him closer to her. He came willingly, desperate for her. For hours his body had ached, his brain throbbing, all of him desperately needing back the part of himself he had lost to the woman now within his arms.

"Now that you have me," Joan sighed, her eyes filled with mischief, as well as needs all her own, "what are you going to do with me?"

"You told me to take you," London answered, panting, sweat dripping from his forehead, down his arms, his back, across his stomach, pooling around the hairs on his chest. "But you didn't say where."

"Surprise me," said the Pirate Queen. Then, she closed her eyes, her arms encircling London's body even as his slid around hers—one around her perfect waist, the other up and over her shoulder, fingers brushing her neck. The woman gasped at his touch, delight filling every cell of her being.

London felt her skin against his, the deep, growing warmth of her, the tingling, living energy crackling throughout her system. He drank the feeling in, grabbed for it, immersed himself in it, and then, he closed his own eyes, and the two beings merged into one, their flesh mingling, limbs melting, bones dissolving—their combined form blurring from the human to the infinite.

Red hair exploded in running scarlet lines across the throbbing mass of self-indulgent plasma. Powerful appendages—practically hands—extended and the single entity caressed itself, loved itself tightly, overwhelmingly—completely. It raced at transcendent speeds, criss-crossing galaxies in milli-seconds, groping its way blindly through both time and space, shattering the walls of dimensions the way the ocean overwhelmed sand castles—casually, as if physical law was as malleable as pudding. Its journey lasted for years on end, all of it over in the same moment it began.

Then slowly, infused with an overwhelmingly wanton feeling of satisfied regret, the single mass began to reluctantly unravel itself back into the two individuals it had been at the beginning. Moving with giddy hesitation, London and the Pirate Queen robed themselves once more in their regular world clothes, regained their regular world attitudes, and then, they came together once more, their lips hungry for each other as their bodies easily stepped back through the barriers between realities into the dimension they called home.

They arrived where they should—at the point where they had exited, as was natural—in the hallway outside of the office they and the others had been using. Everything exactly the same as when they left.

Except for the fact that the hallway was now dark and wet, and filled with smoke and the shouts of the frightened.

"What is it?" asked Joan. "What happened?"

A moment's inspection of their surroundings told the story. It seemed that the building's electrical power had been interrupted by some unknown force while they were gone. But, other than that, everything was nearly exactly the same as when they left. The only difference was that the hallway had gone dark.

"Us," answered London. "We're what happened."

That and the small detail that the hallway was also split down the middle, its floorboards splintered and smoldering, the walls and ceiling both scorched and collapsed down upon the shattered woodwork. Everywhere around them was the thin smell of bitter smoke, mixed with the wet drizzle of shattered and twisted sprinklers, and the wounded cries of men and women, all of them broken and bleeding and dazed with the wonder of what had just happened.

CHAPTER THIRTEEN

"**S**WEET BRIDE OF THE night," muttered Morcey's voice somewhere off in the darkness, "what the hell was that?"

Going to tell him?

London snarled at the sarcastic voice sneering at him from the back of his brain. Rapidly, the detective forced himself to put aside all that had happened to him on the dreamplane to concentrate on what had taken place in his absence. He could see that he and Joan had not moved. Indeed, from where he could feel her arms, still wrapped about him, he knew the two of them had only been absent for a handful of seconds.

And yet . . .

London let the thought hang in his mind. He had tried to be careful, to not utilize the energy of the dreamplane in the real world. Even though he had ultimately allowed himself to throw all cautions aside, still he had been certain neither of them had done anything on the other side that could have reached back into the their own plane of existence.

Could it?

Screams and shouts continued to sound throughout the darkness. Pushing all distractions from his mind, the detective shut his eyes and concentrated, looking for a connection between the two realities. He thought back to their departure. He could hear Joan's voice once more–

"Good. Let's run up a tab."

Could feel her lips joining his, and then the rapid slipping across, the arrival, the teasing, the games, the chasing and the inevitable capture, the self-contained melding, the travel and the heat and the final separation, the one last kiss . . .

"Oh, God . . ." London's groan drew Joan's attention.

"What is it, lover?"

"This."

His voice was a snarling whisper. As his arms unlocked their hold on the Pirate Queen, he waved them both about himself in the dim light available, indicating the ruin stretching away from the two of them in all directions as he continued, shouting;

"This! All of *this!* Don't you get it; can't you see? This is our doing. We were kissing when we left this realm, when we kissed again over there, this was the result."

Joan unconsciously released her hold on the detective as her eyes strained to take in the damage. At first she made to protest, but instead she went silent—accepting her share of the blame for what had happened. The woman cursed herself inside, knowing the accident would throw walls between herself and London she might not be able to surmount. Even as she struggled to think of a response, suddenly the emergency lights cut in, blinding hard arcs of pure white that flooded the hallways throughout the building, reflecting from the smoke still hanging everywhere.

"Boss," shouted Morcey with relief, "there you are."

"Yeah," answered London. "Here I be. Cantalupo, Krandell, how are they?"

"They're fine. They just came back. See, they're there inside." Morcey pointed behind himself at the door through which he had just passed. "Soon as there was noise, I jumped to, lookin' ta see what'd happened—you know. Hey, like, in our line, you never know what's gonna happen next, I mean . . ."

The ex-maintenance man's voice trailed off suddenly. He had finally focused on the picture before him. As common sense reconstructed the scene as it must have been a moment earlier, he took note of the fact that London and the Pirate Queen must have just been embracing. Caught off guard, he looked away embarrassed as he asked;

"Ahhhhh, anything happen here I should know about? We under some kind of attack or somethin'?"

"Nothing to worry about," answered London. The detective stepped toward his partner, indicating the door as he continued. Giving the man a reassuring wink, he said, "Things were a little hairy for a minute, but I think I've got it under control. Let's get back in there for now before anything else goes wrong."

"Hey, okay. So, this is the deal, then. We're gonna take this case off the city's hands?"

London surveyed the damage once more, then offered with a sigh, "After all this, yes—I think we're going to have to."

It was several hours before London and the others were able to make their way to West Thirty-First Street, specifically to the Greeley Arcade, the building which was home to the London Agency. Crossing the fifteen steps from the elevator to his office door, he took the knob in his hand, then stopped. Holding the bronze sphere within his fingers for a moment, he finally sighed, and then turned the knob and walked in to the inevitable.

"Teddy," Lisa's voice sounded. "I've been so worried."

"Sorry," answered the detective honestly. "I knew you would be."

"Are you all right? Why were you with the police? You said something about taking a case. From them? From the police? I don't understand? You cut off me off so abruptly. And then . . . why didn't you call back?"

London tried to answer, but before he could speak Morcey and Joan moved into the office behind him. The detective watched his partner's face, watched her eyes as they shifted from him to a point somewhere behind him. Specifically to the doorway, or more precisely, to the person framed by the door jamb. Lisa went sharply stiff—her face cold and brittle. She did not ask if Joan were a new client, or a police liaison. She had no need. One look into the other woman's face told her everything she felt she needed to know. The Pirate Queen stared back, her head tilted slightly, eyes filled with mischief.

"What's the word on Pa'sha and his boys and Doc Goward," asked London. "Did everyone get out all right?"

"It seems so," answered Lisa. Her voice strained, but she refused to allow it to crack. Joan shut the door behind herself, making it obvious she was there to stay. Not willing to lose another fraction of an inch to the person she was rapidly sizing up as a viable threat, Lisa shifted her head slightly, pointing with her eyes as she asked;

"Who's our guest?"

"Oh, I'm no guest," answered Joan. Walking forward, the Pirate Queen extended her arm, allowing her most believable French accent to surface as she said, "Mademoiselle Joan de Molina. I've become more, what could you say, how would you describe it, an asset to the company. I'll be . . . hummm, heavens, you know, I don't actually know what I'll be around here. Teddy? Teddy, tell us . . . what will I be around here?"

"Enough!"

London's growl turned all the heads in the reception area. Tired of steadily losing ground, he pushed all the weariness and anxiety and frustration he had gathered over the last few hours away from himself. Like bundles of trash he simply exiled it from his person, not caring what effect he might have on the world as he snagged enough energy out of the ether to neutralize the effects of the previous twenty-four hours. Then, before anyone could speak, he snapped off a series of orders.

Morcey he assigned to find them all some lunch. Joan he told to stay with his partner and to both keep out of the way and out of trouble. Lisa he ushered into his office and shut the door. Outside, the Pirate Queen attempted to follow the pair, but Morcey caught her arm and, wagging his finger in the air, instructed the woman that doing so might be a bad idea. Grinning, knowing immediately that the ex-maintenance man was no threat to her plans, she agreed that he might have a point, and then joined him in his search for sustenance.

In London's office, the detective sat behind his desk, Lisa in one of the leather client chairs on its other side. He told her the entire story of the night before then, tracking Laub, breaking into the museum, their confrontation, what had happened to him and how Joan's intervention had saved his life, and possibly everyone else's in the world.

Then, after a long breath, he also told her of reading Joan's mind, of giving orders to Officer Fergeson, and of the horrible messes he created with both actions. He told her of his first meetings with Krandell and Cantalupo, of the trip to see young John Marshall and the others, and of what had happened when Lai Wan had arrived.

"That's all that happened?"

Lisa asked the question, knowing the answer. London, not knowing what else to do, told her what had happened when he and the others had begun to look into Cantalupo's unsolvable case, including his side trip to the dreamplane and the destruction it caused. When he was finished, Lisa was quiet for several long moments. Then, she finally asked;

"What did you do after that? How did you explain the damage?"

"I didn't," he told her. "Cantalupo asked if we'd been attacked and I told him I thought it was possible. I hinted that it might have been supernatural, but that I didn't have anything to do with it. I'm not sure he believed me. After that, I told him he'd better attend to his station house. I promised that Paul and I would get the ball rolling on his investigation, and then we left and came here to fill you in on everything."

"Why?"

London's head snapped back a fraction of an inch. Of all the responses Lisa might have made, the one he received had not been anything he had been expecting. His mouth felt terribly dry, his jaw refused to move—useless. Pulling saliva free from behind his teeth, he sloshed it around within his mouth, desperate for the ability to talk. Although the first answer that came to him was to simply ask what she meant by her question, he knew better. Almost grateful for his momentary paralysis, he answered instead;

"Why? Because that's what we do around here. No matter what happens, you're still my partner. This is still a business. At the absolute least I think I owe you that much.

"Don't you?"

Lisa sat still in her chair, forcing herself to remain calm, to not answer. She was too young for what was happening, too inexperienced. Maybe, she thought, someone with a different background, a background that was in any way normal, might have been able to handle all that was being thrown at her, but she could not. She loved London dearly for freeing her from her old life, for saving her from the terrors from beyond that would have done unimaginable things to her.

And, she knew that deep within his soul that London loved her as well. But, she had also known from the beginning that there was no way for her to reach that love buried within the detective. He had looked at her across the gulf of all the black and terrible things that wished to destroy him, and afterward he had kept her at arm's length, not daring to get close to her, worried about all those entities which would delight in making her suffer.

Still, she had waited and dared to hope he might be able to forget about a lover's safety, or at least to put such a consideration to the side long enough to find out if they were willing to share such dangers if it meant being able to share other things. And now, looking into his eyes, and Joan's, she could see that finally such had come to pass . . .

With some one else.

The four words burned in the young woman's mind, almost forcing her to tears. Catching herself, refusing to play that role, to burden London with such nonsense when there was obviously something so much larger than the both of them brewing, she turned to the practical instead, asking;

"So, do you have any idea what this thing really is between the two of you—how long it's going to last? Anything? Are you in love with her? Do . . .

"Do you want to be?"

London sat silently, not knowing what to say. Or, more correctly, not able to get a word in between all the voices in his head. Hundreds of his ancestral voices were chiming in, male and female, all either offering advice on how to handle Lisa, or laughing at him for getting into such a damn fool predicament in the first place. Never having been in such a situation before, the detective had never had such a flood to deal with before. Finally, however, after far too many seconds had passed, he managed to dismiss them all with a mental blast which cleared his mind completely after which he said;

"Sorry—I, I couldn't shut down all the chatter in my pea-like brain. Listen, no—I'm not in love with her. I certainly don't want to be. As for how long this mess will continue . . ."

London hesitated, not knowing exactly how to answer, not knowing what the truth was, or would be. Finally, he told Lisa softly;

"I don't know. As far as I'm concerned it's already lasted too long. The feelings I have for her aren't real. You know that. I know that. And, really, I'm sure she knows that. But, that's not the point. They're there, and as long as she keeps pumping emotion into them, I don't know what's going to happen next."

Lisa nodded unconsciously, a tear forming in each of her eyes despite her strong resolve to make certain such a thing did not happen. She had just about structured her poise to where it might possibly protect her when London added;

"I don't."

His voice was plaintive and tired, and it shattered all her hopes of resisting. The tears she had prayed to keep only a possibility began welling, threatening what little composure she had remaining. With all the strength she possessed she held onto the droplets, forcing them to stay within their ducts. Blinking, she spread them across her burning irises, then pushed her chair back with her feet. Standing, she made a gesture indicating London should stay seated.

"We're partners," she said in an even voice, "and my main duty is to keep the office running. That will happen. Have no worries. I'm going to go and call in Morris, or Bennet, or one of the other freelancers to come in and take charge of the day to day operations."

London made to speak, but Lisa put up her hand and wedged it firmly between them, forcing the detective to stay in his seat, and to do so silently.

"Don't speak—please, Teddy. This is hard enough. I know this isn't your fault. It's not like you're some kind of cheating husband. We're not married; we're not engaged. We've never even done anything as simple as go to a movie . . ."

"But, Lisa . . ."

"Teddy, *please.* Just let me talk. There is nothing between us that this can hurt. You had an accident. Either you can be healed, or . . ." the young woman's words choked in her throat. Whatever she had been headed toward saying, she veered off onto terrain she was more certain she could transverse.

"I'm going to go home, and I'm going to stay there for a while. It's not the sophisticated way to handle things, but I'm not a chic New York girl, and I'm not very sophisticated. Knowing that at least gives me the edge that I don't have to embarrass myself while this gets worked out. So, please, just work on this case and, and forget about me . . . for now. I'll see how you are when things are over."

"I would hope so," London told her, a trifle annoyed at her desertion, a bit relieved as well.

"Try and stop me."

And with those words, she opened the door to the reception area and disappeared from sight. London sat behind his desk, staring at the door, staring into space. From the faint noises he could discern, he could follow her movements—back into her own office, the grabbing up of a purse and jacket, stopping by the door for something, pausing for a long moment, then finally heading for the door to the hallway . . .

The detective knew he could enter her mind, listen to her thoughts, influence her—he *knew* he could. But, a quick reminder detailing the disastrous mess he had made of things earlier that day stopped all such thoughts cold. Black thunder rang through his mind, slamming such notions with a searing fury. For a moment he simply could not believe that he could entertain such foolishness for even an instant. As the moment passed, however, he decided against wasting anymore time.

Just how many kids have to die before you get your act together, mister? Or is getting laid that important to you?

Feeling himself sink into a weary calm, London pressed a button on his intercom, and asked, "Paul, how's lunch coming?"

"On its way," the balding man answered. "Anything else, or should I continue to entertain our guest here with my endless bag of jokes and impressions?"

"Tell me, do you have that list of addresses that Cantalupo gave us?"

"Sure thing, boss. You wanta look it over?"

"No," the detective snapped. Pulling Betty from his shoulder holster, he yanked open the drawer in his desk where he kept his ammunition. Then, spilling a box open across his desk, he ejected the spent casings from his battle in the museum and began to reload the weapon with fresh shells.

"No," he repeated as he slid the last new bullet needed into place. "But I want you to figure out a route strategy. Draw up a convenience grid—which ones to visit in what order. We're getting out of here and we're going to go to every one of them that we have to go to until we can figure this damn thing out and get our lives back to normal."

Morcey agreed, and answered in the positive when London told him to be ready to go in five minutes. Seconds later, the food he had ordered arrived from the coffee shop downstairs. The ex-maintenance man paid the delivery boy, then sent him on his way. Returning to his office, he threw the three brown paper bags into a knapsack while informing Joan as to what their plans were. Hoping against hope, he offered;

"You know, it'd probably be easier on everyone if you were to just pull a fade right about now."

"Why, aren't you sweet?" asked Joan in an almost pleasant tone. "Not too fast on the uptake, but loyalty has its virtues, I suppose."

Choosing not to answer, the ex-maintenance man checked his own weapon, thinking;

Oh, yeah—this one is just goin' ta be bags o' fun. Then, he reached into his bottom drawer for his back-up pistol and ankle holster.

"Just in case," he said quietly, rolling his head on his shoulders as he did so. "Just in case."

CHAPTER
FOURTEEN

JOAN AND MORCEY SAT in the comfortable living room of Peggy Lynn and Norman Chamberlain, waiting for London to finish in the bedroom. Peg and Norm sat with them. The bedroom in question was not theirs, but that of their son, Terry. The police had gone over the room before, of course. They had also questioned Terry's parents in great detail, as well as a number of their friends and neighbors and even a large number of Terry's classmates.

Terry Chamberlain had been the first victim found after the authorities had become convinced they might have some sort of epidemic on their hands. He had been the first to be investigated in every way the police could think of. None of it had helped. None of it had mattered. Now, while London went over the late youngster's room, his partner and the Pirate Queen questioned his mother and father, succeeding only in reminding the couple of the previous vast failures.

"Again, we're really sorry to have to bother you folks with all of this."

"That's okay," answered Norm, cautiously. "I didn't mean to offend, or anything—just wanted to check, you know. Even though you came with a police car, you yourselves aren't cops, I mean police officers, I mean . . ."

"Don't sweat it," interrupted Morcey, halting the man's rambling. As if he had been working with the police as a community liaison for decades, the ex-maintenance man launched into a highly effective spiel that put both parents much more at ease almost instantly.

In the meantime, London sat on the edge of the late Terry Chamberlain's bed, his eyes wandering about the room. This was the fifth such bedroom he had inspected so far since they had left their building. He and the others, as well as an officer Shaub, sent along as a token of comfort to keep people at ease, had managed two inspections before finally stopping to eat the bagged lunches Morcey had brought along. Notes compared at that time led the team in no particular new directions. Now they were on their third post-lunch visit, most likely the last one they were going to be able to make before the sun went down.

Shaub proved useful then in so much as he had been one of the uniformed officers handling crowd control and other minor tasks at quite a number of the previous interrogations. While the police detectives had first questioned the various grieving parents about the habits and hobbies of their dying or already deceased children, he had soaked in much of the atmosphere. It allowed him to give the others an extremely clear picture of the desperate futility of such exercises.

"It was sad," he said, water bottle in hand. He held it absently, almost as if he had forgotten about its existence. "So many of these people, sittin' there thinking that somehow we were goin' to be fixin' everything—like we could start their kids breathin' again. Or, the other end, like we somehow stopped them from breathin' in the first place."

"Serious question—do you think we're likely to get anywhere now that some time has passed?" London made his query with little hope of a positive answer. He was not disappointed.

"I wouldn't think so," answered Shaub honestly. "My guess would be the ones who were expectin' miracles are just gonna get more excited, and the ones who weren't are gonna be more hostile than they were the first time around."

The officer's prediction had proved to be quite prescient. No one made trouble for the team, but none of the parents proved very helpful, either. Norm Chamberlain was one to question everything, looking for negatives behind every imagined shadow. Peg Chamberlain allowed her husband to do most of the talking. Noting this, Morcey made a suggestion.

"Norman, and, ah, is it okay if I call you 'Norman?'" A slight nod gave the balding man the permission he was looking for. "Thanks, man. Listen—you spend any time with Terry here in the house in any one spot? Back yard? Basement? Doin' projects? Goin' to the movies? Watchin' television? Anything like that—father/son stuff?"

Norman thought for a moment. There had been nothing for so long he almost dismissed the question. Ever since all those damn Japanese cartoons came along, and the video games, damn Japanese games to go with the TV, even comic books in Japanese, backwards, backwards comics that weren't even in English. What the hell was the boy doing with . . .

The grieving father stopped himself, curtailing the ugly thoughts. His son was dead. Buried. Gone from his life and the world. Such nonsense was useless. With a will beyond many, Norman Chamberlain stopped thinking about himself for a moment and tried to think of something that, even though it might not be able to help his son, might be able to help avenge him.

"The back yard. You know, we used to play a lot of catch out there. Would that be okay?"

"Honey," interjected his wife, pity in her voice, "that was ages ago."

Norman's head jerked, but he said nothing. Was she trying to make him look bad, to say he was a bad father? What was he supposed to do? The kid changed. Overnight—he gave up on sports, gave up on everything they'd ever done. Just all comics and cartoons and video games. Nonsense—just a goddamned buncha . . .

His face going slightly red, Norman calmed himself, a part of him actually marvelling at how quickly his defenses had rallied. He forced himself to go quiet once more, though, reminding his inner voices that there was no one there he needed to defend himself against. With a quiet voice, he asked;

"Does it matter? That we haven't been out there together for a while—a long while?"

"No—not at all." Morcey put down his coffee cup and rose to his feet quickly. He did not really want to see a different place. He merely wanted to remove the father from the mother's presence to allow Joan some time with the woman alone. His hand on Norman's shoulder, Morcey gave the man a conciliatory pat, steering him toward the back of the house.

"Not at all. Let's go see what kind of gardener you are." Then, as the two men began to move for the kitchen, the ex-maintenance man threw his eyes sideways, indicating to Joan that she might want to try and get through to the mother while they were gone.

"So, tell me," started Joan, concentrating on the woman next to her as the men disappeared, timing her question to the precise moment they passed through the back doorway;

"What do you think happened to your son? Don't worry about your answer—just blurt out the first thing that comes to your mind. Tell me anything at all you've thought of since . . . well, since it happened."

In the bedroom, London continued to stare. He took in the colorful posters hanging on the wall, some of them mere paper taped in place, some of them fancier cloth scrolls hanging from nails. His eyes passed over the neat rows of paperback-styled collections of manga, Japanese comic books, stacked on the shelves, situated under the rows of video tapes and DVD boxes.

Normal stuff, he thought. Normal kid stuff. The same normal kid stuff we saw before lunch, that we read about at the station house, before we indulged ourselves and then rent it asunder.

The thought haunted the detective. It did not bother him so much that he had been unfaithful to Lisa. Indeed, he was not even certain the term applied. He and Joan had not had sex. What had happened to them—the dreamplane blending of their flesh and minds and souls—that was something that went far beyond mere physical contact.

Yeah, well, doesn't that make it even worse?

London could not answer the voice. In some ways, mere sex might not have been so bad. It would have been a simple mistake. A simple, human mistake. But what he had done—they had done—that had not been sex, and it had not been a mistake. It had been what both of them had wanted. It had been a complete surrender, a total mixing of their selves until only one personality remained. In truth, a part of the detective had hoped that once would cure everything—one emersion, one taste would satisfy the burning curiosity, and then they could both go their separate ways. It had not worked that way.

If anything, despite one effect he was still hoping for, for the most part things were worse than ever.

"Damnit," sighed London, eyes closed, hands on his legs, fingers unconsciously drumming against his knees. "So what am I supposed to do now?"

Your job.

London sighed again. The voice from the back of his mind had a point. He was getting no where merely moaning about the mess into which he had gotten himself. He would deal with the Pirate Queen, and with what had passed between them, and with what it had done to his relationship with Lisa when it was time to do so. Right then he had a job to do, and from what he had begun to sense, it was going to turn out to be one of those jobs that only he could do. Pushing his problems to the back of his mind, he began to focus on the belongings of Terry Chamberlain once more.

"So," Morcey asked Norman, the two of them leaning on the stained, but unvarnished wooden rail of the deck outside the door to the back yard, "what do you make of all this?"

"Me?" The father was slightly taken aback by the question. "Aren't you the investigator?"

"That's true," agreed Morcey with a thoughtful nod. "But you have to understand, we have to investigate everything, and that includes what you think was goin' on. After all, you were his dad. No matter what you might think was happenin' between you, you still gotta know him better than anyone."

The balding man gave his words a moment to sink in, then added, "You gotta understand, what you tell me might seem insignificant to you, but if you and the next dad tell me the same thing, and then the next one, you never know what kind of pattern I might find in it all."

The pair was quiet for a short moment. Norm broke it first by asking if Morcey minded if he smoked. When the ex-maintenance man indicated it made no difference to him, especially considering that it was Norm's property, the still-despairing father broke out his cigarettes and quickly lit one. His pleasure on making his first drag told Morcey volumes about the man.

"We'd talk on nights like these."

"Talk—what about?"

"It didn't matter, you know? Just come out back and sit and talk about stuff. Girls, school, his mother, TV crap we'd watched, nothing important—just dumb stuff."

"Can you tell me about the last time you guys kicked around some dumb stuff?"

"Awwww, it's been way too . . ."

Norman had started to answer with his usual self-pity, but he caught himself. Something in Morcey's calm manner had brought him to where he could manage to make his way past his grief, to where he could see beyond the things which had separated him from Terry to the places where they came together. As Morcey listened, Norm took another long drag from his cigarette, then let the smoke tumble out over his words as he spoke.

"Actually, it wasn't all that long ago. I sorta dragged him out here, 'why ya avoidin' the old man,' kinda stuff, you know? But he didn't fight me on it or nuthin'. It was like he wanted to talk about somethin'."

"What was that?" asked Morcey.

"Oh, just some game, some new kind of game. He'd been picked to try it out. I never heard about it before—haven't heard anything about it since then, either, but . . . it was kinda nice. You know—to be out here again."

Norman Chamberlain stared off into the dark recesses of his back yard. What he was actually seeing was beyond Morcey's powers of deduction. The balding man did not bother the wounded man. He did not need any of London's extra abilities to catch the sounds in Norman's throat, to know the man was trying hard to cover the sound of his tears.

Inside, Joan was not faring much better with Mrs. Chamberlain. The Pirate Queen had tried the same tact with the mother, working to get the woman to think back on her son's last days, to see if she might be able to remember something she had not told the police. Something of *importance* she had not told the police. So far, Peggy Chamberlain had been able to come up with many things to tell Joan. Many. And not a bit of it, the redhead knew, would be of the slightest use to anyone.

Still, she knew that as long as she could keep the woman busy, she was helping London by giving him the time he needed alone. A small part of her also recognized the good she was doing Peggy by letting the poor woman drone on. This was more than simply grieving. Being able to ramble on about anything that came into her mind about her son to someone working on solving what had happened to her boy allowed the woman a sense of self-worth, a feeling that she was aiding in the fight, that she was not a bad mother—foolish, worthless.

She just wants her taste of revenge, thought the Pirate Queen. Reflecting on how often she had drunk from that cup herself, Joan settled in and let the woman talk, all the while keeping her eyes on the hallway leading to the back of the house. To the bedrooms. To London.

The detective finally stood up, tired of wasting time. Tired of being afraid. He had learned all he could about Terry Chamberlain at police headquarters. There was nothing inefficient about the men under Captain Cantalupo's command. His crime scene investigators knew their jobs. Everything any normal, intelligent human being could learn about someone, they had learned, photographed, and typed up in neat, precise language. London, however, intelligent as the next man, was far from normal.

Time to get this show on the road.

The detective had been holding back, not attempting anything out of the ordinary because of plain and simple fear. It was, of course, completely understandable. Breaking his own rules, in less than twenty-four hours he had nearly driven a man mad, entwined his life, indeed, his very soul, with that of an international thief, most likely ruined the most important relationship in his life, and destroyed a great deal of one floor of a police station. He still marveled that no lives had been lost during that ridiculous shenanigan.

Yeah, the back of his mind sneered, you've been having quite a day today, haven't you?

When Morcey had told Cantalupo that the damage must have been caused by their "enemies," making little quotation marks with his fingers as he said the word, the detective had almost laughed out loud. That he had lost control in such a manner, thought only of himself and his own pleasure while using the dreamplane, brought back to mind every fear he had ever had since the first moment he had stumbled into such power.

Still, if you're done feeling sorry for yourself, you *are* here for a reason, so best to get started.

London had decided to try and use his abilities once more. He would call upon the same power he had used at the museum, but there would be a difference. Both times he had made mistakes early in the day, it was by laying his hands on people. This time, living beings had been removed from the equation. Reaching out, the detective touched Terry Chamberlain's desk.

Closing his eyes, the detective inhaled deeply, pulling air into his lungs and impressions into his mind. Who was Terry Chamberlain, he asked the room. What had he been like? As a student, as a son, as a male? What were his interests? What were his weaknesses, his strengths, his dreams and plans and desires? And, if possible, what had killed him?

Slowly at first, and then in an ever-building flood, one after another the inanimate surroundings released their secrets. As London moved about the room, placing his hands on different objects, asking the same questions over and over, he received thousands upon thousands of impressions, memories and private moments, all of them helping him to build a remarkably complete picture of their former owner.

Then, his hands touched Terry's computer. Information cascaded into his mind like heat waves lashing out from the edges of a forest fire. It was so hideously plentiful that at first, when the one tiny sliver that would make all the difference came along he almost missed it.

Almost.

CHAPTER FIFTEEN

"**I** HOPE THIS LEADS US somewhere, London."

The impatience in Cantalupo's voice was clear. That the detective still had any credibility with the policeman after the destruction of the day before left London grateful. Of course, he and the others had continued to work afterwards—the least they could do, as Morcey had put it—but there was a difference between putting in hours and making requests that forced the police to put in hours as well.

"You and me both, captain," answered the detective. He had debated for some time over telling the police officer about the call he had made the night previous, about the information he was waiting on, but he thought better of it. He already had one card face up on the table. The others he would keep close to his vest for the moment.

London stood with both Cantalupo and his man, lieutenant Krandell, in a Manhattan police warehouse. After his visit to the Chamberlains the evening previous, the detective had called the captain and made a request, one he had hoped could be filled by the next day.

"Do they all have to be turned on?" asked one of the uniformed policemen still getting the area set up for the tests to come. "It's just I don't know if we can come up with enough outlets for all this equipment."

"No, I don't think so," answered London. "Just having them here will be good enough—at least for now."

One of the things the detective had noted that every one of the victims had in common was that they all had a computer. Yes, he had told himself, it was not his father's world. It was not even the world his teenage years had known. Now the things were like toothbrushes. Everybody had a personal computer any more. Grandmothers, farmers, football players and their cheerleading girlfriends—everybody. But, the twenty-seven youngsters taken so far were of a type. They were intelligent and precise. They were all at the top of their class. Their rooms, their notebooks, their drawers, everything about them had shown organizational skills far above those possessed by the average crowd.

"So then," asked Cantalupo, still more hope than irritation in his voice. "That ever so important question answered with a non-commitment—I ask again, are we ready?"

The detective turned toward a noise behind them. It was a practically imperceptible sound, but London could feel the footsteps coming, could hear the breathing of the pair walking down the hall. He nodded in Cantalupo's direction, indicating the far doorway with a shrug and a moving of his eyes. In the seconds it took for the door to open, as all attention was suddenly focused elsewhere, he went over everything that had happened to bring him to the place he was occupying at that moment in time.

Tracking Laub had taken them to the museum, intersecting them with Joan. As he concentrated on Laub, she had concentrated on him. His clumsy groping into her mind had linked them; then she had groped her way into his mind at the police station, and they had set off an earthquake in New York City. Not one of the suburban, outer boroughs, no, they had to strain the solid bedrock of Manhattan Island, an earthquake-proof location if ever one had been built.

Apparently, a little knowledge, a snicker within his head whispered wickedly, is still somewhat of a dangerous thing.

London frowned, silencing the voice—expelling everyone back to memory. His lies about supernatural forces attacking had not really been believed by Cantalupo, but the man had been forced to accept them—he had no choice. Could he explain things any other way? Could he arrest London and the Pirate Queen for creating an earthquake?

Technically, a new voice reminded him, they could. Getting a DA to make it stick would be the hard problem.

Yeah, our government's assumed some pretty unconstitutional powers, thought the detective, but I don't think even this administration is ready to go that far.

That had left the detective and his agency free to continue investigating the bizarre deaths creeping through the city. Home after home they had invaded, one set of parents after another smashing away at them with emotion—itching curiosity, burning anger, violent, shredding hope . . . until finally it had been more than London could bear. Already suffering from the building tension between himself and Lisa, the anxiety he was forced to suffer as he walked in and out of one grieving life after another had been a series of struggles which had rent the detective's soul.

"You know," London muttered in a quiet aside to the approaching Morcey, "They got a saying about ignorance . . ."

London had almost balked the night before. Despite what was happening to his personal life, he did not want to welsh on a deal. Cantalupo had agreed to cover the agency's tracks in return for help with his unsolvable case. That was enough to get the detective involved. Once he saw what was going on, however, he had been moved to help the police because it was clear something was happening that only he might be able to handle.

But, the presence of Joan de Molina had thrown a wrench into everything. It was bad enough, London told himself, that he was the Destroyer, somehow saddled with the duty to protect mankind from dangers from beyond.

Duty, a voice in his mind snorted. That's a funny one. Who voted that one in for us? Who made that decision? I musta been out of the room. I don't remember raising our hand on that one.

London ignored the thought; he understood it, but he had no time to try and go home again. What was—was. If some supernatural nightmare was creeping into the world, who else was there?

The detective's memory flashed to the moment when everything had changed—the night before when he had tried laying hands on Terry Chamberlain's computer. Finally there had come a burst of hope. Amid all the trillions of bites of information stored within the machine, one tiny notation had glowed with a light slightly different from all the others.

London gave Morcey and Lai Wan a short wave. He knew no one else would be with them. Wondering where Lisa was for a tiny instant, he shoved the memory of her face from his mind and moved forward to greet the others. Before he could reach them, he thought of Joan as well. With equal efficiency he removed all thoughts of her from his mind, returning to the tasks at hand. He met his partner and Lai Wan just as they reached the other side of a series of tables holding some forty computers.

"So," asked the psychometrist, "what would you have of me now, Mr. London?"

"Just something simple, for once," answered London, working as much carefree attitude as he could muster into his voice.

"Another I might feel some sympathy for," said Lai Wan. "Someone who had not put me through so much I might allow to lie to me so cavalierly. But, there is nothing simple about what you want me to do here."

London's frame went slightly stiff. He understood Lai Wan's problems with him. He realized all that he had put her through on top of what life itself had put her through even before they had met. Trying to keep them all moving forward as easily as possible, he countered;

"Well, I wouldn't think the task here was all that big a deal, but . . ."

"And that is the problem with you, is it not, Mr. London? Your seemingly constant inability to think about much of anything beyond your own needs."

"Rest assured," he answered coldly, "I thought about this. I pulled something from one of these computers last night—an impression that had been left lingering on one piece of data. All I need from–"

"Is what, Mr. London? For me to risk my sanity by stumbling into some mine field your limited abilities in such matters say has been cleared. Or have you already blown everything to Hell, and now merely need me to come in and clean up the debris . . ."

"I think we could . . ."

"As usual?"

"*Goddamnit, woman–*"

The detective's voice swelled, the air around him frying the ozone. Tiny cracks appeared in the concrete floor beneath his feet even as his fingers curled into fists. He understood his rage was being created by exactly what Lai Wan was describing, but he had also had enough of it. The woman stood before him, defying him, mocking him, her hands-on-hips pose as arrogantly positioned as possible.

It's like she just wants us to take a shot at her.

Other voices within London's brain cried out in agreement, many of them ready to bring the woman down a peg or two. The detective stared into Lai Wan's eyes, tearing through the fear and hate she had thrown across them, itching to find an excuse to lash out at her. And then, as Morcey, Cantalupo and even Krandell moved to intercede, he laughed.

"Okay," growled Morcey, "somebody want to clue me in here on what the big gag is?"

"Nothing to worry about," Lai Wan assured him. "Just a small game your partner and I needed to play."

London grinned sardonically. Finally understanding the psychometrist's recent increasingly hostile attitude, he made a sweeping bow in her direction.

"Does that mean we're finished with the testing, then?"

"This round at least," she told him. Knowing her point had been made, though, she allowed herself the tiniest of grins, a fraction of a second's worth of which only London took note. Scratching his head, Morcey said;:

"Oh man, I'm seein' things beyond me comprehension again."

"My life isn't that complicated, is it, Paul?"

"Mr. London," the balding man said in his sincerest tone, "they ain't got words yet for the kind of knots your life gets tied in. So, tell me . . . what's goin' on? I mean, it is okay if the rest of us slobs know what the heck's been happenin' here—right?"

"Sure, Paul," answered London. "I made some, shall we call them 'errors in judgment' recently—mistakes that Lai Wan here thought might be indications that I was going to keep making more, and possibly bigger mistakes. She's been pushing me to see just how far into playing God I intended to go." The detective looked at the psychometrist with a respectful, but curious gaze.

"You took a bit of a chance there, you know."

"Not really," answered Lai Wan. "The most you would have done was cause me some sort of physical pain—possibly kill me. I have known pain all my life, Mr. London. And, as for death, I have moved across that dance floor as well."

"It's true," said Morcey in an aside to Cantalupo. "I wasn't there, but I heard the story." Then, straight-faced he turned back to Lai Wan and asked;

"Shall we begin?"

Krandell stared at the outsiders, listening to them, trying to fit them and all that had happened since he first met them into his old world view. He could not do it. Sneaking a peek at Cantalupo, he could tell his captain was not doing a great deal better.

"Yeah, we might as well," answered the detective. Indicating the computers crammed together on the tables between them, he said, "I'd like you to lay hands on each of these machines and see what you come up with." When the psychometrist merely stared, London explained further.

"These come from the homes of most of the victims. I know the numbers are wrong. Some of them had laptops and personal computers, some used their own machines and their parents' as well. Last night I figured I couldn't mess anything up too greatly by seeing what I could come up with, just laying hands on one of them. I hit a small bite of information stored in one, well, maybe not so much information, as a memory of something. Like finding a fingerprint instead of a finger. I don't want to say what it was, because I don't want to prejudice your search."

"And we need to find this same thing in every machine?"

"Not every one, maybe," answered London. "But if we find it in more than one, in a majority, then we're onto something. If we did find it in every one . . . well, you know . . ."

The detective spread his hands wide and smiled. Understanding the gesture, the woman sat down in front of the first machine. Steadying her breathing, she closed her eyes, and then let the fingers of her left hand graze the keyboard while her right stroked the machine itself. After only a few seconds her eyes opened. They were stark. Unblinking.

"I may see what you mean," she said with a hint of emotion. She looked at the next computer with a focused and wary gaze for just a moment. The near-shudder London sensed in the woman's eyes disturbed him greatly. Then, without further comment or hesitation, Lai Wan slid her chair sideways and repeated the process with the next machine. In only a few seconds she broke contact with the computer, her entire body moving in a manner which unconsciously flashed the same message as the last time.

One by one, the psychometrist moved from machine to machine, spending but a few seconds at each. It was all that was needed. Several of the computers registered no results, but each and every time those machines were the property of one of the victims who had possessed access to more than one computer. In two cases both machines gave Lai Wan the result for which she knew London was looking. By the time she was only a third of the way through she was certain she had the answer needed. But, in the interests of being thorough, she continued up one side of the tables and down the other, laying hands on one after another.

When she finished with the last one, the psychometrist turned not to London, but to Captain Cantalupo instead. Walking toward the spot where the officer and his lieutenant had positioned themselves, she spoke directly to him in a voice filled with sympathy.

"I am sorry for your burden," she told him. Touching his arm, she whispered, "Truly sorry."

"I, ah," the captain hesitated, "don't understand."

"You will." Then, turning back toward London, she pursed her lips for a moment, not wanting to speak, then released the words no one wanted to hear.

"In all the machines I designated, thirty-nine of them, I believe, I found exactly what you thought I would. You were referring to the mention of a new computer game, 'El Dorado,' were you not?"

London nodded in agreement. Cantalupo's eyes narrowed. As Lai Wan pulled her shawl more tightly around her shoulders, the captain of police spoke up, his voice tinged with both frustration and the beginnings of anger.

"Excuse me," he growled. "I reassign an entire squadron to go out and basically seize all this private property on your say so, London—I piss off citizens left and right; I don't explain myself to anyone, and you tell me it was so you could confirm that all these kids were into the same fucking video game?!"

"Not exactly," answered the detective.

"Please be calm, captain," interrupted the psychometrist. Catching Cantalupo's eyes with hers, she asked, "Do you remember when I examined young John Marshall?" The officer assured her he would remember that day for as long as he lived. Accepting his answer, the woman told him;

"Do you remember what I told you I found within his mind, within his soul? The humming I mentioned, and the voice, the one asking about 'gold?'" When Cantalupo nodded, admitting in as few words as possible that that was something else he would never forget, she told him;

"That hum, and the sound of that flat, hissing voice I told you about . . . it is in every single one of the designated machines."

Speaking the words seemed to take a great deal out of the woman. Only London understood why.

When inside Marshall's rapidly fading mind, the psychometrist had brushed up against a force, some kind of hunting intelligence that had frightened her greatly. For all she knew, it was a creature as powerful, and as close to entering the physical world's plane of reality as Q'talu had been only months previous. The mere suspicion of such a thing made her shudder. Pulling her shawl even more tightly about her, she said;

"You were looking for a common thread that linked all of the dead together? Diligence has rewarded you, Mr. London. Now you have one. Everything you asked about, everything you suspected—it is all there."

With a shudder, and then a flourish, the tired, frightened woman headed for the door. As far as she was concerned, her work was finished.

No one tried to stop her.

INTERLUDE

D R. DAVID HARDY WALKED down the thickly carpeted hallway briskly, racing for the large doors at its end. Growing short of breath, when he finally entered the main meeting chamber of Future Images, Inc., he did so just a little too quickly. He had his reasons. The scientist had stayed too long at his desk, ignoring the clock, praying the numbers he had been crunching would add up to his salvation. When they did not for the ten thousandth time in a row, he had thrown his calculator across his lab, shattering it against the nearest wall.

Hardy did not see the splintering plastic, or the scattering pieces. He was too busy running for the elevator. Minutes later, *minutes late*, he hurried into the company's inner sanctum where Harlan Mortonson was waiting for him, along with a small assembly of the company's head people. Most of those present were from the marketing department. The thought of what that meant made Hardy shudder deep inside, all his fears leaping out from their hiding places to snipe at him in unison.

"David," shouted Harlan, maybe a shade too friendly, "come in, come in. Everyone's dying to meet you."

"Come on now, Harlan, you'll make the poor boy think none of us remember him from the last time you showed him off."

Hardy smiled pleasantly at the vice president who had just spoken, grabbing hold of his anger before it could spill out of him over the man.

Dying, thought the scientist, freezing his smile onto his face with a grimness which actually hurt. Burning anger churning his intestines, his mind snarled, I'll show you dying.

Hardy did nothing, though. The image of pulling the chuckling management flunky across the table filled his mind. With it came a tingling in his hands, a sensation so vivid he could almost feel the pain of slapping the man repeatedly. All of it helped the scientist keep his false smile fixed in place. He did allow the dream to fill his entire field of vision for a long moment, though, his right hand holding the vice president by his tie, his left hand swinging back and forth, knocking the idiot's empty head to and fro, to and fro . . .

Yessssssssssss, his mind purred, that would be nice.

Then, the scientist was at his seat. Snapping his attention back into focus, he smiled at everyone around the table as he slid into his chair. Mortonson chattered with this and that individual for a moment longer, then took his place at the head of the table. Pushing himself into business mode, he quickly got the attention of everyone else in the room entirely focused onto the reason they all were there.

"Now, David," he started, seeming to give over all his attention to the scientist, "I know you're still years away from a home version of your fabulous machine, but we thought that today we'd get a little company focus going. Bring everyone else up to speed, let them see what it is you're doing down in that dungeon of yours."

"Pretty much still just spinning my wheels, sir," answered Hardy through a sick smile.

"Dr. Hardy," the speaker was a woman in her late thirties, still good looking enough to hold onto her seat near the front of the table, "let's not worry about where your work is at present. Days or years, a decade, that doesn't matter."

"A decade, oooohhh," interrupted one of the men across the table from the woman. "I'm not certain Harlan would agree with that."

The man was a sniper—one comfortable feathering his nest with blood spoils torn from others. He mentally chalked up two points for himself as his comment snagged the polite laughter he was after. The woman nodded toward the speaker, her smile as phony as her breasts, then continued, saying;

"Really, Dr. Hardy, what we want to do here is get a feel for what's coming. How we can integrate it into other facets of the company's operations, where we can cross-develop ideas—you understand, I'm certain."

"In case we're not being obvious enough, what we're searching after today are the money angles, David," said Mortonson with deliberate seriousness, just enough to allow everyone around the table to chuckle without allowing their attention to drift. "We understand that they might still be a long while off, but the more prepared we are to corral them, the easier they'll be to herd inside the stockyard when they do arrive."

"What do you need?"

"Everyone here knows bits and pieces, and that's the problem. I really would have preferred to have this meeting a year or two from now, but there's too much rumor and not enough fact floating around this building, and it's going to hurt us if allowed to rampage unchecked. So, rather than letting us stumble in the dark any longer, if you could simply explain what you're doing to everyone so we can all be working from the same corner of the diagram, that would be top drawer."

Hardy was just about to speak when the vice president who had spoken to him on his way in interrupted, saying;

"And dumb the technical stuff way down for us farmboys—okay, Doc?"

The polite laughter sliding through the air on its way to oblivion did not offend the scientist nearly as much as the man who had inspired it.

"I'll try my best," answered Hardy, "but you will have to make some effort to keep up."

The vice president bristled, his reaction inspiring more laughter around the room. Letting his most parental features take control of his face, however, Mortonson soon got the upper management of Future Images, Inc. back on track. Finding himself standing at the end of the company's grand mahogany meeting table, all eyes on him, stabbing him, frying him with their glare, Hardy began speaking after a dry-mouthed moment of hesitation.

"You're all aware that we live in an electronic age. No secrets there. But, what does that term mean these days? The electronic age? We've been in the electronic age for over a century. They started working on such mundane things as the electric blanket in 1912. But then, that really didn't involve any *electronics*, did it?"

Hardy watched the dull eyes flicker in some of the heads watching him. Of course, there were many at the table who were following him—were far ahead of him at that point. But the others, those who weren't quite grasping even this simple fact, they would need all the help they could get. Sneering internally, his contempt helping drive down the fear still strangling him, Hardy tried to get to the point as quickly as possible.

"Maybe it's actually more fair to say we've been in an electronic age for only a little over fifty years, ever since vacuum tubes and transistors, printed circuits and all the rest of the hardware we've been turning into juicers and personal computers and navigational systems, et cetera, took over everyone's lives. These inventions spawned countless more products and services. Transistors and chip technology have saved millions of lives in countless ways. They've allowed us to travel to the deepest ocean depths and to walk on the moon. But is that it? Is that as far as we go?"

The marketing people began to grow interested. Hardy could see it in their eyes, in the way their shoulders were moving, their heads craning, faces suddenly pensive.

"At first we used electricity to makes things move, then we used it to power cells that began to make things think. What can I use for a good example?" The scientist pretended to ponder his question for a moment.

"Cars used to be extensions of their drivers. The driver's power turned the wheel, his strength ground the brakes to a halt, his memory got him and his vehicle where they were going. Not anymore. Now onboard computers and power brakes and power steering and power windows do it all. Now we've got satellites to give us directions to where we're going." As heads nodded around the table, he added;

"They've already tested a working model of an onboard computer that, working with electronics built into a roadway, can actually take over the driving—run every car up within six inches of one another. Really, it's now come to the point where the car isn't just an extension of the driver, it's rapidly becoming the driver, and the schmoe behind the steering wheel is on his way to being just another passenger."

"So where do we go next, David?"

"Next," answered Hardy, responding to Mortonson's welcomed cue, "next we add electronics to human beings. We've added them to everything else. We've made everything else smarter. Now, it's time to start hardwiring people."

The room went quiet. Not that it had been overly noisy before, but suddenly, even the buzz and static shuffling sounds were gone, replaced by an uneasy fear. Hardy capitalized on that feeling moving its way through the room.

"We're years away from many of the practical applications for this technology, but still, the possibilities . . . ah, and that is why we're here today, simply to ponder the possibilities, right, Mr. Mortonson?"

"That is all for the time being, David. So, if you could go ahead and tell everyone here what it is we're aiming for—the concept that's going to feather all our retirements—I think I can safely so that we would all love you for it."

Every eye froze on the scientist's face, watching his mouth, waiting for his lips to move.

"Think of the Internet existing right inside your head," he told them. "No need for a computer, all you would have to do is simply think about a subject, and everyone's websites would instantly register in your brain, beamed there by satellite. Not sexy enough for you, then try one of these on . . ."

Hardy's voice tightened a notch, anger creeping in, sounding enough like excitement to fool those around the table.

"Why go on vacation when you can simply sit in your living room and feel yourself climbing Everest, or surfing a tidal wave, bungee jumping, wrestling grizzly bears, whatever. Want to walk the Great Wall of China, hang glide the Andes, walk on the bottom of the ocean, dance with Gene Kelly—go ahead. Why not? Why not do anything you want?"

The gathering began to think in their typical dollars and cents fashion, the ideas Hardy was throwing out catching all their attention, gathering it in, bunching it. What he was telling them was actually *better* than the rumors they had been hearing. Seeing how completely he had them, Hardy told them more.

"Why stop there? Want a date? Want to sleep with any of a million beautiful women? Or men?" The scientist smiled, nodding his head to the collection of power-suited ladies present. "Why not? Once a simple sex program is created, the partners can look like anyone—*anyone* the client wants to be with."

"You're saying we're going to be able to do something to people that's going to allow them to, to ah, program themselves? Would that be right?"

"That would be exactly right, Mr. Donnelly. Someone doesn't like the sex they are, they can change it. In their heads, when they look in the mirror, they'll see what they want to see."

One hefty man slapped his bulging stomach, saying, "Hell, who needs to wait? My wife tells me that that's my problem now."

Everyone laughed. Then they began to chatter. Dr. David Hardy directed their conversations, correcting ideas, expanding them, making certain that the leaders of Future Images, Inc. understood exactly what he was going to be doing for them.

"Why go to the movies when you can simply program your own mind to see one, to live it—to put you inside it? Why sit in a theater watching King Kong tear up New York when you can actually be in one of the World War I aircrafts trying to shoot him down. Why play a road race video game when you could actually be in that car, going full throttle? Why let some little pixilated man in an elf's cap defeat an army and marry a princess, when you could be doing it yourself?"

The buzz around the room leaped in greedy fits and starts. Questions by the dozen began to be aimed at Dr. Hardy. Nothing about his process, of course. How he was going to make such things possible, no one cared about. No, the questions all concerned money—how much of it this and that would take, how much could be made, how much more could be made, would it be possible to do this or that or even something else and how much money would all of those possibilities make. To Hardy the quizzing seemed endless. And pointless.

"You see," said Mortonson in a quiet aside to his chief scientist, "I told you. They know it's going to take years. But, they could care less about that. They're not worried about how much time it will take, just how much money they'll be able to make once it is here."

This is more like it, the CEO beamed to himself, certain he had finally found a way to throw off all of Hardy's worries. Throwing his arm over the scientist's shoulder, he thought, this should be just the ticket to convince David that everything is going to be fine.

Mortonson continued to smile, as did Hardy, although only one of them was aware that Future Images, Inc. would never get to market the scientist's ideas, because he would never live long enough to finish them.

CHAPTER
SIXTEEN

EARLIER WHEN LAI WAN had reached her limit and left the police warehouse, London's first thought had been to send Morcey after her in the hopes his partner could cajole her into returning. Realizing, however, that the women needed time to herself after all he had put her through, the detective decided against it, telling himself;

"You might want to give her a minute before you throw her into another shark tank."

London had sat back at that moment, struggling to obtain a clear picture of what he had to do to get back on track. Admitting to himself that relying further on Lai Wan at that moment would be a futile gesture was a good start. The psychometrist had done as much as she was going to do—as much as she was capable of doing. Pushing her at that point, he knew, would only exacerbate the problems between them.

All right, he asked himself, then how will we do this?

You could see how Morris is doing.

Now there, the detective whispered to the other voices in his mind, is a good idea. I knew I had a reason for letting you guys hang around.

Ex-Marine captain Michael Morris was one of London's regular, and most dependable, field operatives. He had been the first person Lisa had thought of to monitor the office while she took her leave of absence. London backed the idea completely. The former commander had been on his mind as well, and not just to handle routine office maintenance chores in Lisa's absence. The night before the detective had given Morris something slightly more important to follow up on, letting the man know he would need some answers the next day.

"So, Mr. London, do think we might get back to business some time today?"

The detective shook his head as if he had just come out of a long slumber. More and more he had found himself simply slipping out of the normal world, existing inside his head as if no one else was around—as if no one else was real.

Especially, a voice from the back of his mind noted, when Lisa's not around—ehhhh?

Putting aside thoughts of Morris and Lisa and everything outside of what had just transpired there in the police warehouse for the moment, London turned his full attention to Captain Cantalupo. Tilting his head apologetically, he smiled awkwardly, then said;

"Sorry, but when these kinds of cases come along, sometimes I get a little too self-absorbed. Not trying to excuse myself, just explaining."

"We all get those kinds of cases," responded the officer with a sympathetic nod. "Don't worry about it. Just get on with explaining why you've turned half my department into computer wranglers, would you?"

"Certainly," answered London. Taking a deep breath, he threw himself back into focus, then said, "Last night I got the idea to lay hands on one of the kids' computers. I'm sure you can see where I was coming from . . . they all had computers, maybe that was our link, that kind of thing."

"And was it?"

"Well, when I tried it out I felt a surge that I thought might be the same as what Lai Wan had experienced in John Marshall's mind. What I felt was only a fragment of what she had come up against, of course. She found the entity, I only found what I thought was, say, its fingerprint. But she confirmed my guess—I was right. She felt the same dark presence I did, that she'd felt before—and today she felt it in at least one computer for every victim you've got in this case. The same voice, the same strange humming sound, that same singular appeal about 'hunting gold'—all of it."

"Yeah, I got that before. So," the captain asked, "where does this leave us now?"

"I'll let you know in a minute." Flipping open his cell phone, the detective hit the speed dial command that would ring the main switchboard on Lisa's desk. Morris answered. London listened. After a few minutes of terse questions, he thanked the former Marine and then rang off, turning once more to face Cantalupo.

"Last night I got one impression from the machine I thought was worth working on." The captain listened intently. Krandell stood off to one side, eavesdropping as best he could while putting on a face which claimed he could not care less what was said one way or the other.

"I put one of my best people onto my idea," the detective told him. "That was them just now, giving me their report. And, with it in hand I think I can safely say—yes; we do finally have an angle of attack."

"Pray tell." Cantalupo raised one eyebrow. His entire frame shifted, the bulk of it relaxing. Then suddenly the tension returned without warning, settling into the area of his neck and shoulders. It caused his head to quirk oddly as he spoke. "And what might that be?"

"I caught a phrase, a name, last night I felt was tied in with the other hints I sensed. Rather than strain Lai Wan by sending her in a completely different direction than the one in which she was already headed, I gave the job over to someone who could do some real world tracking for us."

"And what did they find?"

"That computer game Lai Wan mentioned earlier," London hinted, "the one she found in every machine . . . it doesn't exist." Cantalupo's eyes narrowed. Krandell pursed his lips, his head cocking to the side. The detective continued. "At least, not officially."

"Meaning . . .?"

"Meaning that it's not in any stores," answered the detective. "And you can't get it on-line. This 'El Dorado,' it's not in any catalogues as an upcoming item. There are no commercials touting it as the next big thing. And yet . . ."

"And yet," filled in Krandell, his eyes bright with flecks of hope, "every one of our teen corpses has a mention of it in their computers."

"More than a mention, right, London," snapped Cantalupo. "They've got the whole damn game. Correct?"

"Yeah," responded London. "Correct-amundo."

"Jeez," added Morcey, a large grin spreading across his face. "Interestin'—ain't it?"

"It's got my interest," agreed the lieutenant.

"I've got a woman coming in to do some further poking around in these things before you return them to their owners," said the detective. "No problem with that, is there?"

Cantalupo shrugged. London nodded in return. The detective gave the captain a slip with the woman's name so the officer in charge would know who was coming. As everyone looked about the room, searching for any last bits of business, Krandell asked;

"It's a hell'va clue, and hats off to you, but the greedy bastard in me has to ask—iz'at it—all we got? Have we shot our wad, or do we have any thing more?"

"One more sliver," added London, "but it's a tasty one. My man turned up a reference in the pages of *Popular Science*; apparently there was an article a few years ago wherein the CEO of some outfit known as Future Images, Inc. was quoted as being on the trail of the next big thing—an interactive computer game that would be *so* revolutionary it would throw every other type of game system in the dumpster."

Cantalupo felt his mouth go dry. Like any cop, he did not much like having a high profile case on his desk which had the interest of the brass upstairs. He also did not like having nowhere to go with such an investigation. Sensing a breakthrough ahead, he knocked a cigarette from his pack into his mouth with practiced ease as he asked;

"And he named it?"

"Indeed he did," answered London. "Now, he was wise enough letting the 'El Dorado' kitty out of the bag to then not say anything more. Not a hint. But, whereas there were no specifics, he did let slip the key words 'computer game' and 'interactive.' This 'El Dorado' he named was to be some new type of computer game which interacted with the person playing it in a way no one else had dreamed of so far."

No one spoke. Cantalupo, Krandell and even Morcey simply pondered the information for a moment—analyzing it, testing it, looking at it from different directions. At almost the same instant, the three of them turned toward London, their faces all showing they had reached the same conclusion.

"You wouldn't happen to have the address of this Future Whatevers handy, would you?"

"Why, Captain," answered London, his smile turning hard, "I thought you'd never ask."

CHAPTER
SEVENTEEN

"**G**ENTLEMEN, NOW THAT WE'RE all comfortable, what exactly is it you people are trying to tell me?"

Harlan Mortonson sat across the meeting room table from London and Cantalupo, his arms resting on the flat surface, fingers braided. He kept his hands rigidly in place, sternly resisting the urge to run a hand through his hair. It was an obvious nervous impulse, and he knew better than to deliver a show of nerves that early in the game. Still, the men in his office were there to help him. They must be. They were the police. And he had done nothing wrong.

Well, nothing they could know about, anyway.

"You have to understand, sir," said London, turning up the intensity of his smile, flooding it with both sincerity and sympathy, "we have to be a bit tight with our information for the moment. Anyone here at this company might be involved in what we've discovered."

"Anyone but me, I assume?"

"No sir," answered the detective. "At this point you're as suspect as anyone. But we have to start somewhere."

Mortonson's head snapped an infinitesimal amount. He had not expected such blunt truth. He still could not imagine what the police were after, but for one of their representatives to come on so strong in the first moments of their opening interview could not be a good sign. The CEO thanked his foresight in having the meeting in a room where the air conditioning was turned to its coldest setting.

Not a good idea to start sweating in the middle of this, he told himself. Allowing his eyes to roll over the faces across from him, he caught the intensity in London's eyes and suppressed a shudder as he thought, no—not a good idea at all.

"To be fair," said Cantalupo, interrupting Mortonson's musings as he smoothly assumed a good cop position to play off London's lead, "it may only be what we 'think' we have discovered. Meaning what we have could all just be a big coincidence. But, we won't know until we start talking to people."

"Whatever," sputtered Mortonson. "Please, let's just start, shall we? And could we start by you telling me all there is that you *can* tell me? I mean—really, gentlemen—how else could I possibly be of any assistance?"

London and Cantalupo looked at each other for a moment as if giving the CEO any information at all was some sort of major security risk. Then, with a well-practiced look of defeat, the captain released all the facts they had planned to give the man from the beginning.

"Well, all right. We can probably tell you at least this much," he said in a conspiratorial tone. "While working on a string of homicides, we've come across information concerning a property being developed here—we believe it to be a computer game with at least the working title of 'El Dorado.' Would you like to confirm this, sir?"

Mortonson took a long look at Cantalupo. His security people had, of course, checked the officer out thoroughly before allowing him past the lobby, let alone into the executive suite. He was indeed a New York City precinct captain coordinating the city's efforts to determine what was behind a string of quite horrible, and so-far, unexplainable deaths. His people had requested the information from the officer's own station house, then had it corroborated by the corporate liaison at City Hall, not settling for less than a fax of both his identification and a separate photo ID from both sources.

No, Mortonson had to believe the man sitting across his desk at that moment was Captain Michael Cantalupo of the New York City police force. A Captain Michael Cantalupo of the NYPD who knew about his company's most highly guarded piece of experimental intellectual property. And, worse yet, the man was a Captain Michael Cantalupo who was now calmly insinuating that said experimental, intellectual property, which his company had poured millions into, was somehow connected to a string of horrible, unexplainable deaths.

But, he asked himself, how? How could anyone have heard about what we're doing? And why would people be dying; *how* could they be dying? It doesn't make sense.

The man silenced the thought as soon as it entered his brain. That someone had heard about what they were doing was proven by the fact that a policeman was sitting across from him at that very moment quoting him the name of their test application.

Find out what you can, old man, the CEO told himself. You didn't get to the top by doing things the easy way, goddamnit. Now find out what's going on.

At the same moment, Lieutenant William Krandell and Joan de Molina were in the office of Future Images' head of security. Mr. Adam Potts was a slender man, a person of average height with modest features. He was pensive and withdrawn, with nothing about him which anyone would notice quickly. He was an individual about whom it had to be said that ultimately there was not only nothing flashy or intense or intriguing about him at all, but also that there probably had never been a time in his life when these things were not true. Which was, of course, essentially the perfect look for someone in his line of work.

"So, Mr. Potts," asked Krandell with an easy tone of camaraderie, one lawman to another, "what can you tell us about this 'El Dorado' thing anyway?"

"Security is my racket here, detective," he responded in a sleepy, somewhat faraway voice. "Even if I had come across this thing you're talking about, if I was to tell you anything about any of the products here, that would be a breach of security. That wouldn't be doing my job now, would it?"

"So," Joan purred, "you're not even willing to confirm that 'El Dorado' is being developed here?"

"That's really not my place, ma'am," he responded easily. "There's plenty of others you can talk to here that can do that for you. You understand how it is."

The security chief watched the two people across his desk with seemingly only the slightest interest. He had studied them quite carefully by camera when they, along with London and Cantalupo, had been kept cooling their heels at reception. Now, he made only causal eye contact, often not looking at them at all as they spoke. Eye contact would only interfere with his current attempt to analyze the pair on the other side of his desk. He was studying them with his ears, listening to their questions and their responses, measuring their breathing, gauging the amount of fidgeting they did in their chairs and what it might mean. Potts had long ago memorized and catalogued every noise the chairs in his office made. He knew exactly what kind of squirming people were doing to recreate any of them.

"Don't you have any questions about our security here?"

"I do," answered Krandell. "Plenty of them. Let's say, for the sake of conjecture, that you do have a computer game being developed here called 'El Dorado.' What I want to know is, where would you be doing that kind of work, and how is it protected? If someone is after it, or if they've already cut into your research, how could they be getting to it? How can we set a trap for them? How is it your own security hasn't caught wind of this yet?"

"And if it has," purred de Molina, asking her question as if it had just occurred to her, "why is it you haven't contacted the authorities with such information?"

Potts stiffened slightly at the digs. They were baiting him. It was obvious. Still, the security chief had to wonder, why were the police there? Homicides involving a product that hadn't made it out of R&D? A thing not announced, no fanfare? It didn't seem likely. Of course, if the police were telling the truth, and there was no reason as of yet to suspect they were not, then something was dangerously out of kilter.

"Can we cut through any of this dance to whatever it really is that you people want?"

"Sorry to have to tell you this," answered Krandell, his tone notching upward toward impatience. "But we've already given you that. But I'll give you a freebie so that perhaps you'll stop yankin' our licorice and understand we're all on the same side on this thing—so far."

Potts stiffened slightly at the lieutenant's implication that there might be something sinister going on at Future Images. Then, he reminded himself that there just might be something sinister going on—something of which he, the head of security, was not aware. Reining in his anger, he listened patiently as Krandell continued.

"We've got the computers of over forty New York City citizens impounded right now. Every one of them is dead or close to it, and every single one of them had this 'El Dorado' on their hard drives."

"Yes," the Pirate Queen followed up smoothly, "which basically has us wondering who here is your leak, and what kinds of protection you have both from the outside world and from insiders getting things to the outside world. I mean, if this person could be found, maybe your company wouldn't lose the millions it's probably invested in this game." Then, as if it were another afterthought, she added;

"Oh, and maybe children might stop dying and staining your corporate logo with the blood of the innocent. If that wouldn't be too much of a bother for you . . ."

Potts smiled toward Joan, nodding that there was nothing bothersome about her request. Spreading his hands wide before him, he told her;

"No, ma'am, no bother at all. The only problem is, why would we be worried about a product that isn't even ours?"

There, the security man thought. There's the absolute denial you've been waiting for. Now, I've thrown out my best defense, let's see your retaliation card.

"So then," Joan answered slyly, "you and your corporation would have no problem with us releasing all the information to be found on all those computers we mentioned? I mean, if 'El Dorado' isn't your product, maybe we could just make an industry wide appeal, ask every computer company in the world to look at what we have to see if they could shed some light on things. I mean, we are talking the deaths of over two dozen children."

"Yeah," added Krandell, enjoying seeing cracks forming in their adversary's armor. "And a few more before the end of the night. That kind of bad publicity could cripple a company, I mean, when it gets out that whoever it is that made this game allowed it to be used so irresponsibly, then tried to not only protect their corporate secrets, but also deflect responsibility for such a horrible set of crimes by claiming ignorance over their own product . . ."

Potts sighed audibly. He did it on purpose, a noise meant to signal polite defeat. He had known he did not possess very many good cards from the beginning of their little game, but he had played those he had as reasonably well as could be expected. Mortonson had personally told him to cooperate with the police in every way possible without breaching company policy or security. With his hands tied only loosely, Potts smiled at the pair across from him.

"Oh, *that* 'El Dorado.' Of course we would want to help in any way possible. Now, obviously when speaking of our security, I'll have to do so in the broadest of terms. Meaning, that while I might tell you the fourth level has pressurized flooring, I won't necessarily tell you how much pressure it takes to trip a response, or exactly what that response might be. Can I assume that would be adequate for now?"

The Pirate Queen smiled in a way meant to indicate that, for the moment, at least, that would be enough.

INTERLUDE

"YES," HARDY SHOUTED. "YES, that's what I mean—get me Mr. Gallbendo—yes, *now,* goddamnit!"

The secretary on the other end of the phone said she would attempt to find her employer as quickly as possible. The scientist listened to the click indicating that he had been put on hold. Listening to the gentle music in the background Hardy wondered if those seconds of quiet harmony would be the last he would know. Sweat beaded across his forehead as he tried to formulate what he would say to the gangster when he came on the line.

It was not often that Hardy contacted Albert Gallbendo. Usually—almost always—it was the other way around. Gallbendo called all the shots between the two. He said "when" and he said "where." He named a height and Hardy attempted to leap to that exact point in space and to then hang there suspended for as long as possible.

But, the instance in question was different. At that particular moment, Hardy had called Gallbendo because the police had come to Future Images. Because they had come asking questions about "El Dorado." Because they had connected the dead he had strewn across the city one to another. And because after that, they had somehow then drawn a line from each and every one of the corpses first to each other, and then back to Future Images. Hardy could not imagine it would be long before his company's corporate defenses would be breached, and the lines would be drawn to him. And then from him to . . .

"Please hold for Mr. Gallbendo."

Hardy's fingers trembled, the receiver almost falling from his hand. He was terrified, but he did not know what had him more frightened. Yes, he was scared by the fact that the police had come looking for him, that it did not seem more than a matter of time before they would have him. He was more frightened, however, over how Gallbendo would react to the news his investment was in danger of going to prison, and of involving him in more than two dozen murders.

"David," came the sloppy, heavily accented voice. "I'm told you're a bit upset."

"Upset? Upset?" the scientist repeated. His words tumbling out of him in a frantic slew, he shouted, "The police know about 'El Dorado.' They know about the bodies. They're closing in on me. They're going to figure everything out." When there was no immediate response to his news, Hardy shouted into his phone.

"Didn't you hear me? The police know about 'El Dorado.' They know the game is being produced by my company. They know the game is what's killing people. They *know!*"

"This seems to have you somewhat concerned, David."

"Concerned? What in the name of God is wrong with you? The police are here. They are here, right now, at Future Images. They are apparently talking with my boss and with our head of security at this very moment. How long do you think it's going to be before they show up at my office, you stupid wop bastard? How long?!"

"David," Gallbendo said the name softly, with just a touch of impatience, as if trying to explain thunder to a frightened child. "Getting yourself all worked up is not going to help you in any way now, is it?"

"You're not listening to me. I said . . ."

"David," this time the mob boss said the name sharper, louder. The sting of a rolled newspaper implied in its tone. "You are the one who isn't listening. Hear me when I speak to you—getting yourself all worked up is not going to help you in any way now, is it?"

Hardy shook from the combination of fear and rage flashing through his system. How had he allowed himself to be maneuvered into such a corner? What had he done wrong?

Locked your wife away in a sanitarium, slept with your teenaged assistant, jumped ahead with a questionable, unstable technology, gambled your children's lives against making it work by borrowing money from killers—the droning voice hummed from the back of his mind—did I leave anything out . . . besides all the dead bodies?

The scientist's mouth fell open. The part of him that had been urging him on the last few years now suddenly was sneering at him. Laughing in his face.

"David," came Gallbendo's soothing tones, "are you still on the line?"

"Yes," he answered the mobster, his voice subdued—uncertain. "Yes, sir. I'm, I'm sorry. I got . . . distracted."

"And you are a bit calmer now?" When Hardy assured Gallbendo he had control of himself, the gang boss told him, "that's good. Yes, David, I understand that the police being there is certainly not a good thing. Not a thing that any of us might want. But panicking over such things only makes them worse—understand?"

"Yes, sir."

"Very good. Excellent. Now, you listen to me, this is what we're going to do."

Swiftly, the mob boss outlined a plan of action for Hardy to follow. First, Gallbendo was certain the police were merely on a "fishing expedition," searching for clues they did not yet have. They might have evidence enough to point them toward Future Images, but the gang leader knew that if they could link the scientist conclusively to the deaths of the test subjects that there would have been no pleasant talks with Hardy's superiors.

"They would have simply arrested you and anyone who got in their way. They would be tearing your lab apart and seizing your papers and equipment."

Having calmed himself, Hardy knew what he was being told was the truth. The police did not act like the lawmen in old television shows. The modern legal system was far too complicated for such tactics. Gallbendo let him know it was quite likely they would not even talk to him that day.

"Understand me, if they didn't put the grab on you immediately, then they're there to do exactly what they did. Shake you up—make you act without thinking. Not even you, but 'whoever.' At this point it is safe to assume they have no idea who they want, or what they want. Future Images is simply something that smells like a bone to them, and so their muzzles are filled with saliva."

Then, Gallbendo paused for a moment, his voice dropping a note as he asked;

"David, did you call me on the cell phone I gave you?"

Hardy had. The mob boss complimented him on not falling apart to the point where he forgot the single rule he had been given. After that, the mob boss's instructions were swift. Hardy was to bring the phone with him that night, along with all the work he could turn over at that time—whatever was available. They would meet at their usual place. Hardy was to make certain he was not followed. As Gallbendo put it;

"Some deals go well, some others do not. I will take back my phone, accept what you have for me of this new technology, and we shall cancel your debt to us."

"Just like that?"

"David, you will be watched now. Investigated. If we were to come near you at this time, we would only involve ourselves. We shall give you the services of one of our best attorneys. I'm certain our investment will be met by what you have for us. Yes, it would be nice to have acquired the entire package, but things did not work . . ." The older man sighed forlornly, then added;

"I've been told life is not perfect. I guess those who said so were correct."

"And, and . . ." Hardy stammered. "That's all? That's it?"

"That is it for us. You will not be out of the woods. As I said, you will be watched. You will be investigated. If they can connect you to the children, you will certainly go to trial. But, at least you will not have to worry about anyone except the police."

Hardy gasped down three great lungsful of air, one after another, exhaling and inhaling rapidly. Making himself almost giddy, he promised to do all he had been told exactly as it had been outlined to him, then broke the connection. As he stared at the silent cell phone in his hand, he could scarcely believe things had gone so easily.

Rapidly he began to throw together copies of everything he would need to give Gallbendo's people that evening. He laughed as he did so, marvelling at how easily he was getting off the hook to which he had thought himself permanently affixed. Now it turned out the mob was just as frightened of the police and jail time as he was. More so.

After all, they were running scared from jail sentences. His terror was born of the fear of being tortured to death by the very gangsters he was now watching fade into the darkness. As he tossed the last discs and sets of printouts into his bag along wiht several portable drives, he thought;

Amazing—I get to keep everything. If I can stonewall the cops, pull a dummy on them—*I know nothing*—I can get out of this with everything.

Everything.

David Hardy stared at his over-stuffed bag for a moment. As he thought about all that had happened to him recently, about where he had believed his life was headed, and now where things had gone instead, he found himself becoming somewhat hysterical. Laughter trickled out of the corners of his mouth. Not quiet, hard-to-notice giggles, but full blown howls of merriment.

Before he knew it, Hardy was slamming his fist against his desk, mad cackles escaping his lips in a torrent as he crushed his eyes closed against the tears of joy splashing freely down his cheeks. He was, he realized, the luckiest man on the face of the planet. Grabbing up a stale cup of coffee left over from that morning, he held it aloft, shouting;

"I don't know who I owe all my good fortune to, but here's to them. Thank you, sweet savior, from the bottom of my eternally grateful heart."

Hardy drained the sour brew, brown rivulets sluicing out of the corners of his mouth. Coffee dribbling down his chin, the scientist ran his tongue around the inner rim of the cup, then crumpled it and threw it over his shoulder. Not caring where it landed, he grabbed up his over-stuffed bag and left his office on time for once—for the first time in over a year to be exact. There was a bounce to his step he found wonderfully refreshing.

Once in the parking lot, he stashed his load in the backseat of his car then took a quick look about to see if anyone was watching his vehicle. He saw no one, but he had not expected to do so. Anyone planning on watching him, he told himself, would probably be more professional than to allow someone like him to spot them. Knowing that, however, the scientist scanned the road outside the parking lot as well.

He saw no suspiciously parked cars, no people sitting in their driver's seat attempting to appear casual. Finally, not wanting to appear suspicious himself, Hardy got into his car and started it up. Pulling out, he watched the traffic around him diligently in his rear and sideview mirrors, both leaving the corporate headquarters and out on the roadway. Carefully as he studied the traffic around him, however, he could find no one attempting to follow him.

That meant if he did not go home, there was no way possible for anyone to follow him to his meeting that night, which meant there was no way he could screw things up and lead the police to Gallbendo.

I've got it made, he told himself, tears again smearing his face. All I have to do now is find something to do until midnight. Then I just go to the restaurant, turn everything over to Gallbendo, and I'm home free.

It seemed too good to be true.

A movie, he thought. Dinner and a movie. A few drinks afterward, and that's it. I'll be free.

And, like all things which seemed that way . . .

CHAPTER
EIGHTEEN

L ONDON WALKED INTO THE employee parking area of Future Images, Inc. just shortly after 11:00 that evening. The detective was dressed in all black, wearing rubber-soled shoes and a hood which made him look more or less like some sort of movie ninja. The industrial park the corporation was a part of was easily accessible from a score of different directions. Such an open atmosphere had not been arranged because its various corporate residents had nothing to fear from vandals. Far from it. They simply had, in their opinion, a certain image to present to the public.

Building high walls, installing formidable gates, stationing armed guards to question all who enter it was well known to give the impression that those doing the entering were thrusting themselves into some sort of militarized zone—not a nice, secure place to do business. Not at all the image the fine lords of the Golden Investments Park located in the very upscale town of Melville, Long Island, wished to convey.

No—Golden Investments was a well manicured fifteen acres, restful to the eye, tranquil in all its outward appearances. Security for each corporate headquarters within its boundaries was left strictly up to the masters of each individual domain. Some did relatively nothing in the matter of security—relying on the strength of their neighbors to ward off thieves. Future Images was not that type of corporation.

"Pa'sha," London whispered into his headset, "I'm in position. Are you and yours ready to rumble?"

"All is as planned, little brother," the weaponeer's voice crackled in the detective's ear. "You give the word, we will see what we can do to accommodate your wishes."

London smiled faintly. He and the large islander had been friends since the detective had first come to New York City. Pa'sha, born in Haiti, said he did not mind living in Manhattan because "it's an island, ain't it now, man. Dey all the same. The mosquitoes here, maybe they wear three piece suits and Rolexes, but dey still suck blood just dey same." London trusted no one else at his back the way he did Pa'sha. Looking at his watch, he kept his eye on the second hand, saying;

"We're coming up on five after—perfect time to make a little 'boom boom.'"

They watched the seconds ticking by together—twenty-three, twenty-two, twenty-one . . .

"Everyone is in position, Theodore," the weaponeer added. "But your main worry will be the local police. Remember, my sources tell me their response time is most impressive."

Eighteen, seventeen, sixteen . . .

"Don't think that's going to be a problem, but thanks for the concern."

Twelve, eleven . . .,

London waited in the shadow of the stand of four trees he had picked earlier that day for the assault he knew he would be making that evening. When things broke loose, he knew exactly where he wanted to go and what he was looking for. He had no one with him because, for once, he was determined to use his new-found abilities to his full advantage.

Ten, nine . . .

What did it matter, he had thought, if doing so would disrupt the area around him? Future Images was killing children. Wrecking a little havoc within their corporate headquarters was not a concept with which he had much trouble. Certainly he would be trying to not hurt anyone. After all, he had no way of knowing how many people at the company knew anything about what was going on with 'El Dorado.' Maybe none of them knew about the deaths; maybe only a few–

Six, five . . .,

Certainly none of the cleaning staff are in on it, he thought as his second hand clicked past the "11." Or their security guards, either, for that matter.

Three . . .

London took a deep breath. Pa'sha raised his hand to signal those all around him.

Two . . .

The detective stood, moving to the very edge of the shadows. On the other side of the Future Images complex, his oldest friend gave the last of his preliminary hand signals to his staff. The Murder Dogs began moving forward.

One . . .

London ran for the building as a series of explosions rocked the other end of the corporate headquarters. Pa'sha and his people had set off a series of concussion bombs—noisy, smokey, powerful enough to vibrate everything close by quite violently—nerve-wracking devices to be certain, but not terribly destructive. Nothing would be destroyed, but to those inside that notion would seem like an impossibility.

"Gas bags," shouted the large man. "First five—go!"

As the security system's cameras all clicked to see what was happening on the far end of the buildings, as men and women hurried to windows, to phones or the appropriate emergency panels, London continued his all out run at the only building for which he had any use. As he came within the last few feet of the massive, one inch thick plate glass windows which made up the walls of the entire first floor, he threw himself into the air even as five gas bags were ignited at the opposite end of the complex.

Flames splashed in all directions, curling, rolling along the ground like waves rushing up a beach. At the same instant, London hit the glass—or, more precisely, he did not hit the slab of glass before him, but rather he passed through it. He did not shatter it, crack it, move it aside or affect it in any other way. He merely spread his atoms thin so that they could pour through those comprising the glass. At the moment he landed on the floor inside, the second brace of gas bags was ignited. The flames splattering in all directions at the other end of the complex were so massive in scope they spew such a light London could see it as brief flickers casting shadows through the parking lot outside despite both the distance and the blocking angles of the buildings.

That, he thought, is going to bring a whole lot of attention down on us. Fast.

When last he had seen Captain Cantalupo, London had told him to expect a woman who would take a last look at the impounded computers. She had arrived shortly after the detective and the others had left. Her name was Cat. She was an electronics expert London had met through Pa'sha. He knew if anyone could break the secrets of 'El Dorado' in a short amount of time, she could, so he had sent her in to dig out whatever she might be able to find in the time they had.

If the game had still existed intact within any of the impounded computers, the police's case against Future Images would have been made. It was not, however. The traces London and Lai Wan had both picked up had been just that, only glimmers of the game—left-over crumbs. Such was not supposed to be possible; no matter what kind of deletion program one had, everything that ever went into one's computer was theoretically still there somewhere jamming up their hard drive. But, that had not been the case with 'El Dorado.'

Somehow, it had been removed from the computers of the children it had slain, even though those who put it there should have had no access to the machines—certainly not all of them. London had set Cat to recovering what fragments she could of the game. It was a job a team of experts could have easily justified spending a month on. Cat was given five hours. In the end, she uncovered enough bits and pieces to bundle together a rough skeleton of the game. As she handed the disc upon which she had saved her findings to London, she told the detective;

"I haven't got the faintest idea what the hell these cheese-winders used to clean these machines, but it's new, it's thorough, and it practically circumvents everything out there that the rest of us know about."

"Meaning . . .?"

"Meaning," she growled, "that these freaks are skimming across the pond light years ahead of the rest of us. Remote, selective cleansing of a hard drive isn't supposed to be possible. I'm not saying it's sinister, but it's sure the hell advanced."

As the woman stood on the other side of London's desk, the detective stared at the disc in his hand for a long moment. Then, suddenly he shifted his gaze to Cat, his mouth curling into a one-sided grin. As he simply stared, the woman blushed, then demanded;

"What?" London smiled broadly, then asked;

"Cheese-winders?"

"Y-Yeah," Cat stammered. "Cheese, wind—eat cheese, make wind. If you were from Wisconsin you'd get it."

The detective grinned as he remembered the moment. He rarely saw the strawberry blonde that flustered. Then, shoving the image aside, he pulled the disc Cat had given him from his inside pocket. Quickly removing his glove, he held the disc in his naked hand. Touching the plastic circle to his forehead, he closed his eyes and muttered;

"All right, now—where are you?"

Feeling a pull downward and to the left, London checked with his companions outside, asking for a time estimate. He was given four minutes—tops. Understanding the urgency of the situation, he thought;

Well then, let's just cut loose this once and see what the hell happens.

Willing himself to simply "be" wherever 'El Dorado' was within the complex, he felt his body begin to slide across the room. Chairs and desks were knocked from his path by some invisible shield he had not consciously brought into being. His body passed through several walls, then began a downward descent. His eyes still closed, not wanting to break his concentration, he continued to wish himself to the point in the complex where the game was housed. Mere seconds after he had thought his command, the detective's feet came to a halt. He opened his eyes to find himself in the laboratory of Dr. David Hardy.

Outside Pa'sha and his Murder Dogs continued to monitor the situation. From their remote position on the grounds of the next corporate park over, they had continued to bombard the Future Images complex. Using small remote control planes designed for military scouting purposes, they both kept an eye on the entire headquarters as well as delivered their payloads.

The firebombs they were using were mostly for show. The gasbags were the same type used by special effects people in motion pictures. They threw out great amounts of flame and deadly looking black smoke; they would also leave vicious scorch marks on everything around. But, they were merely distractions, not meant to cause any real damage.

The crew had also severed the corporate headquarters' communications grid at the moment their diversion began, which had gained them a large handful of extra seconds—possibly as much as half a minute. Thus, automatic relays tripped to summon the fire department and the police lay dormant. Phones sat dead, unresponsive to any commands. With Cat to aid him, the weaponeer could have thrown a grounding blanket over the area which would have dampened cell phone activity as well, but London had nixed the idea, not seeing the reason for such elaborate preparations, or for the expense.

"Hey," he had said, "I think I can be in and out fast enough that we don't need to bother. After all, I'm assuming we're talking more than pocket change to pull something like that off—yes?" When his friend has assured the detective that such a maneuver would indeed cost them, he had said;

"Well then, forget it. We're sinking deeper into the red every second on this one. Let's remember, no one's paying us any of this. But, the money's got to come from somewhere, and so far it's all coming out of my bank account."

"But, Teddy," Pa'sha had responded in a tone of mock confusion, "I don't understand. On the TV, the heroes run off on missions of mercy and the good-est of will all the time, and no one ever has to pay for anything."

"Whoever said I was a hero?" London had grumbled.

The words came back to him as he moved forward into Hardy's lab. He surveyed his entrance point. His body had literally melted its way through the floor—several floors, actually—and yet he had not felt the slightest increase in temperature. He had landed within the lab noiselessly, with but the lightest of touches. The detective had only taken a few steps forward, however, when he felt the presence of another human being in the room.

"You've got my people running around like lunatics upstairs, you know."

London turned to find Future Image's Adam Potts holding a gun on him. Before the detective could react, four of the security chief's people came into the room from various vantage points. All of them were armed with very serious-looking automatic weapons. All of them had their serious-looking weapons trained on London. And, just as Potts began to move forward, carefully—he had, after all, seen the detective's mode of entry—announcing his intentions to unmask him, Pa'sha's voice sounded in his ear;

"The police, little brother, have found their way here. Doing things your way, that means you are now officially on your own."

Sigh, after all these years, London thought, *now* I start to get my own way.

CHAPTER NINETEEN

"**A**ND SO," POTTS SAID, drawing closer to London, "just whom do we have under here?"

The security chief did not reach out for the detective's mask, nor make any other kind of overt gesture. Adam Potts was not a foolish man. He had fully witnessed the dramatic entrance made into the laboratory by the intruder before him. He had seen the impossible—watched the ceiling first glow, then shimmer and bubble. He had heard the odd, flat hissing sound before the affected area evaporated away in a pale steam of molecules that simply dissipated before his very eyes. Then, while still trying to comprehend what he had observed, he had watched further as the figure before him streaked down from above, landing without sound or impact.

"Someone rather clever, I would think."

That he could walk toward this mysterious individual, speak to him calmly, showed Potts he had a greater reserve of courage than he himself had ever imagined. Like any man, he had always wondered what he might do when faced with the unbelievable. It gave him comfort to feel his feet moving across the floor, to hear his voice still steady and clear. The security chief knew it was only his example that had kept his people from fleeing the room. Indeed, a part of his mind was congratulating him quite briskly for maintaining his professional detachment when he could smell the mounting levels of fear and astonishment all about him.

I guess, a part of his mind whispered, *it's nice to know the old dog can still keep ahead of the puppies.*

Potts acknowledged the thought—grinned slightly at it with a self-satisfaction another part of his mind told him could be preparing him for the slaughter—each smug morsel merely another bucket of slop for the hog just before Christmas. He gave that thought its due as well, thinking on the example of his, perhaps wisely-frightened, team all about him.

They're young, he reminded himself needlessly. *Wouldn't have blamed any of them if they'd fled—think I know how they feel, actually. Feeling the urge myself.*

And yet, still another region of his consciousness hissed at him, *you keep walking forward. You know there isn't the slightest possibility that this doesn't tie in with what you found out this afternoon. Why are you setting yourself up to take a fall over this—what do you care? What do you think you owe* anyone at this point?

Despite the urgent pleas shouting out from the back of his mind for bold-ness or retreat, Potts continued to circle London, keeping just out of arm's reach of the detective. His stride was tight and controlled, and yet managed to appear casual. The security chief was calling on every bit of training and experience he had to keep his actions just so as he tried to figure out what exactly he was supposed to do next.

Children are dead, the part of his brain in charge of self-preservation barked. Future Images is to blame. Do you think this fucking avenger is going to stop and consider that you think you're just doing your job? That you were "only following orders?"

Potts did not question the word "avenger" when it sounded in his mind. He had done several tours as a military policeman—had been decorated for meritorious service—had put in twenty years with the Detroit police after that. He came to Future Images with a gold shield and twenty-six years of practical experience they found highly valuable. When he had talked with the lieutenant and the woman earlier that afternoon, watched the tapes of the police captain and the private citizen with Mortonson, he knew deep within his soul that something would be coming.

And that, once again, his value would be sorely tested.

You don't get mixed up with the corpses of more than two dozen kids without bringing trouble down on yourself, he thought bitterly. Moving his eyes slightly to the left, then the right, Potts took in the lab around them, wondering, just what the hell were you up to in here, Hardy?

"That is the big question," said London. "Isn't it?"

"My, my; surprise, surprise—it speaks."

And then, after answering the figure before him, the security chief realized abruptly the question answered had been unvoiced. He had not said anything aloud for the intruder to hear. Instantly his eyes widened—mouth drying, tongue growing itchy, feeling thick and heavy within his mouth.

"Sir, should we–"

"Not now, Bradley."

Potts stopped moving, except to step backward, unconsciously circling back behind one of the laboratory's heavy counters to put something of substance between himself and the figure in the center of the room.

"Sir, I think–"

"Quiet!"

Potts did not mean to snap at his man, but he could not have him asking a question for which the security chief had no answer. At that moment it was of monumental importance for him to maintain his illusion of superiority—both between himself and his people, and himself and himself. Things had moved so quickly, he had reacted so automatically to the break-in that much of what had actually occurred was just beginning to sink in on him.

Just what the hell was going on, Potts wondered. What was Future Images getting itself into? How had the man before him done all he had done? Potts kept abreast of things, technical advances and the such, but he knew of no hardware, military or private, that could accomplish the things he had just seen. He had not even heard of anything in basic development that could allow the wonders he had just witnessed.

Even as he tried to put together what few facts he had, the com-link on his belt was alive with summonses from his other people stationed around the complex. A score of his advance guards were in the far parking lots, searching for the cause of the explosions, trying to contain the still raging seas of fire which had flooded four key areas. More than a score of police officials as well as the truck chiefs of four different fire brigades were also demanding to talk with him.

Potts ignored them all, switching the machine to silence—something he had never done before. It was something the man had never even considered doing in the past—not even during his private down time, let alone a crisis situation, but it could not be helped. At that moment, with his brain peculating from all he had witnessed, he simply could not afford any distractions. Even though he and the intruder had already been within each other's presence for nearly a minute, he still had no idea whatsoever as to what he was dealing with.

In the meantime, London had been using the time afforded him by the security chief's unprecedented hesitation to carry out his mission. During the time that Cat had been piecing together what she could of the game 'El Dorado' for him, the detective had been working with Lai Wan. The psychometrist had been coaching him, trying to help him secure a handle on how best to use his powers that evening to get to the bottom of Future Images involvement in the London Agency's current case.

Ignoring the men around him, not concerned about their guns and threats, he had, from the first moment of his arrival, cleared his mind and begun a search for anything concerned with either 'El Dorado,' or the deaths of the children the game had caused. It was how he had entered Potts' mind earlier—not because he had wanted to, but because the security chief's own thoughts had invited him inside. It had only taken him a moment to find what he was after.

This is amazing, thought the detective, feeling the information he needed simply come to him within his mind. Inexperienced as he was at such a search, still the framework Cat had put together for him was all the hook he needed to zero in on 'El Dorado.' His senses came across the game in seconds, then began bringing him every other detail about it as well.

"Interesting game, this 'El Dorado,'" he said, now keeping his masked face aimed toward the security chief. "The player actually gets to experience the game as if they were living it. In fact, it seems that once they enter the game, they don't even realize that the game world isn't their own."

Potts froze at London's words. Even the security chief himself was not supposed to know that much about the game. He did, of course, but only because he had always made it his business to know those private things wherever he found himself. But, this man before him, he had just arrived. He had not had even a millisecond's time with the computers. How, wondered the security chief, could he know?

Anything?

How?

"So that's it," exclaimed London, his voice betraying a degree of surprise. "You're using nano technology. You inject the player with biological machinery that rebuilds them from the inside. The nanites stimulate the player's brain, cause them to 'live' the game within their own minds. That way, interesting . . . they really feel pain; if it's raining they would actually feel wet, could smell the smells . . ."

London stood transfixed. The more of the inner workings of 'El Dorado' that were revealed to him, the more fascinated he became. Potts watched the detective, desperate to understand how the intruder could possibly be telling him so much about the company's most secret project. But, even as the two men continued to entrance one another, one of the other security men began to feel the strain of the moment.

He was, like all of Potts' people, a man possessed of a steady hand and a cool head. Under any normal circumstance he was a soldier to whom the security chief would not have hesitated to entrust his life. But, there was nothing normal about that evening. No one had ever expected an entertainment company to be bombed in the middle of the night, or to be invaded by characters out of a comic book—masked figures that levitated. That read the minds of men. And machines.

That melted their way through walls.

We're supposed to protect whatever's in this lab, the man thought, and yet Potts is just standing there, listening to this spook yak on about all our secrets. He's got Potts under some kind of spell—I've got to do something.

Even as the guard began to move slowly forward, London continued to absorb all the factors involved with 'El Dorado.' Like most people he had heard about nanites, but he only understood them in the abstract. They were to be something like tiny engines that could be installed within a person's bloodstream. If the patient had a cancer, the nanites could be programmed to move through the body to where the tumorous areas were and to then remove them. Like most people, he had never thought much more on the idea after he first heard about it. It was just another scientific advance that would never happen—like the flying cars and instant weight loss pills people had been talking about forever.

But, as the detective continued to amass data within his head, he found himself suddenly overwhelmed. As the ideas that had been accomplished by David Hardy were revealed to him, he staggered under the implications. The scientist, it seemed, had not simply created a new step forward in gaming, he had utterly shattered the last wall between God and man.

This doesn't make any sense, thought London. With these things—these nanites—you, you could do anything. You could cure any disease, build an elevator to the moon; you could engineer anything you wanted, anything at all, at the molecular level—mountains of diamonds, an ocean of oil, unlimited supplies of food, of gold bricks, ice cream sandwiches, clean water, steel girders, ivory, cream cheese, ozone . . . you could have has much as you wanted of, of . . . anything.

Anything.

The detective's mind raced wildly, unable to keep up with the overwhelming influx of ideas flooding through it. David Hardy had unlocked the elemental building blocks of the universe. He had learned to engineer machines at impossible sizes, which ultimately meant he had, for all intents and purposes, uncovered the philosopher's stone—lead into gold, straw into bologna, left-over carbon dioxide into a new Marilyn Monroe.

This guy has tinkered together the power of mind over matter, thought the detective. He putters around, engineers up the power of God for himself, and all he's using it for is *to create a game?*

The concept stunned London, left him speechless, immobile. Moment after moment, he stood in the center of the room, still drawing more information to himself, already paralyzed by that which he was still working to comprehend. Eventually, as the mounting slivers of time turned into a second complete minute, Potts began to realize that the intruder was no longer paying him any attention, that the man had become distracted by something more important than the security chief and the ring of armed men all about him.

Potts was just about to try and decide how best to use that information to his advantage when the member of his team that had realized the same fact a second and a half before him fired his first shot, sending a bullet into London which send the detective stumbling across the room, blood arcing out behind him.

CHAPTER
TWENTY

S OME TEN MINUTES BEFORE the first bullet caught Teddy London off-guard, tearing through the detective's body, spinning him around and slamming him against the lab counter behind him, David Hardy was waiting where he was supposed to, his eyes grazing his watch once more.

Ten more minutes.

The scientist had arrived more than twenty minutes early for what he had been assured—and did at least hope—was his final appointment with Mr. Albert Gallbendo. Since that moment he had consulted his watch some sixty-two times. Many of them were just nervous glances, second after second unconscious reconfirmations that the mobster was not late, had not stood him up, would still come—still accept all the scientist had stolen from his lab.

Still release him from his debt.

"Like a refill?"

Hardy nodded, allowing the short, plump brunette to perfunctorily top off his cup once more. He watched the black liquid pour into his cup, watched it swirl, noted the steam drifting away to nothingness. He stared at the coffee, considered adding his customary amounts of milk and sugar, but his hands did not—could not—move. Instead, his eyes followed the still-diminishing ripples within his cup, concentrated on watching as each crashed against the surrounding white china walls, the entire surface slowly settling into a flat plane once more.

"Keen powers of observation," he reminded himself in a rueful tone, "the hallmark of a good scientist."

Eventually, a tilt of his eyes let him know he had been peering into his coffee cup for close to five minutes. Surprised he could actually focus his attention for such a length, Hardy tried to recall any of his thoughts during the period. His brain actually registered little surprise when he realized he could bring nothing to mind. He had simply stared, vacantly putting himself into a peaceful state for which his entire body seemed grateful.

He was going to make it, he knew. He was going to be all right. The police could be bluffed; they had nothing to go on—certainly nothing on him.

Hardy thought for a moment with self-congratulatory amusement on the idea of police scientists attempting to understand what he had wrought. The notion made him giddy to the point of laughter. The sound leaked out of him quietly at first, a gentle noise little more than a cheerful mumble. But, the longer he thought on the idea of public servants trying to decipher his greatest achievement, looking to unlock the road map of his Promethean climb, the louder his volume grew until finally full belly-laughs were pouring out of his mouth.

"Something funny about the coffee?"

Hardy looked up to see his waitress returned. He understood immediately that she was there to see if he had some sort of problem she should relate to the bouncers tucked away in the kitchen. Gallbendo's favorite restaurant did not tolerate much in the way of shenanigans. Hardy reined in his merry amusement, telling the woman;

"Forgive me, please," he started. His manner stuck halfway between giddy and downcast, he told her, "I apologize to one and all. I got caught up for a moment, is all. Earlier today, what can I tell you?" He paused for an instant, staring upward with a sheepish grin, then confided, "it looked as if the sky was caving in on me. But now . . . well, now . . ."

He spread his hands wide apart, shrugging his shoulders, indicating to the waitress that he did not actually know how things were going, but that they certainly seemed to be going better. The woman nodded, giving Hardy an understanding smile. The scientist returned it, and started to finally lift his coffee cup to take a straight shot of it black and hot, just to do something different for once, when he spotted Gallbendo's men coming through the door.

"Hey," called out one of them. "Let's go."

The two men stood in the doorway waiting for Hardy to join them. At first the scientist merely stared at the pair, uncertain as to what he was supposed to do. When they continued to simply stand and stare back at him, he called out;

"Where's Mr. Gallbendo?"

"He's waitin' for you in the limo. Now if it ain't too much trouble, perhaps you could fuckin' join him there?"

Hardy noted that even though the man had a question in his voice, his attitude did nothing to indicate he was doing anything other than giving a command.

Still, the scientist thought as he gathered up all the materials he had brought with him, whatever it took to get out from under the strain he had been trapped by for so long was worth the effort. Leaving his coffee untouched, he secured his bundles then headed for the door.

At fairly much the same instant that Hardy began to pull his bundles together, Joan de Molina was brushing her hair absently with her hand, making herself ready to move forward. She was standing in a hallway staring at a door. It contained two locks. One, a simple plated latch—the other a deadbolt. Neither device was of a make or model possessing any innovation offering much of a challenge to one of her skill. Still, she did not advance toward it, but rather simply continued to stare forward, debating her next move.

All right, she asked herself, honest hesitation welling within her for once, what do we do next?

To be so uncertain of her motives, her thinking, her self—of what she wanted to do, of why she wanted to do it—this was not normal for her. It had been long over ten years since she had been so indecisive, since the Pirate Queen had not simply outlined a simple and direct course of action for herself, then followed it through.

This is absurd, she told herself. The voice speaking within her brain, one woven from her sternest tones, shrieked at her. The words tore through her skull, vibrating within her mind.

Do you hear me—*absurd!*

The redhead raised her hand to knock on the door, but did not move it forward. Her fingers shook for a moment, trembled, actually, then retreated back toward her shoulder unbidden. A section of the Pirate Queen's brain rebuked her, pouring heated chastisement over her insecurity even while another thanked her in endless squeaks for not knocking on the door.

"Oh, how the mighty have fallen," she muttered, drawing her still wavering fingers to the corner of her mouth. She held them there for a moment, then allowed them to snare the tear rolling over her cheek before it could dribble all the way to her chin.

Joan stared at the door for another long drag of seconds. Inside her, her two opposing opinions continued to war. While they did, a third voice entered the debate. It slammed at both the other view points, roundly chastising the Pirate Queen for considering either of their courses of action.

Before she realized it, her hand moved forward and rapped on the door before her. Joan gasped, her hand racing back to her face, covering her mouth. She was not ready, did not know what she would say, what she would do—did not even know why she was there really, not really–

What was I thinking; why would I come here; what did I think I could accomplish–

And then, the door opened.

"Yes," the voice came from the doorway, wrapped in the casual sounds of inquisitive ignorance, a noncommittal greeting offered while the one opening the door awaited visual confirmation of whom exactly they were greeting. "Can I help . . ."

And then, the barrier between them opened far enough for Joan de Molina and Lisa Hutchinson to see each other face to face. The Pirate Queen stood stock still and silent; Lisa did not.

"What do you want—" And then, as quickly as her anger possessed her, other thoughts flooded the young woman's mind and she acted on them just as quickly.

"Is it Teddy?" she demanded. "Is he hurt? What is it? Why didn't you just call? Where is–"

"Please," Joan blurted the word. "I came here to see you. To talk to you." Lisa stared, not understanding what the Pirate Queen wanted—not caring. "I think we need to."

Lisa continued to stare for a moment longer, then considered stepping aside to give the woman on her threshold just room enough to enter her home.

At approximately the same moment the first bullet tore through Teddy London's body, David Hardy was standing in the parking lot outside the restaurant, waiting for the taller of Gallbendo's men to unlock the door of the black limousine before them all. He watched the action, his mind still swimming in the relieving feeling born from the marvelous fact he was about to be set free. Still, a smaller, less marvelous fact nagged at him.

Riddle me this, science man, he asked himself, if Gallbendo's in the car, why did they lock it?

Hardy's eyes went wide, his mouth opening at the same time. His jaw opened and closed, opened and closed—small strangling noises coming from his throat.

He's not in the car. He's not in there—they're not letting me off any hook. They're here to kill me!

The scientist turned to run, but his attempt was too late, too half-hearted. If he had acted on his thoughts at once, wheeled around and run for his life, he might possibly have escaped. But, he did not. Too great a part of him wanted to continue to believe the lies he had been told, that he had told himself.

Did you really think you were going to get out of this in one piece? The voice from the back of his mind chuckled at him, even as the hands of the smaller of Gallbendo's thugs grabbed him by the shoulders.

You stupid wop bastard!

He heard the words again, for the first time, actually, suddenly remembering, suddenly hearing what he had said, what he had called the mob boss.

You stupid wop bastard!

You moron, the voice laughed wickedly within his head. They'll kill you just for that.

The man who had caught hold of Hardy tossed him forward into the back seat of the limousine, following him inside quickly before the scientist could think to scramble forward and escape out the other side. In the meantime, the second thug shut the door behind the smaller man, then circled around to the driver's door and let himself in. Cringing in the back seat, Hardy performed like so many who had gone before him, offering any reward that came into his mind if the men taking him to his end would only let him go. The brutal indifference of their laughter calmed him into silence.

CHAPTER
TWENTY-ONE

A SECOND BULLET TORE THROUGH London before he could hit the floor. Potts had blinked hard at the first shot, part of him amazed that something as simple as mere bullets could actually knock over the intruder—that anything at all could reach him. Even as the notion blinked through his mind, however, the guard that had fired the first and second rounds began moving forward rapidly, searching for a third clear shot.

Youth, thought the security chief, not blinded by common sense, not needing to *know*. That's what keeps them from making the same kind of idiotic mistake you were just making.

His hand reaching for his own sidearm, Potts began moving forward on the black-garbed figure himself. He dismissed the notion of further self-chastisement for the moment, the idea the intruder was more than just a man adequately dispelled. Switching completely back into his normal mode, with a motion of his other hand he began the rest of his men moving forward as well.

In the meantime, London had not quite given up on the idea of self-chastisement.

Christ, he thought, pain ripping through his consciousness, distracting him on a hundred levels at once. That's about as stupid as you've been since, since . . . well . . . forever.

He wanted to snarl at himself, thunder with rage over how he could be so foolish. Ten score voices lashed at him from the back of his mind–

Destroy them all
What are you waiting for?
Do it Do it Do it!
With your powers, you let this happen?
Something like this? To you?!
To us!?

London growled within his head, dismissing his ancestors. Yes, he knew he had been foolish, but he was not ready to compound his earlier mistakes by making more.

Still, he thought, on the other hand, I'm not dying here—not tonight!

With the slightest concentration, the detective reached into the floor and pulled the strength from it. All about him men, machines and furniture fell through the weakened floor into the sub-basement level below. Reeling from the effort, London pushed himself further, using the energy he had stolen to dissolve the lead pellets within his body.

They're just pieces of metal, he reminded himself. Just little lumps of lead. Nothing more. Nothing that can hurt us. Don't you go into shock on me, you bastard.

The detective sat against the section of wall he had reached, curled on the only piece of flooring he had left substantial. As flecks of rotted wood and steel and tile continued to fizzle away to become his fuel, he infused himself with energy, mending his torn flesh, repairing ruptured arteries and organs. Since he did not yet know within his conscious mind how to force such repairs, he had to trust to his body's own mechanisms, wasting great quantities of power as he pulled himself back together as best he could.

"Fire!"

From the sub-basement, a great volley was unleashed by Potts and his men. Bullets slammed all about London, gouging into the wall around him or the floor beneath him. Many of the shots were well placed, and would have struck the detective, save that he had already covered himself with an absorbing shield. Indeed, each projectile which struck it only made its powers greater—London absorbing not just the lead of the bullets, but their propelling force which his shield sucked up greedily.

Recovered, London quickly reviewed all the information he had acquired. His mind reviewed all of it at light speed—Hardy's notes, lists of possibilities, endless streams of data on experimentation, implementation, the recording of results, journal entries, phone calls--everything electronic that had been stored within or passed through the machinery in the scientist's office was now part of the detective's memories as well.

Standing up, London continued to ignore the constant hail of bullets coming at him, not only from the basement, but from the same floor as more guards jammed into the area in response to radio calls from Potts. The detective sighed, watching the men firing taking damage from ricochets while he casually ignored the melee. A side of him, angered at the effrontery of the man who had fired first, viciously urged London to funnel away all the lives before him, or at least that of the man who had wounded him.

Nearly killed us, you know.

The detective ignored the voice. Killing a man for doing his duty was simply murder. He understood the urge boiling within himself, wanted to act on it. On the other hand, however, it seemed so petty, somehow. London looked down to his chest, his side, to the spots where he had been shot. Even his clothing had been repaired according to his wishes.

What's the point, he asked himself. You start letting a moment of discomfort equal homicide . . .

Then, before he could finish his thought he noticed the guards were moving about, changing their positions, trying to find a firing point from where their bullets might be more effective. He also heard Potts calling to his men to cease fire, saw him giving futile hand signals to the same effect. Some stopped. Most, however, were too interested in being the one to bring down the intruder.

Potts understands, thought London. He knows they're just hurting themselves and wasting ammo. If they stopped shooting, and started thinking, maybe they could come up with something, he's thinking. But he knows they'll never . . .

And then, suddenly it hit him. He was as bad as those below. Sitting on his ledge behind his shield, thinking cosmic thoughts about the balance of power when he should be getting about his own business. Refocusing his attention on the part of his brain holding the recent influx of messages, log entries, and experiment notations which had been made under Hardy's time in the lab complex, he resumed scanning them for information as he prepared to leave. Then suddenly, he came across one of the key pieces of data for which he had been looking.

"Holy Christ in Heaven."

Anger burned through the detective as his brain digested that which he had just found. Questions flooded his brain at the same time. Did those below, the uniformed lackeys littering the atmosphere all about him with lead—did they know what had happened there, did they know what they were defending?

Were they, he asked himself, suddenly willing to reverse his mercy, aware of what they were trying to safeguard?

Of a sudden the guards no longer seemed like men doing their duty. In London's eyes they became like all who accepted money to impose cruelty and suffering on the world. He remembered the deaths their employer was already responsible for, revisited all the empty children's bedrooms he had just explored, stared once more into all the desperate eyes of their parents, begging him to somehow bring them back their slaughtered sons and daughters–

Dead, his mind growled. Children, murdered—dozens of them—just to make a fucking video game!

So why not kill them, whispered a voice in his mind. Why not cleanse the world of all such creatures?

London could feel power growing in his hands. Unconsciously he was gathering the force he needed to simply throw forth the energy needed to obliterate the guards below him. Then, a different notion struck him. A hungry one.

It had only been a few weeks since his clash with a coven of vampires. Not the cartoon vampires of the cinema with their fangs and daytime coffins, but the murderous force which took lives to extend their own. Such a simple thing, to stop siphoning energy from desks and walls and windows, and to do so from human beings—bodies soaking in power, bubbling over with energy—men who deserved to die.

Deserve to die

For a moment, the detective strongly considered doing so, then another bit of information flashed through his mind, pushing all other considerations aside. It was a minor tidbit, an almost meaningless scribble. But, combined with others, the single line of data sobered him back to a reality far more important than a matter as trivial as revenge.

Using the already gathered force, London descended to the floor, landing next to Potts. Extending his shield around the security chief, he snuffed out the noise coming through the barrier so the man could hear him as he asked;

"No games, Potts—do you want the deaths of all those children on your conscience or not?"

"No."

London stared into the man's eyes. He was tempted to use the same talent he had on Joan and Officer Carl Fergeson to go into the man's mind and make certain he was telling the truth. He declined, instead simply doing what he had done all his career before he had been selected by Fate to be the Destroyer. He watched Potts' eyes, studied his face and body language, searched for clues to the man's true intentions.

After a handful of seconds, he decided that like most mortals, Potts had a conscience. All around the two, the security chief's men threw themselves at London, slamming at him with fists and gun butts, attempting to break through his shield. Like the bullets before, he accepted the energy they expended, storing it all as he told Potts;

"I believe you. And, I'm thinking I might need your help with what I have to do next. Care to offer it?"

"Whatever it takes."

London smiled beneath his mask. Reaching out to the security chief, he gestured for Potts to give him his hand. He did so, and as the detective wrapped his fingers around those offered, the rest of the security force stepped away from the pair, all of them experiencing varying shades of fear and amazement as the two men simply lifted into the air and floated away.

Chapter Twenty-Two

L ONDON AND POTTS FLASHED through the in-between space known as the dreamplane, using it as a conduit to where the detective wished to be, to where the last bit of information he had taken conscious note of told him he *had* to be.

"What, what . . . what the hell was *that?*"

"That was the dreamplane," London explained calmly. "I can use it to move from place to place when I have to. It takes a lot of energy to get there with a passenger, but then your people provided that by throwing all that lead around."

Potts was shaking. One moment, to be in one place, a place you knew—knew well/the next instant . . .

"How . . ."

To be in another . . . a place not recognized, a place unknown, frightening, alien—

In an instant, the security chief thought, his soul freezing in his chest, *in an instant—*

"W-Where?" Potts stammered, cursing himself for the weakness, marveling all the while he could function at all. "Where are we? And . . ."

"Why?" The security man nodded as London asked his question for him. The detective told him;

"Hardy's been taking money from the mob to hand 'El Dorado' over to them a piece at a time. That's why he moved into a crash program—he needed quick results for them."

London stretched his back out, pulling himself back together after the dual exertions of repairing his body and then stepping through space with a passenger. He knew he had to balance the information he fed Potts with bits of time with which the man could absorb it all. He had to keep in mind that not only was he asking the security man to accept great quantities of unsavory information about people he knew, as well as dirty secrets which could jeopardize his company's future and thus his own, but he was forcing the man to shatter one world-image after another at a staggering rate.

In the past handful of minutes Potts had witnessed a man levitate, shrug off multiple gunshot wounds, shatter matter at its atomic level, shield himself telekinetically, and disassemble the laws of physics. And yet, the things he had remaining to reveal made the ones on which he had shed light seem like sideshow come-ons and parlor tricks.

"We're here in this parking lot," the detective told Potts, "because Hardy made an arrangement with an Albert Gallbendo to meet here tonight."

London scanned the lot for Hardy's car. He did not have a vision of it, but he did have the information from the scientist's driver's license and registration. As he spotted it, he added;

"The conversation he had with the mafioso had all the earmarks of a final meeting. I need to know if he's inside. While I look for his car, you go in and see if he's there. Let me know as soon as you can."

The security chief stumbled off toward the restaurant. London found Hardy's car a moment later. That told him the scientist had arrived. Less than a minute later Potts returned to let him know Hardy had been in the restaurant but had left.

"No one inside," reported the security chief with an exaggerated drawl, "and believe it or not, no one will confirm that Hardy left with anyone. In fact, there are some fairly emphatic about swearing that he didn't. Then, there are plenty of others who say he wasn't even here tonight."

"There's a reason people only eat in certain places," London answered. Shutting his eyes for a moment, he opened them again and stared into Potts'.

"Listen—they took him and they're going to kill him. Then they're going to take the secrets he stole from your company and take them back to their boss—and that, believe me, is something both of us want to prevent."

"I can understand why I wouldn't want it to happen," answered the security man, still conscious of his duties. "But why both of us?"

"Because," London told him, staring off into the darkness, "it will mean the end of the world."

"Wha . . . what do you mean? What are you saying?"

"Hardy's game, the operational system," London explained. "It has more than one use. Hell—it has millions—billions. It can feed the hungry, it can cure the blind, make diamonds from coal—anything, it can do anything. Get me?

"*Anything.*"

Potts' concentration seemed to shift, lose focus. The detective could see that the man was reaching his breaking point. Boiling his pitch down to its simplest level, giving the security chief something to focus on, he told the man;

"What I'm saying is, maybe Hardy can't see the forest for the trees with what he's using, but others will. This technology can't fall into the hands of . . ."

Potts stared as London suddenly interrupted himself with laughter. His head bowed, body shaking, the detective felt tears running down his face as he howled into the night.

"Oh, yes," London finally managed to choke out the words, still chuckling as he did so, feeling his body begin to go weary once more. Wondering just how difficult it was to tell when you were finally insane, he managed to say, "God forbid the Mafia get a hold on this. Christ, as if they'd be the big problem."

Potts simply continued to stare, not knowing what to say. Pulling himself together, London finally reined in his laughter, then grabbed the security chief by the shoulders.

"Nobody can have this," he snarled. "No one. Period. Not the police, not any churches, certainly not the government—not any government. We've got to find them and stop them before this goes a step further."

"But, but . . ." Potts stammered again. Cursed himself again. "Why? I mean, I don't mean 'why not let the Mafia have it,' but why can't anyone have it?" London's pupils expanded frighteningly—his eyes frosting over dark with fury.

"Are you kidding me," the detective shouted. "And just who is it *you* would trust with the power of God?" Potts stayed silent for a long second, then finally he swept in a deep breath and said;

"It does seem you're asking me to trust you with it."

London stopped for a second, tired and angry and frightened. Capping off all the voices exploding within his head, he answered quietly;

"No, I'm not. You listen to me—I didn't ask for this to happen to me. I don't want you to trust me with this power. I don't want anyone to trust me with this power."

The detective paused again, the last few days tumbling through his memory like so much fresh magma burning down a virgin hillside of timber. Remembering all the horror and destruction he had seen since he had been "blessed" with the seemingly never-ending catalog of abilities he now possessed, he whispered;

"God, man . . . I don't even trust me with this power."

Potts nodded. He understood what London was trying to tell him, even though the security man barely understood anything else that had happened around him since the invasion of Future Images had begun. The detective nodded back. Both men took in deep breaths, then Potts asked;

"I'm in—I'll help you . . . but I need to know something. You're saying that Dr. Hardy invented some process that can do anything at all, but that he's only using it for 'El Dorado?' I'm not arguing with you, I just don't understand . . . wouldn't someone as intelligent as David Hardy realize he had come up with something as powerful as you say it is? I mean, wouldn't that be like inventing the gun and not understanding that it could hurt people?"

London nodded again.

"I've been wondering that, too. Care to go find the answers?"

"You seem to be in for a pound," answered Potts. "I think I can stand good for the penny."

The detective smiled tightly, then placed one hand on the security chief's shoulder. Nodding once, he closed his eyes and began to study the heat trails running out of the parking lot. When he found the one he wanted, he gave Potts one last look, offering the man a final chance to step back. The security man only slipped a new clip into his sidearm and said;

"We're going to have to take your ride . . . mine's still back at the office."

London reached out toward the scientist's abandoned car there in the lot before him. With a gesture he consumed it. Then he turned his senses toward searching for the limousine Albert Gallbendo had sent to pick up David Hardy. Finding the location in seconds, he folded time and space and pulled Potts and himself some twenty miles away.

CHAPTER
TWENTY-THREE

"**W**HAT WOULD YOU LIKE to talk about?"

"Darling, I don't actually think I'm going to 'like' any of this, but I do think we need to get some things out of the way, you know, before . . ."

"Before what? Before one of us kills the other?"

The Pirate Queen stared at Lisa, the conflicting voices within her head driving her to distraction. She still did not know why she had taken herself to the other woman's apartment, still did not know what she wanted to say, thought she might accomplish—none of it. Joan de Molina knew herself well enough to understand that she would not have done such without a reason. Somewhere within her, she always had a reason for everything she did.

Yes, that's me, she thought, the woman with all the answers. Well, I certainly wish I knew what question I believed I could answer by putting myself into *this* situation.

Steeling herself, fortifying her will reflexively as she had done a thousand times before breaking into a heavily guarded area, or fighting her way out of one, she forced herself into a place of serenity, then asked;

"Really, aren't you going to invite me in?"

"You know what they say," answered Lisa. "A vampire can't enter your home until you step aside and ask it in. I'm not certain there's any real advantage to doing that here."

A part of Lisa was almost shocked at her bluntness. Up until a few months previous, she had been the most sheltered of women. Her father had raised her for a specific purpose, none of which required her to develop any kind of self-preservation skills. Catching on to the fact that her father did not see any use in her becoming very clear-witted, she had played dutiful and cowed to the point where he had not seen the harm in letting her go to college. Doing so helped him protect himself from the observations of others. After all her years of working to convince him she could not possibly respect a thought he had not sanctioned, he allowed her that bit of freedom. His one mercy toward her, self-serving as it had been, had been his undoing.

Now, Lisa searched the face of her enemy, the woman who had swooped into her life grasping after the man she loved, desperate to identify whatever self-serving crumb of pity had brought her there at that moment. She had serious doubts as to whether or not she could handle herself around Joan, and no idea whatsoever as to what the Pirate Queen could want from her.

There is, a thought whispered through her mind, one way to find out.

Yeah, spat another, kill her, incinerate the body, scatter the ashes, then get a Ouija board and ask her.

Lisa smiled at the notion. She could not stop herself, did not want to, actually. Joan could not help but notice the change, but refrained from commenting. Finally, after three more intolerably long seconds, Lisa stepped back, saying;

"Okay, I'm as curious as the last dead cat. Come in, won't you? It's so good to see you again."

Joan moved stiffly past Lisa, coming into the apartment's mid-sized kitchen. Her instincts honed from years of sizing up spaces against the possibility of late-night break-in returns, the Pirate Queen developed a mental blueprint of the place instantly. Bathroom to the right of the kitchen, living room to the left. Two bedrooms extended away from there—the smaller one used for sleeping, the larger as an office/storage room/et cetera.

"I can tolerate a certain amount of sarcasm and ill-will from you," Joan responded, "but I hope we can get past such, or there's little point in us meeting at all."

"You know where the door is," Lisa snapped. "And, being a thief, I'm sure you've already scoped out where all the other exits are. Do feel free to avail yourself of any of them at any time. I think the four story drop to the street is closest."

The Pirate Queen stopped short, one foot in the living room, one in the kitchen. She felt herself trembling, could feel her fingers curling into fists. Her body rigid, she stared straight ahead as she admitted;

"You know, this isn't easy for me, either."

"Why not," snapped Lisa, moving forward, her face closing on the back of the Pirate Queen's head, mouth aimed at her right ear, "you're the one with all the quick answers. You're the invader, just rolling in over those with something to lose—taking what you want without–"

Anger flushing her system, Joan spun around—sharp and quick, her reflexes polished. As she did, her eyes went wide as she saw Lisa's hand come up with equal speed, a .45 automatic in it, leveling with her opponent's midsection.

"What are you doing?" Joan stepped back, taken so completely by surprise her concentration vanished. Even with all of London's knowledge of Lisa, all his impressions and notions and imaginings of her within her own mind, the Pirate Queen had not anticipated such an action.

"Protecting myself from a known criminal," snapped Lisa. Using her weapon as a blunt threat, she backed Joan into the living room, telling her;

"Joan de Molina, aka the Pirate Queen, wanted across Europe and Asia in connection with seventeen out of twenty-one of the world's major, still unsolved art thefts. B&E expert, master gambler, known to be armed at all times, also highly skilled in hand-to-hand techniques. Known thief, known whore, known murderer. What? Was I supposed to make tea and put out a plate of Oreos before I let you do whatever the hell it is you came here to do to me?"

Joan sat down on the room's only couch slowly. Setting her handbag on the coffee table before her, she then extended her arms out to both sides, resting them on the couch's crest. Calmly, she told her host;

"There is a snub nose derringer in my bag. The throwing stars and knives I'm far more comfortable with are hidden on my person. I didn't come here to use them—didn't think about them, really. I just put them on this morning the way I would my bra.

"I didn't come here to hurt you, Lisa."

"Why not?"

"Because . . ." she said slowly, her voice going quiet to avoid going shrill, "I could never have Teddy if I did such a thing."

Lisa's head snapped backward slightly. She certainly knew what Joan wanted, but hearing her say so was still more than she could stand. She felt the .45 growing heavy in her hand. She had taken it from its holster positioned at the small of her back without realizing it, a part of her screaming for her to use it ever since it had filled her hand. She had not been expecting Joan; the weapon was something she put on every morning as naturally as the Pirate Queen adorned herself with her blades.

Sitting down in the easy chair across from the couch, Lisa rested her automatic on the padded arm beneath her hand. Sliding her finger from inside the trigger guard, but not breaking contact with the weapon, she answered;

"At least you know him that well."

"I know him inside and out," the Pirate Queen purred. Her voice teased Lisa, hinting at everything the younger woman had feared since first setting eyes on the redhead. "And that's why we're going to have to come to some sort of understanding."

"Explain yourself."

"Theodore will not choose between us. He will worry himself, question himself, dizzy himself in a thousand ways, but he will not choose." Joan watched Lisa's face, using all her own instincts coupled with the knowledge she had of the younger woman taken from London's mind. Seeing agreement within Lisa's eyes, she continued, saying;

"And it's all so foolish. He and I, even if it all came about by accident, are now thoroughly intertwined. Our souls are perfectly enmeshed one within the other. You, you're just someone he felt sorry for, someone he protected and now doesn't know what to do with."

The Pirate Queen enjoyed the steam she noted building behind Lisa's eyes, pretended not to notice.

"Because of the events of a few months previous, now he is saddled with these useless paternal feelings for you. And you, instead of understanding, you continue to hang on, hoping he's going to suddenly sweep you into his arms and ride off into the sunset, even though the two of you have never even kissed . . ."

"Very nice try," answered Lisa, far more calmly that Joan had desired. "But you're losing ground with me with every word. Teddy and I are partners. His business has more than doubled with me running the office. He's not keeping me around out of pity. You on the other hand . . ."

"Enough."

Joan accompanied her single word with a dismissive wave of her hand. Tossing her head, enough to cause her hair to ripple slightly, she added;

"We could keep at this for some great length, I'm certain. Both of us could present great quantities of reasoning as to why we should be the one to be with Theodore, but I say we look at the facts, and the facts are thus: we both want him. He will make himself crazy before choosing between us. Which means we have to choose for him."

The Pirate Queen let her last sentence hang in the air, then finished her thought by saying;

"One of us is going to have to step out of the picture."

With Lisa watching her carefully, Joan went into her bag and brought forth a small box. The shape was instantly recognizable as the kind used to hold decks of cards. Thumbing the top open, she shook the container gently, allowing a standard deck still tightly bound in plastic to slide outward into her palm. Then, extending her hand toward Lisa, she said;

"It's a fresh deck. Check it out if you need to."

"Why would I need to?"

"Because I think this is the only way to settle things between us. We both draw a card—high card wins."

Lisa glanced across at the deck, her attention focused not so much on it, but on the notion of what it represented. She felt heat extending outward from the small rectangle, crawling across the room toward her as she tried to wrap her mind around the idea of it all.

"Whoever gets the high card stays with Theodore," said Joan softly. "The other simply walks away."

Lisa stared for only an instant longer, then gave her answer.

CHAPTER
TWENTY-FOUR

"GET OUT OF THE car, Hardy." The speaker was the man next to him in the back seat. "The door's open. Use it."

"I don't understand," the scientist lied. Sliding further away from the open door and the smaller man waiting outside it, he begged, "Why are you doing this?"

"We're just followin' orders—just like you." Sighing, the speaker added, "You were told what to do tonight. So was we. Now be a good boy and do what you're told."

Tired of waiting, the man on the outside lowered his massive frame until he could see inside the back seat.

"Get outta da car, ya little freak or . . ."

"Or what?" shouted Hardy. Squeezing himself into the limousine's corner, pushing himself mindlessly into the smaller thug, he held his bags and papers tightly to his chest as he screamed, "Or what? What?!"

"Christ a'fuckin' mighty," muttered the driver. "I hate when they go chicken shit."

Reaching inside the car, he slapped Hardy roughly even as his smaller partner pushed the scientist off of himself. Tugging with only a minimum effort, the driver jerked Hardy from the back of the limo with ease. Savvy enough to realize their employer would want every single scrap of paper Hardy had brought with him in perfect condition, the smaller thug quickly began gathering up anything the scientist dropped, chasing them down with the aid of the limo's headlights while his partner shook him brutally for defying them in even the minute way he had.

"You mooky little weasel," the driver growled. "Stop droppin' shit everywhere."

The larger man slapped Hardy, pulling the bags the scientist was holding from his grasp at the same time. The scientist staggered backward a few steps, free from the larger man's grasp for the moment. His first instinct was to run, but common sense was quickly overturned by other fears as he stared about into the darkness and asked himself;

Where could I go . . . that they wouldn't find me?

Hardy stared out over the marshy dunes before him. Where had such a wilderness even come from, he wondered. A distant memory reminded him that most of New York State was undeveloped, but a lifetime in and around

New York City had left him with little imagination for anything but concrete and glass. If he had been told the sand and weeds and broken rock stretching out before him were part of a time portal that had been opened to the Jurassic, he would have believed it just as easily.

Watching the scientist's head bobbing, scanning the darkness before him, the driver told Hardy;

"You're thinkin' you could get away, ain't ya?"

"No, actually," admitted the scientist, "I was thinking how pitiful I am, that I had all that time when you weren't really watching me, time I could have used to run, and I was too afraid of try."

The thug watched Hardy's face, glowing oddly in the reflection of the headlights, keenly aware that the scientist was talking more to himself than he was anyone else. As his partner approached, the driver made a motion cautioning the other man to silence.

"I've been so afraid of everything for such a long time now, and I'm not even certain why. Afraid of losing my job, afraid of losing my children's love. After I lost that, afraid to lose their respect. And after I lost that, afraid I'd lose even their tolerance of me."

The larger of the two thugs narrowed his eyes, indicating he did not understand what was going on—neither what Hardy was saying nor why he and his partner were not proceeding with their job. Drawing closer, the smaller told him softly;

"I just wanta hear what he's got to say. Go put his papers and shit in the car if you don't wanta listen."

The larger man trudged back to the limousine, not understanding his partner's curiosity but not caring enough to argue with him. He understood enough to know that if he started an argument he might attract their assignment's attention—might stop him from talking. And, if his partner was listening for something special, something Mr. Gallbendo had told him to listen for . . .

The larger man turned and stopped on his way to the limo, listening himself, trying to determine what had fascinated his partner so. Hardy continued rambling, not aware anyone was listening—not actually aware he was speaking.

"I don't know what made me do it, really. I was working on something totally different. I had dreams, of course, had always thought about how it could be done . . . oh, the nights I lay awake, thinking about it, dreaming about it . . . but, it couldn't work, you know. Not really."

Hardy looked up suddenly, his eyes seemingly focusing on the driver. Still silhouetted in the headlight's glare, still speaking in the same faraway voice, he continued to chatter more to himself than anyone else.

"And then, one day, I just had it. It all came so clear, how to make it work. It was like a vision—really—like some medieval vision, sent by God to . . ."

He turned to the smaller of the two thugs then, his arms outstretched, eyes imploring, as he said, "I could see my hands, working the machines, slicing atoms apart, building the nanites, teaching them, making them work . . ."

Several yards away, the larger man bent slightly, whispering into his partner's ear.

"He saying anything worth the hearing?"

"I don't know," responded the driver. "At first it was kinda funny, you know? Him carpin' about his kids and shit, but . . . ah, it's kinda lost its power to amuse, if you know what I mean."

"Oddly enough," came a voice from behind the pair, "I know exactly what you mean."

Both the thugs wheeled about, surprised to find two other men behind them. They recognized neither of the intruders. Both went for their guns. Potts, his sidearm already in his hand, waved it menacingly at them.

"Gentlemen, let's all of us keep this friendly, shall we?"

"Fuck you two," snarled the driver. "What the fuck do you shits want here? You'll get yer drippin' backdoors outta here if you know what's good for you!"

London stepped forward, smiling, shaking his head gently.

"What a funny fellow," the detective said, his motions soft and casual. "Let me tell you, Chumly, if I knew what was good for me, why . . . my, my, I wouldn't be in nearly as much trouble as I am now."

As the two men simply stared, not knowing what the newcomers wanted, not knowing if the smaller of the two would use the .45 he held so evenly, London told them;

"I mean, dead children everywhere, ghost voices echoing in their computers, in their dying skulls, hints of boiling trouble pouring through the walls of space and time, all headed our way, all because of that dimwitted boob over there . . ." the detective's hand pointed at Hardy. The scientist, who had yet to notice anyone new had arrived, continued to ramble.

"There he is, the key to everything, the center of the entire universe right now, the answer to whether or not we all die—horribly and painfully–"

"What the fuck are you talkin' about?" The larger man put his hands on his hips, London's low volume bolstering his courage.

"Me?" The detective pointed at his chest. "Why, I'm talking about the end of the world. Didn't you know? Every time I get up in the morning and have a cup of tea, every time I tie my tie and walk out the front door, it's another chance for the doomsayers to prove themselves right."

"Look, funny man," snarled the driver, "what the hell is this? Do you want something or don't you? 'Cause, if you don't, we got us a job to do."

"Yes," answered London. His tone suddenly filled with a frigid steel so terrible it made both the thugs take an involuntary step backward as he told them, "you were sent to slaughter that gibbering lunatic over there. You brought him here because it's a convenient dumping ground for such work."

Gallbendo's men looked at each other. Was London a policeman, they wondered. From another family? Someone who knew their own boss? Suddenly the larger man let his defiant stance falter, his arms sliding slowly back to his sides.

"I don't think we can allow you to do any of that."

"An-And . . ." the driver asked, "just what are we supposed to do?"

"You?" London said the word menacingly, as if the thought of the two men made him physically ill. "I'll tell you what we're all going to do. My friend here, he and I are going to take Dr. Hardy and see if we can prevent the continents from sinking into the sea. And you two, you're going to go to church. And you're going to pray—you're going to pray I don't decide to just drain the life out of your useless bodies. Then, after you finish praying, you're going to turn yourselves in to the police, confess all your crimes, and then turn state's evidence on Gallbendo and anyone associated with him."

"Yeah, sure," snickered the larger thug. "Right; we'll be sure to do that."

"And if we don't?"

The detective stared into the driver's eyes, then growled, "Oh, you will—or I'll find you and teach you about pain the way your first grade teacher taught you about the alphabet—slowly, and with patience, until you understand everything there is to know about it."

"And how do you think you're going to do that?" demanded the driver.

"Easy," answered London, raising his hand to snap his fingers, "the same way I'm doing this."

The detective pushed his thumb across his middle finger, and suddenly Gallbendo's men found themselves in the center of St. Patrick's Cathedral in Manhattan. The pair jumped as everything changed around them, both letting out vulgar epithets. Staggering from the effort, London told Potts;

"Get Hardy, will you? Bring him to the limo."

"Right," answered the security man. Taking note of the detective's condition, he asked, "You going to be all right?"

"Just get him in the front seat," he said, handing the man one of his business cards at the same time, "and then drive him to this address."

"What are you going to do?"

London pulled open the back door of the limousine and tumbled inside, barely conscious as he answered;

"Sleep . . ."

Then, as Potts went after Hardy, the detective closed his eyes, thinking;

And maybe do a little praying of my own.

CHAPTER TWENTY-FIVE

"YOU WANT ME TO cut cards, for the man I love? You expect me to risk everything, to hinge the entire world's safety . . . in a card game? With a known gambling cheat? Using her deck?" Lisa laughed, the sound growing in her throat until she nearly choked.

"What kind of idiot do you take me for?"

"Then what do you propose we do?"

Lisa stared at the Pirate Queen, her emotions strained in more directions than she could count. A great deal of her was caught up in a violent rage, wanting to simply grab hold of the redhead and strangle her. Part of her still regretted that she did not gut shoot the woman sitting across from her and then simply watch her bleed to death.

"I'll tell you what I propose," the younger woman said finally, in a voice far calmer than she believed possible. "You're supposed to have all of Teddy's memories and feelings tucked away in your brain. All right, go through them. Use them as you will. See what he really thinks of me—figure out what he and I mean to each other."

"I've already done that," answered Joan in a voice filled with purring scorn.

"No," Lisa returned. Her voice even calmer than before, she added, "I don't think you have. I think you're a grasping opportunist who's waltzed through life taking whatever she wanted at the moment and never thinking about the consequences."

"And I believe you're an empty-headed child who's mistaken compassion for understanding and pity for love." Lisa's eyes narrowed, her chestnut brows darkening as the Pirate Queen added;

"You've gotten it into your head that Theodore's entire universe revolves around you, that he can't make a move without you, that somehow a man who can challenge the gods needs a clinging little mouse to make his life complete."

"Get out of my home."

Lisa's hand flashed for the coffee table. Her fingers still tight about her weapon, she used the barrel of the automatic to flip Joan's bag back to her. The slim pocketbook landed in the redhead's lap. The Pirate Queen considered it for a moment, as if it had fallen from the sky. Then, she reached out her hand slowly and picked it up, chicly folding it against her arm. Glancing at her watch causally as she did so, Joan announced;

"My, look at the time. I'm afraid I must be going. We must do this again some time."

Lisa did not speak. Already standing, her gun hand holding her automatic rigid at waist level, trigger finger in place, she simply waited wordlessly for the Pirate Queen to finally rise and make her way to the door. The redhead did so, proceeding forward in a slow and deliberate fashion, her body moving in a warm, sensual pattern. Lisa ignored the distracting sway of the woman, as well as her breezy chatter. Knowing there would be nothing in it except for offense and doubt, she allowed the words to wash over her, acknowledged but unheard.

Such a tactic worked while her adversary was walking away from her. At the door, however, Joan turned back to address her host face to face one last time.

"This has all been charming," the Pirate Queen murmured, "but I must be off. Teddy will be returning from tonight's operation soon, and I must be there to advise him."

The redhead smiled then, wide and lushly, her eyes bright with satisfaction. She blinked several times as she held her pose, her coyness meant to shatter Lisa's confidence, or at least to disrupt it further. Her mouth held tight, her lips bent in a bitter scowl, the younger woman told her;

"You do your worst—okay? You do whatever you think you can get away with to come between me and Teddy."

"Why," the redhead said with a breezy innocence, "I already have. Theodore and I have been to the stars and back again. Quite literally." She let her sentence hang in the air for a terrible moment, then added;

"Didn't you know?"

Lisa could tell that, whatever the woman was implying, she was telling the truth. She also believed, deep within the part of her soul that could not lie to her, that nothing could have happened between London and the redhead the way the Pirate Queen was trying to make it sound. In fact, she suddenly realized as she looked into Joan's eyes that the woman's words were all lies.

Yes, she knew something must have happened between the thief before her and her Teddy, but whatever it was it was not what was being implied.

"You're a sad, sad piece of work," said Lisa, the anger and hate that had been sustaining her leaking away.

"How amusing," answered Joan. Turning her back on the younger woman, she headed for the elevator, adding, "And here I was just thinking the same thing about you."

Lisa shut her door, then locked it. Reholstering her weapon, she moved back into her apartment, much of her body feeling numb—more of it going numb with each passing second. Returning to her living room, she sat down heavily on her sofa. There was no grace to the motion, nothing feminine about it—something she noticed. She merely positioned herself to be caught by the couch's cushions not caring about anything further.

She sat for a long, soundless time, neither thinking about nor feeling anything. She merely existed, trying to pull all the various edges of herself which the Pirate Queen's visit had rattled back into place. She knew that London would never betray her. She understood what had happened to him, between him and the redhead. She trusted him in a way she trusted no other person— the way no woman had ever trusted any man.

"Oh, Teddy," she murmured, "When is this all going to be over?"

And then, she turned to look at her apartment door, the exit leading to the hall. Staring at it for a long second, she felt a cold rush of anger flushing through her. Feeling her face tighten from the strain of it, she looked past the door, then shouted;

"Bitch!"

After which she fell on her side and cried into her cushions.

CHAPTER
TWENTY-SIX

L ONDON HAD LAIN IN the back of the limousine the entire return trip to Manhattan, rumpled into a small ball of flesh and anxiety. Exhausted from the strain of using his abilities longer and further than he ever had previously, he experienced numerous, terrible dreams, all related to the powers he was finally beginning to understand. They left him screaming, drained and miserable. They left Potts wondering exactly what it was into which he had gotten himself.

The security chief spent quite a number of miles wondering about his situation. He was, after all, supposed to be responsible to Future Images. So, what was he doing? If he continued on the way he was going, he would certainly cause his company nothing but harm. It seemed useless at that point, however, to argue that David Hardy was not the murderer for whom the police had come looking. Of course he was.

But still, shouldn't I be protecting him?

Potts glanced over at the scientist crumpled against the far door in the front seat. In all honesty, the man did not appear to want anyone's protection. Curious, the security chief asked;

"So, tell me, David, what's this all about?"

Hardy turned toward the faraway voice. His eyes were hollow—vacant and grotesquely tired-looking. Indeed, the scientist appeared to have somehow lost a piece of himself, as if suddenly his personality had been shattered. The security chief was somewhat unnerved at the sight.

"David, are you feeling all right?"

Hardy did not answer, but simply continued to stare forward through the windshield with eyes Potts felt were seeing nothing at all. The security chief did not take the man's silence personally. He realized the scientist had to be at the end of his rope. Hardy was about to lose his job, his family, his freedom—everything. What had he been going on about when he and London had first arrived on the scene?

"I don't know what made me do it, really. I was working on something totally different. I had always thought about how it could be done . . . oh, the nights I lay awake, thinking about it, dreaming about it . . . but, it couldn't work—not really."

Potts remembered his tone as he spoke—defeated, lost. And then, he had started down a different memory path, and his entire manner had changed. He had become lighter, buoyant, practically effervescent.

"And then, one day, I just had it. It all came so clear, how to make it work. It was like a vision—really—like some medieval vision, sent by God to . . . I could see my hands, working the machines, slicing atoms apart, building the nanites, teaching them, making them work . . ."

It all came back to Potts; he had heard Hardy jabbering about nanites. The security man had heard about nanites previously, of course—years earlier—when everyone had; they were supposed to be machines as small as atoms. The news talked about them for weeks, the new miracle. Once we had nanotechnology, everything and anything was supposed to be possible. Then, as always, all mention of them was dropped when the next interesting fad idea came along.

So, Potts wondered, glancing once more at the scientist, if you actually had the power to do everything and anything, what made you use it to run a video game?

The only answers the scientist gave to Potts' musings were to continue to stare blankly, and to allow a tiny line of drool to begin to escape from the left corner of his mouth.

♦ ♦ ♦

It was close to two-thirty in the morning when London and Potts finally made it to the detective's office with Hardy in tow. Most who had offices at the Greeley Arcade would not have been able to enter at such a time, but London had long ago made arrangements with the building's owners to have twenty-four hour access. The detective's progress was slow. Not only were he and Potts having to practically carry the collapsed Hardy along, but they had taken all of his bags and books when they abandoned Gallbendo's limo next to a fire hydrant.

While relocking the front door, one of the building's maintenance workers entered the lobby. Recognizing the man, the detective greeted him, then asked if he would give Morcey, the workman's former boss, a call, asking him to come into the office as soon as he could. With a chuckle, the man answered;

"Ain't no need, Mr. London. He already upstairs." The detective showed a moment's surprise, then just smiled.

"There you go," added the maintenance man. "That's why he the best. You tell him for me, if'n he ever get tired of playin' cops and robbers, we'all could sure use him back."

"I will make a point to do that, Roger," London answered, giving the man an open smile. "But don't be surprised if I'm not in a hurry to let him go."

Just as the elevator came the maintenance worker leaned his mop against the wall for a moment, then pointed at Hardy whom London and Potts were having to hold up, and asked;

"You need any help with that guy? Or maybe all that other mess you gots there?"

"Appreciated, Roger," the detective answered honestly. "Really—but I think we've got it all. Besides, this is one of *those* cases."

Roger sent his hand back to his mop, fingers wrapping around it unconsciously, more as a way for the worker to steady his nerves than anything else. As the two men across the lobby from him moved their charge into the elevator, the maintenance man called out;

"Yeah, that's cool. Try not to mess up the building too much."

"You getting lazy on me, Roger?"

"No, sir—the owners just don't want to shell out no overtime no mo'."

London chuckled, then threw the other man a wave just as the elevator doors were closing, careful not to break the electric eye and re-open the doors. The trio rode upward to the detective's floor in silence, crossed the fifteen paces from the elevator bank to the door to London's offices the same way. Once there, Potts held Hardy up as the detective went for his keys. Then, remembering Morcey was already there, he simply reached out and grabbed the doorknob. It turned freely.

"Boss!"

On the other side of the door London found not only his partner, but his friend Pa'sha, as well as several of the Murder Dogs, Lai Wan and Professor Goward. While Potts settled Hardy into a chair, London introduced the pair to everyone else. The security chief acknowledged the others, but Hardy's near complete lack of response concerned the man greatly. He suggested London fill his people in on everything that had happened while he took a more careful look at the scientist's condition.

The detective was grateful for the chance to sprawl in one of the comfortable chairs in the waiting room. Kicking off his shoes, he told the story of what had happened from the time he had entered Future Images until the point where he had discovered that Hardy was to be eliminated that night by Gallbendo's men. He described how he could feel the mobster's intent through the pulling of his conversation with Hardy out of the air, how it had chilled him to realize he could read the man's desires simply by hearing a memory of his voice.

"Hey, that reminds me," he said. "Dearon, know any chop shops that would be interested in a tripped-out limo? Only last year's model."

"What make?"

"BMW, wasn't it?" When Potts agreed with London's guess, the Murder Dog captain smiled and answered;

"There might be a bit of change to be gathered from such a toy."

The security chief threw the man the keys, letting him know where he could find the limousine. Pa'sha sent his other lieutenants with Dearon. He was as amused with the idea of sending the mob boss's limo to one of his rival's car-stripping operations, but he never sent just one of his people into any situation. Even when his men did the weekly grocery shopping for the weaponeer's mother, they did it in pairs.

"Sorry about havin' the whole gang here, boss," said Morcey. "But when you went an hour overdue without givin' us even a phone jingle, I thought maybe we'd better start preparin' for the worst."

"Good thinking, Paul," the detective answered. "No problem. Still might need some help tonight for all I know." London paused to give out with a surprisingly large yawn. The action caused the professor to yawn, which then sent Pa'sha's hand to his mouth.

"You know, little brother," the weaponeer said, "if you could just remember to use your cell phone once in a while, impromptu gatherings like this might not be found necessary."

"Sorry, everyone," apologized London. "But this case has been kind of a strain so far. The museum was bad enough, but then, after the fiasco with that cop, and our own personal jewel thief . . . then everything I ended up doing tonight . . ."

The detective stopped for a moment, then swallowed. Looking from face to face in the room, he admitted, "I'll tell you, I'm having real trouble with all of this. I've started to get some actual control, now—the energy I need for what I do, I can take it from where I want to. That's if, of course I have the time to think about it and, well, I thought that would make it easier, but . . . but it's not."

Everyone in the room simply waited quietly. London accepted the silence gratefully, using it to clear his head. After a handful of moments, he said;

"It's just all so . . . so scary, really. What are the limits? What's right and what's wrong? Who's to decide—me? Professor, you said this was all Fate's doing, that I was Destiny's hand-picked boy for dispensing justice, protecting the world from evil. Well, all I can say is, lucky me."

"You are not the only one who has had to make such adjustments," countered Lai Wan.

"True enough," answered the detective. "But I'm the one who's had to make the biggest ones, and in the least time. It's only been a handful of weeks, *weeks*, for Christ's sake, since this was all dumped in my lap. It was only a few weeks ago when you were in the hospital, Paul. Near death. The doctors had given up on you—only a matter of time, they said." London buried his face in his hands for a moment, then said through his fingers;

"Only a matter of time. You remember that?"

"I've got some small memory of da moment—yeah, so?"

"So," London uncovered his face. Staring into his friend's eyes, tears streaking both cheeks, he answered in a whisper, "It didn't even dawn on me that I could just snap my fingers and save you myself."

Both men's minds swam back to the moment. Everyone had thought the final confrontation between London and the vampire Jorsha would be an epic struggle—titanic to behold. In the end, however, it was found the vampire had tired of his life, and brought it to a close by sacrificing the energies he had stolen to restore not only Morcey's vitality, but to cure practically every injured and damaged soul in the hospital.

"And would you now?"

"Would I what?"

"If I was dyin' now," answered Morcey. "Would you snap your fingers and cheat death for me? Again?" The balding man let the question hang for half a second, then added;

"No—don't even answer, 'cause I'll tell you—you're not goin' ta do it, 'cause I don't want you to."

"Paul–"

"Now, don't all of ya get in an uproar. Just hear me out. I've been watchin' what all this puts you through, boss. And I don't think it's gonna get any easier on ya any time soon, neither. So, let me tell you right now, one resurrection is enough for me." The ex-maintenance man lowered his head, running his teeth over his lower lip. Raising his head once more, he locked his eyes with London's, then continued, saying;

"Boss, I'm gettin' a real handle on this dreamplane stuff, and I'll tell you right now, it's scarin' the ever-lovin' crap outta me. I've watched you make some decisions these past months . . . my God, what . . . you threw away two million lives to save the universe. You had a few lousy seconds to make up your mind what to do. To my mind you made the right choice, but there ain't no one here who don't know what it cost you." Then, jerking his thumb in Potts' direction, he added;

"Okay, maybe he don't, but you know what I mean. So understand it when I say this—if the situation ever comes up again, please, just let me go. Because the longer I'm around this stuff, the more I'm startin' ta think I can handle it, too. And honestly, I don't want ta be around long enough to find out."

The assembly sat in silence. Morcey had stolen all the wind in the room, turned everyone's attention inward. Finally, however, London said;

"Well, there isn't much point in all of us just sitting around here. I didn't go to the trouble to save Hardy from Gallbendo's thugs because I liked his looks." Addressing Potts directly, the detective asked;

"Think he's come around enough to answer some questions? Seriously, I for one would like to get this damned case over and done with."

The security man nodded to London, then turned back to Hardy. He touched the man's shoulder, then took his wrist. While he felt for a pulse, Lai Wan said;

"Do not trouble yourself, Mr. Potts. Mr. Hardy is dead."

None of the others bothered to question how the psychometrist could know such a thing even though she was on the other side of the room. Potts kept trying to find some indication of life within the scientist, but pulse, heart beat, breathing, all functions seemed halted. He turned to London, his face showing naught but confusion. Taking his pipe from his mouth, Goward asked;

"So, what now, Theodore?"

"Now?" repeated the detective. "Hell, I guess we do things the hard way."

CHAPTER
TWENTY-SEVEN

"EVEN THOUGH I BELIEVE you must know such to be true already, still I feel I must tell you that I do not believe this to be a good idea."

Lai Wan sat next to the corpse of David Hardy. The body separated her from London who sat on the other side of the scientist's remains. Hardy's body had been stretched out on a folding table which had been set up in Morcey's office. While the balding man and Potts had attended to that, London had called Cantalupo's precinct. The captain had left instructions he was to be alerted no matter where he was if word came in from the detective. Even though he had been home asleep, he was at 132 W. 31st St. within a half hour of receiving London's message. Krandell arrived only eight minutes after his captain with a quite unexpected extra officer tagging along.

"Officer Fergeson," London said with mild surprise. "You'll pardon my not expecting to see you again so soon."

"Yeah," the policeman answered with a guarded manner, "Surprises me, too."

"Don't believe him," interrupted Krandell. "This was his idea. Practically threatened me when word got out where I was goin'."

London looked Fergeson over for a moment, then asked, "You sure you want to be here? I mean . . . considering . . ."

"Yeah," the officer answered. His tone slightly bitter, but filled with something bordering on excitement, he added, "Considering what happened between us before, yeah—this is exactly where I want to be."

"Oh, oh," laughed Morcey. "We got us one with the bug."

"I'll bug you, you fat prick–"

"Whoa, big fella," said London. "Save it for the bad stuff. In fact, let's get it in the open right here and now—why exactly are you here?"

Fergeson looked at the detective defiantly, then to Cantalupo, finally to Krandell. When neither of his fellow officers came to his aid, he fell back on belligerence.

"What I'm doin' here is my business. You, after what you did to me, you owe me, and I'll put myself anywhere I please and you will do nothing about it except take it. You read me?" London considered the officer for a short moment, then turned to Morcey and said dismissively;

"Get this clown out of here."

"Let's move it, greasepaint. Time for you to peddle your vaudeville some-where else."

As the ex-maintenance man moved on Fergeson, the officer threw up his hands defensively and shouted, "All right, all right—back off, will ya? I just want in."

"Why?"

London stabbed the single word at the man, flinging it with a tone that forced all the eyes in the room to follow it as it splattered against Fergeson's consciousness. The officer could feel the others watching him, waiting for his reply. After a moment, he admitted;

"Okay, listen . . . maybe this is stupid, but ever since you and me, ever since I saw . . . damn it, I mean–"

"Ever since you saw into his mind," interrupted Morcey, mercifully filling in the words the officer felt too embarrassed to say, "and you saw and heard and felt everything Mr. London has, you haven't been able to figure it all out—right? Even with Ms. Lai Wan layin' hands on you an' all, you're still wonderin' if it's all real, or if you're just crazy. That about it?"

"Yeah," answered Fergeson, still embarrassed, but in some ways greatly relieved. "How'd you know? He pull the same mess on you?"

"Ha—I should be so lucky. No, I've had a front row seat for most all the crap he's been through—seen it myself. And I'll tell you right now, sometimes I don't believe it, either."

"I'd like to get started here," said London with a bit of impatience.

"Listen, Professor," Morcey called to Goward. "Why don't you take officer Fergeson here over to Lisa's office and try and fill him in on things. If anyone could get this guy up to speed . . ."

"Good idea," added London. "You go with Zak; he should be able to not only field any questions you have, but give you a better idea of what we've been through the last few months than anyone. Even me."

Fergeson considered the suggestion for only a trio of seconds, then agreed. As Goward and the officer headed for the door, London added;

"And trust me, if after he fills you in on how goddamned insane and danger-ous this all is, if you want in, believe me, we'll take you. Extra cannon fodder is always appreciated." Goward put his arm around Fergeson's shoulders and moved him through the door, telling him;

"Yes, quite. Come along, and the first thing I'll be certain to explain is the level of gallows humor we're known for around here."

"I'm N.Y.P.D.," the officer responded. "We know something about that."

Then, before the group in Morcey's office could begin their examination of Hardy, suddenly the front door to the Agency opened. All within could tell from the amount of noise made and the time taken to close the door that only one person had entered. Only London knew who that person was.

"Lisa," he called, all thoughts of Hardy forgotten. "In here."

As she entered, the detective's eyes met with hers, and he knew instantly of her confrontation with Joan. Coming to his feet rapidly, he moved around the desk, practically shouting;

"Are you all right? Did anything happen? Did she–"

Lisa put two fingers to London's lips, the warmth and calmness of her touch putting him instantly at ease. Without wasting a moment, he turned to Lai Wan and asked if she could handle things with Hardy without him. The psychometrist sniffed rudely, indicating that "without him" was the way she preferred things. The detective turned away silently and headed straight for his office with Lisa.

Shutting the door, he moved the pair of them to the couch against his back wall. The two sat, simply staring at each other for a long moment. Their hands sought each others out, their fingers intertwining of their own volition. Finally London asked Lisa what had happened. She told him all of it. By the end they were laughing.

"Wow, sounds like you two almost had yourselves an Asian Cinema moment—two beauties, guns blazing, knives flying—could've been great fun for the cat fight fans of the world."

"I doubt it," Lisa answered. "Gun play and hand-to-hand combat aren't exactly my specialties."

"I don't know," answered London softly, his eyes darting down toward their interwoven fingers. "I think you've got great hand-to-hand skills."

"Teddy," Lisa answered, blushing slightly as she did, "I never would have brought anything like this up before. But with this woman here all of a sudden, I have to."

"Whatever you want to know," he told her.

"Us," she said. "I mean, is there an 'us?' Do you want there to be one? I won't fight with you. And I won't cause a scene. You're too important–"

"What?" London's tone betrayed his utter confusion. "I'm too important? What're you talking about?"

"To the world," she answered. "To everyone and everything. You're the Destroyer, picked by Destiny, or Karma, or whatever, to defend the whole world—at least the world. Maybe the whole universe—I don't know. What I do know is that you're important. You're necessary, and if you're being confused or distracted or annoyed by life, it could mean the end of everything."

Holding his hands tightly, a large part of her ready to accept the fact that moment of contact might be the last one between them ever, she could not control the tears building in her eyes as she told him;

"I love you, Teddy . . . I've tried not to burden you with that, but I do. But I don't want you so badly that I'm willing to bring about the end of everything."

"Then," he told her, pulling her closer, "you're less selfish than I am, because I don't give a rat's ass about the rest of the world. If I can't have you, it can all fall into the sun for all I care."

Lisa's lips parted, the slightest of gasps escaping from them. London stared at them, longed for them, but stayed back for another moment. Somehow, without either of them knowing how it happened, their fingers disengaged so their hands could pulls their arms forward, each wrapping themselves about the other. Staring down into Lisa's eyes, London told her gently;

"Since I've met you I've been to Hell and back, and I've made some fairly bizarre side trips in between. My brains have basically been unhinged a half dozen times, and by rights I should have been carted off to the Laughing Academy a long time ago. There's been so many moments I wanted to just give up, and there's only been one thing that's kept me fighting on . . ."

Pulling Lisa closer, leaning into her, nestling his head against hers, cheek to cheek, chin to shoulder, eyes closed to the world so he could more clearly see the path to her heart, he whispered;

"You."

Lisa's arms doubled their grasp reflexively, dragging the detective closer to her. The pair clung to each other so desperately that even solitary atoms were squeezed from between them. More tears than she could count flowed from her, dribbling down her face to spill into London's shoulder. Then, she suddenly realized she could feel moisture on her own shoulder, a new drop splashing against her every time she felt the detective's lashes brush against her neck.

"Oh, Teddy," she sighed, barely able to contain her sudden happiness, "Are you sure? You could have anything. Anyone. I'm just . . . I'm nobody. I'm–"

"You're the woman I love," he whispered.

Lisa's heart froze, missing two entire beats before the paralyzing constriction which had seized her chest released its grasp upon her. Blood flowing again, pounding through her veins, she felt wonderfully dizzy as he said;

"You're the only person I can trust to keep me sane. If you still want me after this whole Pirate Queen mess, then I'm just the luckiest boy in the world. I'm so sor–"

Lisa pulled away from London then, moving her hand to his mouth, smothering his apology.

"No," she told him. "We haven't got very long before it's all going to come crashing in on us again. Don't waste what time we have with things that aren't important."

London looked into the ever-deepening blue of Lisa's eyes, losing himself, forgetting everything except the moment and the woman with whom he was sharing it. In an instant he relived every second of his life since she had first come into it. In many ways he had known nothing but pain and insanity since he had first laid eyes on her. True as that thought was, however, he also knew it had all been worth it.

His flashback covered the seemingly never-ending parade of monsters and madmen Fate had thrown into his path; he saw again the death of close friends, the slaughter of millions, the destruction of cities, all of it dictated by his decisions, all of it done to protect the universe. And, every step of the way, the only consolation he had known, when one terror after another had flayed him or yet another massive swirl of death and destruction was laid at his feet, was the woman in his arms. As the split second of his flashback raced to a close, bringing him from the moment he had first met Lisa up to their current embrace, his mind replayed the last words she had spoken.

"Don't waste what time we have with things that aren't important."

Knowing good advice when he heard it, the detective leaned forward and kissed the woman he loved, the woman he had proved he needed more than life itself. Of course, she kissed him back, matching his urgency and passion, feeling as he did, the rest of the universe slipping away into the darkness. Not caring, as he did, where it went or how long it stayed there.

CHAPTER TWENTY-EIGHT

"**Y**OU WANT THE LONG version or the short one?"

Glancing at the clock, London told his partner, "Much as I hate to say it, I don't think we can afford to miss anything here. Make it the long version."

"Really, Lai Wan, it's pretty much your show. Why don't'cha give the boss da scoop on what you found?"

"Your Mr. Hardy here," the psychometrist indicated the corpse behind them with both the pointing of a finger and the wrinkling of her nose, as if an offensive odor was hanging in the air, "he died in the same manner as the children."

"What?" London tilted his head, somewhat confused. "He was hooked into 'El Dorado,' too?"

"No." Lai Wan said the single word with an unusual tone, one that implied there was a great deal of story to come. "I do not know how else to say this, except to simply tell you that there is no game by that name, at least, not of Mr. Hardy's invention."

The detective's eyes darted from the psychometrist to Cantalupo. Understanding his look, the captain told him;

"She was just explaining all this when you came in. I'll be honest, we weren't getting it, either."

"What we found in the computers we searched was the set-up for a game—its outline and objective, rules, things of this nature. But, the actual mechanics of the game—they do not exist. They never did."

"Then," asked Krandell, his tone revealing a deep impatience with his not being able to understand anything he was being told, "What killed those kids? What killed Hardy? What's this all been about?"

"I believe, in some way I can not actually understand, and certainly he did not, either," Lai Wan started, "our Mr. Hardy here somehow managed to enter into an old-fashioned deal with the Devil. I believe he sold his soul."

Everyone simply stared. Several made noises as if they were about to say something, then went silent once more. With no questions or comments to contend with, the psychometrist continued, telling the assembly;

"Understand that I had to pull much of what I am about to tell you from sources other than Mr. Hardy's remains. Like young John Marshall, Hardy's mind was completely emptied of memory. His clothing was good for a few random impressions, but the thing trying to cover its tracks by sucking its victims dry does not understand our cultures well enough. It does not, for instance, seem to comprehend the significance of the wedding ring."

As several in the room started to form questions, Lai Wan cut them off, saying;

"I have lived with these abilities for some time now. I know how they work. If you wish, for instance, to tap into a man's power fantasies, all you need are his car keys. If you want to see into his secret guilts, all you need is his wedding ring.

"We all have subconscious desires and shames," she continued. "And simple creatures that we are, we all seem to work fairly much in the same manner."

"Hey, hey," asked Morcey with a chuckle, "what about smart guys like me dat ain't got no noose around us yet? Where do we hide our guilt?"

"Someday," Lai Wan answered him quietly, "when you are married, I shall tell you."

"All right," snapped London. "Forgive my mood but I'm tired and getting the feeling our time is running out. C'mon, spill—what's going on? What're we up against? And most important, just what are we going to have to do next?"

"As I am certain you might well imagine," the psychometrist told London, "I am in no way happy about having to give you this information. As best I can tell, Hardy wanted so desperately to be a success, he began to radiate a willingness to do almost anything to become one—especially in his dreams, the place where the subconscious can run wild.

"Something out there somewhere could feel his frustration and, using every iota of power it had, it managed to connect to Hardy. It was a thing sealed away from mankind long ago–"

"Wait a minute," interrupted Cantalupo. "I don't get it. Not that I get much of this, but . . . listen, I'm trying to understand all this. I really am. To be honest, I keep pretending I'm watching a horror movie, and I keep looking at each thing that happens as if I was trying to figure out its plot."

"I've done that," admitted Morcey. "It helps to stick to the British ones." The captain glared, not caring if the ex-maintenance man was joking or not. Forcing himself to continue, he said;

"Okay, whatever—I don't get that last bit. If this thing we're talking about all of a sudden was locked away from the world, how can it reach anyone?"

"A fair and intelligent question, captain," answered Lai Wan. "I suspect two reasons. First, barriers can be weakened over thousands of years, especially if the one imprisoned has been beating against the bars of its cage all along. Second, yes, we all dream at night of things we might wish to possess or become—whathaveyou—but Mr. Hardy, as I said, he was willing to do *anything* to acquire that which he desired." The psychometrist stopped to take a deep breath, struggling with how to explain what she had to get across to so many newcomers. Finally, taking a hint from what the captain himself had said, she continued.

"As in one of your horror movies, the better ones, anyway, Satan never comes looking for people to make deals with for their souls, they always have to start the negotiations by shouting something like, 'I would sell my soul for . . .' whatever they would sell it for. It is the same here. Mr. Hardy liked to pose as a dutiful husband and father, but secretly, what he wanted were the fame and wealth and the home and women such things generally bring one."

"So," London said, "he wants a hot babe and a big house, and he wants them so bad he sends a message out into the ether generally announcing that he'll deal with anything out there that can deliver."

"Quite."

"Y-You mean," officer Fergeson asked, "you really can sell your soul to the Devil?"

"Not the red-faced, pointy-bearded fellow one finds on *The Twilight Zone* or the such," offered Goward, "but oh, indeed, there are demonic things out there, just beyond the veil, always eager to drag some fool off with them."

"Especially someone like Hardy," said London. Suddenly inspired, his mind putting all the pieces together, he blurted, "this thing, it didn't latch onto Hardy just because he was offering his spirit energy up for dinner. This thing saw more potential in him than that. Maybe it didn't understand what a computer game was, but it, it . . ."

The detective stumbled over his words, struggling to line up everything that had just flashed through his mind. Getting back on track after only a second's delay, he blurted;

"My Christ, this thing took energy from Hardy, maybe it was even the force that weakened his first wife. He wants a fancy wife, that gives the thing carte blanche to suck her dry. He wants fame and wealth, and in his mind he sees this game as the way for it to happen. The thing makes him think the game works; he creates what he thinks are nanites, injects them into his subjects–"

"Injections?" Krandell blurted the word with force. "What injections? What're you–"

"I did a little recon out at Future Images tonight," the detective said, cutting the lieutenant off. "Mr. Potts here has pounds of papers and stuff to turn over to you. But the point is, I learned that Hardy gave these kids injections of biological machines, or at least, what he *thought* were machines he'd created, that would allow them to see this game in their heads. But, what happened was, their acceptance of the injection gave this thing access to them. They wanted what was offered, they got it."

Suddenly it was clear to all that London was no longer talking to them, but to himself. Now that he had finally linked all the information they had gathered together, the finished puzzle was pouring out of him.

"Once this thing had its hooks in them," he practically shouted, "to get their souls, it had to give them what they wanted. So, it gave them access to the dreamplane. They created the game themselves within their own minds. And, the closer they got to victory, the more energy they had to surrender. When they finally reached the end of the game, whatever they thought it was, they had to pay up."

"Jesus on a halfshell," muttered Fergeson. "That's goddamned messed-up. But, if that's the case, then at least it's all over now—right? I mean, this Hardy, he's dead. He can't inject nobody else, so . . ." London was just about to agree with the officer, when Lai Wan interrupted them both, saying;

"I'm afraid it's not that simple."

All eyes turned back to the psychometrist.

"This thing with which we are dealing, it has been planning an escape from its prison for millennia. We were very close to stopping it, but we had a disadvantage. There is one thing Mr. Hardy did not write down, which he did not record anywhere, even within his own memory."

Suddenly the room went cold. As tendrils of fear wrapped themselves around the assembly, everyone unconsciously began drawing whatever available heat there was to themselves to help push away the terror clawing at them. Her eyes heavy with sadness, Lai Wan announced;

"This horror we face, apparently it knew exactly how much power it would need to break its bonds. We all know it has beaten us to the lives of twenty-some children and Mr. Hardy here. As we watched young Marshall pass on, we thought he was the end of the food chain. He was not."

"You mean . . ."

"Yes, captain," answered the psychometrist, her voice filled with sorrow, "Mr. Hardy injected some fifty-nine test subjects. And, before any of you ask—no, I am sorry, but I have no more information on them. I can not tell you anything else about them—when they were injected, if they have died, or not, if they gave up trying to win the game—nothing.

"I can only tell you that this thing, whatever it is, its access point to us is in the American Southwest. It is there, just beyond the door that bars it from our world, gathering strength. And, apparently it need gather only a few more souls, and it shall be among us."

CHAPTER
TWENTY-NINE

S EVERAL HOURS LATER FOUND the London Agency in a state of near chaos. Many of those assembled had not slept in over twenty-four hours and the strain was beginning to show. London himself had managed to catch a bit of a nap in the back of Gallbendo's limousine, but it had been a fitful, nightmare-plagued sleep which by the time the sun was coming up the next morning the detective was thinking might have done him more harm than good.

Groggy and finding his temper drawing shorter by the moment, he tried to both calm himself and focus his attention before any more time escaped their ability to use it against what was coming. Afterward, he attempted to get everyone organized and working once more. Cantalupo and his officers he dismissed to start combing the area for any more deaths or comas that would fit the already established pattern. Morcey suggested they make particular inquires at Jewish medical facilities, reminding everyone;

"You know my people like to get that meat in the ground in less than twenty-four hours. It's Hebrew law and it's caused rabbis and doctors to look the other way in more than one occasion that I know of, and I haven't actually been lookin'. Considerin' the ratio of nerds in the wonderful world of Jewish teens . . ."

The captain decided that the ex-maintenance man might have something and assigned Fergeson to the combing of every hospital, clinic or hospice in the tri-state area where they knew the Torah on sight. The officer grumbled something about the rewards of volunteering, then smiled to indicate he was kidding and headed for the elevator. Krandell was given the rest of the New York City metropolitan area to handle.

For himself, Cantalupo saved the chore of going to both the mayor's office and the district attorney's so he could outline what they had discovered about Future Images. With what they now knew, as well as the hard evidence they now had in hand—especially with Hardy dead—he did not think the corporation would be much trouble. Certainly not, he assured everyone, with Potts basically in their camp.

The security chief's task was to coordinate with his company and the city the making of an announcement concerning 'El Dorado.' It was a long shot, but if anyone else who had been injected by Hardy could be found still alive, there was a chance the group could find a way to deny those sacrifices to whatever it was they were fighting.

Pa'sha was asked to check out the available talent—the kind he specialized in—rounding up the best of the available pool on stand-by, in case they had to suddenly take physical action against their still unknown adversary. Taking the weaponeer into his office, London told his old friend;

"Listen, I know I'm asking a lot . . . hell, it seems like every time I turn around, I'm asking a lot—from everyone—but, I, God, man—I just don't know what else to do."

"Little brother," Pa'sha said quietly, "t'ere be no need for despair. My men be mercenaries. You 'ave always paid t'em when you've used them . . ."

"Not what they're worth. You've been giving me bullshit rates and I've been taking them because every time I turn around things just get worse. And here, here I am telling you to line up all the talent you can find, just in case . . . and . . ."

"And what, Theodore?"

London sucked down several deep breaths, rubbing his eyes at the same time. The skin on his fingers felt raw, gritty against his eye lids. His already-throbbing eyes resisted the pressure, rewarding his efforts with further pain. Moving his hand finally, he started in on his entire face, massaging the flesh of it in the hopes of dragging just a few more minutes of consciousness out of some until-then-hidden recess. As he did, he answered his oldest friend;

"And . . . I don't know what good it will do because I'm broke." As Pa'sha simply stared, he explained, "All that's happened since I became the Destroyer, I'm close to tapped out. Lai Wan says this thing's out West somewhere. How am I supposed to get all of us out there? And move weapons, no less? Then there's food and lodging and transportation once we get there–"

"Little brother," interrupted Pa'sha, "w'en did you become such a banker?" The weaponeer said the word as if interchangeable with heroin dealer, necrophiliac or senator. Smiling gently, he offered;

"Please, let us find our enemy and make certain he needs confronting before we worry about de battle. At least, let us do t'is before we worry about paying for de battle."

"Yeah, I could get lucky and get killed before the bills come due."

"Now, t'at's de spirit," laughed the larger man. Slapping the detective on the back, he headed for the door, saying, "If you ask us to secure plastic explosives for an IRA cell, it will indeed be money up front. But, w'en asking us to help save de world, as I 'ave told you before, de mere act of joining into such a noble venture is a form of currency in itself, don't you know. A man can live many years on dough and water, but he can become immortal by drawing a line in de sand against de devils of t'is life and t'en standing resolute on de other side of it."

"May be," answered London, "but last time I looked, bullets still cost money, and we won't be able to buy any lead if we ain't got the bread."

"Auuucchhh," groaned the larger man. "Leave de bad rhymes to de gutter snipes who t'ink t'ey de music." Pulling aside his jacket just enough to reveal the stock of the compact machine gun hanging there, Pa'sha said, "t'is is the sweetest boom-boom t'ere is, and all de poetry we will need."

The two men faced each other for a moment, then both moved forward at the same instant, enfolding each other in their arms. They did not so much hug as they did hold onto each other, drawing one another closer until the very molecules of their skin began to mesh. Professor Goward had once explained that such an action between any two people was a throwback to ancient times when people believed that doing such would mingle their auras, giving each party strength as the current surrounding their bodies fused one unto the other.

Of course, he had explained, strangers rarely received more than a tiny degree of benefit from such behavior. It was something that worked between either those who knew each other well, and with affection, or between those so open and honest with the world and those around them they could do no other.

After they released one another, Pa'sha slapped London on the back and headed for the door. As he turned the knob, the detective asked his friend to send in Lai Wan and Goward. When the two came in, looking just as drawn and tired as everyone else, he asked first if the psychometrist had come any closer to pin-pointing their adversary. She told him;

"Yes, actually. It seems that since the creature was obliging enough to leave traces of itself all over the Internet, I was, with Lisa's help, able to track it back to its lair. It is, as was suspected earlier, in the Southwest. To be more specific, it is within the region of the Grand Canyon."

"You've got it zeroed," the detective asked. "I mean, you can find it on a map?"

After Lai Wan assured London this was the case, he turned to his middle desk drawer as he asked Goward to come forward. As the professor came around to the side of his desk where the detective indicated, he asked;

"What have you got there?" London pulled a small bundle from his drawer, a thing the size and shape of a bulky fountain pen wrapped in a dark piece of cloth.

"I turned over all the papers, discs, worksheets and all the such which Hardy had smuggled out of Future Images to Cantalupo," the detective answered as he rolled up his shirt sleeve, "all but this."

Unwrapping the slight package, London revealed a hypodermic containing an orange liquid. Handing it to Goward, he told him;

"This is the crap Hardy used to send those kids into the clutches of whatever is out there. The easiest way for us to do any surveillance on what we're up against is for you to slug this one way ticket into my veins."

Goward instantly began to protest, but London put up his hand, cutting the professor off. Turning to Lai Wan, he asked the psychometrist;

"You know more about this thing we're up against, what it can do, how easily it can grab or hold onto someone, et cetera, than any of us. I'm asking you, what do you think my chances are of being able to get close to this thing, study it, find out what it is, and get away again?"

The woman considered the detective for a moment, then finally said, "I think you are right to want to do this. We do not know what this thing is, what it can do, nothing."

"But, it's only a placebo . . ."

"It's the thing we're looking for's placebo," said London. "That's connection enough."

"Now, surely . . ." Lai Wan cut Goward off with a stare, telling him;

"Zackary, there is no other way. Our Mr. London is headstrong and rash. He is careless and unpredictable. But, he is none of these things in the service of anything but the highest ideals. As much as I would deeply wish to continue to dislike him, it is hard to do so and to also maintain one's self-respect."

"But . . ."

Goward struggled to protest, but the look of determination in both London's and Lai Wan's eyes let him know such was useless. After only a few minutes more of bluster and whining, the professor found a vein in the detective's extended arm and injected the oddly-swirling orange fluid into it.

It only took a handful of seconds for London to pass into an unconscious state.

It took even less time for him to begin screaming.

CHAPTER THIRTY

*B*IT BY BIT, FOLLOW *the gold* . . .
   Darkness broke through the void of time, burrowing its way along the fabric of existence with crab-clawed pincers that never ceased in their single-minded efforts. It was a hushed attack, a concerted, focused attempt to assault the curved wall erected countless eons in the past to restrain the assault's master over the millennium. And one powdery crumb at a time, the darkness did its work.

Near-countless centuries had been put forth toward reaching the barrier. A veritably endless system of curbs and hindrances had been placed around that which needed to be confined. Fetters both physical and extraordinary had been employed, magic and iron alloyed and set to entomb the horror that would elsewise walk the world unrestricted. But, those limits had been set when the world was fresh borne, and thinking man an unanticipated future inhabitant.

London stepped into the dreamplane, focusing on the hissing voice, following the orange trail of slime-encrusted blobs it had littered across the purple plains. His vision was partially obscured by the images of El Dorado his opponent had learned to project, but he ignored the phantoms, refusing to allow them even the partial life of the game pattern.

The detective could tell he was working his way inside a prison, one where all but the final boundary had been breached. Over the millennium, the multiple, complicated restraints had aged, weakened, giving that which was hobbled within the opportunity to work toward escaping its shackles—toward roaming the galaxy at will once more.

Free.

Of both bonds and conscience. Free to do as it would, without hindrance or repression. As it did in the past, when the universe ran cold with oceans of death, and the Darkness smiled.

Bit by bit, follow the gold . . .

London inspected the mortar of time used in the last obstruction of the prison, found it splintered and crumbled. Beyond the singular barrier he felt the silent claws as they continued to rend the last of the yoking walls.

What the goddamned hell is back there, wondered the detective. He felt a terrible shudder passing through the scenery all about him, heard the tinkling of faraway warning bells set in place by forces so far removed from Earth and humanity he could not even begin to speculate on their origins.

How in God's name did you find your way to us?

Beyond the furthest boundaries of human understanding, the bonding fabric of the final ancient rampart ignored London's question as it continued to be undermined. Slowly, with a wicked caution borne of diabolically cold calculation, some new horror was dragging itself toward the Earth once more. With exceptional cunning, it had reined in its essence, masking itself and its actions completely.

It had prepared for this moment since before the beginning of time. It was not about to fail, this it knew. It would be free. It would.

Bit by bit, it continued to whisper, *bit by bit* . . .

Within its mind, the pulsing horror thought to itself with rare contentment that soon the cosmic balance it was owed would finally be put aright. Its eternal imprisonment would be compensated, avenged and made just by the destruction of the Earth and the subjugation of each soul ever to have existed on the planet. When it was done, it promised itself, every spirit ever brought to glorious life from the beginning of time would be sucked away into its black grip. And that, of course, would only be the beginning.

For with that much power gathered, finally the moment would be prime for the grandest of challenges—the extreme and elemental contest—the ultimate conquest of the universe, its long-awaited assault on its brothers, their father, the end of its ordeal, the sweeping away of mankind. The conquest of the stars.

The New Order.

At last.

London stood on the wind-swept dreamplane, staring at the dark wall before him. Behind it was something that was struggling to reach the Earth. Its entrance point there was the American Southwest but, he realized, it could be stopped there on the dreamplane as well as at home—had been stopped, in fact, some long time ago by . . .

By whom, he wondered. As he did, a hundred voices within his mind spoke up, some offering the names of long gone alien shamans and priests, most wailing that whoever had locked the hidden terror away did not matter. The encroaching smell of the thing beyond screamed of its intentions toward mankind, its sucking greed to have all the souls that ever existed, to harvest, thrash, enslave and finally digest them merely as energy for some conflict to come was all too clear.

After his wandering moment of curiosity, though, London finally decided it did not matter who or what it was that had turned the key and locked the thing he was so near to away. His main concern, he decided, was that it needed to be secured once more and that if it had once been imprisoned, it could damn well be imprisoned again.

But how, the detective asked himself. Running his hands over and through the mystical entrapments before him, his mind reeled at the complexity of the mystic seals he was encountering.

Who had done this? What had done this? And more importantly, how was it accomplished? And, could it possibly be accomplished once more?

Could it, he wondered. Would Goward know how? Would anyone?

Would anyone know what?

London froze. It was one thing to have the monstrosity within his head sending out its random message, but to have the thing address him directly . . .

So, he thought, it's aware of my presence. It's still on the other side of the barrier. That has to count for something.

Yes, Still—but not for long, little london thing, not for long . . .

The detective turned involuntarily, as if whatever he was facing had somehow escaped, was suddenly festering there beside him. In the far away distance, lightning shattered the ever-growing mountaintops, illuminating everything in every direction, including the figure that has somehow come to within a few feet of London undetected.

Bit by bit, the voice continued monotonously, *bit by bit . . .*

CHAPTER
THIRTY-ONE

S OME TIME HAD PASSED since London had received the injection which had allowed him to track the thing they were searching for to its lair. After his initial violent meeting, his eyelids had lowered, his breathing had gone shallow and his body had reclined, slumped sideways in his chair behind his desk. Goward sat next to him, monitoring his condition. For the last half hour, Lisa had sat in the same room on the couch opposite the detective's desk. She did not bother the professor with needless questions. She simply sat—waiting.

The woman had raced for London's office, with Morcey right behind her, when the detective had first begun screaming almost immediately after his injection. He had not struggled, passing almost instantly into unconsciousness. And yet, even limp, half-sliding out of his chair, he had continued to cry out until Lai Wan had gone into his mind and eased the pain triggering his automatic defenses. As she had then explained;

"He has entered the dreamplane, has found the thing I so briefly encountered earlier."

"You weren't in any pain," Lisa blurted. "Why is Teddy screaming?"

"I only met the merest tendril of the thing we seek, and even then I met it in, pardon the expression, our own back yard. Theodore has obviously taken himself to some meeting place far closer. I do not believe his soul is in any pain. It is his body, reacting to the strain of coming so close to this thing, which was in pain, at least, initially. I have blocked his nerve centers, however. His body should rest now."

"But," Lisa questioned, "I don't understand. What's causing the pain?"

"This thing eats souls," Goward reminded her. "Theodore has now placed his soul, brimming over with power as it is, in close proximity to our enemy. It was, most likely, the force of this thing's hunger that tore at Theodore so."

Lisa had gone back to her own office after that and continued to work for a while. It had not been long, however, before she had returned to the suite's main office. Taking up her position as far from Goward and London as possible, she strove to remain as removed from the area as she could to keep from interfering. She refused to accidentally disrupt the proceedings, to allow her love for the detective to trigger some sort of tragedy. But, on the other hand she simply had to be near him—had to be able to see him, to be able to train all her senses on him.

Having no immediate assignment, Morcey had taken up a position on the couch in the front reception area. He knew he would fall asleep in moments, but he also knew the slight noise of the front door would awaken him instantly. The ex-maintenance man believed he was far too tense to fall into a deep sleep. His theory was confirmed some twenty minutes after Lisa had returned to London's office when the slight creak of the suite's front door knob being turned brought him instantly awake. Before the door could open, he had his over-sized automatic in his hand, waiting to see who or what might enter.

"Such a greeting, Mr. Morcey," sighed the Pirate Queen. "Why is it everyone involved with this establishment wants to point weapons at me?"

"That shouldn't really be all that hard for you to figure out, should it," responded the balding man. "I mean, I thought you were supposed to be some kinda smart. But, anyway, any particular type of trouble you came by to cause today?"

"No trouble," she said quietly. "Please, I just want to help. Is Teddy here?"

"Teddy," came Lisa's voice from the doorway of the detective's office, "is indisposed right now." Her tone cold and even and begging for an excuse to growl, she added;

"I don't know, or really care, if you believe me or not, but right now we really have more important things to do than deal with your stupid infatuations. We have a world to save–"

"I know; that's why I came."

Morcey sat on the couch feeling vastly uncomfortable between the two women and somewhat foolish still holding his weapon at the ready. Quietly, he asked;

"Could ya close the door, sweetheart, just so if anything's followin' ya the noise of it breakin' in will give us a second or two to react." Smiling, Joan stepped into the reception area and closed the door behind her. Once it was secured, she turned back to Lisa and said;

"Listen to me, please; you know that everything has passed from between Theodore and myself, everything mystical, anyway. But it is–"

This time it was Lisa's turn to cut the older woman off.

"What are you talking about?"

"Theodore, he . . ." the Pirate Queen stared for an instant, and then a sad smile crossed her face as she added, "ahhhh, he did not tell you. Of course not. Why would he? So much easier for him to punish himself if you did not know."

The older woman shuddered then, making a pitiful noise which begged such sympathy from the room that Morcey reholstered his weapon unconsciously. Lisa took several steps forward into the room with realizing it, then stopped as the Pirate Queen lifted her head once more. Shaking her head slightly, sadly, she whispered;

"Perhaps if I was to tell you all that has happened, maybe it will make up for some of the problems I have caused." Sitting on the couch opposite the one Morcey had claimed earlier, Joan told the pair everything that had happened since first she had seen London in the museum. The woman kept her story short, sticking to the facts as best she could, taking the pair quickly up to the moment when she and London had been left alone in the precinct house hallway.

"At that point, either Theodore tricked me into taking him to the dreamplane, or he hatched a plan rather quickly once there. Either way, he got me to merge our souls into one being." As Lisa's eyebrows went up, the Pirate Queen laughed softly;

"Please, do not think of it as sex. Yes, it was a wonderful feeling, and beautiful, but it was not a thing of love." She made to explain the moment, paused for a second, then started once more, saying;

"When a parent first holds their child in their hands, in that first moment of contact after birth, there is a flow between them, when for just an instant they become one being. That is the point to where he took me. But, while I was caught up in the moment, he was using it to pull from me all he had previously allowed to enter."

Joan sat quietly, letting her words sink in. As Lisa digested it all, she searched the Pirate Queen's face for traces of deception. She found none. Still not completely convinced, however, she asked;

"That wasn't your story when you came to my apartment."

"I know," Joan admitted. "My ultimate foolishness. When I realized finally that Theodore had severed his connection with me, I hoped to win him by tricking you into severing your connection with him. It was silly, and desperate—I know. But love sometimes makes people do desperate things."

Slowly Lisa crossed the room to the couch, taking a seat near the Pirate Queen. As Lai Wan entered the room behind her, the psychometrist said to the general assembly;

"We are caught in the middle of a terrible conflict, and have no time for distractions. Allow me to assure you both," she narrowed her words to just Lisa and Joan, "that each of you has been telling the other the truth. This is good, for it makes what I am about to propose that much simpler."

Both women turned to stare at Lai Wan, as did Morcey. Pulling her shawl more tightly around her, the psychometrist said;

"It has been made clear that for the Earth to be spared the disaster currently headed in its direction, a great deal of currency is going to have to be acquired."

"Yeah," replied Morcey. "Guns, ammo, men, movin' it all out West, gettin' vehicles . . ."

"Thank you," responded Lai Wan, cutting the balding man off sharply. "Once Mr. London recovers from his coma, and I am fully confident he shall, this will become the next stumbling block in our path. I believe I have a suggestion on how we might remove it for him."

All three of the others simply continued to stare. Seeing they had no questions, Lai Wan told them in a quieter voice;

"It has become a game I play within my mind for some time now, the thought of how I could use my abilities to raise great quantities of money quickly. Understand, until now I have never actually considered acting on any of these ideas. Doing so has merely been a form of relaxation for me, my answer to doing crossword puzzles, as it were.

"Be all that as it may," she said quietly, "there is one scenario we might be able to accomplish in less than half a day. It is a scheme I have worked out quite completely, actually. The only problem is, it requires the assistance of a talented second. Someone familiar with such things as the spinning of roulette wheels, the playing of cards, et cetera. Do you know of anyone whom might fit such a bill, Ms. De Molina?"

The Pirate Queen smiled. Stretching out her arms, eliminating the kinks and cramps which lack of sleep had started to build, she purred;

"I might be able to suggest someone for you—quite easily, in fact."

"Mr. Morcey," said Lai Wan, "I am certain the professor should remain here by Mr. London's side. In the meantime, do you think you could find a vehicle and a driver to take the rest of us to Atlantic City?"

The ex-maintenance man jumped to his feet, excitement animating every cell in his body as he shouted;

"All right—road trip!"

CHAPTER
THIRTY-TWO

L ONDON SCREAMED, HIS EYES bulging, throat torn raw. His arms waving, feet kicking, he threw himself over backwards, crashing his chair against the back wall, his shoes scuffing the large window behind him before he fell into a crumpled heap on the floor. Goward, violently startled by the detective's sudden return to consciousness, nearly fell out of his own chair. Half-asleep when London's first cry cut through the air, he threw himself forward, grabbing hold of the flailing detective as best he could, shouting;

"Theodore, Theodore! For God's sake, snap out of it! Wake up, wake up before you throttle me to death!"

Others crowded into the office as London slowly returned to consciousness. Second by second his violence contained itself as the various facets of his mind readjusted themselves to the normal, waking world.

"I'm, I'm back," he muttered slowly, rubbing at his face, working the fatigue out of his eyes.

"You are, indeed, boss," responded Morcey. "'Bout time, too. We was beginnin' ta think you were gonna take up permanent residence in dreamland there."

"No . . . no, not yet, anyway . . ."

London rose from the floor slowly, half-helping Goward to his feet, half being helped by him. Looking around himself, the detective noted the position of the sun in the sky and quickly realized he had been out for quite some time. Shaking hands with the professor, he also shook his head to clear his mind, asking at the same time;

"Looks like I've been out for a while. What time is it, anyway?"

"About two in the afternoon," responded his partner. "You've been gone for about a day and a half. Learn anything useful?"

London asked for something to drink, hot if possible. Morcey exited for a moment, returning with a cup of coffee from the agency's small kitchen set-up. The detective sipped carefully, using the heat of the brew to help sooth his blistered throat. As he did so, he told his partner as well as Goward of his time on the dreamplane.

He let them know he had not seen their adversary, that he had only come close to it. He described the system of magical seals which had been used to imprison the thing, both those broken as well as those still holding. The detective described the power he could feel beyond, as well as the incalculable, rampaging anger and lust of the creature being contained. Then, he told them of his encounter.

"Things got easier for me after a while—I'm guessing Lai Wan performed some tender mercy for which, believe me, I'm grateful. Anyway, it didn't take long to establish that we'd pinpointed the thing we're after. While I was trying to figure out what we could do against it, though . . ." London grew quiet for a long moment, then finally added;

"I had a visitor."

"What?" Goward shook his head violently, startled beyond his ability to contain himself.

"Who dropped in on you there, boss?"

"It was the Spud."

Before the detective had become the Destroyer, his best friend in the world had been Timothy Bodenfelt, an unassuming, but outspoken doctor who ran a small clinic in Manhattan's Village district. He was much beloved by the community, known by all as the Spud, a friend to any in need. When London had needed help to stop the invasion of the universe by an unspeakable force from beyond, he had been a friend to all mankind by sacrificing his life for the greater good. The only problem for London was the fact it was the detective who had been forced to take his friend's life so that greater good might be achieved.

"The Doc showed up," asked Morcey, trying to make light of the subject. "How's he doin'?"

"Still dead," answered London grimly. "But he sends his regards."

"Tell me, Theodore," said Goward, "I'm certain there must be a degree of pain in talking about him, but what was he doing there? What part could he have in all this?"

"None yet. But, you know, it seems I can't go to the dreamplane for very long before he shows up. Anyway, it seems that the creature we're after didn't get Hardy after all. The Spud did."

London explained that from his side of the veil, his old friend had been watching much of what had been happening. Bodenfelt's specter had not been aware of the situation until the detective and the others had been pulled into it. Afterward, however, it had waited for whatever chance it might have to lend assistance.

"Some others have died as well, but the Spud's been holding them up, just like Hardy. In fact, if it wasn't for him, the game would already be over."

"What do you mean, Theodore?"

"I mean this critter that's trying to get at us, if it'd gathered the rest of the souls the Spud is keeping from it, it would already've busted out. It's tearing him apart, atom by atom, but he's holding on, trying to give us the time we need to get our act together, but . . ."

London paused, tormented by the vision of his friend being fragmented by the monster attempting to tear down the walls of its prison. Taking a deep breath, however, he raised his head and said;

"There's so much. This thing, it's connected to . . . to so much. As it's tortured the Spud, every contact between them has revealed more of its origins. This thing has three, for lack of a better word, 'brothers,' that are all locked away from this world, too. Care to guess who 'daddy' is?"

Goward stared, flustered. Morcey looked deep into London's eyes, then said;

"Oh, you're shittin' me."

"That's right—its name is Fai'gnaner, brother to Ythogtha, Zoth-Ommog and Ghatanothoa. They're the four sons of Q'talu, and they're all in a race to get back here and destroy the universe."

The two men simply stared at London. They had no words. The detective had no more at the moment, either. Sipping at his coffee, working to relive his strained throat, he finally said;

"We were lucky we stopped Laub when we did. Hardy's weakening of the barriers holding Fai'gnaner are what allowed Q'talu to work through his son to empower Laub. That boob's soul's also part of what's powering this thing's prison break . . ."

"Serves the asshole right."

"Well, I can't argue with that, Paul," agreed London weakly. "But we've got a problem, and it's a big one. This thing's entrance to our world is in the Grand Canyon all right; it's below the Colorado River, and it's sitting on the focal point of three gigantic hot spots. They're hundreds of miles apart—fault zones where the magma never broke through the surface but is still there, bubbling, waiting to smash through to the surface."

"I saw somethin' about that on the History Channel. You mean like the San Francisco volcanic field, which for some reason is over in Arizona? And that lava field on that Indian reservation, some kind of dome . . ."

London nodded his head slowly—sadly.

"That sounds right. The area between them covers thousands of square miles. Thousands. If we fail, it we can't stop this thing . . . the entire Western half of the country will simply fall into the ground in the first few seconds of its release." The detective sipped his coffee again, then added;

"There'll be volcanoes breaking out everywhere, a maelstrom of hurricanes of fire will spread out in every direction. Earthquakes that ramble across states, then into other countries. In minutes cracks will split open the shores, Grand Canyon-sized fissures will break open and let the oceans run into the center of the Earth." London paused for a moment, looked at both the men in his office, then laughed weakly as he said;

"You can guess how long the world will hold together after that." The detective threw back the last of his coffee. Setting his cup down on his desk, he swallowed gingerly, testing the strained section of his throat. Finding it feeling somewhat soothed, he stretched his head to the right then the left, pulling the kinks out of it. As he did, Morcey said;

"But, like the guy said in 'Holy Grail,' we're not dead yet. We still got a chance—right?"

"I don't know," answered London wearily. "An effort like this . . . we're going to need a lot of fire power to take this thing down. It's too close to our world to just hold back through magical means. What I'm saying is, from what the Spud could tell me, from what I could see, this Fai'gnaner thing has already partially reached our plane of existence. That means we're going to have to go in and drive it back in person before anyone can seal the gates again. Men you hire to go on suicide runs generally want big bucks and they want it up front.

"I just don't know where we're going to be able to get the money in time." Then, London's mood shifted, his lethargy transformed into a rage by his growing desperation. Slamming his desk top with both hands, he shouted;

"In time? There is no time. We couldn't even go out and steal enough money in time. We'd need to be set to go right now—on our way . . . Goddamnit, I don't–"

It was at that moment the detective noticed Morcey's attempts to attract his attention. As he calmed down once more, he realized his partner had been waving his hands, trying to distract him from his worries since he had first mentioned their need for capital. Focusing himself, London asked;

"Yes? Something I should know?"

"Boss, we are ready to go." As the detective raised one eyebrow, Morcey smiled with self-satisfaction while Goward explained;

"Yes, Theodore, Lai Wan, Lisa and Ms. de Molina took it upon themselves to go to Atlantic City and try their hands at some of the gaming tables."

"I drove," said Morcey. Standing, he headed for the door to the foyer, throwing over his shoulder, "and when the money bags got too heavy I hired bell boys to carry them."

"What? What are you two telling me?"

"We're saying," answered Goward, reaching into his jacket pocket for his pipe and pouch, "that the ladies made a united front and went from casino to casino until they had reached a tally of some two million and three quarters dollars." Stuffing the bowl of his pipe, he added;

"Apparently one million was won at one time on a giant gimmick slot machine that everyone gets one shot at. Lai Wan simply set it off when Paul here pulled it. The officials were quite chagrined, I'm told."

"If that means they was as pissed off as metal heads at a Trapp Family Singers festival," laughed Morcey, returning to his partner's office, "then yeah, they surely was."

Setting fire to the tobacco in his pipe, Goward drew in a great breath of smoke, then released it, adding, "Pa'sha said it was more than enough to do everything needed. He's already in Las Vegas, organizing your troops."

"You bet," added Morcey. Sunglasses mounted on his face and a promotional cap for the movie "Alien" on his head, one which pronounced him the captain of the Nostromo, the balding man added, "he said he was able to get a great deal on some rocket launchers. So, when ya wanta leave?"

London took in everything he had been told slowly. His eyes went from Morcey's face to Goward's, then back again. Standing slowly, he placed his hands in the small of his back, then pushed, forcing the cramped pain which had settled there out of his body. A grumbling sigh escaped his lips, chasing the last of the tension from his system. He stood quietly for a moment, then told the pair before him;

"You know this is no lark, don't you? People are going to die. Plenty of them. People we know. Maybe some we know real well."

"It's true," agreed Morcey. "But hey—it's better than every one, every where dyin', ain't it, boss?"

London turned to Goward. The professor shrugged, exhaling a thick cloud of firm-smelling smoke as he added, "The man makes a good point—really."

Pulling open his bottom drawer, the detective pulled out his shoulder holster and the sheath for his knife. His .38, Betty, and his blade, Veronica, were firmly secured within their pockets. As he pulled them quickly into place, Goward asked;

"You might want to rethink your choice of accessories there, Theodore. Most airports don't allow such things, you know."

"Airports?" London said the word with a comical Mexican accent, then snapped his fingers as he added, "we don't need no stinkin' airports."

CHAPTER THIRTY-THREE

THE NEXT MOMENT FOUND London, Morcey and Goward standing in the heat of the Nevada sun. Goward shuddered, the passage through the dreamplane, even though somewhat expected, left him more than slightly shaken. The older man had spent his lifetime investigating the supernatural, making enemies beyond the veil. Passing through territory where one of his past encounters might catch up to him, where any of them might sense him—remember him, come after him once again—left him more than a little unsettled. Morcey, on the other hand felt somewhat differently.

"E-Yow!" he exclaimed. Throwing his cap in the air, his foot-long ponytail flapping in the dry, desert breeze, he shouted, "Now that's entertainment. Can we ride again, Daddy?"

"Not now, son," answered London, a sudden lightness coming over his manner. "Daddy's got work to do."

Keying in on Morcey's thoughts, the detective had simply moved the three of them to the point where his partner knew Pa'sha and the others to be. Adjusting to their surroundings, the trio found themselves in front of a massive building, one their eyes could only register as a black shape due to the blasting light of the desert sun pouring down upon them. Looking past the driving rays with other senses, however, London could see that the structure was an airplane hangar, one that seemed perfect for their needs.

The hulk was large, but old, forgotten—a thing obviously unused for quite some time. The landscape surrounding told him no one came through the area very often; indeed, throwing his abilities out to their fullest, the detective could tell that outside of the activity the place had seen in the last two days, no one had set foot within a mile of the hanger in over eight months.

"Hey," cried London, making his voice loud enough to announce their sudden arrival. "What's a guy got to do to get a drink of water around this dump?" The detective's question was answered by the sound of a chain running through a wheel, the rusted front exitway rolling up into the rafters, and the words;

"Why, he just have to be asken, man . . . don't chu know, now?"

Dearon and several other of the Murder Dogs came forth out of the interior of the hanger. Clasping London on the shoulder with one hand while taking the detective's right with the other, the younger man said;

"Dot's some kind of silent approach you've got there. Maybe you be teachin' it to me sometime."

London shook the wiry Jamaican's hand with a solid grasp, then pulled the man close into his body for a hug. As they embraced, he whispered to him;

"If we live through this, I just might try."

"T'ere we go, dey happy-go-lucky white boy we all know and love, I tol' dey Daddy-man you'd be returnin' to us." Dearon stepped back from the detective, smiling, asking him;

"You are back up to speed—right, man? We ain't be got to hold your hand no more dis time?"

"Yeah, I think you can stop charging the Agency the nursemaid rate, and go ahead and move it on up to the bad ass rate."

"Now," answered the thin man, slapping his hands together, then forming them into two tight fists which he held close to either side of his face, "those be dey words dat make dey whole world happy."

Several of the Murder Dogs laughed at the comment, as well as Morcey. London ignored them all, concentrating on knocking back as much of the water he had been brought as possible. Downing the entire bottle in two gulps, he wiped his mouth and then asked for another. The detective, of course, was not simply trying to cool himself in the face of the desert's heat. He was severely dehydrated, not having eaten or drunk anything for over two days while his consciousness had been wrestling with the outer reaches of Fai'gnaner's consciousness. Indeed, he had gone so long without, London did not even realize he was hungry until he had slaked his thirst.

Finishing his third water, the detective immediately asked if there was anything to eat at the hanger. Dearon returned with a large cardboard box which he deposited in front of London. Inside, the detective found a variety of slim, brown cardboard boxes. Picking one up for inspection, he turned it over in his hands, saying slowly;

"And . . . what have we here?"

"Oh my stars and garters," laughed Morcey. "C-rations." When London simply narrowed his eyes, the balding man explained, "MREs—Meals Ready to Eat—it's Army field chow, dehydrated food. When I volunteer at the local synagogue back home, takin' the kids campin' and stuff, we use this all the time."

"And *you*," the detective pointed at his partner, "enjoy meals made out of *this?*"

"Hey, you're goin' campin', not to da Ritz." Morcey laughed, then added, "Whatd'ya want, egg in yer beer? Suck it up, boss."

London studied the small brown packet he had picked at random, which turned out to be Omelet With Ham. The extremely plain cardboard box gave him the usual list of ingredients, told him the total weight of the contents was six ounces, that it had been packed by Land O'Frost, Inc., who were somewhere in Lansing, Illinois, and that it had all been inspected and passed by the Department of Agriculture. Opening the box he found a small packet made of some kind of silver material half way between plastic and metal.

"Oh," he complained, "you have got to be kidding me."

"Sorry," answered Dearon with a smile which threw suspicion on his apology, "but it's the desert. Daddy-man told us to be bringin' in men and guns. He didn't say nuthin' bout no refrigerators, so dis is what you get."

By this point even Goward was beginning to find London's consternation amusing. The detective rifled through the container once more, this time pulling out two more boxes like the first, one promising Potatoes Au Gratin, the another containing Applesauce. All three boxes were the same size, made of the same dull cardboard. Beginning to feel sorry for his partner, Morcey held up some other selections, announcing;

"Ahhhh, it ain't so bad. Look—I got a Roast Beef dinner here; and here's Macaroni & Cheese. C'mon, what'll be, boss?"

Putting the three boxes he was holding in one hand, London picked up several others, then stooped down to grab an old, rusted wheel rim that happened to be under the table on which Dearon had first set down his crate. Placing all his selections inside the rim, the detective sighed, then simply absorbed everything he was holding into his system.

"Man," exclaimed Morcey, "and people call me a fussy eater."

Most of the Murder Dogs laughed, slapping each other on the palm. Morcey and Goward returned to trying to make their own selections. While they did so, London returned to the front of the hanger. His intention was to walk around the building, making a tour of inspection as it were. He was halted by the sight of several heavy-duty military vehicles approaching from the distance. A quick mental inspection assured him that Pa'sha had the shotgun position in the first truck.

Strolling out onto the tarmac, the detective waited for the vehicles to arrive. As the first one rolled into the gated area in front of the hanger, Pa'sha threw open his door and was actually crossing the distance between himself and his old friend before the truck had come to a complete halt. London had just enough time to see officer Fergeson, as well as Lieutenant Krandell, Captain Cantalupo and security chief Potts disembark as well before the weaponeer reached the detective's position and threw his arms about him.

"Little brother," he said softly as the two embraced, "how quickly you move these days."

"Yeah," croaked London, the breath crushed from him as always when he found himself in Pa'sha's grip, "good to see you, too."

"You are well?" the weaponeer's eyes scanned his friend's face with concern, while he asked;

"You are ready—yes? No? T'is has taken too much out of you, maybe? Tell me."

The detective was just about to comply when the front and side doors opened on a smaller transport that had been hidden in the middle of the larger vehicles. Lai Wan, Lisa, and Joan exited, all of them heading for the two men's position.

"Well," he said, greeting the trio, "this answers my first question. Now I know where you all are."

"And," asked the Pirate Queen, "are you pleased to find us all in one place?"

"We're not going to find too many volunteers for a deal like this," he answered honestly, "so all hands are welcome. Besides, if you three can make it work . . ."

Lisa rolled her eyes, then placing both her index fingers against London's chest, she asked;

"Maintaining a relationship with you is going to be a little bit trickier than with most men, isn't it?"

"With moi?" The detective said the phrase with comic exaggeration, then said, "Hey, you think life with me is tough, wait until you see what Pa'sha brought home for dinner."

CHAPTER
THIRTY-FOUR

S OME SEVEN HOURS LATER, the team assembled in the desert was finally ready to begin its assault. Dinner had turned out to be far more substantial than originally indicated. The C-rations had been Dearon's little joke on London. Those stationed at the hanger had indeed been using them, but the Murder Dog lieutenant had known Pa'sha was bringing more substantial provisions with him when he returned with the rest of the attack squad.

Under the spectacular glory of the desert sky the, by then, quite large assembly had feasted on roasted chickens and beef, baked potatoes and carrots and corn on the cob, as well as all manner of breads. The weaponeer knew something of battle psychology, at least, the way it applied to the types of warriors he lead. Open pits had been dug and lined with rocks. Wood had been piled into vented pyramids and their food had been cooked. Simply, basically—wonderfully.

Gathered together in the dark, sitting on the ground, eating with their hands, the mercenaries quickly fell into a fast and easy comradeship with each other. Throwing hot food one to another, drinking and laughing, whether or not they knew the warrior next to them before dinner began or not, by the time the initial logs had turned to embers, the bonding Pa'sha needed had begun. To ensure its growth, he staggered to his feet, pretending to feel the drag of too many potatoes more than he did. Approaching the largest of their cooking fires, he made hand gestures and throat clearing noises that indicated he wanted everyone's attention. Once he had it, he announced;

"I am so very delighted to have you all here tonight, dey have not made de words for me to express my joy. But now t'at everyone has filled their bellies and washed down de sand from t'is afternoon's little drive, I thought I might say a few words."

London sat on the ground, his back against a make-shift wall of ammo crates and parachute packs, his arm around Lisa. He knew where his friend was going, had been there several times before when the weaponeer had made the same journey. Pulling Lisa closer, he pushed his back into the packs behind him and closed his eyes, listening to the stir of the crowd as his big brother announced;

"In just a few hours, we be goin' up against somet'ing like none of you has ever seen before. Now, I tell you true, every man and woman here, I don't t'ink any of you is the shy type."

The weaponeer's words brought roars of laughter from around the fire. Besides his own Murder Dog squad, Pa'sha had brought in nearly two hundred of the top professional soldiers who could be hired on such short notice. They were all battle-hardened, reliable individuals. They were not yet, however, a team. Sharing a meal had been step one to getting them there. Sharing a good laugh was step two.

"But, tonight, I tell you right now, you goin' to be seein' t'ings, if you ain't white now, dere be one damn big chance you be white by morning."

"That's great, brother," cried out a voice in the darkness. "Then maybe I won't have so many assholes givin' me the willy-eye on the subway."

"Dat ain't cause yo black," laughed the man next to the first. "Dat just cause yo ugly."

The response was followed by the sound of a solid punch which was then met by another. More laughter sprang up around the camp. Pa'sha chuckled himself, then set his deep, booming voice against all other sound until he had his audience back. While two of the Murder Dogs came up on either side of the fire before him, the weaponeer shouted;

"Tonight, I tell you now, I tell you like it is, we be goin' into Hell itself. You was told t'is before, but I be makin' sure now you understands what is bein' said to you—make no mistake about it—before de night is through, you all goin' to be seein' t'ings you ain't *never* seen before. Am I lyin' to dese boys, little brother?"

London maintained his seat, but opened his eyes wide as he shouted in response;

"I wish it was lies. I'd give everything I have if even just half of it was lies."

"T'ere's de facts, you jackals. Dis man, he know. He done been t'ere; he done seen de big evil up close and personal. He done kick its ass, too; he done bust its head. I know, cause I been t'ere each time."

The crowd grew quiet as Pa'sha spoke. Some continued to chew at their food, sip their drinks, but all were listening. Sensing their attention focusing sharply, the weaponeer shouted;

"But t'ese contests with de t'ings beyond, t'ey cost. T'ey done cost us in gold and blood and tears. We done buried too many good men—too many. And I tell you true, tomorrow, we goin' to be diggin' in the sand, and burin' more. But, if we don't, t'en I tell you one more true t'ing, de whole damn world goin' to know de feel of fire, 'cause at dis shinin' moment in time, we de only damn t'ing between the gates of Hell and everyt'ing else."

While Pa'sha spoke, his men had begun fanning the flames in the pit before him. As the coals had turned from a dull red to an intense orange, they continued on, bringing them to a searing yellow-white. The coals radiated, the heat of them beginning to bake the weaponeer intently. Steam began to filter forth from Pa'sha's boots and pants, the white haze of it swirling about his body as he spoke.

"T'at's why I be tellin' you now, any body don't t'ink t'ey up to t'is job, you say so now. No body be t'inkin' de less o'you. I be tellin' you true, t'is no game—not tonight. Tonight, you bein' asked to walk up to de Devil hisself, to grab him by de throat and to choke him for all you got. And, dat's just for startin'."

As the two Murder Dogs continued fanning the coals, two more approached their positions, both carrying fuel canisters.

"Dat's why I be tellin' you now, any one of you, you ain't up to t'is job, you been paid half your fee already. You want—we give you t'ey rest right now and take you back to Vegas. T'is be a serious offer, cause what we goin' do tonight, ain't never been done before. I don't know what to tell you to expect, except t'at it goin' be some shit like you ain't never seen. You goin' fight monsters. You goin' see de deep crazy. And if you can't handle it—you goin' be dead."

Leaning over the fire pit, sweat pouring off his meaty face, dripping onto the shimmering coals below, drizzling spirals of smoke leaping upward in response, Pa'sha shouted;

"What I be sayin' here be, I don't need no soldiers tonight. I don't be needin' tough guys. I be needin' snakes and wolves and bears with fangs like daggers and eyes blazin' with a need to rip darkness a new asshole. I be needin' gorillas t'at can spit lead and eat fire, dat will climb mountains of glass, wrestle with demons, and cut off t'eir own arm if t'ey need a club what to beat Satan in de head with."

Making a slight nod to his men, Pa'sha took a deep breath as they both prepared their canisters—unplugging their nozzles, holding them to the ready.

"What I need be my own damn devils, ready to walk t'rough fire and back. Ready to follow me t'rough de flames of Hell and laugh while t'ey do it."

And then, as Pa'sha stepped into the fire pit before him, his men poured gasoline onto the coals from both sides as the weaponeer shouted;

"I be walkin'. Who be followin'?"

The initial splash of fuel dampened the coals at first, causing a monstrous billow of thick black smoke to hurl itself upward around Pa'sha's massive body. Then, as the gas streams evaporated and heated, suddenly the fuel burst into flames, a fantastic gas ball flashing upward into the sky, back-lighting the weaponeer just as he stepped forward out of the pit. As he stood before the assembly, flames licking his arms and back, smoke steaming away from his head and face, legs and torso, he stood as if unaffected, shouting;

"Who be followin'?"

Savage screams and shouts went up across the desert. Instantly men and women both leaped to their feet, scores of them racing for the firepit, all eager to be the first to follow Pa'sha through the suddenly dwindling flames. Cries went up for more fuel and more wood to be thrown into the pit as one after another ran through the growing blaze.

"Man o'Christ," said Fergeson softly, pointing at the mercenaries. "He's telling them that they're going to get murdered by Satan in a few hours, and they're celebrating like he's handing out free beer. What a bunch of crackheads."

"Yeah," chuckled Morcey sitting several feet away from the policeman. "Not smart like us."

CHAPTER
THIRTY-FIVE

EVERY SINGLE MAN AND woman had stayed.
"I mean, really," Goward whispered to London, "it's almost impossible to believe. Look at it; you got up there after Pa'sha—you told them what they were going to be up against. You made certain they knew *exactly* what was coming—in all its mindless horror," the professor moved his glasses to wipe away a line of sweat from between his eyes. Blinking, he slid his glasses back into place, not noticing the gesture as he said;

"And it will be a mindless horror—my God, this thing, if it awakens, tries to bring its consciousness in line with the one surrounding . . . I mean, if it actually can force its reality onto the rest of us. Think of it, the horrors people will . . ." Goward shuddered, his body smashed immobile for the moment following by the power of his imagination. After an awkward pause, he firmed his chin, then whispered;

"And after you got that—all of that—across to them, they stayed. Every one of them."

"Well," responded London, "that could just mean Pa'sha knows how to pick his troops. But, honestly, either way—isn't that a good thing?" Goward studied the detective, wondering if the man was toying with him. Giving the older man as much of a grin as he could manage, the detective said;

"Hey, in some ways, really, it gives me faith we might just get through this." As the professor flashed him a curious glance, London told him;

"Let's face it, those guys out there, for the most part, anyway, are people that've been thrown away by society. Bad home lives, bad relationships—not able to hold regular jobs, not very comfortable playing by society's piss ant rules. Zack, these are the poster children for 'Camp Does Not Play Well With Others.' And I tell you right now . . ."

As Goward filled his pipe, the detective lowered his voice to something akin to a snarl. The note charged his next sentence, gave it a tone demanding attention.

"These are my people. They do what they want to do for a living. They do what they feel like. They do what they feel is right. It doesn't matter that they're getting paid. It matters that we outlined a suicide mission to them, and they're practically foaming at the mouth for the chance to be a part of this."

"A lot of people," Goward inserted, "would be losing their minds right about now."

London grinned, his eyes sparkling with mischief for a glinting instant. He fell back into the moment immediately, but he seemed to the professor somehow lighter. Pointing out at the somewhat wild troops at their disposal, he said;

"Yeah, there's a lot who'd be losing their minds just imagining what's coming, but not these guys. They grew up on this stuff. *The Invaders, Godzilla, Alien, Predator, Star Trek,* these are Captain Kirk fans, Zack. They're not scared of monsters."

"No?"

"No. Seriously, if anything frightens these guys, it's the same thing that frightens me—that we're the universe's first line of defense. And what I'm saying by that is, if you think about it, it's preposterous." London stopped talking for an instant, his mouth drawing tight. Tilting his head, taking a deep breath, he asked;

"I mean, seriously, the government—any government, or one of the religions—any one of them—is anyone official, anyone in charge, doing *anything* about this . . . does anyone else outside of the NYPD even *know* about this?"

London closed his eyes and shook his head, snapping shut the part of him trying to rationalize why he was the person Fate continually slapped with such trials.

Because, a part of his mind reminded him sadly, that's simply the way it is. You be that guy. Period. That's all there is to it.

He might have accepted the job by default, but he *had* accepted it. And he knew it. His left hand tightening into a fist, his shoulder shaking from the force of it, the detective released his fingers, whispering;

"It's just not fair."

Then, throwing away his fatigue, London simply altered his mood before he allowed it to defeat him. Forcing himself back into the game, he slapped the professor lightly on the back, saying;

"Anyway, those guys out there, there's no one else I'd trust my life to tonight before I would these guys."

"A battalion or two of Marines wouldn't get the job done?" inquired Goward. "Wouldn't make you feel even a tad safer?"

"Not really," the detective answered. Twisting his head, chasing away the last little kinks, he explained, "Regular troops, for the most part, they're made up of regular guys. They know how to follow orders, pay bills, make love to their wives, et cetera. The world they understand is the fake world, the glimmer world . . . the world group consensus points toward when we're supposed to be talking about the so-called 'real world.' But these guys . . ."

London nodded toward the now shadowy shapes waiting in the low light of the waning moon. His finger stabbed toward one heavy-set, balding man with a fantastic red beard. The thing ended in two long braids, each of them slapping against the suit of body armor he was assembling with every move he made. Focusing on the fierce, scarred individual, the detective said;

"These guys, they know that world isn't real. Let a natural disaster sweep through an area, these are the guys who know how to handle themselves. Most people, you cut their hot water, or turn off the power and they're crying desperate. 'Boo hoo, my computer can't tell me what to do. Wah—I'm helpless.'"

"Being a little harsh, aren't you, Theodore?"

"No, not really." London stared at Goward for a moment, then began checking over Betty one last time. Inspecting each of the rounds in her cylinder, he said, "We're getting ready to try and stop the end of the world. Those guys out there, they're not going to fold on me. You know why? Because most of them have already seen the end of at least one world. Wives walked out on them, kids turned against them, chased out of 'decent' places just because they want to look or act or think a certain way."

The man with the braided beard had just been slapped in the back of the head by a large black woman. He spun around, a fine and quiet edge aimed at whomever was behind him, his face a fierce twist of fiery hatred. Then, just as suddenly, the knife disappeared as did his expression, and the balding man grabbed the woman and squeezed her to him, the pair of them laughing at his reaction. Sliding his .38 into its shoulder holster, London said;

"No, that guy, right there, I wouldn't trade him for twenty Marines."

"Wise decision," offered Pa'sha, walking up toward the pair. "I was t'ere de night he put some twelve assorted servicemen in the hospital. T'ey did do him some damage, t'ough. T'at be de night he got de scar on his right cheek. He be most proud of it."

The professor stared at the two men as if they had just spit on him. It was not a look of anger, but rather confusion. Indeed, both the detective and the weaponeer thought, if it had been a look of anger, he would have understood their thinking. Pa'sha winked at Goward, then handed his little brother Veronica, saying;

"My boy, Qaumel, he put a nice edge back on your girl here, poor t'ing, she is. What you been doin'? Usin' her to stir mayonnaise?"

London inspected the edge, nodding approvingly. Sliding the weapon into its sheath, he shrugged an answer to Pa'sha, then turned to Lisa as she approached.

"Teddy?" she asked, "everything is set in the hanger."

"Give me a rundown," the detective closed his eyes, listening intently as she told him;

"All one hundred, ninety-seven mercenaries, as well as all fifteen of the Murder Dogs, have been issued headsets. All have been tested. Pa'sha is in complete com-link with all his troops."

"T'at is good to hear, Lisa girl."

"All sensors placed around the hanger appear operational. Automatic defenses check out as well. If anything approaches the hanger during the evening,

I should be able to locate, target and fire upon it. If the automatic defenses aren't enough, our three upstanding members of New York's finest will be here to back them up. And, if the automatic sensors need a boost . . ."

"Automatic sensors," Lai Wan sniffed, saying the words as if quoting pornography, "if we need those, we are in more trouble than we think."

Two of the mercenaries, the man with the braided beard and the black woman who had teased him, approached Goward with a suit of combat armor. As his eyes widened, Pa'sha reminded him;

"Doctor-man, you know you goin' in with us, to tell us what we be seein' and how we can kill it. You de one body we don't want to see burned up into little bitty professor meatballs."

"C'mon," said the bearded man with a surprisingly pleasant voice, "let's get you done up here. My name's Elmer, and this here is Latesha. A passel of us drew straws, and we copped duty keeping you alive so'en you could keep everybody else alive."

"It just seems like good business sense, don't you know," Latesha said with a smile. "See, Elmer—those business classes momma done made me take are paying off."

The redhead groaned, then clapped Goward on the back, telling him, "You just stay between us, we'll keep your britches outta the crosshairs."

"Or die trying," said the woman softly, "right, baby?"

"Oh yeah," shouted Elmer with a wicked enthusiasm. "You wild bitch, you!"

Latesha laughed and stuck out her hand, indicating she wanted Goward to surrender his jacket and tie. He handed the woman the jacket, but refused to give up his tie, telling her;

"Young lady, I have been a working man for, I would imagine, about two decades longer than you've drawn breath. On exceptionally hot days, I have been known to put aside my jacket, and perhaps even loosen my tie. It is, however, beyond my capacity to face the idea of going out into this night without it."

"Let him keep it, girl," laughed the bearded man. "After all, you can't tell me you ain't got that damn troll of yours in your kit."

Latesha unsnapped a pocket on her flak vest, pulling out a small plastic doll with outrageously long pink hair. Smiling in a pouty, baby doll pose, she answered in an outrageously high voice, "And how could you expect me to place myself in danger without little Voodoo here to keep me safe? My babies would never forgive me if I did such a thing."

Elmer laughed and flipped his hand in a get-out-of-here gesture while kneeling in front of Goward. Strapping a shin guard in place on the older man's left leg, the mercenary said;

"Don't sweat it, professor. We all got our ticks. That's what makes us human—right?"

"Yes," Goward answered, nodding his head absently, his voice far away. "Yes, I do believe it does."

While Goward was secured within the protective suit Pa'sha had put together for him, Morcey came up to London, reporting;

"All chutes inspected and distributed. Everyone's ready to rock and roll. Got your bed all set, too. Come check it out."

London turned, falling in behind his partners as they headed back into the hanger. They brought the detective to a central location, one set with a plain table loaded with electrical equipment, a number of chairs, and a crate large enough inside for a man to lie down within. Upon inspection, the detective found the crate filled to a great depth with blankets and cushions. The walls of it had been lined with foam and blankets as well.

"Looks comfy."

"Hey, it better be," exclaimed Morcey. "After all, we can't have you wakin' up in da middle of dis thing. That would be bad for everyone."

London looked about, commenting to the balding man, "I don't see anything for you."

"If I remember da plan correctly," Morcey countered, "I ain't gonna be in there dat long to need one. You walk me in, and as soon as you need me to send in da troops, back out I come. Right?"

"Yes," agreed the detective. "I guess so."

London looked about the hanger. Fergeson, Krandell and Cantalupo were all armored and waiting. Krandell was checking his weapon. The captain was talking with Fergeson, most likely getting him ready for what was coming. Lai Wan was seated quietly off to one side in the darkness. The psychometrist's chair was a recliner, and she had it at half tilt. Though her eyes were closed, London did not believe she was asleep. Even as he entertained the thought, the woman called out;

"In case anyone is interested, I believe this evening's transportation is nearly here."

London smiled. Some sixty-eight seconds later, even as Potts came walking up to the detective, Pa'sha's radio man announced that the planes they were expecting were requesting landing lights. The weaponeer acknowledged the message, then signaled his people to guide the planes down. In the far distance, two 55 gallon drums were uncapped and the fuel inside them ignited. As the first two were lit, so were pair after pair leading up to the hanger.

Three massive, wide-bodied transports came down out of the sky, one after another, landing on the barren desert floor and then rolling up into their simply marked positions. The planes did not kill their engines, but instead stood ready as the waiting mercenaries clamored aboard. Black-garbed warriors disappearing inside all the aircraft, Potts told London;

"I guess this is my cue."

"Thanks for coming along," said the detective. Taking the security man's outstretched hand, he gave it a solid shake, telling him, "You could still make a run for it, you know."

"I know," Potts answered over the roaring sound of the aircraft engines. "But I've spent too many years now simply being a caretaker. This world of ours doesn't really offer too many chances to make a difference anymore. I'm a couple of months from fifty years old . . ." Letting go of London's hand, the security man ran for his plane, shouting over his shoulder;

"Really, what would be the point of hitting the big five oh if I let something like this pass by?"

Even as Potts disappeared into the darkness, Pa'sha moved forward to say his own goodbye to his little brother. London and the weaponeer grabbed each other in a fierce hug, an action which left the much smaller detective somewhat crushed—as it always did. Turning, following his men into the night, Pa'sha shouted;

"Time to make some boom-boom."

"Yeah," the detective said, "it's probably about time for all of us to go to work."

"That in mind, where's the Pirate Queen," called out Cantalupo. "Why isn't our continental cupcake here making her usual obnoxious comments?" Curious, all heads turned toward London. Climbing into his crate, the detective answered;

"I had an assignment for Ms. De Molina that was best known only by her. Like the old 'Mission Impossible' idea, if no one knows where she is, no one can tell the enemy. We are up against things that can read minds—remember?"

Heads around the hanger nodded. Morcey positioned himself in a battered old recliner in his own dark corner of the structure while London settled into his protective padding. As the first of the transports returned to the air, Lisa grabbed the sides of the detective's head and pulled him to her. Her eyes pleaded with his, begged him for all things. Their lips finding each other, her eyes closed and she simply loved him all she could for a moment. Then she released him, watching him move into position as she told him;

"You at least *try* and come back to me in one piece, you hear me?"

"Let 'em *try* and stop me."

As the second transport followed the first into the sky, London looked up into the worried face above him and smiled. Then, in the moment of evaporating noise that hushed across the desert as the third transport left the ground, he winked at her, and closed his eyes.

As she walked to her place at the monitors, Lisa concentrated on London's wink. As she did, a thought came to her. And suddenly, Lisa Hutchinson realized she knew something no other being in the universe knew, and that the best thing she could do would to be to put what she knew as completely out of her mind as possible.

CHAPTER
THIRTY-SIX

TEDDY LONDON CLOSED HIS eyes, and in seconds found his astral self on the dreamplane. Unlike earlier that day when he had walked physically across the shadow dimension, Morcey and Goward in tow, he sent only his soul there that night. The physical slowed one's reactions, was harder to maintain away from the Earth's magnetic fields. Besides, knowing he had an intense struggle ahead of him, the detective had put together a bit of a plan which required his body remain behind.

Like so much he had been forced to attempt over the past few months of his life, his idea was something he had never tried before, had never conceived of before. But, he hoped it would give him some small advantage, as a reserve, if nothing else—the way a gambler might insert a derringer up his sleeve. He also hoped, much like said gambler, that things could be accomplished without gunplay.

It's so much smoother that way.

As he chuckled wryly at the thought, London sensed Morcey's presence. Reaching out through the velvet darkness all about him, the detective located his partner and drew the man's astral form toward his own. As the two came within sight of each other, the ex-maintenance man said in a nervous voice;

"Hey, I love this job. I mean, who else gets travel options like this?"

"No one I know of," answered London. Barely conscious of the scarlet lightening shattering against the distant mountains, the detective closed his eyes for a moment, then pointed to their left, saying, "We need to go this way."

"All right then," answered Morcey. Levitating his astral form up from the ground, he gulped, then shook his head, grinning as he added, "Let's fly."

London nodded, and the two set out in search of the prison of Fai'gnaner, both of them secretly praying its walls were still standing.

"My mark tells me we should be close."

"You can tell time," the pilot of the third transport told Pa'sha with a grin. "I'll give you that."

"Save your noise for someone who might be unfortunate enough to love you," the weaponeer answered without amusement. "I left all my extra charity in my other suit, don't you know."

"That's all right, friend. With pay like this, who needs charity?"

"Now, t'at's de spirit." Consulting his watch once more, Pa'sha asked, "What are we now—two minutes out? Two point twenty, perhaps?"

"Close enough," answered the pilot. "Get ready for a dead set at two minutes in . . . five, four, three, two . . . now." Pa'sha punched in the stop watch feature on his wrist watch, marking two minutes until drop. As he did, the pilot asked;

"I know it ain't kosher, but the cat is begging to lose another life, so I have got to ask . . . any chance you can crank me in on what you guys are doing?"

"Certainly, my friend," answered the weaponeer. "You are flying us into de Grand Canyon. We are dropping in via black chutes because we do not want to be detected. You, of course, have already logged your flight plans as trainee missions, and I would imagine t'at even now your radio man is assuring de National Park Service t'at you 'trainees' are off course and will be gathered up soon—yes?"

"Oh yeah, that was the deal. You guys need to get in there fast, I know. But, even though you look to be taking enough fire power to bag every moose, cougar and goddamned duck from here to Utah, you don't look much like hunters. And, dropping into a pit deep enough where you could hide the Empire State Building in any of a thousand corners, in the dark, yet—whooo-wieee—now that takes some Teddy Roosevelt-sized balls, man." The pilot made an appreciative whistle, then continued, saying;

"Our decoy planes'll land back in Phoenix and deal with the feds while we proceed to a safe stash we've got in the Mojave. I mean, when they find you guys all busted up on the rocks, it ain't going to be too hard for them to put two and two together. But the planes we say were over the canyon, they'll be clean, so no one can touch us. But, dude, seriously, what're you guys doing?"

"I will tell you," answered Pa'sha. Glancing at his watch, he gauged his words, saying, "t'ere is a powerful evil from beyond time and space headed t'is way, man. Yes, t'is is a true thing I speak. We be goin' into de canyon to where it's physical form be imprisoned so we can blow it back to Hell, don't you know. If we fail, t'en de whole world stands to be destroyed, which is why we got men goin' to be flyin' with you, and keepin' you and yours quiet."

Seeing the second hand of his time piece hit the "9" on his watch, Pa'sha gave the fifteen second gesture to the man next to him. As everyone prepared to jump, the weaponeer turned back to the pilot and said;

"I don't expect you to believe such crazy talk, but I do need you to understand t'at if you and yours try to leave t'ese planes after t'ey have landed, before my men receive word, t'ey will be forced to stop you."

"Stop us? You mean kill us?"

"Let us hope it does not come to t'at." As Pa'sha headed for the back of the large cargo plane, Dearon stepped into the pilot's cabin, letting the man plainly see the detonator in his hand as he said;

"Hello, my friend. I will be your terrorist for t'is flight. Let's make certain all trays and seats have been returned to de upright position. Shall we?"

On the dreamplane, London and his partner made their way as quietly as possible to the point they wished to reach. Occasionally things flew overhead, or raced past them in the shadows. Each time the pair drew in on themselves. It was not that they were necessarily fearful of those others moving about through the dimension—they simply could not afford to waste time or energy on any of them. London had not been completely certain he could find his way back to Fai'gnaner's prison. The spectral end of its confinement had been created in a manner which caused it to shift positions. The detective had found his way back to where he had encountered the prison earlier. Now he and his partner were tracking it through the ether, straining to rediscover it. Realizing their time was running low, London growled under his breath, trying desperately to get his bearings. As he did, Morcey said;

"Hey, boss, I got a idea. You're concentratin' on this prison and you ain't gettin' nowhere—right?" When the detective assured his partner that was the case, the balding man said, "Didn't you say the Spud was there, tryin' to keep the thing inside contained? If that's the case, why not–"

"Just concentrate on finding the Spud," said London abruptly, cutting Morcey off. "I knew there was a reason I pay you."

Clearing his mind, the detective switched from trying to rediscover the all-too-elusive mystic trap, and instead set his senses to finding his friend. In only seconds he had located the specter of Timothy Bodenfelt. Reaching out, he placed his hand on his partner's arm and shifted them across the dreamplane instantaneously.

"Sweet bride of the night," sputtered Morcey as he beheld Fai'gnaner's prison. "What in all the hells they ever dreamed up is that?!"

The god-thing lay in the center of a mass of swirling, pulsating energies—some of them bright and shining silver, many of them black, or dark umber. Certain of the molten colors moved with a steady rhythm, others rocked and spasmed, jerking as if close to rupturing. It was obvious to see that the imprisoned monstrosity was close to corrupting the last of the bindings holding it back from entering the physical world.

"Spud," shouted London over the noise of the growing wind all about them, "what's happening? How close is that thing to busting loose?"

The ghostly remains of Timothy Bodenfelt turned to answer, when a terrible green darkness cut through the dreamplane, ushering in the end of the world.

CHAPTER
THIRTY-SEVEN

PA'SHA AND HIS FORCES were strung out across the sky when the bubbling lights first began to appear. Much to their surprise, the mercenary force found themselves landing at exactly the same moment that a vile, putrid yellow-green dazzle began to seep upward from between the rocks, followed by a vulgar hissing and sprays of super-heated steam. As his parachute lowered him all too quickly toward the ground, the weaponeer studied the phenomenon carefully.

The first thing to catch his attention was the unnerving shades of green reflecting in the growing phosphorescence. The churning swirls were not any of the healthy colors of nature—not that of pine or fir, grass or tree leaves. Instead it embraced the hues of decay, the sick, rotting color of peppers or onions gone bad, the bubbling pus shimmer of long-still water, choked with too many layers of algae.

Watching the changing colors in the light, he noted that they were spreading rapidly, not only across the floor of the canyon, but upward over its northern wall as well. Though the lights had no central point of origin, still the shimmering lines seemed to be coming together in a sort of recognizable pattern.

"A spider's web," whispered Pa'sha. "Or perhaps a maze."

The lights did not take on either form exactly, but in some ways resembled both. The weaponeer was just about to radio Goward to ask his opinion of what he was seeing, when the professor broke in on the line, calling him.

"Pa'sha," the older man's voice screamed, "tell your men to avoid the colors. Don't let them land inside the area being claimed by the colored lights."

The weaponeer was not one to ask foolish questions. He trusted Goward, and did not need to know his reasons for making his request. Switching to wide band transmission, he was just about to do as the professor had said when the lights stopped moving. As Pa'sha took note of the change, the last lines of glimmer crossed, and the world exploded.

On the dreamplane, chaos ruled. Fai'gnaner's prison was gone, destroyed in an explosion of dark, sopping music which splashed against the ears of all, forcing both the living and the dead into retching states of revulsion. The Spud, as well as the spectral remains of those still surviving victims of Fai'gnaner which had been assisting him in holding the god-thing at bay, were sent whirling across the landscape, their disembodied selves splattering against the rocks and each other.

London and his partner fared no better. So unexpectedly had the wave of pain-soaked noise exploded against them that the pair were buffeted as helplessly as the others. They were thrown light years across the shadow dimension, left floundering and breathless in a sea of warm, but rotting color. London pulled himself together first, but the fact did no one any good.

"We're too late."

"Gee—ya think?"

Not bothering to answer, the detective pulled his focus together, centering his attention on the Fai'gnaner entity. Shutting his eyes, he cleared his mind, allowing his senses to find the now freed god-thing. Pulling in on himself, summoning all his power, gathering still more from the random bits of free energy moving on the furious, hot winds all about them, London began preparing himself. The majority of his attention focused on the monster halfway across eternity from him, another part of his mind worked his mouth, telling Morcey;

"You've got to get back now, let them know this thing's gotten loose–"

"Got'cha, boss." The ex-maintenance man prepared to wake his sleeping self, but London spoke once more, telling him;

"And then, you've got to come back."

Morcey blinked several times, holding his hands out in front of himself awkwardly as he did so. Swallowing once, then again, he asked;

"Come back? You want me to . . . come back? On my own? To fight the thing what just threw us across a galaxy?"

"Yes," the detective's voice answered calmly. "Fai'gnaner's prison disguised much of his essence from me. This thing is far more terrible than I ever imagined. I'm going to need you. The whole world is going to need you. Get back as soon as you can."

"Yeah, yeah—oh yeah."

The balding man felt his astral form sweating. He did not know how that was possible. Wasn't he only a spirit? Wasn't he just dreaming? Hundreds of questions flooded through his mind, each one more frightening than the last. Weaving his way through all of them, however, Morcey ground his teeth together for a moment, then asked simply;

"And where will you be when I get back?"

London opened his eyes suddenly, then pointed off into the shimmering distance to the speck of light which they both knew was the still exploding prison of Fai'gnaner and said;

"Over there."

The detective winked, then threw himself into the void, hurling his astral form toward the still rupturing cell, bending time as he did so in the hopes of arriving there at the same second he was first hurled away from it. Shaking his head at the sight, feeling his pony tail sliding across his back as he did so, Morcey muttered;

"My brother-in-law ever complains about how hard his job is to me again, so help me, I'm gonna punch his lights out. I don't care what my sister says."

The balding man smiled at the mental image and then did everything he could to force himself awake.

Pa'sha screamed commands for his people to withdraw to any point they could reach outside the spewing hiss of lights. Bubbling phosphorescence crackled its way to the surface, burning away soil, vegetation and rocks, atomizing anything in its path. Mercenaries still in the air worked desperately to sling their guide lines so as to direct them out of harm's way. Those already on the ground scurried frantically to avoid the deadly green hues. High above it all, Elmer's meaty fist caught a hold of Goward's shoulder. Pulling the professor toward him, he shouted;

"Take it easy, Doc. Relax. We got the right drift goin' here. We'll be okay."

"At least," Goward croaked through dry lips, his eyes bulging at the sight below, "we won't have to search all that hard for the entrance."

The mercenary appreciated his charge trying to put a light face on things. Still, knowing precise information was far more helpful than wishes, he asked;

"All kiddin' aside, this is bad. Right?"

"My friend," answered the professor, his stomach twisting in knots, "you are as correct with that statement as any man has ever been."

Elmer stared down into the exploding landscape, watching the ground erupt and his friends die. Jerking hard on his guide lines to continue forcing himself and Goward out of harm's way, he muttered;

"Yeah, that's me. The master of understatement."

And then, as if to give counterpoint to his words, the massive center of the blazing maze of lights below them flared, erupting molten rock in every direction, including upward.

London flew across the darkened dreamplane at a speed unimaginable. For a moment he had considered simply transporting himself across the distance instantaneously, but at the last second he had decided to try something different.

Hold the line, boys, he thought to himself, just stall that damn thing for a couple of lousy minutes.

As he scorched across the void, the detective's mind worked to coordinate all the information he was receiving. From ahead he could sense that

Fai'gnaner was still in the process of emerging from its lair. The nothingness around him seemed clear of any obstructions. That made sense to him. Even those travelers of the dreamplane with little or no experience would sense the cataclysmic eruption of the god-thing's prison and either avoid the area or depart entirely. Those things wishing to confront London would hardly want to tangle with Fai'gnaner as well.

His ability to detect what was happening at the monster's entry point to Earth itself was masked by the speed at which he was traveling. Try as he might, he could not maintain his pace and keep a clear picture of what was occurring there. Grimly, he shut down that part of him trying to be in two places as once and concentrated on building his speed. Pulling inward on himself as he moved, London worked at condensing his atoms, at making himself as dense as possible.

I'm only going to get one chance at this, the detective told himself. Here's hoping I get it right.

And with that, the detective closed his senses to the growing scent and sounds of death coming from the god-thing before him, and redoubled his efforts. He could tell he would arrive at the ruins of Fai'gnaner's prison in less than thirty seconds. He thought of saying a prayer, then laughed madly as a voice from the back of his mind asked to whom it was he thought they should pray.

CHAPTER THIRTY-EIGHT

MORCEY AWOKE SUDDENLY, EYES flung wide. His throat constricted when he first tried to speak, but necessity drove him to strain his throat to its limits.

"The damn thing's loose," he croaked, his voice so twisted it drew the attention of everyone within the hanger. Indeed, so abrupt was his return to consciousness that his body was flung forward out of his chair by his fearful excitement.

"It's already loose," he shouted as he picked himself painfully up off the floor. Ignoring the throbbing beginning within the knee upon which all his weight had landed, he added, "Its spirit form is loose from its dreamplane prison."

"We know," answered Lisa without turning from her screens. "It's escaped its restraints here as well. I'm monitoring Pa'sha's radio messages."

"How they doing out there?" Cantalupo crossed the hanger at a trot as he asked his question. Fergeson and Krandell stayed at their posts, but both turned their heads, eager to hear the answer. Still not looking up, Lisa told them all;

"Not good from what I can tell."

Morcey ran his tongue lightly over his lips.

"Damn," he muttered. "This is not the way this is supposed to be goin'. But, speakin' of goin', that's what I gotta do."

"Going?" Krandell said the word as if he did not understand it. "What do you mean? You're not supposed to go anywhere."

"Change'a plans," responded the balding man, heading back to his chair. Forcing his throat to loosen, embarrassed by the fear that had closed it, he forced a wad of phlegm and blood up into his mouth, then spit it out onto the concrete floor of the hanger.

"God, that was delightful," he muttered, then explained to the others, "The boss told me he needs me back on da dreamplane. It ain't my idea of a good time, but . . . he signs the checks, so . . ." Shoving himself into the corner of the tattered chair, Morcey moved himself this way and that, looking for the same comfortable spot that had helped him get to sleep so quickly the first time. Easing himself into it once more, he added;

"Keep your fingers crossed that you get to see my smilin' face again."

As the ex-maintenance man tried to relax, forcing himself into as calm a state as possible, Fergeson quipped;

"What's he talkin' about? I mean, even if he gets his soul or spirit or whatever creamed on this dreamplane, he's leavin' his smilin' face right here."

Krandell smiled as widely at the officer's comment as Cantalupo frowned. Both lawmen were about to add a few words of their own, when all within the hanger heard the clawing noises on the roof.

♦　　♦　　♦

"What the *shit* is *that?!*"

"Believe it or not," whispered Goward, his voice unable to raise itself any higher, "that's what you came here to kill."

Elmer shook his head, his eyes wide, pupils small, answering;

"God love a turkey, now don't that make me look foolish?"

The red-bearded man simply stared, unable to move. Latesha stood next to him, equally immobile. The god-thing dragging itself up out of the ground was impossibly big. It dwarfed any dinosaur of which either of them had ever heard, rivaled the tallest creations of man. The monstrosity seemed to pull itself forth from its ever-widening split in the Earth forever, trumping even the size of Japanese film monsters. But whereas it matched its cinematic rivals in size, it resembled none of them.

The thing did not have legs in any understandable sense. Appendages extended from it in all directions, long, armored multi-jointed things that grabbed at any and all surfaces, pulling themselves upward, lugging the enormous girth of their host body into the free air which it had been denied so long. A thick, nausea-inducing yellow film covered the god-thing's body, a curd-like paste which blew forth from the great, manhole-sized pores covering its armored torso. An ocean of the horrid ooze fell away from it like dandruff, the great, refrigerator-sized flakes splashing against the surface, burning all they touched.

Everywhere about the area the mercenary forces continued to retreat from the crumbling section of the canyon. The molten rock spewing forth around Fai'gnaner did not hamper the creature, but was an extreme hazard for any human that got too close. Certainly the flowing magma would incinerate any it covered, but even simply breathing in the noxious clouds of burning ash filling the air was certain death.

As the mercenaries continued to flee the sight of Fai'gnaner, their headsets came to life as Pa'sha's voice flowed across the override channel. Barely able to believe what he was seeing himself, still the weaponeer drew his nerve together and commanded;

"What be going on here? Did you not think t'at big yellow bastard was what you came here to kill? Are you waiting for sweet Jesus to come down and teach you how to pull your triggers? Turn around, you dandies, grab your nerve, and send t'at t'ing back to Hell!"

And then, unlimbering the grenade launcher strapped to his back, Pa'sha took aim and sent a steady stream of projectiles flying at Fai'gnaner. Before his first missile could find its target, some two score weapons from around the area opened fire as well. Explosions large and small shattered against the towering body, blasting great festoons of the yellow treacle outward from its grotesque form.

Having turned the tide of retreat, Pa'sha switched to the channel reserved for Goward. Breaking through the static being caused by Fai'gnaner's presence, the weaponeer shouted;

"What's happened? Why is it free?"

"There's no predicting these things precisely, you know," Goward answered, still staggering away from the god-thing as fast as he could. "We were simply too late. Theodore must have been too late as well."

"So, what do we do?"

"We're out of my ballpark now, Pa'sha, old boy," answered the professor grimly. As the nightmare firefight raged all about him, he screamed to be heard over the continual explosions and the roar of their target. "I came to look over its prison, to interpret signs and seals. That's all blown to bits now," he bellowed, pointing into the chasm, "down there—under ten tons or rubble. The only chance we have now is for you and your people to keep doing what you're doing—which is to blast the ever-loving crap out of it and hope you hit something vital."

Pa'sha turned all his attention on the advancing god-thing, staring at the monstrous form continuing to claw its way upward. All around him men and women were dying. Fai'gnaner spewed crimson ice and a gelatinous green fire which took more of the mercenaries with every passing moment. For seventeen terribly long seconds, the weaponeer stood frozen, unable to formulate a plan, incapable of seeing anything they could do that might hold back the mountainous bulk.

T'ere is no way to beat it, man, a voice whispered within his head. Pa'sha nodded, knowing the words were true. Then, bitterly, he shouted;

"T'ere be no beating t'is t'ing—you all be knowin' t'at. But t'ere's no one sayin' we can't die trying, either." Unlimbering the rocket launcher he had brought with him, the weaponeer shouted over his general link;

"So let's be gettin' to it t'en!"

It was at that moment of redoubled effort that the first of the black winged horrors descended from out of the ebony night sky to begin their attack.

"On the roof," snapped Lisa, "bodies, moving about. Four, no five of them, more dropping out of the sky." Remote turning one of the cameras Dearon had installed, she snapped on the lights he had rigged as well.

"Wings," she cried. "They're flying in under their own power. Wing spans varied—three to six, seven feet. Claws, fangs, skin looks thick enough to be armored."

A crashing noise from outside and above was accompanied by one of Lisa's screens flashing back to darkness, its only illumination coming from those stars visible that night.

"They got the lights!" Cantalupo narrowed his eyes, telling a suddenly embarrassed Fergeson;

"Thank you, Sherlock Holmes."

"Good thing we don't need lights to do this."

Lisa's finger stabbed a button and from all four corners of the hanger roof, swivel-mounted Ma Deuce .50 caliber machine guns began blasting away at the intruders. Shells capable of slicing through inch thick metal cut down the flying invaders, slaughtering them by the dozens. But, fast as the computers at Lisa's command were, they could not move their weapons in two directions at once. Before long, the never-ending flood of beasts managed to silence all four of the guns as they had extinguished the lights. Then, above the heads of the crew, thick claws began to slice their way through the rusting corrugated metal of the roof. Cantalupo turned to Lai Wan, asking;

"Where'd these bastards come from? I thought you could sense these things?"

"I can," the psychometrist answered. "But they did not approach us by coming across the desert. They simply appeared above the hanger, as they seem to be appearing over Pa'sha and his men right now as well."

"They're here for Teddy," shouted Lisa, her voice tense—straining. As she turned her head for the first time since she sat down at her monitors, her eyes caught Lai Wan's. The psychometrist simply nodded her head.

"Screw 'em," growled Krandell. "They may be here for him, but it's a lead lunch they're going to take home with them."

All three of the policemen cocked their weapons. Lisa stared at her monitors, all of her capabilities neutralized. Lai Wan moved to Morcey's chair, pushing it toward the center of the hanger, grateful the old recliner was the type that came on wheels. After that, all five of the defenders simply stared upward until the first reptilian face poked its way through the roof. Then, they were all deafened by the futile noise of weapons fire.

CHAPTER THIRTY-NINE

"**I** HATE THIS, I HATE this, ouughhh, how I goddamn *hate* this!"
Morcey raced across the dreamplane, desperate to reach
Fai'gnaner's prison. All about him, in the ever-increasing darkness,
chittering voices whispered at his passing, the horrid, tiny sounds working to
distract him, draw him in, steal his focus.

"I ain't listenin'," he told the air around him, told himself. "I ain't listenin.'"

The ex-maintenance man forged his way forward, ignoring the ever-increasing gloom as best he could, but the whispering terrors plagued his every step. Was he going the right way? Could he possibly find his way back? Could he find his way there in time? What good could he do when he got there? If the thing they sought to stop could knock London halfway across the universe—without even trying—what chance did he have?

Morcey shuddered as he raced along the ever-blasted plane in the lightning-split darkness. He was out of his depth, the sibilant voices told him, helpless in the face of what was coming. He would be ground up and utterly consumed before he knew what had found him. He would be destroyed, annihilated, atomized. Like everything else in the sad human equation, he would be vaporized, slaughtered, forgotten.

But, the voices told him, it didn't have to be. No—not if he ran. Fai'gnaner would be a long time in consuming the universe. One who started running now in the other direction could survive.

Live, the thousand tiny voices urged, *flee and live, survive— survive.*

Images of blood-soaked destruction filled the balding man's head, his brain afire with hundreds upon hundreds of rapid flashes, each displaying for him the future end of a different world. Tears rolled down his face, soaking his shirt and jacket, drenching his pants as he watched his entire family die endlessly—brutalized, tortured, raped.

Don't be a fool, the horrid voices slithered to his ears. *Why die needlessly; Why? Why?!*

Eyes closed, ears ringing, Morcey ran blindly across the dreamplane, the shadows of his tormentors ever-gaining on him. High above the retreating form of the balding man, those whispering within his mind grinned to themselves as to how all-too-easy his destruction was going to be.

◆　◆　◆

Krandell was the first to react. He peppered the ceiling above them with bullets, firing a dozen rapid, controlled bursts through the first hole the invading creatures had torn in the hanger roof. Initially a splatter of fluids fell to the concrete below, then a severed head, followed by three bodies—two mostly intact, one decapitated.

"To your left," Lisa screamed at Fergeson, but the officer could not hear. Indeed, despite the precautionary earplugs they all were wearing, everyone within the hanger had been deafened by Krandell's shooting. Feeling her friend's words, however, Lai Wan put the sense of them into the officer's mind.

"Holy Jesus!"

Fergeson turned just in time to let loose a wild volley at two of the winged horrors as they swooped down from the ceiling directly at him. His shots mostly went wild, but they diverted his attackers which made the lieutenant happy enough. Abandoning her monitors, all of them mostly useless now that the flying horrors were swarming over them, Lisa grabbed up one of the three compact Uzi machine guns Pa'sha had left for her.

How? She aimed the thought at Lai Wan. How did they get so close? Without us knowing it? Without the machines sensing them? Without *you* sensing them?

They came through the dreamplane, the psychometrist answered, placing the answer into her friend's mind as she had the warning into Fergeson's. Just as they did at the museum.

Cantalupo had joined in the melee, pumping shotgun shells one after another into the air. In the first five minutes of their struggle, the three officers had littered the concrete flooring with the remains of more than three score of the creatures. The air curdled with the scent of gunpowder and alien blood. It smelled harsh and thick, and it choked all living things in the hanger, even the flying terrors spilling it.

"Look," shouted Lisa; "they're leaving!"

No one could hear her, of course, but all took note of the same occurrence. The monstrosities were all heading for the holes they had torn in the ceiling and the walls, disappearing outward into the darkness. Quickly Lisa returned to her monitors to try and determine whether or not the creatures were returning to the dreamplane. While she did, each of the policemen worked at reloading those weapons they had emptied.

Lai Wan concerned herself with Morcey and London. Focusing her powers completely on the two men, she checked their heart rates, their breathing, made certain the gunpowder smog was not choking them. Neither of them could be allowed to awaken accidentally. Knowing that was of paramount importance, the psychometrist threw herself into making certain both men were all right.

Sadly, thus distracted, she could warn no one when the winged nightmares reversed their retreat and flew back into the hanger at top speed.

◆　◆　◆

Pa'sha shuddered as Fai'gnaner dragged its entire bulk upward out of the ground. He and his men were not quite as ants to the behemoth, but the comparison was close. The weaponeer could see that the missiles and shells they were throwing at the god-thing by the thousands were having but the slightest effect.

The best we can do is keep this thing occupied, Pa'sha thought. And that, only barely.

More than half the mercenaries had already been slaughtered along with seven of the weaponeer's Murder Dogs. Not merely killed, but devastated, the energy of their bodies captured, their souls plucked, savaged—devoured. Their screams rolled across the desert long after their flesh had been atomized.

That had been before the arrival of the same winged horrors that were attacking the hanger. Dropping out of the sky in hunting packs of twenty or more, the fanged monstrosities tore into the rapidly shrinking assault force from every angle. And, they were not the only extra danger with which Pa'sha's warriors had to contend.

Magma had begun to pump its way to the surface, following the path cleared by Fai'gnaner. In some places it bubbled and oozed, in others it flung itself forcefully from the ground, burning all it touched, including the air.

Also, enormous dust devils had sprung up throughout the canyon, and to both sides of it as well. The heat tornados whirled madly, cutting through one another, grabbing up sand and pebbles, plants and rocks, insects, small animals, droppings, litter, burning cinders, loose globs of lava—anything in their path. They swirled that which they captured faster and faster, battering anything they came across, knocking men to the ground, scarring their flesh— pummeling them. Blinding them.

From the vantage point Pa'sha had reached, he directed his troops as best he could, reminding them to protect the back of the man next to them—to keep at least one eye open for the incredibly swift, fanged terrors which had slaughtered so many of them already. Charting the direction of both the magma and the tornadoes as best he could, he managed to keep scores of his people from death.

And then, suddenly an alien tone cut through all the chatter on the weaponeer's various com links, slicing its way cleanly through all his thoughts. Capturing Pa'sha's attention immediately, the corrupt hiss told him;

You—you are the one who keeps them annoying me so. You are the one that must be eliminated.

Involuntarily, the weaponeer looked up. When he did, all he could see was a long, groping appendage as big around as a subway train, suspended thousands of feet above him for an instant, then descending straight for him.

Chapter
Forty

L ONDON WOULD REACH THE god-thing in less than a minute. His speed was a thing unimaginable, faster than any man-made conveyance could obtain, swifter than the pace set by galaxy-roaming comets. Moving at the speed of thought, he gathered every molecule of weight he could as he continued on toward Fai'gnaner, increasing his mass as he went to make their eventual contact a moment of monumental impact.

Closing rapidly, finally separated by no more than some eight times the diameter of the solar system, the detective's internal radar conformed for him that he would intersect with the god-thing in some forty seconds.

Not a whole hell of a lot of time, he thought. Sure hope this works, because I'm guessing it's a little late now to try something else.

Despite the distance, London could still feel the spirit of the Spud far ahead of him, crumpled and exhausted, spread thin across thousands of miles of the dreamplane. Those few others assisting the specter, the last remaining victims of Fai'gnaner's millennia of scheming, were strewn about the firmament along with Bodenfelt, barely conscious—spent. Finished. As best London could tell, no force remained on the dreamplane to oppose Fai'gnaner outside of himself. Hoping to discover some further clue to assist him, the detective released his consciousness forward, throwing himself into the barest outer walls of the god-thing's mental defenses. Amazingly, he found himself able to move freely.

This means one of two things, thought London, thirty-five seconds from impact, either it's been so long since he's had to protect himself he's not quite realized he should be getting his defenses in place, or . . .

Or, came the voice in his mind which spoke to the detective but rarely, *Fai'gnaner is luring you into a trap.*

Twenty-nine seconds from the god-thing, London abandoned caution and hurled himself into every aspect of the monstrosity's consciousness into which he could penetrate. Much washed over him without the slightest adhesion, thoughts and feelings so alien he could not begin to describe them. Like a blind man with no nerve endings trying to sort mountains of cloth, the majority of what he encountered left him confused—puzzled.

Shifting down into Fai'gnaner's lower functions, however, the detective discovered the reason for the horror's distraction. The god-thing had gathered those last souls it had lured to itself with Hardy's help. But rather than simply absorb them, it was first seasoning them with realization—enhancing their flavor with understanding. Only twenty-two seconds from impact, London was stunned to discover that the first spirit slated to be devoured was Hardy's.

"For centuries, you have all been so pitifully, predictably alike."

The god-thing squatted in the ruins of its prison, cosmically charged bars and mortar broken and ruined all about it. Having waited for so many thousands of millennia, it could not help but savor its moment of triumph. Not realizing it was but nineteen seconds from the commencement of London's attack, the monstrosity bellowed;

"Promises of riches, baubles of commerce, and you have flocked from every backward pocket of your detestable fetid sphere of muck." Fai'gnaner played with the last vital strands of Hardy's being, pouring the feeble molecules of it from one appendage to another, sneering;

"For so horribly long I kept at it. The miserable Elder Things, they were the ones, they sank Mu beneath the waves, sent my brothers into exile—save timorous Zoth-Ommog, whom hides still at our father's side in distant R'lyeh. They split this world, crushed all life on the side where they buried me . . . but I endured."

London listened intently, even as he continued to increase his speed. Dragging the weight of several worlds along with him—muscles straining, brain shrieking, nerves aflame—he felt he was as ready for impact as he would ever be.

Still a long way to go, he thought. Pulling in on himself, trying to mask his aura and all other signs of his approach, the detective prayed, seventeen more seconds—just keep talking, Fai'gnaner, you over-sized bastard. Just keep jabbering and paying no attention to me.

"Slowly I learned to reach through the bars of my prison. The Elder Things, fools that they were, thought I would break my spirit against the walls of my physical confinement, but I soon realized that was a waste of energy. And so I set about gathering a harvest of human souls, dragging them to me with promises of anything that would satisfy their greed."

Gold, thought London. That's what all the talk of gold was about. He's been at it forever. Who knows how many he's taken—the conquistadors, the gold rushes . . . Hardy. That's how he got Hardy, too—got him to bring him so many more souls.

Continuing to dangle the still-sentient bits and tatters of the scientist's soul from its claw-tipped appendages, Fai'gnaner emitted a noise which seemed to translate as appreciation.

"But, the power you brought me, so many at one time, so quickly, so clean, delicious–"

London's speed doubled once more. Ten seconds from impact, the detective swallowed a vast gulp of air, determined to hold it until he made contact with Fai'gnaner, not wanting to give away his approach with even so tiny a noise as the slightest expansion of his lungs.

"You have brought about the end of a universe, davidhardy. I hope the rewards you garnered by doing so pleased you, for your time is over . . ."

Seven seconds to impact–

"And that of Fai'gnaner, son of Q'talu . . ."

Six seconds more–

"Most powerful of the four horsemen . . ."

Five seconds–

"Is about to begin."

Four–

"All I need do now," bellowed the god-thing, tossing the last remains of David Hardy into its vast and horrific maw . . .

Three–

"Is destroy you, little london thing . . ."

And, with those words, Fai'gnaner swallowed his prey, then turned with a speed blinding and met the approaching detective with a resounding blow—one which knocked London from the sky and plunged the entire dreamplane into thick and utter darkness.

CHAPTER
FORTY-ONE

L ONDON EXPLODED, HIS BODY shattered, atoms spilled across the darkened plane in a light-year wide arc. The mass he had been dragging along behind him flew off wildly causing terrible destruction in all directions.

"Foolish little london thing . . . it is not for the miserable likes of you, so foully, miserably human, to take such a magnificence as Fai'gnaner unawares."

The god-thing surveyed the still wavering cosmos all about it, the reality of it still working to reshape itself after the hideous battering of Fai'gnaner's blow. Smiling to itself, the monstrosity surveyed all the levels of opposition working against it at that moment. Cutting through time, it observed all its foes, laughing at their inevitable destruction.

In the Grand Canyon, the humans London had brought to bare on him were routed—finished. The detective's best friend was but moments from being crushed by the god-thing's molten bulk. Fai'gnaner pictured the future moment, looked on the image of Pa'sha's body, sizzling, stuck to the bottom of the monstrosity's blazing foot, and chuckled with a tittering glee.

"So long denied, so long starved and shunned and hidden away—so long without amusement . . ."

At the same time, the god-thing observed Lisa and the others in the hanger, all of them slowly being moved toward each other, herded, backed step by step into an ever shrinking circle by the shrieking nightmares Fai'gnaner had sent to them. The god-thing's already hearty amusement grew as it tasted the mounting fear in the lonely building, doubled as it gently licked at the flickering tatters of hope remaining there.

"Slowly," it whispered, sending the order to its hovering minions. "Bind yourselves with restraint—allow this moment to endure." As a terrible din rose from the flying horrors, the god-thing relented, like a parent whose child simply can not wait until dinnertime, telling them;

"Very well, there is such a thing as too much drama. You may take the weak one now."

Instantly the horde descended toward officer Fergeson. Lisa barely had time to scream as the creatures overwhelmed the police man, ripping his body to shreds with their fangs and claws, even as the others splattered several dozen of them with gunfire. Leathery bodies piled up everywhere—to no real advantage. Fai'gnaner showed multiple rows of fangs as it grinned.

It was too late. Everything they wanted to accomplish, it was simply too late. Fai'gnaner had freed itself both in the physical world and on the dreamplane. Its prisons were shattered; they could not be rebuilt. Its confinement was at an end. In seconds all of its enemies on the Earth would be destroyed. The dreamplane had been swept clean, all save for London's barely surviving remains. Turning back to the detective, Fai'gnaner lowered itself to a position from where it could scoop London into a more manageable pile. Sifting the ground, the immense horror had almost pulled the widely scattered bits and pieces together when to the god-thing's surprise, Morcey arrived at its feet.

"You," the monstrosity said, half-surprised, half-amused.

"Yeah," the ex-maintenance man said. "Me. Me . . ." He looked at the wild rumple of atomic particles being swept up by Fai'gnaner, somehow recognizing them as the basic building blocks of London's astral body. His voice going shallow, straining, he whispered;

"The guy the boss was countin' on." Turning away from the sight, closing his eyes against the surrounding darkness, he added, "The guy who showed up too goddamned late."

"And," the god-thing's voice echoed within Morcey's mind, pleased at the timely distraction, "exactly what would you have done if you had not 'showed up too goddamned late?'"

"I . . . I don't know. I don't even know why Mr. London wanted me to come back. He just said he needed me, so . . . so I, I . . ."

The balding man was amazed to discover that his spirit form could shed tears. Fai'gnaner turned its bulk toward Morcey, studying him as he tried to pull himself together. Suddenly aware of the god-thing's proximity, the ex-maintenance man asked;

"How is it we're even talkin'? I thought you were all about rulin' the universe—of course, I'm just hearin' things in my head. Maybe this shit has finally knocked me for the big one."

"Now that I am free, my tiny lump," Fai'gnaner said to the balding man, "I have all the time of eternity. I will spend the next, I can not yet know how many millions of years, harvesting all human souls. I shall gather every past one from every preceding century, all the lovely tastes which should have been mine, and when they have all been consumed, then I shall feast on the living."

Morcey sat down on whatever was beneath his feet in the darkness, not caring about anything anymore. If London had been destroyed then everything was finished. The ex-maintenance man knew he could do nothing against the taunting god-thing hovering over him. Fai'gnaner's mind had been made open to him. He had seen what was happening in the hanger, at the Grand Canyon.

It was over.

They had lost.

London was gone, and hope had deserted the universe. Soaking in Morcey's thoughts, the god-thing stretched itself, uncurling its long, unused muscles, preparing for the joyful business of slaughtering all life, past and present.

"Your world is but a stepping stone for me," it thought to the ex-maintenance man. "By the time I am done, all life that ever was, that is now, or that ever will be, shall be incorporated within my magnificence." Its many appendages finally finished with the task Fai'gnaner had set them to, the horror gathered London's astral form into a recognizable shape. As Morcey stared, helpless, not seeing any move he could make that could possibly matter, the god-thing said;

"Unlike so many of those beings which might almost be considered my peers, I have enjoyed speaking with you, my lump. Insight is always valuable—but then, so is a good meal."

Drawing London's still inert form to its vast and wicked maw, Fai'gnaner was just about to toss it within itself, when suddenly a tiny voice echoed within the god-thing's mind.

"You know what else is valuable," it asked, "the time one can gather playing possum."

And with those words, London's eyes flashed open. Instantly his form blazed as he burned his way free from Fai'gnaner's grasp.

"Now, moi cheri?"

"Now."

Joan de Molina came forth from her hiding place deep within the detective's consciousness and the two combined as they had once before. Crimson crystals scratching their way across the polished landscape all about them, their bodies fell apart at the atomic level, layers of desire—that burning, crackling hunger, so all-consuming that reason and sanity wilted in their presence—blending them completely–

"Teddy–"

"Embrace it–"

Their very thoughts blurred one into another as their blinding ravenousness poured around and over and through both flesh and mind. Then, one mind, one body, one life—one memory—they drank the feeling in, grabbed for it, emersed themselves in it–

"Oh, little london thing . . ."

Flesh mingled, nerves meshed, limbs molten–

"No wonder father loves you best . . ."

Their combined form blurring from the human to the infinite. As Fai'gnaner began to realize what it was holding, red hair exploded in running scarlet lines across the throbbing mass of self-indulgent plasma. Two minds, dancing around one another at transcendent speeds, slashing their way blindly through the walls of dimensions, with a mad laugh, they devoured each other, throwing themselves forward through the startled god-thing, setting its spirit body aflame, blasting it apart and lighting the entire dreamplane with its smoldering essence.

EPILOGUE

IT HAD BEEN DECIDED in advance of their night in the desert that any and all survivors would meet in New York City as soon as possible. Some one hundred and twenty-three hours passed before all involved managed to make their separate ways home. Of the hundreds who went out into the night, enough returned to fill only a mid-sized side room in a medium-sized Chinese restaurant.

"I hope they start bringin' somethin' fattenin' soon," announced Morcey in a too-loud voice. "After the last couple of weeks I've had on the job, I've decided I need to live a little."

Many chuckled. The relative handful of survivors sat at four tables—each of which could service no more than ten comfortably. Only one of them was full to capacity.

"You and me both, me brother."

Dearon toasted the ex-maintenance man with a glass of black plum wine. Morcey lifted his bottle of Tsingtao, a Chinese beer he found nicely sturdy. Glass met glass, then lips. The two were sitting with Pa'sha and a number of the surviving mercenaries and Murder Dogs. The next table was filled with nine more of their number. Another quartet of them sat with Lieutenant Krandell and Cat, both of whom had chosen the table because they wanted to sit next to two others whom had chosen it—the electronics expert next to Lai Wan, the lieutenant next to the Pirate Queen. Cat accused the officer of being a "touch too high school." Krandell made a point of moving his head and neck, using the pain of his movements for emphasis as he said;

"Hahehah," the lieutenant half-laughed, half-groaned, "I *wish* I was still in high school, lady. Stuff like what happened to us out there wouldn't have hurt near so bad back then."

London and Lisa sat together. Next to them was an empty place setting, next to which were Professor Goward then Elmer, the red-bearded mercenary charged with keeping him alive. Across the table from the empty place setting was Cantalupo, who himself was surrounded by more unattended plates, glasses and napkins.

"We couldn't even fill four tables," London said with a sigh.

Staring at one of the vacant place settings, Lisa answered him softly;

"I'm sorry that poor officer Fergeson didn't make it. Those things that killed him, they were just toying with us—he just happened to get picked first."

London merely nodded. He remembered telling the young man how happy he would be to include him on their team, heard the words over and over he had told the officer so glibly;

"Extra cannon fodder is always appreciated."

And don't forget, the back of his mind whispered to him, after you get done beating yourself up over him you can start feeling sorry for Potts, too.

The detective frowned. He could not get the security man's last words out of his head, either.

"Really, what would be the point of hitting the big five oh if I let something like this pass by?"

Pa'sha had told him Potts had not even made it to the ground, had been smothered in mid-air by Fai'gnaner's burning foam. Just like so many others—smothered, frozen, incinerated—slaughtered. The images sat within his mind as the first course was brought into the room.

The London Agency had not rented the banquet space for the evening for anything as mundane as debriefing the troops. That had been done as each member of their party had found their way home. Some had been shaken, traumatized by what they had witnessed. Most had taken it all in stride, more broken by the amount of their fellows lost in the horrific battle than anything else.

As for their silence, the Agency had little to worry about. For most, receiving the second half of their payment was sufficient incentive to remain quiet about that which they had seen. Staying out of the hands of the law, or the nearest insane asylum were also good motivators toward buttoned lips. The news media was filled with empty guesses about what had happened within the Grand Canyon, but so far no one seemed to have come close to putting anything like the truth together.

No, the survivors were gathered simply so all could drink together in a private place where they could discuss whatever they wanted while enjoying a ten course meal. This meant every table would be brought an appetizer, soup, eight following courses, and then a few extras before dessert. Each group would receive identical amounts of every dish, brought out and set on a large, rotating glass plate which covered most of the center of the table. Anything needed for the meal, condiments, ice, pots of tea, et cetera, could be found there and brought before oneself with but a flick or two of the wrist. For those willing to consider their escapade a victory, it was a wonderful evening.

The first platter brought to each table was a mixed meat plate—one-to-two bite-sized strips of barbecued pork and roast duck. Many in the side room knew how to use chop sticks and started in immediately. The majority needed forks, however, and were delayed a moment as the waiters passed them out.

The meats were still warm, succulent in their separate sauces, and they disappeared quickly. None of the tables had finished their appetizer, however, when their waiters returned with tureens of seafood soup, a thick brothed potion rich in crab, shrimp and lobster. Quickly dished out into hand-sized bowls previously set out on the glass wheels, those who wished soup took the bowl in front of them—a few clever enough to recognize the condiment dishes containing vinegar adding a tart red spoonful or two to theirs.

These courses were rapidly followed by more. Baskets of mixed seafood and vegetables came next—shrimp and scallops, mushrooms, snow peas and carrots and more. The baskets turned out to be edible, interwoven strips of fried yam, made all the more delicious from having soaked up the juices of their contents.

A platter of bok choi with garlic followed, coming at the same time as a dish made from a heap of broccoli topped with shrimp in white sauce and candied walnuts coated in sesame seeds. While the attendees were still marveling over these, two more dishes were brought out—servings of barbecued porkchops, thick in a tangy red sauce and platters of tiny, flash-fried fish coated in a wonderfully light batter.

Food and drink flowed. Chicken with skin cooked so perfectly it had become paper thin and fall leaf crisp, spinach with Chinese mushrooms, and a set of large, steamed fishes completed the main courses. Afterwards, just in case anyone was still peckish, good-sized bowls of fried rice and lo mein were delivered to each table as well.

Most of the assembly enjoyed themselves greatly. For the mercenaries and the Murder Dogs, it was a well-earned bonus. They toasted fallen brothers and sisters, collected donations for some of their families—Latesha's children drawing particular sympathy. Most had no one to worry about, or to worry about them, and a simple clinking of glasses was all their memory warranted.

After one such round at their table, Morcey wondered aloud if he could survive another such memorial service. He and Pa'sha and the others in their group had paid homage to close to a hundred of the fallen. More than two score bottles—beer, wine and stronger libations—had been removed from their table alone. Noting that another of their number had just fallen asleep, the weaponeer laughed, then added;

"And so, my little brother comes t'rough for us again."

"I guess so," answered the balding man in a non-committal tone.

"Please," said Pa'sha, the end of the word interrupted by a belch all could tell was only a down payment on future wind, "if you had been in t'at damn canyon, with t'at goddamned foot coming down on you . . . oh, you would sing his praises like the sweetest of the jungle birds."

"Ahhh no," admitted the balding man, "when him and the Pirate Queen blew Fai'gnaner to Hell and back, my ass was a two-step away from bein' toasted, too. I ain't arguin' nuthin' like that. I . . . I just, I don't know . . ."

"I do . . ." answered Pa'sha softly. "You worry more about him than you do yourself."

The two smiled at each other, each determined to keep drinking until the other one capsized. Fumbling with the cap of a bottle of Jack Daniels Black Label, Morcey began searching for the name of the next of the fallen to toast. Many in the room, including several of the waiters, had begun betting on the outcome of their contest since the barbecued pork chops. It was a much needed release for them all.

Watching the arm-bending gladiators, but not partaking himself, London continued to brood on those they had left behind in his own way—among other things.

Too many, he thought, too many good lives wasted.

Noting his discomfort, Lisa moved her hand near his arm, grazed it with her fingertips. She said nothing, merely applied the slightest pressure, guiding her nails against his shirt, plowing a gentle path between the hairs on his arm. He glanced at her, trying to make his eyes playful. She returned his look, masking her concern, working at appearing light and breezy.

"I'm sorry," he said, unable to meet her even halfway. "I don't seem to be very much fun. Maybe you shouldn't have worked so hard on getting me back."

"Teddy, how can you say that?"

"Oh, just feeling sorry for myself."

"But, darling," Lisa hesitated for just a second, then finished, "why? We won. You did it. You did all of it. You're like a superhero—you saved the world. Again. This is the third time you've saved the entire planet and everyone in it."

"Not everyone," he answered, his voice tiny and hollow. His mind flashed over the past few months—Manhattan, Elizabeth, Geneva, Chernobyl— millions dead. Burned, smothered, poisoned, crushed. Millions. "Not as many as usual . . . but enough."

"You didn't choose to kill anyone," she said to him. Pointing to the others at the table, she said, "Ask anybody here. Nobody blames you for what happened."

Goward immediately made sympathetic noises, as did Cantalupo. London tried not to argue with anyone, tried to convince them he would be fine. No one believed him. The person with the most reason to not believe him watched his eyes from her table, and the pain cutting through the detective made her own body ache. Masking her intent from the others, she gathered her things and said;

"As much fun as this has been, I think I hear the midnight plane to Lisbon being called for boarding. I think it's time for a trip to the ladies room and then an 'au revoir' to you all, until next time."

The Pirate Queen rose, smiling to all the others at her table, slightly surprised when Lai Wan stood at the same time. The psychometrist made a comment about women always needing someone to go to the restroom with them and left the table without waiting for Joan. Catching up to her outside the banquet room, the Pirate Queen asked;

"You are not a subtle person, Ms. Wan. To what do I owe the honor of your escort? Wanting to make certain I leave?"

"I am not your rival for London," Lai Wan answered. "Nor do I seek to become your companion. I only wanted to have a moment alone with you so we might speak." Standing in the small corridor which led to the lavatories, the psychometrist looked Joan squarely in the eyes and told her;

"There has been much tension in this group since you were pulled into it. Like some, I will not be sorry to see you depart. But, there is also no denying that without your presence, the world would be in ruin right now. Oceans would be boiling, the sky would be burning, and all would be dead or dying, and not in any pleasant ways."

The Pirate Queen stood still for a moment, the slightest hint of how stunned she was showing past the always erected mask she kept across her eyes. Perfect as her training was, she could not keep anything from Lai Wan, of course. Despite the fact the psychometrist was not probing her at that moment, still there was no way Joan could contain her emotions from her.

"Thank you," she said finally. "I wasn't certain anyone had noticed."

"Tosh," Lai Wan made the dismissive noise as she waved her hand before her. "London has not broadcast the story of what happened simply not to embarrass Lisa. He lied to her, to everyone, about having been able to cut the connection between the two of you because he was actually planning that far ahead."

"He is a remarkable man, cheri."

"He is clever, rash and lucky, but we are all alive because of it, so I can not complain with conviction. Still, I was curious as to what your plans were?"

"My plans for Theodore, I take it?" When Lai Wan merely stared, the Pirate Queen laughed sweetly. "You scare many with that look, don't you?"

"You distract equal numbers with your charm, I imagine. Did you have an answer for me?"

Joan smiled, tilting her head first upward, then down. Finally, biting her lower lip gently, she made a shrugging gesture with both her shoulders and her eyes, then said;

"What else can I do? She is his; he is hers. What he did to the two of us is done. I will love him forever, and he will love me, and never will that change."

"I feel sorry for you."

The Pirate Queen's eyes jumped slightly, registering her surprise at Lai Wan's words. The psychometrist appeared instantly embarrassed, obviously regretting her statement. When questioned as to whether or not her abilities gave her some second sight of a future tragedy in store for Joan, Lai Wan answered;

"No, I have no real ability to predict that which is to come. I only meant, not as a psychometrist but . . . as a woman," she paused, then finished her thought as calmly as she could, the slightest shiver in her voice, "I do . . . I feel sorry for you."

It was an honest and kind sentiment, one woman to another. And the Pirate Queen's eyes sparkled as she smiled.

"Please, don't feel sorry for me. Really." The ripple of her body was as honest as had been Lai Wan's voice. Joan stared at the psychometrist for a heartbeat, then added;

"I might not have your particular talents, but I believe I know you well enough to say with authority that you are no stranger to being loved by a man, and being loved back by him. My Theodore . . . he's the one they're talking about when they jabber on about 'better to have loved and lost . . .'"

The redhead giggled, and then blushed to hear herself so young. She turned away for a moment, enjoying a memory, and then turned back.

"It is very sweet of you to care, but trust me, I'll be all right."

Lai Wan nodded. Joan started to leave at that moment, then turned back and cast the psychometrist a wicked glance. Hooding her eyes, she dropped her voice to a suggestive octave, and asked;

"You know, *you've* never let it be known what you really think of my Theodore, have you?"

And suddenly, everything changed.

Thrown such an abrupt challenge, Lai Wan shifted her feelings, pulling everything of herself back inward from the outside world. Without meaning to, she threw a coldness into the narrow hallway which could not help but frighten even the hardened Pirate Queen. Pulling in on herself further just as quickly, however, she made the moment pass, then said;

"And I never shall."

Joan nodded sharply, her mask firmly back in place. With a flourish she cast away every bit of anger, fear or heartbreak, showing the outside world only the face she wanted them to see. Then, turning back to the restaurant, she said;

"Come, help me make my goodbyes. I think some folks will feel much safer with you nearby."

Lai Wan nodded, understanding. In a moment they were at London's table. The waiters had just returned with platters of orange slices and almond cookies. Most of the attention in the room was not on dessert, however, but on the continuing battle of the toasts still raging between Morcey and Pa'sha. The two had begun to sputter their words and spill more than they swallowed, but they were conscious and thoroughly enjoying the open wagering going on around them.

"Men," said Joan, coming up behind London and stopping. "You are all so very silly."

"Well, yeah," he agreed, "but it keeps us off the streets. No wait a minute, we do some of our best silly work in the streets."

The air around the table froze for a charged moment. The detective and the Pirate Queen both thought of a dozen things to say, but turned away from them all for a variety of reasons. Finally, not wanting the awkwardness of the moment to become completely obvious, Joan said;

"It has been a pleasure to meet you all. Elmer, I would like to thank you greatly for watching over our Professor Goward here. He is far too adorable to be allowed to perish." Both men blushed slightly, making trifling farewells. Turning to Cantalupo, she told him;

"As for you, Captain, I'm afraid I must confess, I am not really a member of the London Agency."

"Nooo," answered Cantalupo, feigning shock. "And here I was, all taken in and everything. My goodness, what a chump you made out of me." As the Pirate Queen laughed graciously, the captain continued, telling her;

"Oh, and by the way, I just thought I'd mention that the museum, that wonderful place that brought us all together, reported that besides the cup we had to dispose of, the 'terrorists' seem to have stolen a pair of gold ear rings."

"Really . . .?"

"Yeah," answered Cantalupo with a bit of a growl. "They were a lot like the ones you were wearing when we picked you up that night."

"How interesting." Joan gave the captain a politely interested look. Cantalupo snorted at her gall, then added;

"Un-huh, I know. Here's something else I know." As everyone at the table turned at hearing a certain note in the policeman's voice, he told them, "Remember all those dead kids? And how we found there were more at risk? Seems you and London here were in time to save seventeen of them."

"Really?"

London and Joan said the word at the same moment, with the same inflection. Lisa took great note of the fact, but said nothing. Having given everyone time enough for the information to sink in, Cantalupo added;

"Just some tidbits to let you know that while some things get noticed, there can be reasons for overlooking them as well." Joan made a motion with her eyes to signify she was impressed with the captain. He snorted gently once more, adding;

"Don't consider it a free ticket to come back to our fair city any time soon, however."

"A policeman to the end, eh, captain? What is a girl to do?" Tossing her glorious mane, the Pirate Queen turned to London then and said;

"Teddy, you are far too dull and I think I must go back to Paris to find a man who does not suffer so. All this brooding over people dying. Tell him for me, Lisa, people die all the time. But our seventeen . . . if the concept of saving the world is too large for you, think of them, and let go of all this pain you clutch to yourself."

London stared at the Pirate Queen for a moment, his throat tightening. Dismissing a thousand comebacks in an instant, he finally said simply;

"Well, I'll do my best."

For the briefest of moments Joan thought to mention that if he could actually let go of his pain that he would be leaving with her. Deciding she had seen enough cruelty when passing through Fai'gnaner, she said only;

"I know you will."

The redhead made to leave, then turned back for one last moment. Staring into London's eyes for one last time, she said;

"I would ask a favor of you, though."

"Yes . . .?"

"The next time you see your friend, the Spud, tell him . . . tell him for me, if he ever meets a beautiful seventeen year old boy named Ferris Miller, that he should tell him . . . he will always be loved."

And then, before any further comment could be made, a sudden explosion of laughter and shouts from the next table, accompanied by the sound of a chair and the person in it falling over backwards, announced to all that a winner had been found in the drinking contest. Good cheer flashed instantly throughout the room. Money changed hands for a final time, and glasses were topped off all around as everyone toasted the contestants.

Dearon made a short speech about the strengths and good qualities of both men, and all the survivors toasted their health. All but the Pirate Queen, who was already outside, hailing a taxi with one hand, and hiding her tears with the other.

GLORY AND FAME

Nothing lasts forever except the moon and sky.

—Kansas

"**A**IN'T SEEN YOU IN a while."

"Now there's an understatement . . ."

The apparition let its words trail off softly. It was easier that way—took less energy.

"Yeah, all right, I guess so," said the balding man. "Anyway, Dr. Bodenfelt, I was wonderin' . . ."

His words were extremely disarming. He was the kind of person who talked easily. True, his were the speech patterns of a simple man, sent forth with an accent and pulse of life in his voice that indicated to most that he might possibly be just intelligent enough to be useful–

"The way you keep showing up, and all . . ."

And his words, while indeed probing, were so only in the most inoffensive manner everyday language would allowed. Anyone paying more attention to him than the average joe-in-the-street, someone trying to figure him out, as it were, would have to come to the conclusion that the man was simply too honest to be any kind of real threat to anyone.

"Is there anything in particular you're hanging around for?"

Or perhaps–

"Anything I should know about?"

Too clever to be easily recognized as such.

The apparition condensed itself, struggling to reformulate its being into a more recognizable shape. This was, in a way, mostly a wasted effort, since the fading shimmer had long since lost the ability to appear as once it did when it still inhabited flesh. The wraith could not remember the face with which it had originally grown to manhood, nor any of the other features that had distinguished it from the rest of mankind—hair color, weight, complexion, to what extent its eyes did or did not sparkle—all memory of things of that nature was lost to it now, so completely that, in truth, it did not even realize that which it did not remember.

"No," the ghostly presence answered. "Not that I know of."

Now most of the spirit's time was spent barely corporeal, invisible to the grand majority—unseen, unheard. Wandering and waiting. At times like the present, however, when it needed to communicate, it would make an effort, concentrating itself until it began to resemble once more a human being. It remembered being human quite clearly actually, for when alive it had embraced the juice and thrill and responsibility of life with remarkable verve.

Its name had been Timothy Bodenfelt, though most all folks of its acquaintance had called it "the Spud." As a man it had been a doctor, a healer with a deep and caring soul, and it had given up the flesh decades earlier than infirmity would have beckoned it to do so, so that others might survive.

"Are you sure about that there, Dr. Bodenfelt?"

The spirit all had called the Spud when alive gathered what strength it could and halted its casual drift, flashing with purple electricity as it hissed its answer.

"What do you want of me, Paul?"

The balding questioner before it was one Paul Morcey, a partner in the London Agency, a firm specializing, if somewhat reluctantly, in supernatural investigations. Theodore London, who had founded the firm, had been Bodenfelt's best friend when the spirit had still been alive. They knew each other as Ted and the Spud, and at a moment when the universe had been in monumental peril, Bodenfelt had offered himself as bait for that which held doom in its terrible hand.

The man had gambled that London would understand his sacrifice and agree with it. The detective had, and with regret chewing on his soul most strenuously, London had pulled the trigger which had saved the woman he loved along with his city, his world, his galaxy, and quite possibly the universe and all of creation from destruction.

"Yeah, okay, I guess I got you here for a reason at that . . ."

All he had been forced to do to achieve such was to obliterate his best friend.

"Tell me, Mr. Bodenfelt, why do ya keep hangin' around Mr. London? I mean, are you hauntin' him, or what?"

The apparition stopped short. Its color diffused at the query, paling considerably. The leg and arm facsimiles it had been producing ceased growing, the ends wisping on the breeze. It considered the balding man for a long moment, then finally spoke once more, filling the air with its speechless words.

"You care for Ted a great deal, don't you?"

Slightly embarrassed, Morcey answered;

"Hey, we ain't pickin' out china patterns or nuthin', but I watch out for him. That's my job."

"I thought you were . . . a janitor, wasn't it? You saved Ted's life, and he invited you to stick around . . . but that was . . . long ago. Why are you still with him? What concern is he to you?"

"Hey," growled the balding man, "the boss needs me. I gave up my old job that day you said, when I pulled his bacon outta the fire. But I'm workin' on becomin' a real detective. I carry my weight at the agency, normal cases and . . . the others."

"Mr. Morcey," the spirit's whispering voice echoed within the ex-maintenance man's head, "I do not doubt you do these things. I did not challenge such. I asked you *why* you do so. And again I ask, *what* concern is he to you?"

The balding man stared, unable to find words to give the apparition before him. Within his head, a voice from the back of his mind prodded him.

You had better start getting somewhere with this thing, or you're going to have gone to a lot of trouble for nothing.

It was true. Having become concerned over the spirit's continued presence, as well as its effect on his partner, Morcey had attempted something he had thought far beyond his capabilities. Consulting with Zachery Goward, a professor the London Agency used quite often due to the man's extensive knowledge of the supernatural, he had worked out a method for reaching the dreamplane—not with his partner as he had done in the past, but on his own.

He had decided to do so when he realized that London's friend had come to him far more than once after the detective had been forced to end the Spud's life to save everyone and everything else. He had also noted a disturbing corollary between the wraith's visits and London's mental health. Seeing the departed spirit bothered the detective on some subconscious level, disturbing him in a manner so profound that it worried Morcey greatly.

And so, it had come to pass that the ex-maintenance man had decided to attempt to do something about the apparition's visits. Thus it was that now, his body sleeping peacefully in his bed, Goward sitting at its side, watching over the shallowly-breathing carcass, his intellect, his soul, the electrical essence which was *him*, stood in between worlds with the spirit he had hoped to contact. Sadly, however, after so much effort he seemed to be accomplishing nothing.

Oh brother, Morcey thought, if I don't get on the ball here, I could end up making things worse.

"Sweet bride of the night," the balding man blurted, "Bodenfelt, what'dya think I'm doin' here? I'm tryin' ta find out what you're up to? What is Teddy London ta me? He's the Destroyer—all right? He's God's hand-picked, right-hand man. When shit comes around, it's his job ta deal with it, and it's my job ta be there at his side."

"Interesting . . ."

The whisper hung cold in the violet reaches of the dark realm in between worlds. Morcey did not know how to effect the ether universe, did not want to, had not come to it to create or destroy. He had come there searching for a ghost, hoping to remove it from the real world once and for all.

"What the hell's that supposed to mean?"

"I asked you what concern Ted is to you, and you tell me that to you he is God's hand-picked, right-hand man. You think of him as that which you must stand beside. Very well . . . tell me then, Paul . . ." the voice faded from within the ex-maintenance man's head for a moment, as if it were having trouble remaining focused. Then, after a small cluster of seconds, it found itself once more, and asked;

"If that is how you see Ted, how is it you see yourself?"

Morcey shivered, the reality of his position starting to finally dawn on him. He was not dreaming; he was not awake. He was, as it were, standing at a right angle to such concepts. He was outside the simple geometry of that world which was controlled by so simple a clock as mere consciousness. He had stepped into the shadows of death, but had not died—returned to the space he had flown through while his forming body had gestated within his mother's womb.

All about him was the energy saints and monsters had used since the beginning of time, floating along in pulsating clusters. He dare not immerse himself in any of it, though, he knew. To do such might lead him to other worlds, to beings a trillion times removed from him in scope and power. Goward had warned him that by sending himself to the dreamplane he was courting myriad forms of disaster—quite possibly death. He considered the professor's words seriously, then went ahead and did what he felt he had to do.

"Look, Bodenfelt," he said finally, "how I see myself ain't important. It's how I see the boss that's important. The way it looks, he's all the chance the world's got. If he loses even one'a dese battles, then most likely it's all over for everyone."

The apparition merely hung in the air silently, neither confirming nor denying anything Morcey said.

"Every time you show up, he's bothered for a long time after. Seein' you depresses him. You oughta be able to figure that out. You were his best friend, for Christ's sake. Ta save everyone he had ta kill you. There was no other way— it had to be done. You knew that, that's why you did what you did."

Morcey stopped for a moment, mentally catching his breath. He was partially surprised that he even needed to breathe where he was, but only partially. Goward had admonished him sternly to the fact that when he was on the dreamplane he still had to act as if he could die.

"Keep a low profile," the professor had urged him. "Get in, do what you want to and get back out. Don't attract attention to yourself, don't get foolish. The old saw about dying in the real world if you die in a dream, it's no joke. Sleep leads to dreams, dreams lead to the dreamplane, and once there, the slightest letting down of your guard can bring the worst things imaginable to you."

The older man's eyes had blazed with warning, and Morcey had known the professor was not exaggerating in any way. Gathering his strength, he tightened his grip on the situation and continued, saying;

"What you did back then, that was an awesome move on your part. You saved the world and everything as much as any of us did. But . . . it's killin' da boss ta see ya. Don't you get it? Yeah, he's got all these powers an' all, but he couldn't stop what happened without sacrificin' you. And now, it seems every time we turn around, you're floatin' around somewhere remindin' him'a what he had to do to you. I'm tellin' you, it's tearin' his heart out."

"Good."

Morcey's head jerked back slightly, as if he had not heard the spirit correctly. Staring at the insubstantial entity before him, his shock and surprise were so great that his emotions began to churn the air about them both, sending out invitations into the darkness to those others who might be nearby. Reining in his mental outburst, his eyes narrowing, voice dropping to a growl, the balding man snarled at the apparition;

"And what in Hell do you mean by that?"

"I think it means it's best if Ted regrets killing me," the spirit answered. "It was the only way to cleanse the universe of that which was trying to possess it. I knew it. That's why I did what I did. Ted knew it as well; that's why he did what he did. It should have been a simple thing—one life given so all life everywhere could survive, and yet he struggled so greatly before he could do it."

Morcey remembered the story as it had been told to him, as he had seen it in London's eyes. The detective had used his field glasses, had spotted his friend atop the faraway tank he had chosen as the platform from which to lure their enemy to its doom, his leather shoes slippery on the rain-slick metal. There the Spud waited for the beyond horror they all sought to stop, hoping his end would not be as terrible as he was imagining it would. Spotting London in the distance, the Spud had waved to his friend, and both their eyes had filled with tears.

After that, the detective had forced himself to go cold inside. He had cut away those memories and feelings that might stay his hand, divorced himself of emotion, focusing his attention instead on preparing his missile. He had worked slowly, deliberately, aiming the rocket at the base of the tank, waiting until the exact moment when his friend's sacrifice would do the most good. Then, when the time was perfect, his finger curled around the trigger, the Destroyer had closed his tearing eyes and lived up to his name.

"I see you remember the moment."

The spirit's words echoed several times within Morcey's head. Before he could comment, the thing asked him;

"It was hard for him to kill his best friend, but he did it. But now, the next time, how hard will it be for him to kill another to save the world? And, after that . . . will it be all right to murder ten to save half the world? Fifty to save a quarter? A thousand to save a million? A hundred thousand to save a half million?

"When does it stop?"

And in that moment, Morcey comprehended what the wraith was trying to say. Having already thought the same things, the balding man retorted;

"It don't stop, because it ain't never gonna begin. Mr. London's the Destroyer, all right. That he is. And he got picked to be that by Fate or Destiny or whatever 'cause the world ain't got no better than him. And he don't need you hangin' around clawin' at his nut all the time."

"I wish that were so."

The words limped through the air, weak and frail, thin as shadow against the sun, but resonant with a clean and shining honesty which rang undeniable in the cold light of the dreamplane. Summoning enough energy which, in the real world would have toppled a continent, the apparition found the strength to form itself anew. Legs and arms extended completely, the illusion of toes and fingers winking in and out of existence at their ends. Upon its shoulders a head formed, a thing with hair and eyes and ears, a nose with nostrils and a mouth which actually opened and closed. It was not a mirror image of Timothy Bodenfelt, as he had been, but it was humanoid and erect and it was close enough to do what the wraith wanted it to do.

"The Destroyer before Ted, did he not fall? Give in to his baser levels? Do you think it can not happen once more?"

"Anything can happen," Morcey answered. "Nuthin's impossible—that's what makes life so damn interestin'. But Mr. London ain't the type to crap out in the last innin'. So if you're stickin' around 'cause you're worried about the boss suddenly snappin' his fingers and tearin' the fabric of the universe apart every time he wants an ice tea, I think you can safely pack it in."

Pulling forth every spare bit of energy the dreamplane had to offer it, the spirit smashed the seams of time sufficiently to be able to remember what a smile was. Then, rearranging the molecules of its physical presentation long enough to flash a sad one across its continence, it told the ex-maintenance man;

"You don't understand, Paul. Whether I come or go is not up to me. It's up to Ted." As Morcey stared, the wraith whispered;

"Ghosts do not populate the world because they want to—not usually, anyway. No; we are trapped within the world of man by those who cling to us."

The balding man turned his head slightly to the left, leaning it down slightly toward his shoulder. Staring unblinking, understanding began to light within his eyes as the apparition added;

"It is not my desire that I remain near Ted, coming back into his life on occasion, Marley to his Scrooge, warning him of what might lie ahead—no. It is *his* desire that I do so."

"You mean . . ."

"Yes; it is he who wants me near him. It is Ted who thinks he needs a reminder. Not me."

Morcey shrunk in upon himself, feeling somewhat awkward—a touch foolish. He raised his arms from his side, holding his hands out before him, trying to explain himself. Needing no explanation, the spirit raised one of its already dissolving arms toward its dissipating head. Placing an almost completely disintegrated finger before its no longer moving mouth, it made a reassuring noise calling for quiet. Then, collapsing back into its more comfortable form, it told Morcey;

"They say in Rome, when the great Ceasars would return from battle, they would march their captives and their booty before them. All of Rome would see the display as it moved through the streets, slaves, gold and gems and ivory, spices and silks and whatever else they'd brought back. As his legions marched before him, displaying all this splendor he'd brought back to the glory of the empire, there would be a solitary slave riding in his chariot with him."

Bit by bit the wraith continued to fade from sight, becoming more just a lighter color hanging in the air against the blackness of the dreamplane than anything else. The sound of it seemed to cause the color to rise and fall, each word uttered diminishing the whole a bit further.

"This slave had only one duty, to ride with the emperor, to stand with him at royal games, to remain at his side when he went to the Senate, et cetera. Indeed, he traveled with the emperor everywhere, and his one job was to every once in a while, just lean forward and whisper in his master's ear . . .

"'All glory is ash, all fame is fleeting.'"

Morcey stood quietly, his arms dropping once more to his sides.

"You are no slave," the wraith whispered. "But you have his ear. Stick your two cents in once in a while. He needs it. Or, at least, he thinks he needs it."

And then, having discovered all he had traveled to find, Morcey began to fade from the dreamplane, the same as the presence which he had brought to it. Grateful, relieved, he called out to the fading apparition;

"Thanks, Dr. Bodenfelt; thanks for everything."

Resisting dissolution for a final moment, the wraith whispered;

"Remember, Paul . . .."

And then, Morcey awoke in his bed, the professor at his side, with three words ringing in his head.

"Glory and fame . . ."